TIME MAGAZINE CALLS JOYCE HABER
"HOLLYWOOD'S NO. 1 VOYEUR."

HER BOOK, *THE USERS*,
IS THE MOST SHOCKING NOVEL EVER
WRITTEN ABOUT HOLLYWOOD.

NO ONE ELSE COULD HAVE WRITTEN IT.

NO ONE ELSE WOULD HAVE DARED!

"*THE USERS* IS HOT!! Joyce Haber's prose is interesting and intimidating. She's obviously had one ear to the keyhole of half the bedrooms in Beverly Hills."

—Rod McKuen

"THE HOLLYWOOD *ROMAN À CLEF* TO TOP THEM ALL!"

—*Penthouse*

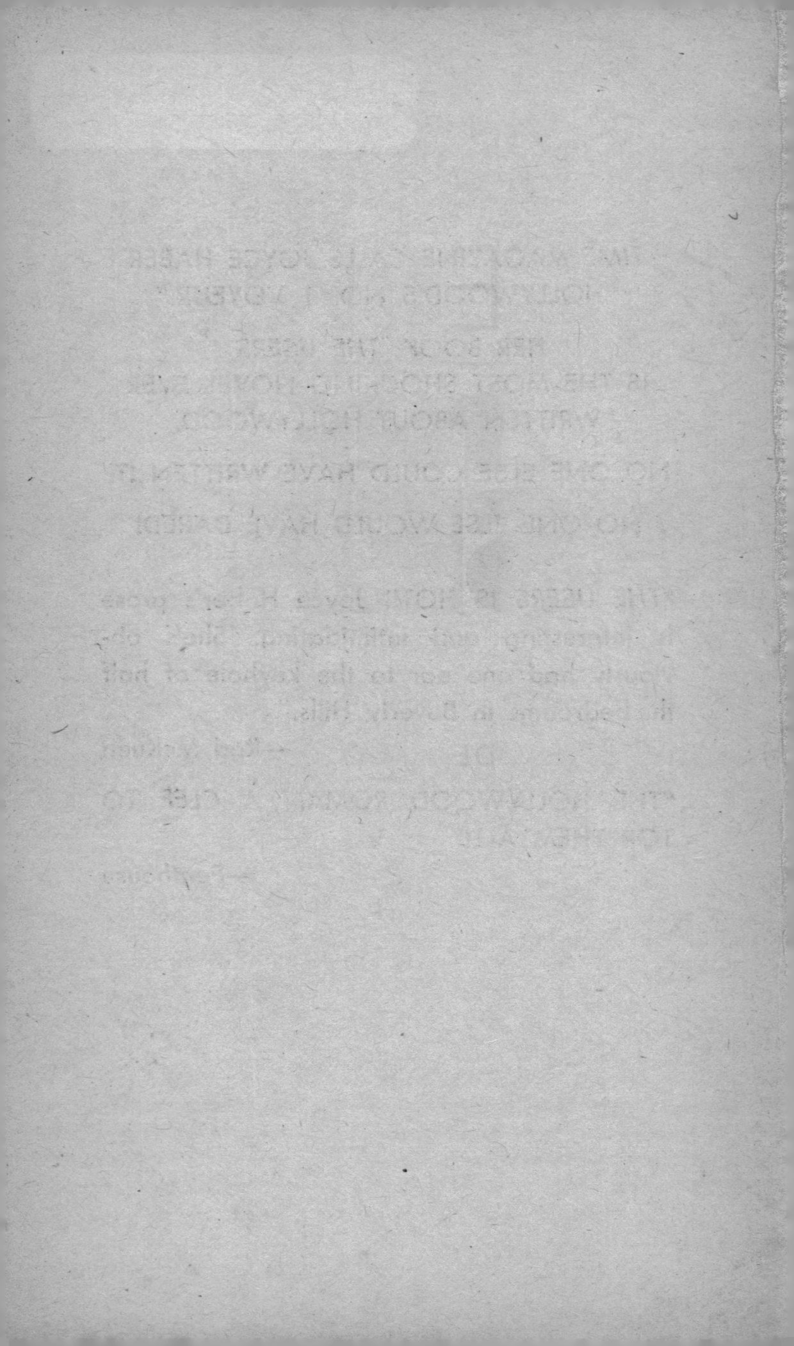

A DELL BOOK

Published by
DELL PUBLISHING CO., INC.
I Dag Hammarskjold Plaza
New York, New York 10017

ISBN: 0-440-19264-1

Reprinted by arrangement with Delacorte Press
Printed in the United States of America
First Dell printing—July 1977

For
COURTNEY and DOUGLAS
Who May Read This Book
in Fifteen Years

"Under the spreading chestnut tree,
I sold you and you sold me."
—George Orwell, *1984*

"Under the spreading chestnut tree,
I screwed you and you screwed me."
—Warren Ambrose, 1976

BOOK ONE
THE PARTY

1

"I ran into Mel Ferrer the other day," Harvey Parkes said. "He's furious with me. I used to do him, but then I stopped returning his phone calls. I won't work south of Wilshire. I'm just too busy, and I've had to make it a rule."

"I suppose one of these days you won't have time for me," Elena said. She was in her black leotards, lying on the white rug in the den, stretching. Harvey was sitting on the leather hassock, looking down at her through steel-rimmed glasses.

"You're the last person I'd *ever* drop," Harvey said, pretending to be annoyed at her for suggesting such an idea. He sat cross-legged, his thigh muscles stretching the imported French fabric of his white pants. There was no fat whatsoever, not a ripple, where his navy polo shirt tucked in. It had become his trademark to wear pants and short-sleeved polo shirts, which he seemed to own in infinite numbers and varieties of colors. They always looked new, as if he never wore them twice. Elena envisioned miles of clothes racks, filled with pairs of tight trousers and polo shirts. Always color co-ordinated and skin-tight, they were all of the thinnest, finest fabrics. Today it was white and navy, with Adidas to match. And the narrow link chain (given to him by Mrs. Norton Simon for Christmas) that circled his neck and drew attention to the chiseled definition of his sternomastoid muscles, was gold, like the buckle of his navy linen belt.

"I'm not a very rewarding client," Elena said. "I never do the exercises anymore. Only when you're here."

"Well, that's why I'm here."

"Let's face it, Harvey. I don't really do them, anyway."

"No, you don't," he said.

"My mind wanders. I'm not an exercise person."

"Actually, you don't need them. You have good body efficiency, you're lucky, your tensions work *for* you."

Elena had learned that such comments from Harvey were compliments. From the way he had been observing her for almost two years, she knew that her body pleased him. Bodies were his business and he discussed them in appropriate terms. It had never occured to her, before she knew Harvey, that men didn't talk to you about your body, unless they were lovers, admirers, or doctors. Lovers and admirers were not objective. They observed you lustfully or, less frequently, with love. But Harvey looked at you with a professional eye. His saying that you had good body efficiency was equivalent to another man telling you that you had an attractive body, but without the sexual connotation. In that sense, his compliments were more meaningful, because they were objective. But she had never been able to figure out how, or when, or if Harvey thought about her body the way other men did.

"But let's at least try to do the lower back," Harvey said. "*That* you need. And *that* you should do every day."

"Because it's the one I detest," Elena said. She rolled over onto her stomach and arched her body, lifting her legs and her head, obeying his suggestion that she was a rocker on a chair, an archer's bow, imagining that a string was drawn tight from the back of her head to her feet.

Harvey got up and paced, watching her. "Now relax. Now again. Tense and tight. Feel the string." He went to the mirror where he could watch her while he also looked at himself. He liked to see himself in other people's mirrors. It was instructive. No two mirrors gave the same perspective.

"Harvey, I *hate* what I'm doing," Elena said. "Enough, it's enough." She rolled over onto her back, groaning with relief, and stared up at the vaulted, beamed ceiling. "What do you hear? What's going on?"

"Not very much," he said, which was the way he always began, reluctantly. She watched him scratch the palm of his left hand, a trick he had devised to enable him to look at his wristwatch which he wore face in.

"You have to go," she said.

"Not yet," he said, pretending annoyance, as before. It was part of their foreplay. He arrived every Tuesday at one-thirty, and for a few minutes they pretended to work at the exercises. Then they gosspied for the rest of the hour.

Elena smiled and sat up and got a cigarette from the coffee table while Harvey returned to his place on the hassock. He discouraged his clients from smoking in his presence, but she was an exception. For she was a favorite client of his, and he enjoyed their long visits. But he knew it wasn't ethical, and sensed it wasn't manly, to talk about his clients. Still, he found it irresistible to gossip with her.

Then, too, Elena was responsible for his unique success, and even though he could never feel really free with her, he tried to think of her not as a client but as a friend. That helped him not to resent the free hour he had been giving her once a week for the past eighteen months, even now when his schedule had become so heavy he had no business wasting even a minute. He was extremely punctual about time, and his clients—even those who arrived compulsively late to every other appointment and engagement of their lives—were intimidated to the point of panic at the thought of being late for Harvey Parkes. It wasn't enough simply to be ready when Harvey arrived. You had to be waiting for him, in your leotards or your sweat suit; and no children, maids, dogs, cats, telephone calls, or any of life's crises were allowed to intrude.

Elena had made a deal with Harvey. He would do her and Randy on the cuff, and in exchange she would introduce him to important, select clients. Randy hadn't been offered a picture since their arrival from Europe, and it had been suggested by his then-agent that it might be helpful if he lost a few pounds and got back in shape. What really concerned the agent was that Randy had been drinking too much and was beginning to look bloated. Elena had made inquiries and learned about Harvey, a qualified physical therapist who ran a small gym in Santa Monica. Since he didn't know it was *déclassé* to live south of Wilshire, he could be persuaded to make house calls—especially if the client was a celebrity.

In the area known as West Los Angeles, which encompasses everything between Beverly Hills and the ocean within jogging distance of Sunset Boulevard, the lives of shopkeepers, bank personnel, gas station attendants, as well as professional and service people—physicians, dentists, attorneys, accountants, hairdressers—are enriched by the celebrities they keep. It is a geographic impossibility in that area for a professional person or a business establishment to be without a celebrity quota and still enjoy a feeling of importance in the world of mass media entertainment.

Paul Lynde's accountant felt important.

At the Vicente Foods market in Brentwood, the word would pass with the rapid-tap of computerized cash registers, along the row of checkout stands, to the checkers and boxboys and the customers waiting in lines, that Mrs. James Garner had come in. Mrs. James Garner would be sought and located and pointed out, and then she would be scrutinized, openly or secretly, by everyone, including those who were not clear about exactly who Mr. James Garner was.

At the Standard station in Westwood, an attendant said to another, "You know who that was? Jim Nabors' mother." "No shit," said the other, turning from the car window he was wiping. "Where, where?" came the cry of the woman in the car who, in a burst of excitement, threw open the door with such suddenness and wanton strength it caught the attendant across the back and hurled him into the gas pumps where he fell unconscious.

Celebrity name-dropping was a status game in which even the most distinguished and dedicated members of the medical profession competed. A nose and throat specialist could always find time to treat Barbra Streisand for a minor sinus infection.

Harvey Parkes had the requisite number of minor celebrity photographs, signed and framed, on the walls of his modest gym in Santa Monica. Most of them had been given to him by his clients, the wives of minor actors and television personalities, who rushed to him between errands three midmornings a week after driving the children to school. As evidence of his professional familiarity with celebrities, he pointed the photographs out to Elena when she came to discuss her proposal. At that time he was too weight-lifter heavy for his height, and he broke into a perspiration and trembled noticeably at the prospect of dealing with a celebrity of Randy's stature. He was suspicious of business arrangements where no money changed hands and decided that he was probably being used and that Elena wouldn't live up to her part of the bargain.

But she did. As a result of her sponsorship, as well as her guidance ("Darling, you must limit yourself to house calls, and set your own terms, and you must make it a point to be difficult. Not too difficult, but difficult.") Harvey had come the distance. The gym had been sold, and Harvey could not accommodate the numbers of clients who called. His secretary informed you that there was a waiting list. If you were a "Super-A" celebrity, Harvey would try to work you in, until he could create an opening for you by dropping a lesser luminary.

In the beginning, he would arrive at your house, wearing a no-iron jumpsuit, in an immaculate red Volkswagen, bringing a portable massage table. Now he came in a Jaguar and carried a wafer-thin Gucci attaché case in which he kept his appointment calendar, your exercise chart, and his book of phone numbers. He gave you three-quarters of an hour to the minute, without discounting the time he spent on your telephone checking with his office and rearranging his day's appointments to accommodate cancelations and emergencies. He analyzed your body's trouble areas, custom created your individual regimen and taught you how to perform the exercises properly. Thereafter, he came to you one to five days a week to make sure you did them.

Aware that he had become a celebrity himself, as well as a status symbol (grander than a Bentley, because there was only one of him), he began to re-educate himself, observing his clients, gathering clues and picking up pieces of information, learning what mattered most—what was "in" and what was not "in," and what was "class" and what was "no class." When he realized that it exposed a lack of class to cultivate over-developed muscles, he trimmed off fifty pounds and revised his daily workouts to concentrate on symmetry, definition, and grace of movement. Now he secretly prided himself that no film star in his age range—with the possible exception of Burt Lancaster—could match his not overstated physical perfection.

"Well?" Elena said. "What's been happening, Harvey? What do you know?"

"Let's see," Harvey said. "I know you're giving a dinner party a week from Friday." He liked to start off with news that wasn't news.

"Mm."

"And Victor Kroll's coming."

"Mm. Who told you that?"

"Gosh . . ." As always, he couldn't remember. "I heard it three or four places."

"Tell."

"I'm trying to remember."

"Harvey, for God's sake . . ."

"Oh," he said. "Mrs. Barry Springfield."

Anybody else would have said "Mrs. Springfield" or "Helen Springfield," but Harvey always referred to his clients by the way their names appeared in the columns . . . Mrs. David Begelman, Mrs. Aaron Spelling, Mrs. Dick Shepherd (Judy Shepherd was the late L. B. Mayer's granddaughter). Even when his female clients were stars in their own right, and were accorded that status by the press, Harvey Parkes still deferred to their husbands. Jean Simmons became "Mrs. Richard Brooks," Martha Hyer "Mrs. Hal Wallis."

Unlike Elena, Helen Springfield was merely a fringe member of the New Hollywood's social hierarchy (known as the "A Group") and the international jet set; she was not accorded recognition by the notable press of the world as a celebrity. Again, unlike Elena, she had not achieved the special individuality to qualify for equal (first name) mention with her husband, who was the Board Chairman of one of the biggest aircraft companies. Wives of prominent men, unless they were actresses or otherwise professional, seldom did.

In this regard, Elena was unique. In the remarkably short period of three years, since her marriage in Europe to Randall Brent and their arrival in Hollywood, she had charmed her way into the elite circle of the A Group and had moved up through the ranks of its pecking order to a position of prominence, as social arbiter and as one of the press-noted hostesses of the world, celebrated and envied for her talent at knowing how to give the most successful parties.

In the society pages, the gossip columns, and in magazines like *Town & Country,* where her photograph appeared constantly as the very incarnation of chic, acknowledgment of her individuality gave evidence of her importance by the way her name was printed. Rarely anymore did her name appear, among those prominent at the ladies' luncheons, as "Mrs. Randall Brent"; it was "Elena Brent." And even when she was mentioned with Randall, she was granted equal billing with her movie actor husband, as "Elena and Randall Brent."

Nothing satisfied Elena more than this kind of recognition. And no bit of gossip, however delicious, interested her more than hearing what others, especially her friends, were saying about her.

"What did Mrs. Barry Springfield say?" she asked, sitting on the floor, looking up at Harvey. Her eyes sparkled with excitement. At the moment she looked like a naughty child who smoked.

"Well," Harvey said, "she's all worked up about it. You know. She's out looking for something to wear. . . ."

"I love it. . . . What did she *say?*"

"I'm telling you . . ."

"No, you're telling me *about* it," she said, impatiently. He was so exasperating about details that she had to *drag* things out of him. He had no judgment about what was important and what wasn't.

There were also times when she could have killed him for not having gotten more information, for not following through. He didn't have the intelligence to pursue a remark by asking the next logical question. He just listened, like a nitwit, to whatever *they* told him. And half the time he didn't even do that. He cared hardly at all about *what* his celebrity clients were saying. It mattered only that they were celebrities and that they were saying it to *him*. But his physical access to information was unique, and his value to her was priceless.

It was the desired goal among members of the A Group to know everything about everybody. And in Elena's circle of close friends, the A Group hierarchy, the unofficial, self-appointed executive board, the ones who set the rules and decided who was coming in and who was going out, and who was loved and who was not loved, possession of information was power.

"I don't remember her exact words," Harvey said. "What difference does it make?"

"It makes a difference."

He never knew what she was doing. Questioning him, probing, cross-examining, she had been able to extract pieces of information that seemed meaningless to him; and by fitting them together with the abundance of news that came to her over the telephone every day, she accumulated material she was able to use in ways that would have astonished Harvey.

"I'm sure Mrs. Barry Springfield didn't say, 'I'm out looking for something to wear,'" Elena said. "I want to know *where* she's looking, that's my point. Not that I care, in *this* case."

"That's *my* point," Harvey said.

"*Forget* Mrs. Barry Springfield. She's totally insane. She's out looking for something to wear. . . . She bought three Norells at the showing last month. Three. She drove poor Gus stark raving crazy trying to make decisions. She wanted *everything* . . . except one, the one he wanted her to have, because after all, what does he know? She pestered him unmercifully. . . . Here is this poor, talented, sensitive man, with dozens of important people and admirers and friends he cares about, waiting to congratulate him. . . . It was a marvelous collection . . . and it was his moment of glory, and he wanted it, and he deserved it . . . he even *paid* for it . . . and he was of course *exhausted* from weeks of preparation and all the last-minute hectic things that go on, and no sleep for days, because that's the way it is. . . . And the poor man, an *idiot* would know, wanted only to stand there in his spotlight, in his terrible exhaustion and sip his brandy and let everybody tell him he was marvelous. He didn't want to be turned into a dress salesman by Mrs. Barry Springfield."

"God," Harvey said.

"Actually, she wanted to buy six . . . literally *six*. At up to five thousand each. But she couldn't 'afford' six . . . she can afford sixty . . . and Gus was expected to ignore everything else and right then and there haggle with her all night if necessary until she made up her mind. What did she say about Victor Kroll?"

"Well . . . she can't wait to meet him."

"I wonder why."

Harvey looked puzzled. Victor Kroll was the White House *éminence grise*. Through the long wake of Watergate, he had embraced his position as economist and statesman, assumed an aloofness to the machinations of politics, and had emerged above reproach, the Administration's sole survivor. And, therefore, its Man of the Moment, a hero by default. His prestige had soared, and the media had begun to use the word "charisma."

"I mean," Elena said, "so he can admire her new dress?"

Harvey laughed, feeling a slight twinge of guilt toward Mrs. Barry Springfield. Elena was always surprising him. Anybody else would be serious about the idea of entertaining Victor Kroll. Or nervous. But she made jokes. Though it confused him, he felt privileged to be sharing a joke that concerned Victor Kroll. And that inspired him to begin to recall the others who had talked with anticipation about the party, impressed by Elena's acquisition of one of the most powerful men in the world.

She still had to press for details, stop him again and again to ask questions, pulling and dragging the pieces out of him. And though she didn't get nearly enough, Elena listened with secret delight, savoring every word, her pleasure undiminished by her private knowledge that Victor Kroll was *not* coming to the party.

She had received a telephone call from Washington yesterday, from Kroll's appointments' secretary, saying that Kroll's schedule was in process of being revised and that his trip to Los Angeles would have to be canceled.

She had been disappointed, but not surprised. Kroll's acceptance of her invitation, several weeks ago, was contingent upon his being in Southern California on the weekend of her party, and he told her quite frankly that his proposed trip looked doubtful.

He had taken her call personally. In a warm, friendly voice, he said he would be delighted to come, but she must not count on it. And in that event, he hoped there would be a raincheck. She assured him there would be.

He liked her, she was sure of that. She had met him last year at a party on Long Island and had seen him again during the summer at a dinner in Malibu given by Mickey and Paul Ziffren. He had been charming and, even nicer, seemed charmed.

When she had issued her party invitations, promising Victor Kroll's appearance to everyone, Elena looked upon it as a justifiable deception. For she was a superb party-giver. Like a great actress, she had the talent, instincts, and ability to improvise, and she had the energy and drive to excel. She had learned that an atmosphere of anticipation was a key element to a really successful party. She understood that anticipation was more than half the fun. By promising Victor Kroll, she was providing that element, giving everyone something to look forward to. It was not a deception because he had, in fact, accepted. She was merely proceeding on the premise that he would be able to attend. And if, at the last moment, he was forced to cancel because he had been called away by affairs of state, could she be faulted?

Even the cancelation, properly used, would offer excitement. "Darling, I just got a phone call from Washington, from Victor Kroll. He has to cancel. He's been called to Brussels, for some secret Common Market talks. Apparently there's been a sudden development. Of course, he couldn't talk about it, but he implied. . . ." Thus, in exchange for the disappointment, the guests would have the bonus of feeling privy to top-level affairs of state.

But it was too soon, and there was no reason, to break the news. The party was still more than a week away, and Elena knew it was important to keep the excitement alive as long as possible. The phrase used by Kroll's secretary on the phone yesterday, that his schedule was "in process of being revised," suggested to Elena that there would be no immediate announcement that his trip to California was canceled. That gave her a margin. She would delay breaking the news until a day or two before the party. If the news broke in the media before that time, she would say that she had just received a phone call from Kroll himself. In the meantime, she would concentrate on trying to find a replacement, a new attraction or a surprise. She hadn't had time to consider who it might be. There were times, like this, when one had to improvise. It was not essential. Her party would be successful in any case. But it was a challenge and an excitement, and that's what she enjoyed.

For the moment, courtesy of Harvey Parkes, she was allowing herself to enjoy the reports of her current success. Whatever happened next week, this week Elena Brent was giving the most talked-about party of the season.

The phone rang. Elena picked it up quickly and said hello in the hurried voice she used when she wanted to establish at once that she couldn't talk.

"Hel-lo, dear," said Grace St. George, slowly. "Am I catching you at the wrong time?"

"Eternally, dear," is what Elena wanted to say, but she answered, "Yes, dear. Harvey Parkes is here." People always referred to Harvey by both names, running them together to sound like one word. You said "Harveyparkes," and when you answered the phone and said he was here, your caller replied, "Callyouback," and instantly hung up.

Except Grace St. George, who was inordinately gauche and lacking in judgment. "Oh, give him my love, dear, and tell him I won't keep you. Just one quick thing . . . how are you . . . ?"

"Fine, darling. Look, let me call you back."

"Be sure. It's important. There's somebody I want you to meet. Let me just tell you this one thing, I won't keep you. . . . He's *very* special and bright, you'll be impressed, he's from the East, and he's come out here to do a picture. He's optioned a marvelous property, with a part that was *made* for Randy. I'm saying this fast, because I don't want to keep you. . . . Dear, you know I don't go around casting pictures, because I'm not qualified and I don't presume, but Adam gave me this property to read, and I read it, and I had dinner with him last night. And I said, Adam, I am going to mention a name to you, for your picture, and I don't want you to say anything, I want you to think about it. . . ."

"Grace, I'm dying to hear about it, but Harvey is glaring at me, and. . . ."

"I'll let you go, dear. Just one thing. Adam is *very* interested, he's very excited, and I don't want us to let go of this for Randy. I told Adam we'd arrange something. . . ."

"Darling, that sounds exciting and I'll call you back."

"As soon as possible."

"Yes, dear." She hung up.

Harvey had picked up the other phone to call his office, and had carried it to the mirror, where he had watched himself while he talked briefly to his secretary.

"Ohh," Elena groaned, "that woman is so abominable!"

"Poor Grace," Harvey said, and Elena looked at him, thinking, isn't it amazing that even Harvey has learned to say "Poor Grace." Grace was a "closet" press agent, the only one of her kind, and she had been around for more years than most people were old enough to remember. She was employed secretly—because she was an embarrassment—by the wives of C stars and by newcomers to Hollywood. Among her clientele were rich Mexicans, Manhattan stockbrokers moved West, near-authentic jet setters, television millionaires with socially ambitious wives—people who wanted to get into the celebrity-gossip-column world but didn't want it known that they were using a flack. When one of her former clients told another she'd seen Grace, the other inevitably said, "How's poor Grace?" Never "How's Grace?" Most of them denied ever having had any connection with her. Because she was lonely—deservedly—some of them felt sorry for her and allowed her to hang on, inviting her to parties that were big enough to withstand her.

"She's such an unbelievable slob," Elena said. "She's found another promoter who is allegedly going to produce a picture, and *she's* casting it, no less, and offering the lead to Randy."

"Maybe it's something," Harvey said.

"*No*, dear, it's clumsy. And annoying. She wants to use my party. I'm supposed to invite her, with the promoter. So he can exploit my friends. And we know everybody's crazy about her."

"God," he said, looking in the mirror, troubled. "That's incredible." Then he said, "I'm beginning to have Ronald Reagan's mouth."

Elena looked at him.

"Thin lips," he said. "I've always had thin lips, but lately they've been getting a prissy look. See what I mean?" He turned and showed her.

"Really, I don't," she said, though she did. She wondered but didn't ask why it mattered. He was in his fifties. Did he expect to be discovered by a talent scout at Schwab's? "I think you're very handsome."

"I'm not," he said. "I just hate that prissy look. As you get older, your lips get thinner. I've been trying some exercises, but so far I don't see any results."

He showed her the facial exercises which were supposed to keep the lips full. He turned his lips outward, inward, one at a time; he pressed them together hard; he pursed them for a kiss and stretched them out as far as he could, like a camel; he held them loosely together and blew air through them, to bring greater circulation to the outer layers.

"Harvey," Elena said, "come with me, I want some coffee. Do you want coffee, or juice, or something?"

He didn't, but he followed her into the breakfast room, saying, "Facials are very beneficial. If you really work at them, you can keep everything firm and never have to have a face lift. Your face is full of muscles, did you know that? People don't know that and they go around all their lives never moving their faces. They just let them hang there, so naturally they gradually fall."

"Can you teach me?"

"You don't need them," he said.

"Why not?"

"You have good bones. And you move your face. Besides, you're young."

He sat at the table in the breakfast room, which opened off the kitchen, and watched her pour coffee from the electric percolator which was plugged into the wall beside the sink. The sink was filled with unwashed dishes. Pots and pans, empty bottles, sections of newspapers and pieces of mail crowded the counters.

Harvey was accustomed to the mess in the kitchen. Elena had explained that Fannie had Mondays off and didn't return until late on Tuesday afternoon. "It gets to be a mess," Elena had told him, "but it upsets her if I do it, so I ignore it."

Harvey watched Elena rinse out one of the unwashed cups and negotiate the percolator past obstacles and pour herself a cup of coffee.

"You know who ought to do the facials, just between you and me," he said. "Randy."

"I don't think we'll mention that," she said. She brought her coffee to the table in the breakfast room and sat down across from him.

"Oh, I wasn't going to," he said. "I was just mentioning it to you."

Thinking of Randy, Elena observed, had caused Harvey's lips to tighten and turn inward. Randy had been Harvey's first important client and his first failure. He had endured the sessions with Harvey for two angry months and then quit. Harvey took it as a personal rejection, though Elena had tried to reassure him it was not, explaining that Randy was not an exercise person, just as she was not an exercise person.

But Harvey still felt that Randy had taken a personal dislike to him, and Elena had never been able to convince him otherwise, no matter how persuasively she lied. When inspired—and the most fleeting glimpse of Harvey, seen from the upstairs window as he parked his Jaguar and crossed the circular driveway to the front door, was enough to inspire him—Randy could do twenty violent minutes just on Harvey's "Posturepedic tight-assed" walk.

"How's he been?" Harvey asked. "Anything happening?"

As always, she told him that Randy was considering various offers, making it a point to specify at least one. She was extremely adroit at the game of assuring people that Randy was active and busy. She knew how to fabricate details that had the ring of truth, and she knew to vary her stories and her attitudes, even to dropping occasional words of discouragement or concern at times, to support credibility at others. The only thing that worked against her was time, time's evidence that Randy hadn't done a picture in three years.

"He's been working very hard," she said, "to finish the script. The writer was here last night, and they were still working at three when I went to sleep."

Harvey was vague about the nature of the project, though she had been telling him about it for the past few months. He was vague because the project didn't exist, but that never occurred to him. He believed her, and that enabled him to sound appropriately convincing around town, when anybody asked about Randy.

Harvey looked at his watch. It was time for him to leave. Then he snapped his fingers and said, as though he had just remembered it, "I *knew* I had something to tell you . . . and I almost forgot."

Elena saw that he was smiling the certain smile—narrow-lipped and prissy, she realized—he used when he played his favorite game. It indicated that he had a choice piece of gossip and had deliberately delayed telling her until the last minute.

She could have thrashed him for being such a tiresome fool about it, but she played his game to please him. She lowered her eyelids and made a prissy-mouth back at him, and said, "Harvey—you—are—*wick-ed!*"

He threw back his head and laughed. There, she thought, you've moved your face.

He loved this game because it paid her back for all the times she had acted disappointed by the news he brought her. He liked to show her that he had no problem about remembering details when it came to something significant.

He loved to bring her a really juicy piece of gossip. He loved it so much, he hated to part with it.

"What *is* it, Harvey?" she demanded, dying to know.

"Marina Vaughan . . . " Harvey said, taking his time watching her. He could feel her mind working. She glanced off to the side, at nothing, then back at him, then away.

Elena put out her cigarette and lit another, watching Harvey, her mind racing to the possibilities. Marina Vaughan was news. She was one of the brightest young stars in show business. And one of the few super-stars of the world.

Was it drugs? An overdose? A breakdown? Suicide attempt?

Any of those were possible. All had been predicted by people who knew Marina and worried about her.

Sex? What sexual experimentation could it be that Marina had not already explored?

Had she fired her manager, a loyal and patient man who had guided her career from the beginning? That, too, had been predicted.

Had she been beaten up by her lover, Rick Navarro? Was he in jail?

"Rick Navarro," Harvey said, and before he finished the sentence, Elena knew . . . "moved out last night."

She could hardly wait for Harvey to tell the rest. As much as she wanted to hear the details, she wanted him to leave, so that she could phone Natalie. She had to control herself from picking up the phone right then and there, while he was still talking.

Oh, how it would delight Natalie's bitter heart!

And, oh, how she wanted to be the one who gave Natalie the news!

She had to get rid of Harvey before Natalie heard it from somebody else. If Natalie heard it from somebody else, she would kill Harvey for playing his game, for letting precious time go by, for having waited until he was ready to *leave!*

If Harvey's report was reliable—and his answers to a few key questions satisfied her that it was—nobody knew about it yet, except the Mexican maid and Harvey, who had arrived at Marina's this morning to keep their regular appointment, and had heard the story from the maid, in Spanish, with gestures and tears, and evidence in the house of incredible havoc. Marina was asleep, heavily sedated, to be sure. But asleep, not dead. And Rick Navarro "*ya se fue*" in the Porsche with all his belongings, driving away at dawn, stoned out of his gourd and turning up the tape deck to blast out the sound of Marina's voice screaming at him from the latticed veranda while the Mexican maid sobbed on her knees and prayed to God in her room behind the garage.

Elena had become so caught up in the story that she didn't hear Randy come into the kitchen.

"Hi there," Harvey said, looking past her with an expression of dismay.

Elena turned to see Randy, barefoot and in his robe, his hair in all directions, his face unshaven and swollen, his hung over eyes almost shut, contemplating the sinkful of dishes and the rubble-entrapped percolator with a look of rage she associated in that moment of confusion with the rage of Rick Navarro.

"Darling," she said, pleasantly, "I didn't hear you get up." She came into the kitchen to greet him, but the look he gave her told her it would be a mistake to pursue pleasantries for Harvey's benefit. So she went to the cupboard for a cup and saucer. "Dear, don't try to cope with this mess. Let me help you. Why don't you go into the den and I'll bring you your coffee."

Randy was never at his best in the morning, but rarely had she seen him this hung over. Harvey had gotten up from the table, and she was aware of him standing there in the breakfast room, not knowing what to do next, unnerved by the way Randy totally ignored him, and shocked by his appearance. Harvey hadn't seen him in months, because Randy made a point of never coming downstairs until he was sure Harvey had left.

"Go on, dear," she said. "The paper's in there." And she busied herself fixing the coffee, praying that he would just go, with no words for Harvey to hear, none of the poisonous hostility that had begun to erupt last evening.

Randy put his hands in the pockets of his robe and stood up straight, lifting his head and looking out of the slits of his eyes into the breakfast room. "Good to see you Harvey," he said, and went out to the den.

"I've got to get going," Harvey said, and then looked frightened. "Oh. My case . . . is in the den."

"I'll get it, dear," Elena said.

He followed her out and waited in the hallway, where he could hear Randy's voice coming from the den: ". . . dumb fuck's car wasn't out there, how am I supposed to know he's still here?"

When Harvey had arrived, water from the sprinklers next door had been hitting the driveway, so he had parked in the street.

Elena appeared with his attaché case. She was smiling, and she shook her head to indicate that Randy was being impossible today. "It's one of those mornings," she whispered.

That put things in perspective for Harvey. He drove away, realizing that Randy was the same as ever. He'd been up late, working—and drinking too much, as always—and it was just one of those mornings.

But he still didn't like him. And he very much resented being called a dumb fuck. He discovered he was holding his lips pressed tight. He relaxed them and blew out air, letting them flap loose and easy.

2

After saying goodbye to Harvey, Elena had rushed upstairs to the bedroom to telephone Natalie. She avoided the den because she knew, at times like these, to stay out of Randy's way. He despised you if you spoke to him, or appeared to look at him. You were supposed to go about your business, pretending he wasn't there, ignoring him. But once you had been intimidated, he would move in like a sniper and begin to shoot at you. She was sympathetic to his suffering. She understood the misery he endured during these periods of depression, but you had to protect yourself.

She knew by the way he had behaved that he was lying in wait, and she was determined not to let him snag her and delay her call to Natalie. She headed for the stairs and literally ran past the doorway of the den, determined, should he call out to her, to pretend she hadn't heard him.

He didn't call out. She escaped, free, into the bedroom, and closed the door. She went to the telephone and dialed Natalie's number and got a busy signal. She dialed Natalie's other number, and got a busy signal. Naturally. She considered having the operator break in, on the pretense that it was an emergency, but decided to give it a few more minutes. If both lines were still busy, she'd have the operator cut in. Who knew, in fact, that it was not an emergency?

She wondered if Natalie had gotten the news, if that's why both lines were busy. Natalie would be the first person Marina would call, providing Marina were conscious and functioning.

Before her affair with Rick Navarro, Marina phoned Natalie daily, at all hours of the day and night, from all over the world, wherever she happened to be. She had turned Natalie into her mother surrogate and mother confessor.

It was interesting to Elena that Natalie, small-boned, brittle, nervous, with large dark eyes, resembled Marina's mother, the legendary Bobbie Shaw, a shooting star whose brilliant fire, slowly darkened by alcohol and drugs, burned out and fell to earth—a suicide. But where Bobbie Shaw had been soft and too vulnerable, Natalie, with the brittle face of a malevolent china doll, was hard.

When Marina made a picture, Natalie, along with Marina's agent and manager, was summoned to the studio and consulted about every decision. Natalie was prominent in the entourage that went to Vegas for Marina's casino openings. And the men in Marina's life were subject to Natalie's opinion and approval. Not one of them ever rivaled Natalie's importance to Marina.

When Marina began going with Rick Navarro, who had arranged a series of concert tours for her, Natalie thought he was sweet and inoffensive. He smoked grass and sniffed a little coke, smiled a lot and seemed rather passive. And he was devoted to Marina, so devoted that Marina gradually needed other people less and less. At first, Natalie was relieved. It was a respite from demands that had become too frequent and too exhausting.

Then one day Natalie realized that Marina had stopped consulting her, and she learned that Marina had also stopped consulting her agent and her manager. Marina saw none of her old friends, and she stopped going to parties. Rick had taught her a new set of values; the real meaning and purpose of life, he'd told her, was a man and a woman together. Alone. And she had never been happier, had never felt so loved or so cared for. Rick devoted himself to her, gave her his body, his mind, his heart, his soul, and all of his time. It was a demanding devotion. He delegated much of his work as founder and Chairman of Navarro Records to his President in order to manage Marina's career. Because he was the one who knew her and loved her best, he began to choose her scripts, produce her pictures, her record albums, her club engagements, and her television specials.

And he helped her to realize that she'd been used by opportunistic people—like her agent, her manager, Natalie, and her former friends.

It was Marina and Rick against the world. Rick was in, and everybody else was out.

* * *

When Elena tried Natalie again, the maid answered and said that Natalie was on the other phone. Elena asked her to tell Natalie it was urgent. She returned to say that Natalie couldn't get off the other phone, but would call her back as soon as possible.

Again bypassing the den, Elena went downstairs to the kitchen for a cup of coffee. Randy was there, pouring himself a gin and orange juice.

"Forgive me," he said. "I'm in your way."

"You're not in my way," she said, knowing it was a mistake to say anything. And a mistake to say nothing.

"I'm going," he said. "I have my drink."

She understood about his drink. He knew it was wrong to drink early in the day, and he never did, except at these times when he had to.

"I *need* my drink," he said.

That was one of the deeper traps, and not to be answered.

"Guess what Harvey told me," she said.

"Guess what Harvey told you . . . Let me see . . . That you have a filthy kitchen?"

"Harvey understands about the kitchen."

"Harvey's very understanding. You ought to show him your dressing table and your bathroom."

When she made no reply, he said, "She is maintaining a cautious silence."

The phone rang. Rather than pick it up in the kitchen, she hurried into the den to get away from him.

"Hi, dear," she said.

"Hel-lo," said Grace St. George. "You didn't call back, and I've decided to be a pest."

Natalie would know to call on the other phone, so Elena sank into a chair and let Grace have a few minutes. It was, of course, a repetition of what she had said before, about this person named Adam, and the property he had optioned for a picture, and how bright and attractive and intelligent he was, and how excited he was about the idea of Randy playing the lead. Grace didn't say he was a millionaire, and that was unusual for her, so probably he was destitute. He had produced a play on Broadway and another in London, both successful flops. Grace was the only press agent in the world who was stupid enough to tell you that her clients' plays were flops.

The property that Adam had under option, Grace said, was Harry Waller's novel, *Rogue's Gallery*. Harry Waller was probably the most famous contemporary American novelist, admired for his talent but famous for the extravagances of his personal life—his marriages, affairs, drinking bouts, public displays of political and social protest, and all-around pugnacious and/or clownish behavior. He was also noted for the fact that he did not give movie promoters options on his novels.

"When you meet Adam," Grace said, "you must make him tell you how he got Waller to give him the option, it's marvelous." And then she said, because it was her custom to give you your horoscope, gratis, and because she was so incredibly foolish, "Darling, this is a good month for you, that is to say it can be a good month for you, if you'll make it a point to take advantage of opportunities."

As the conversation—it was one-sided, with Grace saying everything seven times—went on and on, Randy came in with his drink and sat across from Elena, listening to her say, "Uh huh" and "Hm," and watching her with his expression of bemused contempt. It occurred to Elena to hand him the phone, so that Grace could tell him how she was casting him in the part. But she knew how much he detested Grace for being the phony she was, and in his current mood, he would probably tell her that he only considered firm offers and that she could shove Harry Waller's novel up her ass.

Randy suddenly asked, "Who's doing all the talking, Rattley Natalie?"

Elena covered the mouthpiece and said, "It's Grace St. George. Being pushy. And borrrrring."

He looked at her for a moment, shaking his head. "Christ," he said. "You have a vicious mouth on you, enough to chill anybody's goddamned blood." He was going to defend Grace St. George, whom he detested, because Elena had attacked her.

He had started to be this way last evening, on the way home from Kip Nathan's. They had been invited, along with Natalie and Jack Kaufman and the usual crowd, for drinks and coffee and to see a new film that Kip's wife Nancy had seen and adored at the Cannes Festival.

Kip Nathan was the head, in charge of production, of Pacific Pictures, a major Hollywood studio. In an era when most movie companies were run from Wall Street board rooms, the typical studio chief had a life expectancy considerably shorter than that of a Latin American dictator. When a film was good, the president back East took the credit; when it was bad, the studio chief was blamed and ritually sacrificed to the financial gods. Kip, who had just turned forty, had survived these perils for seven years. His success was extraordinary. His wife, Nancy O'Brien, had achieved unique success as a journalist and polemicist, and nation-wide recognition as a glamorous guerrilla on the journalistic-political-sexual scene. And she was only thirty.

Such evenings, spent in the company of top agents, producers, performers, successful, powerful men who controlled the industry, had become more and more difficult for Randy. There was no avoiding them nor did he want to. It was important to belong, but it had become increasingly demoralizing to be on the outside of success. Especially demoralizing was the knowledge that among his closest friends were men like Kip Nathan who, when they could—and did—dictate the casting of pictures, never said more to him about his career than, "What's happening?" Randy didn't want favors from them, or charity. He would have liked to feel that they had respect for his talent, ability, and value as an actor.

As Elena and Randy drove home from Kip's last evening, Randy hadn't spoken. He drove fast through the traffic-empty streets, as though he were late for an appointment. He never so much as glanced at Elena. She was invisible, a phantom, and he drove alone.

She had learned not to attempt to make conversation at such times, so she kept quiet and didn't look at him. When they turned on to Maple Drive, a block away from home, he finally spoke, accusing her of keeping a noticeable silence which, he said, was uncharacteristic of her and, therefore, was her mean-mouthed way of making the point that he was a shit.

At home, when she uttered the bare amenities—in a "natural" tone of voice, lest she be accused of sounding either "phony-polite" or "cunty" —he responded with one-syllable answers, grunts and irritable looks, implying that he found her annoying, boring, and contemptible.

She used to try to figure out what he expected her to do at these times. One day she realized that it didn't matter.

She was not supposed to exist. In this particular game of solitaire, all that mattered was his inner war. It would cripple his intellect and hold him in a vise of depression that would grow tighter over the next days. He would lie in bed, wrapped in his terrycloth robe, and stare at television with an expression of vile hatred. He would try to cheer himself up with a drink in the mornings—permitted only at these times of crisis, when depression gripped him. Finally, something would loosen his tongue—usually something trivial on television, either a starlet on "The Tonight Show" who "had the cutes" or the sight of some cheap sofas being touted by a local dealer who "should be forced by the FCC to read a statement declaring himself a liar and a pig and a felon who sells shit."

That would be the prelude, sometimes lasting for three or four days, to the explosion that would follow, the bitter recital of injustices and mistreatments and misfortunes, major and trivial—the movie they had seen in which he did not star; the picture makers they knew who pretended he was not available; the friends who endured him for her sake, since she was the star of the outfit and he was the dumb wife—that had been collecting over the days and weeks since the last explosion.

She had once tried, at the start of one of these harangues, to help him by pointing out his pattern and urging him to let his anger come out sooner, to get it over with. They were in the kitchen. He had looked at her with a degree of fury she had not seen before. Then he had become extraordinarily calm, and as she watched him cross to the cupboards, she felt a chill of premonition, the certainty that he was going to seize an implement with which to kill her. By the time he brought down the bottle of gin and began to pour himself a drink, she had planned her escape route through the house—*not* stopping for anything, not even the car keys on the table in the foyer—and out the front door and down the middle of the street, out in the open, away from the shadows of shrubbery and trees.

After he had mixed the drink, which he stirred for a long time, he looked over at her and said without raising his voice, "One of the many things you are *not* is a *thinker*. You think like a faggot. You know how to scheme, and haggle, and bargain, and bitch your friends, but you don't know how to *think*. That's okay, it's cute of you. But that doesn't qualify you to be the head shrink in the nut house, does it? Don't you ever dare to hand me that kind of patronizing horseshit, do you understand?"

And then he had taken his drink and gone upstairs to the guest bedroom—which had not yet become his permanent private bedroom as it was now—and slammed the door with such force it bounced immediately open, and he kick-slammed it again. A moment later there was a terrifying crash, which meant something had gotten in his way and he had kicked it over, or had hurled something against the wall.

She had stayed in the kitchen, standing by the sink and smoking, waiting to see what would happen next. She began to believe that her suggestion had worked, that she had provoked the explosion. The thought pleased her, because her theory had seemed to her to make sense. She had strength, and a great capacity for dealing with adversity. The only thing in life she could not tolerate was to be faced with a problem that couldn't be solved.

But it had turned out she was wrong. There were no more crashes. He resumed his silence with a vengeance, and went deeper into the pit of his depression and stayed there longer.

When the other phone rang, Elena picked it up and held it to her other ear. It was Natalie. She talked into both phones, telling Natalie to hold on and telling Grace she had to get off, even though she and Grace had still not settled on a meeting with Grace's latest promoter, Adam Baker.

The sight and the sound of her, talking into the two phones—to two women he abhorred, one a sloppy loose-lipped old cow's udder and the other a mean-cunted dykey bitch—filled Randy with contempt. He shook his head to let her know that he could not go on sitting there, a captive audience to a display of such turgid shit. Then he took his drink and went upstairs.

Elena and Grace promised to phone each other tomorrow, and Elena was alone on the phone with Natalie, at last.

"What did *she* want?" Natalie asked.

"She's been phoning me every five minutes, hounding me to invite one of her clients to my party, can you believe it?"

"Who?"

"Who listens?" Though Natalie was her closest friend, Elena had learned to protect her possibilities, even dim ones presented by Grace St. George.

"A rug merchant?" Natalie said.

"Something like that."

"Maybe he'd like to finance something."

"I'm afraid it's the other way around," Elena said. "Is everything all right?"

"Yes, why?" Natalie asked.

"The way Christine said you couldn't get off the phone."

"I called Nancy to thank her and I couldn't get her off."

"I haven't called her yet. Harvey Parkes just left."

"Are you all right?" Natalie asked.

"Fine."

"Christine said it was an emergency."

"I wanted to be sure I got you before you went out. I called you earlier and both your lines were busy." She was trying to determine if Natalie had heard the news and, if she had, what reason she might have for holding it back.

"How's Randy?" Natalie asked.

"Not now."

"He's right there?"

"No, I mean it's boring. He's all right."

"There was a little tension last night?"

"Was there?"

"When we were leaving, I sensed a little tension."

"Did Nancy say something?"

"*Nancy?* Nancy notices nothing human. Only ideas. When I thanked her, she said, 'What for?' in that offhand tone she gets, that sounds like 'Fuck you.' I wanted to say, 'For shooting off your mouth all through the picture, like the yenta you are, that's what for.' "

"And serving rotten coffee."

"Oh, was that coffee? Did you love the picture?"

"It was forgettable."

"You didn't like it?"

"I seem to keep forgetting it. It's disappearing, piece by piece. I'd better hurry up and phone her."

"You don't have to worry. She'll tell you the whole picture. That's why I couldn't get her off. Who *cares* about a movie to that degree? Aside from Pauline Kael."

"I don't think Kip liked it so much."

"Does he know anymore? He's brainwashed. Have you ever seen such *awe?* He thinks she's the Oracle. I'm beginning to have serious doubts about his IQ."

"I suppose it's typical," Elena said. "I mean, if you were a psychiatrist . . . because it's so entirely the opposite of the way he used to be."

"The dummies were at least nice to look at. And he didn't permit them to talk."

"And there was the turnover."

Before he married Nancy, Kip kept a succession of starlets moving in and out of his bachelor-pad mansion. They all had the same qualities—great bodies, no minds. They hung around as decoratively and inanimately as the decorator-purchased Picassos on the walls. They'd be there for a few days, sometimes a week, never longer than two weeks. And they were never repeated.

"Why did he marry her; can you tell me?" Natalie asked.

"He's impressed. *You* told *me.*"

"She's not even attractive."

"Oh, yes," Elena said. "She's attractive."

"No, dear, she's an incipient hag with too much chin and no tits."

Elena gasped. It was true. Suddenly, she had an entirely different picture of Nancy. Natalie, with insights flaming out of hostility, could always cast a new light.

"She's attractive to him because she's Nancy O'Brien," Elena said.

"A professional ball-breaker."

"He's proved he's man enough to capture a woman who publicly criticizes men for being weak. So that gives him balls."

"Oh shit, I think that's a lot of shit, I really do," Natalie said.

"The dummies bored him. Nancy has brains. He's proud of her; he's like a doting father."

"I'll bet *that* doesn't go down very well, and *speaking* of . . . how do you suppose he adores that? You know she doesn't give him head."

"Darling," Elena said, "don't try to presume what goes on in the bedroom. You never know. Nobody knows."

"In this case the whole world knows. You read her book . . . you couldn't put it down, could you?"

"Natalie, you're arguing with success."

"I hate all that Women's Lib crap. Why doesn't she just admit she hates men?"

"I think she does admit it."

"She plays it both ways. She's a sneak, is what she is."

"I don't remember that she said specifically what she did in bed."

"*Didn't* do. She said specifically that she put down the whole sex culture, especially phallic-worship, which she says is a concept invented by *men*—and that's probably true, but then Bell invented the telephone, so can't I use it?—and she thinks women should quit getting down on their knees."

"Well . . . philosophically."

"Read it again."

"Darling, do you care?"

"Darling, Nancy O'Brien doesn't need you to defend her. I'm trying to understand Kip."

"Darling, he won the liberated woman," Elena said. "So he's king of the mountain. Face it."

"Then he's playing the same game he used to play with the dummies! He's exploiting her. And she lets him get away with that? One thing she is not is a dummy. I think she sees right through him. I think she not only doesn't give him head, I think they don't even fuck. We know he has a problem, don't we? You don't keep an endless parade of dummies unless you're trying to prove something. I used to figure it was because he couldn't get it up."

"No, he can get it up."

"You were there?"

"We once had a very interesting discussion about sex and he was very out in the open about it. He said he wasn't very sex-driven. He loves girls, but his mind isn't on sex, it's on business."

"So he sublimates. But to an extreme. It's not normal not to be sex-driven. Take it from me, he can't get it up."

"She got pregnant."

"Okay, he got it up once. The miracle is that she didn't flush it down the toilet. She went right ahead and debased herself, like a cow. Not only that, she *married* him. And don't think the money and the power didn't have a lot to do with it. She's a phony. She's using him. I think she enjoys not fucking somebody important and powerful. That child can thank God it's a girl. Would you love to be a boy with your balls in her hands?"

"Natalie," Elena said, "not to change the subject, but Harvey Parkes was here . . ."

"Then why aren't we changing the subject?"

"We are . . ."

"Because we know Harvey Parkes doesn't have any—that's a rubber cup he got at Ah Men, isn't it?"

Elena told Natalie about Helen Springfield looking for something to wear to the party: ". . . because the Norells, of course, won't do."

"I agree," Natalie said. "Norell should pay her not to wear them. But there's nothing she can wear. Poor Helen. What can you wear when you have a big head and no neck and a short body and a big ass?"

Elena said, "Oh, you'll love this . . . Harvey says Mel Ferrer is angry with him because he won't return his phone calls. He used to do him, but now he won't. Guess why?"

"Did Mel make a pass at him?"

"Does Mel like boys?"

"Audrey is not a boy?"

"Natalie, try very hard not to think about sex for a minute. He won't do Mel because he refuses to work south of Wilshire."

Natalie laughed so hard she had a coughing spasm and had to leave the phone. When she came back, Elena said, "Have you talked to Marina lately?"

"I don't talk to Marina," Natalie said.

The last time Natalie called Marina, several months ago, Marina had said very irritably, "I don't have time to hang on the phone, Natalie, so if it's something important, just tell me fast." To which Natalie had replied, "Okay. You can go *fuck* yourself, is that fast enough for you?" And hung up. And had not called or heard from Marina since.

"When Rick's finished with her," Natalie said to Elena, "and she's a basket case and needs me, I'll find some compassion and I'll try to paste her together again, but I'll never feel the same about her, because she's a cunt."

"Darling," Elena said. "Rick moved out last night."

"No!?"

Elena related what Harvey had told her. There was not a sound from Natalie, but the silence was perceptible. It breathed, like a hungry beast. Elena gave it meticulous attention, feeding every detail she had been able to extract or interpret from Harvey. She could picture Natalie sitting on the edge of her bed, legs crossed, leaning forward in a kind of crouch, the dark ferret's eyes darting, shifting, as though they listened, the small hand going to the doll mouth where the precise, pretty pointed teeth wanted to pare away at the bitten fingernails, but couldn't because the nails were protected by Juliets, lovely and long.

After she heard the story, Natalie had to hear it again, this time asking questions, to be sure she hadn't missed any part of it, especially the beginning. Then she said, decisively, "Well, I won't call her," and added, "or should I?"

They both knew she would, but it was necessary to discuss the pros and cons.

Elena pointed out that when the news broke, which could happen momentarily—more than likely it would appear in Ballen's column in the Los Angeles *Chronicle* tomorrow—it would be only civil and humane for Natalie to phone Marina.

Natalie felt it would smack a little of the vulture, a role she didn't want to be accused of playing. "Not that I haven't been circling over that love nest," she said, "and I feel I deserve any little scrap of flesh I can get, but I have my pride."

"I agree with you, darling," Elena said.

"I'm entitled."

"Yes . . . but you told me only a few minutes ago that when she needed you, you'd be there to pick up the pieces. And you know you will."

"Who'll thank me?"

"Darling," Elena said, implying that she was not taking that remark seriously.

"Ohhhhh," Natalie said. "Poor scrawny cat . . . she breaks my heart, she's such a fuck-up!"

"Of course," Elena said, as though on second thought, "I'd like it better if *Marina* called *you*."

"I'm *very* aware she hasn't," Natalie said. "It just happened and she can't pull herself together."

"Natalie, you know she's knocked herself out with pills."

"Don't you think somebody ought to get over there and make sure she's not dead?" Natalie said.

"According to the maid, she was asleep and breathing. Harvey made it a point about the breathing."

"Oh, Harvey's an asshole," Natalie said. "And that maid is a lunatic. She wears an onion to bed when she has the flu. I suppose what I ought to do is to call Dr. Dementia," she said, that being her name for Marina's psychiatrist, Dr. Demelius, "but I did that once when I knew she was desperate and suicidal, and I got the very calm voice of God, passing judgments while I tried to plead with him that a *life* was in danger. It was suggested to me that I examine my motives. If he was a plumber and you called him because the house was flooding, he'd tell you to build an ark and bring the animals, two by two. Fuck him, too, I don't need him."

"I agree with you," Elena said.

"I don't need him and I don't need her."

"You're absolutely right, darling," Elena said. And then she helped Natalie to look at the situation objectively: Marina was in trouble. Marina needed her. Natalie was her friend. Natalie was the person Marina had always turned to. Furthermore, Natalie cared. Marina was twenty-five, a child. Natalie was forty-one, a woman.

It was Natalie who must now be strong and understanding and rise above petty feelings of hurt pride and rejection. Natalie must phone Marina and offer her friendship. "And there's no reason to wait until you read about it in the paper. Call now."

"You're right, you're right, you're right," Natalie said, sounding suddenly impatient with Elena.

"Then I won't keep you, darling," Elena said.

"Wait a minute. . . . *Why* am I calling? I mean, how did I hear about it? *Not* from Harvey Parkes . . . or anybody else, for that matter. No, I won't be cast in the role of vulture and gossip. I mean, don't you agree?"

"Darling," Elena said, "it's simple. Do ESP. Tell her you're calling because you couldn't sleep last night for no reason that you know about, but you simply couldn't sleep, and she kept coming into your mind, and you had a very *strong feeling* that something was the matter, and you just simply have to know. 'Marina . . . are you all right?' "

"Don't you think that's a little obvious?"

"She'll adore it. Everybody adores ESP, and who can ever prove otherwise? Darling, in this particular instance, take my word for it, it's the *perfect* way, the best way in the world you can show Marina that you care, because it's *instinct*, you see, it's *felt*, so it proves to her that somebody *really* cares, *really* loves her."

"Which I *do*," Natalie said, "even though she's behaved like an idiot."

"It won't hurt a bit for her to think that you 'felt' it, that you couldn't sleep . . ."

"Not a bit," Natalie said. "Of course, you realize I won't get to talk to her at all, I'm going to get the lunatic maid, and we're going to do idiot-Spanish and she's going to tell me the señorita is 'Dormiendoing' . . . so then I'm stuck with leaving a message."

"Insist that she wake her up. Tell her it's *importante*."

"*Urgente*, dear," Natalie said. "*Urgente* is the magic word. It's the only thing they understand. I'll manage. Just let me get it over with."

"Darling, if you are able to talk to her, try to keep yourself from saying, 'I told you so.' Let *her* tell *you*. Do you know what I'm saying?"

"Yes, yes, I know," Natalie said impatiently. "I'll call you back."

"Right away?"

"Yes, yes."

3

Eventually, Elena went down to the kitchen. It had been on her mind, since Randy's vicious remark earlier, to clean up the mess that had accumulated. She had planned to do it at the end of the day, after she returned from shopping and running errands. There were always seemingly endless numbers of small details to attend to in advance of a party, and she liked to space out the work, doing a little every day.

It was fortunate that the party was more than a week away, because by then Randy's crisis would be over; he was always at his best in the immediate aftermath, before the advent of the next decline. She realized what she had not been wanting to realize: that these episodes had been occurring more frequently and that the better times of relative peace had become shorter.

For today, and tomorrow, having the party to think about was the best possible distraction. She had learned to stay out of his way, and if there were not all the work to do for the party, she would have invented activities to keep herself busy and out of the house as much as possible.

She could cope with the silences and the preliminary, minor-skirmish attacks. And she could tolerate the eventual explosion (though the outburst of violence always filled her with panic) because it was relatively brief and it meant the worst was over. What she dreaded, more than the silence and more than the explosion, was the day of truth which had to follow, when he would begin to unwind his tangled, knotted kite string of hatred, his recital of injustices. He would reveal it all to her, beginning with the specific incidents that were responsible, the remarks, the slights, hers included, the ironies of fate and pieces of rotten luck, the evidences perpetrated upon the screen and the public by talentless shits whose monumental incompetence was matched only by their talent for larceny.

Just as he expected her to be nonexistent during his period of rage-building silence, he expected her prolonged attendance and unwavering attention at the confessional. He would talk on and on, all through the day, into the night, telling it again and again, with less anger each time, with a gradual recovery of reason and perspective, until at last he would perceive the clarity of objectivity. His eyes would narrow, as though he could see it, like a clearing in the woods. Then he would stop, exhausted from the trek and unable to make it the rest of the way. Now was the time to face it: he was weak, and he was a shit.

Along with the recovery of reason, there was always this self-castigation. He would weaken and dwindle, and that's what disturbed her more than anything. She preferred his unreasoning rage, because at least it showed strength. Now, weak, he would come to her like a child and confess that his rage was at himself and that all the injustices had been imagined. He was stricken with self-contempt for all his faults and mistakes, his cruel behavior. Christ, how he had mistreated her! And how *good* she was to him!

She would try to persuade him that there was no reason to apologize, and good reason for him to have become so discouraged. He was not a machine. He was a feeling, sensitive artist.

No, he would say. And then he would cry. She would make him lie down, then bring him a Valium or, if he was inconsolable, a Nembutal, one being enough to calm him but not put him to sleep. Then she would lie down beside him and take him in her arms, telling him there was nothing to forgive and he was being too hard on himself.

He would tell her that she was very good to him, that nobody had ever been so good to him. She would tell him that she cared about him, that it caused her physical pain to see him suffer. He said he cared about her, too, and it caused him pain to know he had made her suffer. Neither of them ever said, "I love you," because that had never been included in their arrangement.

Last night, after their return in silence from Kip's, he had taken his Valium and his two Nembutal and his gin and orange juice. When she came into his room to say good night, he was staring at the late movie, asleep with his eyes open—actually asleep, but afraid to let go and close his eyes.

It was obvious he was not going to leave the house today. He was going to stay in his room, where he'd nurse his gin and his rage. At moments when he felt better, when the gin eased his suffering enough to inspire him to communicate, he'd come out of his room and find her, perversely wanting her attention but not her help. With the momentary easing of anxiety, he would have the strength to level further attacks upon her, a game she had come to find not at all enjoyable. His insults and accusations were attacks that helped him relieve some pressure. But they were never helpful to her, and it was always unnerving to hear what he might say, because it usually contained an element of truth. His accusation about the kitchen, for example.

At times like these, he spoke with the voice of her conscience. At other times, when he was himself, he was understanding about such things. At another time, the condition of the kitchen wouldn't have bothered him so much, or if it did, he'd clean it up himself. He knew that she carried an enormous load of responsibility and that she did more work around the house than either one of them wanted their friends to know. He felt guilty that they could not afford more help. The fact was that Fannie had not had the day off yesterday. Fannie came only once a week, on Fridays, and did all the heavy cleaning that could be done in one day. At least it was sufficient to allow Elena to let things go when she wanted to. At other times, she enjoyed cleaning, a secret never revealed to her peers in the A Group. It was a way for her to use energy and relieve tension. It served somehow to clear away the confusions of life, to sift out what was important and what was not.

Without planning to, she made most of her decisions while she did the dishes, or washed floors, or changed the bed linen.

Loading the dishes into the dishwasher, she remembered that she had decided to call Furio d'Amico because they needed money. She had been going to discuss the problem with Randy, but hadn't wanted to bring it up yesterday, because she knew it would depress him before the evening at Kip's. As it turned out, Randy was depressed anyway. But she had made the right decision. If she had brought it up, his depression would be even more severe, and he would blame her for it and hate himself all the more. There was little point in his knowing about the money. She took charge of finances, because it was an area he couldn't face. And the money Furio would advance would be repaid out of her Swiss bank account. It was Furio who had urged her to open the Swiss account and leave her own money there. She had thought it was unnecessary, but as usual, Furio's advice had been sound. He looked after the account for her. He would disapprove of her dipping into it again, but that could not be helped.

As she dialed Furio's number, Elena decided she would not bring up the matter of the money now, but would ask him if he could come to dinner. It would be helpful to have him around this evening, a way to avoid being alone with Randy. And she needed to see Furio. She realized that she was feeling low, that she needed his company.

His line was busy. She left the phone and went back to the sink, thinking it was not like her to feel this way, wondering what had disturbed her. The obvious answer, of course, was Randy. But his behavior was not new or surprising, and she had learned to be philosophical about it. He needed to work again, and he would work again. It was only a matter of time. She had always been able to keep up her spirits, to be strong. But she had to admit that she felt less patient, less understanding now than a year ago. It was going on too long, it was not changing, except possibly for the worse.

She felt a chill, a wave of anxiety. She thought, I must stop this. What is the matter with me? She reminded herself that nothing had changed, nothing was different from the way it had been. There was no mystery. She understood the problem. It was not necessarily discouraging that nothing had changed. In fact, if nothing was different, there was nothing to be afraid of. There was just as much reason to be hopeful and optimistic now as there was a week ago, a year ago. But a hollow feeling lingered, and she realized that it was fear, like the fear of death, of something ending.

She put soap powder into the dishwasher and turned it on. She got the can of cleanser and the brush and began to scrub the sink. Whatever it was, she would fix it. She determined to revitalize her efforts to help Randy get a job. She had stopped trying, at Randy's request, when one of her attempts misfired. He had warned her not to fuck up his already slim chances by coming on like an agent, because she didn't have the brains or the experience. She had known enough not to argue, but she had been wrong to let him discourage her.

She made the decision to try to help him again. He wouldn't have to know about it; she didn't have to tell him. She put the thought into her mind, gave herself the assignment. Her mind would work on it. She would let herself be free to see opportunities and she'd find ways to use them.

Detestable Grace St. George came into her thoughts. She made a mental note to pick up a copy of the Waller novel at Pickwick's or Hunter's that afternoon. She never made written notes of things to do. She kept everything in her head. Even when she gave a party, she needed no written reminders. The only list she ever made was the guest list.

Victor Kroll came into her mind, and she realized that his cancelation had been a disappointment and was partly the reason she felt the way she did.

She wondered if Natalie had reached Marina, or if she were still trying to get through to the lunatic maid. She wondered if Natalie, whom you had to forgive for a multitude of sins and transgressions, had always stimulated and amused her. The consensus on Natalie was that she wasn't worth it, that her so-called wit was formed out of observations that were cruel. Yes, but always with elements of truth and insight, which was rare. And Natalie did not expect to be liked. In order to appreciate Natalie, you had to recognize that she was engaged in warfare. Everyone else was the enemy. Her hostility toward men was total, matched only by her hostility toward women. She defended herself against men from the trenches, and she attacked women on the front lines.

It was impossible, for example, to talk seriously to Natalie about Kip Nathan. Today was not the first time Elena had tried without success to tell Natalie about the conversation she'd had with Kip about sex, even though sex was Natalie's topic of choice. Though she was obsessed with sex, Natalie refused even to listen to what Kip had told Elena. At the first suggestion that sex was perhaps not the ultimate occupation and reason for existence, Natalie shut her mind and countered with sex jokes. Can he get it up, or can he not get it up? Natalie was a self-professed nymphomaniac. She knew the penile dimensions, erective and staying powers of every man in and out of the A Group who yielded to her invitations. She announced her conquests, rated and scored and broadcasted their attributes or their shortcomings. She gave short shrift (literally) to those who declined, however politely, from engaging, as Randy once described her, "the mouth that won the West." You knew when Natalie scored, because you were given statistics. And you knew when she did not, as in Kip's case, by the nature of the jokes.

Elena and Kip had gotten into the conversation about sex at a party, before his marriage to Nancy O'Brien. He had brought one of his girls, one of the beautiful "dummies," all body and no brains. And, as usual, he was proud of her, wanting others to admire him for his taste.

"Isn't she terrific?" he said to Elena, beaming at the dummy who was engaged in animated listening across the room.

"She's very lovely," Elena said.

Kip looked at her seriously. "You really think lovely?" he asked. He was unusually handsome. He looked ten years younger than his age. In his twenties, he had decided to be an actor and had come to Hollywood. He was "discovered" at the swimming pool of the Beverly Hills Hotel by an aging female star, who was struck by his resemblance to her dead husband. He appeared in a couple of films, but found he was not much of an actor and that he was far more interested in the action on the other side of the camera.

"You're right," he said. " 'Lovely' is the word. She is lovely. And I love to look at her."

"But next week you'll love to look at somebody else."

"Tomorrow," he said, and laughed.

"Why, Kip?" she asked. The stories about his sexual proclivities ran the gamut, because everybody seemed to find an explanation for the fast turnover and the sheer quantity. "He's on number five-thousand-and-six," somebody once said.

"I like girls," he said.

"We know you like girls."

He grinned. "I didn't say I go to bed with them all. I said I liked them. I don't go to bed with them all."

She was surprised to hear him say that, because she had assumed, like everybody else, that his intention was to suggest that he did.

"That would be insane," he said. "Don't you think that would be compulsive?"

"I thought it was," she said.

"I'd never get any work done," he said, "and I'm a very busy man. I enjoy sex, just like anybody else who isn't compulsive about it, and I dig girls, but I don't have a particularly overpowering sex drive. It wouldn't be normal. I used to. When I was eighteen, I turned on to sex in a big way. I mean I lived for it. For about two years, until I was twenty, that's all I did. You think I'm kidding? I mean it was *literally* all I did. Three and four times a day, every day, all day. I never wanted to stop."

"What stopped you?"

"Boredom. What do you think? I outgrew it. Guys who go on that way are just guys who haven't grown up. And they're not enjoying it, because you can't. It loses meaning, and sex is too beautiful to lose meaning. See, it's not a big deal to me. I don't need to prove anything to myself. I know how to fuck. And I enjoy it sometimes, and sometimes I enjoy it less. And lots of times, my mind just turns right off sex and goes to business . . . when I've got lots of things on my mind, and I usually do. You have to realize, I'm dealing ten and twelve hours a day. I've got a hundred things going all the time. I'm not an eighteen-year-old kid with nothing in my life but a hard-on. If that's all I had, well okay. You use the power you have, right? If you have other sources of power, you don't have to restrict yourself to your cock. I have a lot of power and I enjoy it."

Elena never forgot that conversation, because it surprised her to hear any man, and Kip of all people, deny that he was anything but a superstud and that sex was not the most important activity in life.

Most of the women Elena knew were as obsessed with sex as men, not to the degree that Natalie was, but certainly far more conscious of it than she. In her own mind, Elena had questioned Natalie's obsession, because Natalie never talked about men, she talked about their cocks. Her emphasis was always on the object, disassociated from the man's body, or mind, or from any suggestion of feeling or love. She wondered if Natalie was obsessed with the object because—as some analyst might point out—she wanted to have one. And she wondered if, in this way, Natalie also showed her contempt for men—which was apparent in other ways—by focusing there the way some men focus only on a girl's breasts. Though Natalie would deny it, she resented men and was very hostile to them.

Elena had been interested in all of this, because listening to talk she heard every day about sex from women who seemed to think about little else, she had begun to wonder if there was something wrong with her. She was not that interested. She'd had numerous affairs; she'd been able to enjoy sex, at times very much. She'd never had a problem coming to orgasm, as many women apparently did. On the contrary, she was highly responsive.

Until that conversation with Kip, she was puzzled and somewhat troubled by what seemed to be her abnormal repression of sexual desire. Since their talk, she thought a great deal about what Kip said, and she decided that she was very much like him. She decided that she and Kip were more normal than people who lived a kind of prolonged adolescence. Like Kip, her sexual drive was sublimated into her drive for position and power.

Kip's explanation almost satisfied her. One element was missing. He never mentioned love. He talked about sex and sex drives, but where was love? She'd thought about asking him, many times, and perhaps one day she would. She had hesitated, because she sensed it might be a question he couldn't answer. Maybe he had been hurt once. Or maybe he was simply incapable of feeling love.

She had often wondered if that was true of her. Where was love in her life? Not with Randy, because they had agreed to a marriage of convenience. But she had asked the question long before Randy. She had tried to determine, as honestly as she could, if she had ever been *really* in love, or if love really existed at all. Was it a myth? And, if it existed, was she incapable of having it?

She had been sure she was in love with Karl, a boy she had known most of her life. She was eighteen and he was twenty-one, when they made love for the first time. Born during World War II, in East Berlin, they grew up together in the sterile, life-restricting shadow of the Berlin Wall. Elena's father had been a minor opera singer. Her most vivid childhood memories were of backstage, being with him during rehearsals, watching the magical transformation, by lights, costumes, and scenery, of a bare stage into a world larger and more glorious than life. She remained forever impressed by the thrill and excitement of that ambience. She decided she would probably be an actress. She knew that she wanted to do something big and exciting with her life.

When she was twelve, her father retired from the stage to earn a modest living teaching voice. She never revealed to him the profound disappointment she felt. Overnight, it seemed, he ceased to be the heroic figure she adored. He became a nobody, a little man, a teacher. He must have felt the change in himself, because he began to look and to behave like an entirely different person. He seemed to grow small and to become weak. He stooped when he walked, and watched the ground, never looking up. He seemed ashamed. And where he had always shown her great affection, suddenly he would not touch her. He became a stranger, rarely looking at her anymore, seeming not to care about her. Years later, looking back, she realized that, during that period, she had been coming into womanhood and that he no longer knew how to be with her. At the time, she thought he had stopped liking her.

When Elena was fifteen, her father died, and a year later her mother married a Communist bureaucrat, a small man in every way with whom Elena was quickly at odds. She learned to despise him. She had never been able to like her mother, but now she liked her less than ever. Where her father, before his retirement, had been dynamic and full of life, her mother had always been quiet, self-effacing, never smiling. Elena realized now that her mother had been a chronic depressive, so unlike her father, and so unlike her. She inherited her father's disposition. As a child, she had encountered life with a feeling of exhilaration. The world seemed thrilling, overflowing with experiences and opportunities that excited her. She learned early on that she was different from most of the other children. Excitement was physical for her, more physically felt. She could still remember times when, at play with others, sharing in the giddy, laughter-provoking exhilaration of a moment, she felt there would be no containing her excitement, no end to the feeling that she would go higher and higher, that she might rise into the air like a bird in flight, or that she might faint . . . and then she would sense that the others had become aware of her, more aware of her now than of the moment that had excited them.

Instinctively self-protective, she learned to control the expression of her excitement, to rein in her feelings, to draw herself back to earth and be like the others. As she grew up, she learned how to go through life that way, watchful of others, careful to restrict her natural energies and desires, to conform.

Karl was a music student. Like Elena, he disliked his life at home. Together, they decided that life in East Berlin was slow, inflexible, inhuman and, above all, dull.

There was nothing to match the beauty of the experience they shared in each other's arms. They began to dream of a future together in the world on the other side of the Wall, and they spent hours discussing and devising various plans of escape. Karl was serious and cautious. No plan seemed to satisfy him, because none seemed suitably safe, without risk. He kept looking for a better one. Elena came to realize that he would look forever and never go. He would not agree with her that the element of risk was intrinsic and could not be avoided. He said it was not his life he guarded but hers.

Without telling Karl, Elena began to make plans of her own. She had heard stories of girls who had escaped by making arrangements with border guards. She went to the Wall one day to look at the guards, seeing them in a way she had not considered before. As a group, they had always frightened her; they seemed menacing and cruel in their uniforms, like potential murderers. Considering them individually, she saw that they were only boys, some of them no older than Karl. As she walked along, pointedly ignoring their jokes, whistlings, and crude propositions, she knew that she could have her choice of any of them.

She returned again, on other days, gradually becoming familiar with several of the guards, projecting an image of propriety, careful not to let them guess what her motive was. She knew she was afraid, and stalling. At the same time, she was making her choice. She let time and nature take their courses, so that it seemed natural when she appeared at the Wall every day to see Helmut—on her way home from work, she explained—to stop and talk, to bring him something from the bakery, to let him touch her, to receive his first kiss. Helmut was proud, in front of the others, to have won her interest. Elena knew, from the behavior of the others, the remarks and jokes, the nudgings and looks, that they were waiting for Helmut to score. He knew it, too. He had long since begun to ask her. They played the same game every day, in the shadow of the Wall. He asked and she refused.

He reasoned, argued, pleaded. He asked her to come into the shack, near the Wall, assuring her it would be safe, that the others would see that they had privacy. He offered to meet her away from the Wall. He had a furnished room in a part of the city away from people she knew, where she wouldn't be recognized. He told her she was driving him crazy. He said he couldn't sleep. He said she would be responsible if he lost control of himself and raped somebody. When he became too argumentative, she quieted him with kisses.

While he pursued his objective, she pursued hers. She told him about her unhappy life at home. She created the fiction that her father, whom she adored, lived on the other side of the Wall and that it was his dream and hers to arrange for her to join him. She explained how the legalities were complicated by her mother's refusal to sign papers. She said that her stepfather was responsible for her mother's refusal, that he did not want to lose the income Elena brought into the house.

Helmut made her promise that she would never become desperate enough to try to escape over the Wall.

"You will be shot," he said. "They will kill you."

She looked at him a moment. "Would *you?*" she asked.

"I would do what I have to do," he said.

"You would shoot me? Kill me?"

He lit a cigarette, stalling, looking away. Finally, he said, "I don't know." Then he looked into her eyes. "If you will come with me into the shack . . . maybe I will find a way to help you."

I detest you, she thought. She had chosen Helmut because he had seemed the least brutal, but she had never deceived herself that he was a music student. He was, however, more sensitive than the others. His saying, "I don't know," in answer to her question, was evidence that he was not totally without humanity, but she suspected that his decision, if he were forced to make it, would be to do what he "had to do."

She refused to go into the shack with him, because of the others, but agreed to go to his room. It was small and furnished like a cell, with a bed, a dresser, and a chair. There was a sink. The bathroom was in the hall. There were photographs on the dresser of his mother and father, and one of himself in uniform. There were pinups on the wall above the bed of naked girls in pornographic poses, legs spread wide apart, hands framing genitalia, exposing and offering clitorises and vaginal openings. Elena stared at them, too shocked to reveal any reaction at all. She had never seen, nor even imagined, that there were such photographs. More shocking was the revelation to her that a woman could, and would, agree to expose herself that way. Most shocking of all were the lewd and pandering expressions on the faces of the women, the exposed tongues, the open, eager mouths. All of it made sex seem degrading and horrible.

"You are going to show me how you do that," Helmut said. He was standing beside her, and she felt his hand on her buttocks, moving down between her thighs.

In that instant, she was ready to leave, to run out of there. She wondered if he would try to stop her, if he would rape her. She turned her head, to rid herself of the sight of the photographs.

"Will you put out the light?" she said.

"How can I see you?"

"Your eyes will get accustomed to the dark," she said.

"You won't pose for me?"

"I thought you wanted to sleep with me, Helmut."

"I do," he said.

"Then put out the light," she said. And to her surprise and relief, he did.

Going to bed with Helmut made Elena realize that she was not in love with Karl, even though she preferred him as a lover. Though Helmut was different in bed, she found that she was able to experience the physical pleasures of lovemaking as she had with Karl.

She was surprised to discover that she felt no guilt toward Karl. In the ensuing weeks, she continued to go to bed with him while she made frequent visits to Helmut's room. Helmut assured her that he would keep his promise to get her across the border. He said it had to be arranged in a certain way at the right time, that he had to be careful. He had to protect himself.

In bed with Karl, she tried to understand what had happened to the feeling she had thought was love, and she discovered what it was: she had been caught up in Karl's experience, in his expression of love for her. It was as though she had become a part of love by receiving his gift. But it was his, not hers. She was loved by him, therefore she was his lover, therefore she loved him. That was how she had reasoned. Now she saw it differently. She liked him, and she liked to go to bed with him. She enjoyed the sensuality. He was a gentle and considerate lover, because he was able to love *her*.

Helmut's emphasis was upon himself. That first night, the first thing he expected her to do was to go down on him. His desire obviously was not to love her, but to have her service him, as though he were telling it to his friends, the other border guards, "and then she got down on her knees . . ." He was huge, and it was difficult to take him in her mouth. He kept urging her to take more of him, and she knew it gave him pleasure to say, "It's too much for you, hm?" He came quickly and then kept his erection, pushing her back down onto the bed, pushing into her without preparing her, so that it hurt.

As it went on, she was able gradually to respond until it was no longer painful and she was able to experience a degree of pleasure, but not much, because Helmut's remoteness from her kept intruding. He was a strong lover, with admirable endurance, but he didn't move naturally or gracefully the way Karl did. He moved in short, tight, stiff ways, propped up on his hands or elbows, holding his body away from hers. He gasped and groaned, and though she could appreciate his success, she could not match his excitement. His kisses were sudden and harsh. He forced his tongue into her mouth with sudden movements when he deepened his thrust. His attacks upon her breasts were crude, fulfilling his fantasy, but threatening to interfere with hers. He had no concept of *her*. He used her in pieces, fragmented—her mouth, her vagina, her breasts. When he put his mouth voraciously to her breasts the way he did, what was she? And who? She was nothing. Her breast just happened to be there; it was an object for him to focus upon.

On subsequent occasions, knowing now what to expect, she found that she was able to enjoy him more by giving him what he did not give her, by tuning in to his fantasy, joining him in appreciation of his vigor and manhood. Doing that, she discovered, heightened his excitement and gave her more pleasure. She found that sex was something she could use, if she had to, without feeling that she had betrayed herself, and that it didn't require love.

Helmut continued to urge her to make love with him in the shack, near the Wall. She knew his reason, because it was part of his fantasy, which she had already accepted. He wanted the others to know that he was in there with her, doing it. She agreed to it, finally, using his desire as a lever to make him consent to arrange for her escape. She spent half an hour of her last evening in East Berlin in the shack with Helmut, while his friends guarded their privacy. Then, led by him, she made her way west through one of the empty, boarded-up houses at the Wall.

Leaving East Berlin, she wondered how it would feel to know she would never see Karl again. She expected the feeling of loss, the wrench that would tell her she loved him and needed him. Though she never forgot the special feeling of closeness, warmth, and tenderness that she had experienced with him, that she had once thought was love, the wrench never came. There were always others, all different, and in another way, all the same, because she had learned that making love with a man was a matter of perceiving what he wanted and giving it to him.

She also discovered that all men, in bed, were basically either like Karl or like Helmut. In bed, they either made love to *you* or they were involved in their own inner experience.

But no experience ever brought her the recognition that she was in love. She decided that love was a romantic concept, used by people out of need, a need she didn't have. She suspected that she, like Kip, might possibly be stronger than most people, that "falling in love," which entailed being so dependent upon another person, was an emotional trap and a sentimental concept. People lived up to it, out of need, out of loneliness, and because they were conditioned to believe that it was desirable The fact that love was usually accompanied by pain, heartbreak, and the cruelty of separation justified her reasoning.

Arriving in West Berlin, at nineteen, alone, was a frightening and stimulating experience. In those cold-war days, it was a beleaguered city—or rather, half a city—totally surrounded by hostile territory, with the only slender links to the outside world provided by two highways and the narrow air corridors, where commercial planes were often harassed by Russian fighters. Yet despite this feeling of being besieged, or perhaps because of it, West Berlin displayed a hectic gaiety, a come-what-may defiance.

Compared to the drab and dingy East Berlin where she had grown up, with its ghastly fortresslike, oppressive buildings along "Stalin Alley," its pathetically meager shop windows, its dimly lit streets and scarce, dull cafes or beer halls that constituted just about all the "night life"—compared to this dark Utopian reverse, West Berlin was a riot of life and splendor.

The Allied powers occupying the city—especially the Americans—wanted it that way, wanted the city to be a gleaming showcase for the West. They made sure that the necessary money kept flowing in. So the lights glittered away most of the night on the Kurfürstendamm, the main shopping and entertainment street that had been rebuilt from the wartime rubble. It was almost too neat, too harsh a piece of symbolism—light and dark, the blaze of West Berlin that almost literally blinded you if you were not used to it, and the murky half-night of East Berlin, with its oppressive air of menace and boredom.

Elena threw herself into her new freedom like someone who has plunged into a river after almost dying of thirst. Merely walking the streets when she pleased, unobserved, unconstrained, swimming through the anonymous crowds, was a headier experience, she thought, than sex or music. But she quickly found that freedom also had its unsettling side. In her old life, everything had been regulated, preordained. Now everything was uncertain.

A committee working to aid refugees from the east boarded her with a working-class family, gave her enough spending money for a week, and urged her to find a job. The leads provided by the committee were not encouraging. She was not really trained to do anything. The only practical part of her education had been a secretarial course, but she had secretly rebelled against it since it did not fit in with her view of her future; she had gone through the motions, but she managed to forget the squiggly shorthand symbols as fast as they were pounded into her brain, and she treated a typewriter keyboard with a mixture of contempt and confusion.

So the jobs most desired by girls her age—secretary or receptionist, especially with the Americans—were beyond her. Domestic work? She'd had enough of that back home. Waiting on tables? She tried it for three nights in a noisy, smoky restaurant near the Kaiser Wilhelm church, the famous Berlin landmark that had been destroyed during the war except for a brownish stump. She hated the restaurant.

On the third night, walking home through the snowy streets, she passed a nightclub called Die Blaue Katze. A large blue cat was outlined in neon over the entrance; its red eyes blinked on and off, and its tail swayed back and forth. The uniformed doorman eyed Elena. "Looking for work, Miss?" he asked.

And so, almost inevitably it seemed to her in retrospect, she went to work as a B-girl. The routine was simple and standard, the same routine that prevails with minor variations in ten thousand similar places from Berlin to Hamburg to Hong Kong. She was told to get herself a tight black dress—"No brassiere," the manager had warned, "and no panties, either." The idea was to attract a customer, sit with him, and induce him to buy the largest possible quantity of Sekt, the awful, sweet German imitation of champagne, at the then-exorbitant price of twenty dollars a bottle.

The whole thing was organized with Teutonic efficiency. For one or two bottles, the customer was entitled to fondle her anywhere and in any manner he chose. "But you've got to slow him down and make it last," advised one of the older girls. "Then before you let him reach between your legs, he's usually good for another bottle." For three bottles or more she was to unzip his trousers—if he so desired—and bring him to climax under the tablecloth. That would usually rate an extra tip. She found the procedure horrifying only the first time; after that, it seemed to her only messy, and the chief concern was to keep her dress from being splashed.

Most of the customers, of course, wanted more. The girls could not leave until 5 A.M., and the management discouraged them from making outside dates. But if a customer really insisted, he could "buy out" a girl by paying the management the equivalent of what the girl would normally bring in through hustling drinks for the rest of the night.

The accepted B-girl code required that you told the poor sucker you could not be seen leaving the place with him. And so you gave him a phony address at which to meet you later. The first time Elena pulled this trick, her victim was a middle-aged salesman from Frankfurt, and she felt pretty rotten about it. Her cut of the management's take was only ten percent, plus her modest weekly wage, and whatever personal tips she could extract. Still, it added up to three or four times the amount she could have made as a waitress. Elena's second dupe was a young, shy American lieutenant. To her surprise, he reappeared the next night, marched up to her table and said, hoarse with anger: "Damn you, why did you have to do that to me?"

Most of the other victims, she was told, were far too embarrassed to come back and make trouble. The bouncer had the stubborn lieutenant out of the place in half a minute, but Elena could not forget his angry voice and hurt look. She decided never to pull this trick again; she would not promise anything or, if she did, she would deliver. That is how she met Wally Swoboda, the porno movie king.

"King" could be applied to Wally only ironically. He was a slight man with nearly white blond hair and blinking eyes that seemed constantly astonished. He wore white or light beige suits even in winter, and large bow ties that never seemed to be tied quite firmly enough. He was, as he told her that first evening over their first bottle of Sekt, from Czechoslovakia, and had escaped from there to West Berlin three years before. He told her little else, preferring to discuss the other girls in the club—asking how old they were, which ones had steady customers, offering crass opinions of their breasts and legs and behinds.

Even after the second bottle had been popped open by the cheaply ceremonious headwaiter, Wally had not touched Elena. During the third, he asked her to leave with him. Intrigued, she accepted.

His apartment was seedy, with a few "elegant" touches that stood out incongruously: a bronze sculpture of a nude, a small Persian rug, a humming red bar-refrigerator. She began to undress.

"No, wait," he cried, almost in panic.

He came up to her and lowered her dress until one of

her breasts was exposed. Then he drew back to look at the effect. Next he knelt in front of her and slowly lifted the hem of her dress, first from one side, then another, until one of her thighs and her pubic triangle were exposed. He tucked the hem up into her thin rhinestone belt and again drew back to observe.

He went to a closet and produced a slightly mangy black seal coat. "Take off your dress and put this on," he commanded. She did as she was told. "Close the coat tightly—like that," he said, sounding excited. "Now turn. Now open it—tear it open—there. Now close it again."

The coat smelled of mothballs, and she felt increasingly silly, standing there, flapping the coat. At this point, Wally struggled out of his beige suit, approached her and, in the first rough gesture of the evening, pushed her hard and backwards, onto a couch. He thrust his cock into her with rather more authority than she had expected.

"Nudity is not really interesting by itself," he said later, as if revealing a great and new truth. "It's interesting only in combination with clothes. The hidden, the half-hidden, the half-seen—only those really appeal to the imagination."

It was then he told her that he made his living producing pornographic movies—or fuck films, as he called them. She had only a vague idea of what such things were like, and he begged to take her to one the next day. It was being shown in the basement of a third-rate hotel, a private "club"; porno movies had not yet gone public.

She was so startled by the film that she remembered little of what she saw. There was a bored housewife in a loose bathrobe. The mailman arrived. Soon he was screwing her, holding her by the thighs, her back wedged against the wall—why the wall if a bed was available, Elena could not understand. A neighbor arrived who wanted to join the fun. Presently the room was filled with writhing bodies, and the primitive sound track emitted groans and shrieks. Abruptly and absurdly the scene shifted to a placid mountain meadow, where a man in *Lederhosen,* the leather shorts of the Bavarian and Austrian peasants, was chasing a half-nude and very buxom farm girl, who seemed to prefer a large shepherd dog to her human pursuer.

And so it went, interminably, it seemed to Elena, and repetitively. She recalled the pictures on Helmut's wall, here come weirdly to life. There was something unreal about the repeated close-ups of penis pulling in and out of vagina, or mouth moving up and down on penis. Seen through the lens at a distance of only a few inches, veined, hairy, creased, often pimply, the male and female organs looked anything but lovely. Above all, they looked disembodied, mechanical, moving like parts of a strange, fleshy machine.

Wally agreed with her, almost apologetically, when later, over coffee in the sunlight of the Kurfürstendamm, she told him that she had not liked the movie. It was, he conceded, very unimaginative, very trite. He began telling her of the porno films he really would like to make, if only the money men would allow his creative imagination to roam. Slowly, though she knew nothing of such things then, she started to understand that Wally Swoboda was in the grip of an obsession: he wanted to make the perfect fuck film, he wanted (even if it sounded absurd in this context) to burst the bounds of his *métier*.

Patiently, he told her about the Busby Berkeley movies of the thirties, when all those girls in bathing suits would form patterns in the swimming pools, rhythmically moving their arms and legs. Well, in *his* version, he explained as his eyes blinked ever more rapidly, they would be nude from the waist down, and instead of all those silly rhythmic motions they would all be playing with themselves, slowly, gracefully, floating in the water. And then, with perfect timing, they would move into a new formation, by twos, and one girl would go down on the other. Elena tried to follow, but couldn't quite visualize it.

Those Busby Berkeley films, Wally continued, breathing hard, always had a lot of fountains in them which would start spouting just as a row of dancers came floating past. In *his* movie, there wouldn't be any fountains, but a whole long row of erect cocks. And just as the girls danced past, as if at a signal, the cocks would start spouting—streams and streams of graceful white, splashing on the naked breasts of the girls.

At first, Elena thought Wally was joking. Then she realized that he was not—that, in fact, he was a little insane. She learned later that trying to push the pornographic imagination to its extreme was a form of madness; that the Marquis de Sade, among others, had gone mad that way. Wally was haunted by the fact that there was a limit to the variations and combinations of sex, a limit very quickly reached: sooner or later, all pornography becomes repetitive. When he asked Elena to appear in one of his films she said yes, partly because the money was good, but also partly because she had begun to feel sorry for this ridiculous but driven little man.

Wally's studio was a large loft on the outskirts of the city. Beds, sofas, assorted other furniture formed three or four disorderly islands. There were lights dangling from the ceiling and perched on spindly metal stands. Props were strewn about, including a cardboard box full of pinkish objects which, after a few minutes, Elena realized were artificial penises.

Coming to greet her, Wally noticed where she had focused her attention. "Would you like to try one on?" he said, in one of his rare attempts at humor.

With some courtliness, he introduced the rest of the "cast." There was Karl (it *would* be Karl, thought Elena), the "leading man." Karl nodded briefly, as if reluctant to overexert his tall, well-muscled body. There was Horst, the second lead, a rather avuncular-looking man who was busy in front of the mirror slipping a wig on his bald head. Horst gave her a smile. There were two other girls, a statuesque brunette in tall black boots who, said Wally, could do things with a whip that defied belief. And a frizzy brunette who, Wally insisted, had been a rising star at UFA, the big German studio, until she got into trouble with a producer because she wouldn't go to bed with him. (Why not? Elena found herself asking, with incipient cynicism.)

Wally began to explain the "story." In the first scene, Elena was to be a school girl, in a sailor dress, of course, bored and restless. The lodger arrives. He starts fondling her, first her breasts, then everything. She lets him play for a while, but when he tries to get into her, she draws back: Mama has warned her that this is how little girls get into trouble. All right, says the lodger, we'll do something else, something that can't get you into trouble. He shows her how to take his cock into her mouth.

Wally was warming to his story, but at this point he saw Elena shudder. He looked worried. "Surely, you've done this before?" Even though she had, she said nothing. She had hated it with Helmut, and this was a stranger. "I'll tell you what," said Wally. "You're new. I'll tell Karl not to come in your mouth. He'll tap you on the shoulder when he's ready, and you can pull away."

Wally pointed toward a screen behind which Elena could change. What a strange and foolish convention, she reflected, stepping behind a screen to change, when we will all be thrashing around naked soon for the camera. She slipped into her sailor dress and white panties—it would be more titillating, Wally explained, if Karl had to pull them off. She realized for the first time how cold it was in the room. Emerging, she noticed that two electric heaters had been pushed toward the playing area.

"We can't have goosebumps in a fuck film," said Wally.

The action proceeded as Wally had outlined it, while the jaded, elderly cameraman swiveled around on the dolly to get the best angle. Elena felt strangely numb and suspended as Karl, who smelled faintly of schnapps, caressed her, pulled out her breasts, lifted up her skirt and patted her behind. It was, in a way, no different from what she did in the Blaue Katze at night. She felt that she should be embarrassed because she was being watched, but somehow she was not.

"Now turn over and reach between her legs," ordered Wally. "Come in close," he said to the cameraman, who nodded, knowing exactly what was expected of him.

Despite her detachment, she dreaded the moment when she was to take Karl's penis into her mouth. It looked large and red. She bent over it with determination, eager to get through the scene.

"No, no," cried Wally. "You look as though you're going to bite it off. You're a school girl. Hesitate. Be shy."

She obeyed. But when she had finally worked up to the point where Karl's penis was deep in her mouth, she almost gagged. As her mouth moved up and down, she felt Karl's penis stiffen and the sudden surge of blood and muscle under her lips and tongue excited her in a way that had not happened with Helmut. She kept working.

"Very good," said Wally. "You suck beautifully. One would never guess that you'd never done it before."

Karl grew stiffer and stiffer. She felt his tap on her shoulder, the signal that he was about to come, her moment to pull away. Suddenly, impulsively, she decided not to. She shook her head slightly and continued. Now the hot, sticky sperm exploded into her mouth. It tasted, she thought, like soap. In Helmut's case, it had tasted like salted yogurt. (Increasingly, Elena would realize that the taste was as individual as the body smell: it varied with different men.) The shock was greater than she had anticipated. She did pull away now, the liquid dribbling from her lips, and onto Karl's thighs.

"Great," shouted Wally. "You're a natural."

Elena winced at the recollection. Consciously trying to suppress her memories, subconsciously trying to escape the dishes, she crossed the kitchen and again dialed Furio's number.

"Hello," came the gentle voice over the phone.

"*Come stai,* Furio?" she said.

"Ah, I was calling you," he said. "And your phone was busy. You were talking to Natalie."

"How do you know?"

"Were you really?" he asked.

"You know we talk on the phone all day, from morning until night."

"Who else but the two of you," he said.

"Why didn't you call on the other phone?"

"Because it was not important, and you were talking to Natalie and that was important."

"Well it was, as a matter of fact. There is a crisis."

"Tell me."

"Not now."

Furio's Italian accent was softer than most, and whenever Elena talked to him she would begin to hear traces of her own accent returning. Actually, it was not her Germanic accent she heard, but a subtle copy of Furio's. She was proud of the fact that she had lost almost all the guttural Germanic sound. It pleased her that people meeting her for the first time rarely could place her accent. In the years she spent in Italy and France, after she left Germany, she had picked up not only the languages, but the accented English, choosing and using the most pleasing sounds, keeping and using what sounded charming. She had an exceptionally acute ear and an ability to pick up any language quickly—not merely the language of a country, but of a district or a particular class. She did it naturally, through mimicry, and with taste, absorbing the best. It was one of the talents that had made her decide to be an actress, a pursuit she abandoned after she met Furio. He persuaded her it was a poor idea.

"I need a favor," Elena said. "Are you busy tonight?"

"No, I am yours," he said.

"Why don't you come over and we'll have dinner together?"

"Where's Randy?"

"He's here. But I don't think he'll join us. He's depressed."

"Terrific . . . I'm sorry."

"It's a bore. It'll be all right. I have a lot to tell you. What shall I get for dinner? What would you like?"

"Who is going to cook, you or me?"

"What's your mood? Would you like me to cook for you?"

"I would like to cook for you, and you will help me."

She smiled. "Okay. Tell me what to buy."

"I'll bring it."

"No, I have errands to do, and I'll be in the market anyway. So tell me."

"I can't tell you, because I don't know yet. So I will have to bring it. Okay?"

"Okay."

"Elena, are you all right?"

"Of course."

"Randy . . . ?"

"Like other times. You know."

"Yes. Elena, do you need money?"

"Well . . . We'll have to talk about that."

"Mm."

"Are you cross?"

"Unhappy for you, but not cross."

"Furio, never be unhappy for me."

"You are right. What time do you want me?"

"Whenever."

"Seven?"

"Wonderful. I look forward."

"So do I. *Ciao.*"

"Ciao."

Furio d'Amico was the only person in the world she would dare invite into this house tonight, the only person

Randy, in his present mood, would tolerate. He'd not want to join them for dinner because he was holing up in his room, but he would not begrudge her the evening with Furio. Randy even liked him. It was not unusual for people to like Furio. But it had become more and more unusual for Randy to like anybody.

Furio was Elena's closest friend, the only real friend—including lovers—she had ever had. She could not imagine life without him; he knew everything there was to know about her, except for the intimacy of sex. And in a sense, he knew even that, better than most of the men she had slept with, because she and Furio loved each other like children, like true innocents.

In the period before she met Randy, just after her affair with an Italian prince, she went everywhere with Furio, to more parties and weekend houseguestings, picnics, dances, and social events than she had ever imagined there could be. Furio loved to dance, and he loved to dance with her because, he said, he had never known anyone who made herself so completely his partner. "You become like part of me," he said. Though he was shy, he was a good dancer, surprisingly strong and sure. He was not much taller than she, short for a man, and slight. He would hold her in his arms, and they would move together with the music, sometimes for hours, often until the cafe was closing or the musicians were going home.

It was perhaps the happiest time of her life, a strange time and a strange kind of happiness. If she had ever felt real love for anyone, it was for Furio during those months together. She loved him, of course, for the enormous generosity of his friendship. But she had learned a deeper *feeling* of love—more than she had ever felt for a lover—in those slow and sleepy hours she spent in his arms. He would glance down at her, looking into her eyes, and give her a special smile that revealed a secret pleasure. Then he would laugh and hold her closer, but the smile would stay.

It didn't take long for her to straighten up the kitchen. The mess had looked worse than it was. She was pouring herself a cup of coffee to take upstairs, when Natalie phoned again.

"I'm going over there," she said, sounding breathless and anxious.

"What happened?"

"I talked to her. I persuaded the lunatic to tell her I was on the phone. She wasn't asleep, she couldn't sleep. The pills weren't working. She was high as a kite, and instantly with the tears, because I'd called. You were dead center about the ESP. That hit the target. I forgot that Rick was into spiritualism, and she's such a perfect fool she's completely brainwashed on the subject. Anyway, I can't talk now. I promised her I'd get over there as fast as I can, and I've got eighteen things to do before I can get out of here. I'm going to spend the night with her. She pleaded. What could I do?"

"She told you they broke up?"

"Immediately. Sobbing. She couldn't talk about it, but she will. She wants to tell it all, God help me, because if she's this stoned, it will be a torment. But what can I do?"

"Just listen. That's all you *have* to do right now."

"I won't say a word, dear, I'll be a saint."

"Much better," Elena said, "for Marina to be the one who says, 'You tried to tell me, but I didn't listen, and you were right.' "

"Darling, I *got* your message."

"In which case, you should then say, 'Marina, there's no such thing as right or wrong. You're human, you became involved. We're all human, we all become involved. We have to forgive ourselves for being human. It might have worked out very well. It happened not to work out well. That doesn't make me a prophet, and it's not important. You know what you have to do.' "

What Natalie must tell her, Elena suggested, was to pay attention to her work and her career, and as soon as possible, get back into circulation socially. "She needs to for two reasons: for her morale and to discourage any rumors," Elena said.

"Don't you worry about that," Natalie said. "I'll take care of that. *Nobody's* going to get the idea that that shitty little faggot upset her, even if he's *destroyed* her. I'll take care of that."

Elena was only half listening. At that very moment she had heard herself say that Marina must get back into circulation as soon as possible, her attention was caught by the thought that must have been in her mind before she said it: Marina should be ready in about a week to make her first social reappearance. Elena's party was ten days away.

She said to Natalie, "Don't *rush* her, darling. Give her time," and she gave not a hint of the excitement she felt at the image of Marina making her entrance at the party.

She was as eager as Natalie to get off the phone, so she could put her mind to it. She extracted from Natalie the promise that she would phone this evening from Marina's, if she got the chance, to let her know how things were.

Though Elena could be direct with Natalie—and they often told each other what a relief their friendship was, because they never had to play games with each other—and though Natalie was her official "best friend," Natalie was still Natalie. Though Elena maintained the fiction that she was totally direct and trusting with Natalie, she always moved with extreme caution. There were two areas, in particular, where she had learned to operate with downright deceit. One of these was her relationship, especially her nonsexual relationship, with Randy. The other included anything Elena really cared about. She knew instinctively never to let Natalie perceive the degree to which she wanted something. You could rely upon Natalie to be marvelously helpful, unless she sensed that you really cared or desperately wanted something that only she had the power to give you. That is when you could not count on her. Or perhaps you could. Even if it was only a cookie that you wanted, if you wanted it badly enough, you could count on Natalie's perversity, on her soul-deep meanness to rise to the occasion and refuse you.

Elena took her cup of coffee upstairs to the bedroom and cleared a place for it on her cluttered dressing table. The condition of her dressing table was a crime she would have to ignore. While she brushed her ash-blond hair, pulled it back and tied it into a pony tail, she considered the advantages of bringing Marina to the party.

Marina was not a poor substitute for Victor Kroll, not at all. A different quality, another perfume—but equally attractive and effective. With Victor Kroll, the perfume would be noble; a scent of regality and high purpose, of nations in league and history happening now. With Marina, there would also be a quality of regality, because Marina, when she was away from the squalor of her private life, glittered. She was a superstar. The perfume would be theatrical and emotional, like those movie bios of famous stars who played the Palace—like Marina's mother, Bobbie Shaw, and like Marina herself at the Palace, including, as all such stories do, the shadow behind the smile, the heartbreak caused by the wayward lover, Rick Navarro. For some of Elena's guests, there might be the grim speculation that in the near future Marina might die, undoubtedly of an O.D. (following in her mother's footsteps), by intention or accident. Then they could feel that they had participated, had "been there when." Marina qualified as a part of history—perhaps less important and less noble than affairs of state, but to Hollywood's A Group, the most starstruck group of people in the world, it would be their secret preference.

Elena's parties were more successful than most because of her ability to cast well, selecting the right people and the best combinations from the people who qualified as A Group regulars. Most of them were celebrities, socially if not also professionally. She would spend hours on the seating arrangements. Not many hostesses understood that proper seating arrangements predetermined the success of a dinner party, and few knew how to select and combine. You had to understand people in terms of their needs and their effects upon each other. A cardinal rule was that you never sat interesting people with bores. You put all the bores at one table. They didn't know they were bores, and they had a marvelous time. And the interesting people, of course, had no problem having a great time, because they were interesting.

On weekends, the A people encountered each other on tennis courts, at poolsides, on private beaches and at second homes in Palm Springs. They attended screenings in the projection rooms of each other's mini-mansions. During the week, they met for lunch at The Bistro, La Boîte, St. Germain, and at private clubs. They shopped together at Giorgio's, Bonwit's, Gucci's, Amelia Gray's, and the antique shops on Melrose Place. They ran into each other in the waiting rooms of gynecologists, proctologists, and periodontists. It was a challenge to make a party unique for them, to turn up a celebrity for *them,* a celebrities' celebrity.

Marina Vaughan rated as one of the few Super Star-Personalities in the world, and you tried to get her for a party the way you tried to get Victor Kroll. Kroll was better, because Super World Political Figure rated higher than Super Star-Personality, the way a royal flush beat a straight flush. Politicians were not as choice as they had been pre-Watergate. Victor Kroll was an exception, because he was above politics, a figure of history. Certain others, for one reason or another, rated high. Political party preferences were not considered. Charisma counted. Looks helped. Teddy Kennedy would be splendid, because the Kennedy mystique endured. John Lindsay once had potential, but he was adrift. Past and present top political candidates were choice—Goldwater, Tunney, Reagan—as were Brown and governors of other large states.

There were few performers who rated as high as politicians. Marina rated higher than most Super Star-Personalities, because she was a star both in movies and on the stage. No other female could match her for points, except Streisand. Streisand would supersede Marina, earning more points for talent, the greater star of the two, but would lose points because she was a terrible party person who hid in corners and wouldn't come out. When she did, she was unpleasant to people. Her defenders insisted it was shyness, but did that excuse rudeness? The question had been argued on more than one occasion by the ladies of the A Group hierarchy and their acquaintances from the trend-setting press (*Women's Wear Daily, Town & Country,* both *Chronicles,* Los Angeles and San Francisco, and both *Times,* Los Angeles and New York). The fact was, Streisand didn't care enough to bother to make an effort. And that was an attitude that lacked class. It cost Streisand points.

The real reason Streisand was never invited to Group A parties was that she had made it vociferously clear that she wouldn't accept. On rare occasions, she showed up, brought along by somebody else, or as a favor for a friend. And in spite of the consensus, it was worth every effort to try to get her. Lack of class notwithstanding, you'd have Streisand, and your guests would have the advantage of first-hand evidence to report on how she stayed in the corner and was rude. At least they'd be talking about Streisand, which was better than their talking about almost anybody else who didn't hide in corners and was not rude. It made a party important.

Cary Grant headed the roster of male Super Star-

Personalities, and the roster was short. Sinatra, but Sinatra never went to parties—unless they were given by powerful statesmen like Victor Kroll. Kelly. Astaire. Nureyev. (Dancers had an especially super lure for the A Group: Elena had never figured out why.) Greg Peck. John Wayne. Jimmy Stewart. Marlon Brando, like Streisand, had problems. There were very few Super Stars these days. Coop and Bogey were dead.

Certain Author-Personalities qualified—Gore Vidal, Norman Mailer, Truman Capote, all Super Stars. They had their seasons, and timing was important. Capote had become somewhat overexposed by appearing too frequently on the Johnny Carson show, wearing funny hats and becoming familiar to the mass audience, which surely would gain him book sales but lose him status. One paid a price, one lost dignity.

Still, Author-Personality Super Stars made excellent party guests because they were also interesting and articulate, and usually provocative. Mailer sometimes got out of hand, but it would be disappointing if he didn't. He was supposed to.

One had to be terribly careful about actors and actresses, overexposure being a problem there, too. Danger of boredom was a serious threat. You had to know your people.

When you were stuck and couldn't find your Super Personalities, you tried to lure one of the Fun Couples, who could be counted on to enliven a party. But they tended to be independent and had to be in the mood. Last night at Kip's, pretending to watch the tedious movie in the darkness of the projection room but actually thinking about Victor Kroll's cancelation and possibilities for a substitute attraction, Elena had decided to phone the Kanins (Garson and Ruth Gordon), who were visiting town, and the Beans (Jack and Mitzi Gaynor), two reliable Fun Couples, and invite them as insurance. She remembered that now and, in the light of her inspiration about Marina, reconsidered it. She could hold off until tonight, after she talked to Natalie and had a better idea about Marina's condition.

If Natalie were not such an impossible bitch, Elena would lay the idea of Marina's coming to the party right out to her and get a helpful, realistic reaction, the kind she'd give Natalie if their roles were reversed. But it wasn't going to be that simple. She was going to have to let the idea originate with Natalie, and that could take time. Fortunately, she had already laid the groundwork with her advice about getting Marina back into circulation. That was enough for Natalie to pick up on. But Group A parties were not Marina's social preference. She swung with the Quaalude and popper crowd, younger, fringier people, actors and musicians and child executives in the record and music publishing business.

Elena decided to call the Kanins and the Beans and issue invitations. If they could make it, she'd have them, and that would be safest. It would mean four more, bringing her guest list to forty-eight.

The Kanins were out of town until Monday and had not left a forwarding number, so she left a message at the Beverly Hills Hotel that she had called to invite them for a week from Friday and would check back. The Beans were not answering, so she gave their service the information.

She got up from the dressing table and went to the closet, to the mirrored double doors, thinking again about Marina and about a way to drop another suggestion tonight when Natalie phoned. She paused there a moment, thinking, with her hand on the knob of one of the doors, peripherally aware of the sound of the television coming from Randy's room, aware of her image in the mirror, in her leotards. She thought about Harvey saying her tensions worked for her, and about Mrs. Barry Springfield's closetful of Norells, and then she looked up and into her own eyes in surprise, as the idea suddenly appeared, opening up like a blossom . . . Victor Kroll.

Offer Victor Kroll to Marina, her dinner partner for the evening!

Marina would love it. More important, Natalie would love it, because it would provide her with an ideal reentrance into Marina's life, a demonstration of her value and the importance of her connections, scoring high points.

Victor Kroll wouldn't have to love it, because he wouldn't be there.

"Maaaarvelous," she whispered, feeling the heat of excitement and the flush of color that came to her cheeks, the natural color that somehow gave a new expression to her eyes and softened the shine of her blond hair. Even the color of her eyes seemed to have changed, to a deeper green, and her lips seemed fuller, seemed to have a more definite outline. It had always been difficult for her to see herself as beautiful, because in mirrors she had always seen the peasant coarseness of her mother's features, and since she didn't like her mother, she tended to reject part of herself, blinding herself to the true picture of what she looked like.

She opened the closet doors. As she chose what she would wear and laid it out on the bed, she continued to feel the heat of excitement. She got out of her leotards and went into the bathroom and showered, her mind racing with notions to implement her inspiration.

First, she would have to help Natalie get the idea. That would be easy, because now that the lure was Victor Kroll and not just the party, it was simply a matter of saying "Victor Kroll" two or three times to Natalie in the proper context. Natalie, at least, was not stupid. And once the idea came to her, it was as good as certain that Marina would come, because Natalie was undauntable, and Marina was vulnerable, needing Natalie to tell her what to do.

The only contingencies that could keep Marina from the party were the possibility she might be working that night, or that Rick Navarro had left her shattered beyond Natalie's ability to piece her together in time. She'd get that information from Natalie tonight.

Assuming that Marina accepted, Elena would suggest to Natalie that it would be wise not to make a big thing of it, not to let people know, but let it be a kind of surprise. Natalie would like that, because it was secretive and it would be Natalie's surprise. In the meantime, Elena would share the secret with one or two good friends, carefully selected to let the rumor out.

In a day or two, Marina's split-up with Rick would be news and people would be talking, wondering how Marina was taking it and what condition she was in, and of course Natalie would be doling out stories about that anyway, keeping interest alive for as long as she could capitalize on being the source of all knowledge of the situation.

Early next week, the rumor would begin to get around that Marina was coming to the party. When Elena was asked about it, she'd sound hesitant but would finally be forced to admit that she thought so, but didn't like to promise when she wasn't sure. Then she'd impress each caller with the importance of not mentioning the possibility to others, because Marina was nervous about seeing people and would rather just show up unobtrusively. Cautioning people in that way would have the effect of arousing further suspicion that Marina was in a precarious emotional state and, as word got around, anticipation of the party would be heightened.

By Wednesday of the following week, two days before the party, Elena would begin to let people know about Victor Kroll's last-minute cancelation. But disappointment would be painless, because there would be a new excitement about Marina.

Breaking the news about Kroll as late as possible would help. By then, Marina would have adjusted to the idea of coming to the party. More important, Natalie would have adjusted to it, and Elena would have Natalie's help in seeing that Marina followed through. Best would be to find a substitute for Kroll who would appeal to Marina. Elena gave that thought a corner of her mind to work on. Later, she'd have Natalie to help her.

If, despite her efforts and Natalie's persuasions, Marina canceled out at the last minute, there would be, in any case, the benefit to the party of all the advance excitement.

And if worse came to worst, and Marina didn't come and neither of the Fun Couples could make it, people would have built up so much anticipation by then, they'd be determined to have a good time. And Elena would reward them with inside information and anecdotes relating to why neither Marina nor Kroll could make it, what they said, what they were doing . . . and that would be almost as good as having them be there.

She wondered if she ought to call Mary Lazar and find out if Truman Capote was staying in Palm Springs. She decided against it. Better to stick with just Marina, backed up by the Fun Couples. When you gambled, it was best to play for high stakes and play it cool. When you began to hedge your bets, you lost. Besides, Capote was not in season. Vidal was in season, but he was in Rome.

5

She dressed quickly, then hurriedly collected the things she needed—hairbrush, cigarettes, matches, cash, checkbook, credit cards, driver's license, and keys—and threw them into her purse. It had always amazed Randy that she was able to find what she wanted, that she knew exactly where to reach to retrieve them from the littered dressing table, desk and bureau tops, and from the chaos of her bathroom. She told him that she had her own kind of filing system, funky but practical for her. The only time it failed her was after Fannie had been there on Fridays and had tried to straighten things out.

Randy was too much on her mind, and that was the reason she was hurrying. She was trying to get out of the house without a confrontation. She wanted to hold on to her good feeling of excitement, so she could have it with her for the rest of the afternoon. But she knew that she was going to have to talk to him before she left. She had tried to think of a way to avoid it. Leaving him a note wouldn't do. She had to make sure he wasn't planning on using the Mercedes. If she didn't clear it with him, she'd learn later that he'd had to cancel an appointment. He refused to drive the station wagon to appointments. She had never understood or mastered the size of the station wagon and had given up trying to drive it.

Though she couldn't avoid him, she could protect herself and keep in a position of control by establishing that she was in a hurry. She prepared herself to use that device, the way an actress would, employing "hurry" as her *motif*, and she arrived that way at his closed door.

The volume was turned up on his television set, and she could hear the urgent, anxious voices of the soap opera people. She knocked lightly, not wanting to startle him if he had dozed off. When she got no answer, she was tempted to take the chance and leave without telling him, explaining later that she had tried but he was asleep. She compromised, knocking once more, slightly louder.

"Come in!" he shouted.

She opened the door but didn't go beyond the doorway.

"I'm late, I'm hurrying," she said.

He was sprawled on the bed, in his robe, looking like something beached. He kept his eyes on the television set, as though he had to monitor it while he endured her interruption.

"I wanted to make sure you weren't planning on using the Mercedes," she said.

He sighed, implying that her remark was incredible. "Do I look as though I'm planning to go out?"

"I wanted to be sure. Will you be answering the phone? Are you expecting a call from Oscar?"

"I'm expecting shit from Oscar. No, I won't be answering the phone." Oscar Berthel was his new agent. There had been hopeful promises and a brief surge of optimism when he signed with Oscar twelve months ago.

"Then I'll tell the service to pick up."

"I don't give a fuck what you tell the service," he said, slowly and absentmindedly because he had to give special attention to the commercial which had just come on.

"I forgot to tell you that Furio is coming over tonight. He's going to bring dinner and fix it. Do you know if you'll feel like joining us?"

"Have I ever felt like joining you?"

"You might. I don't know."

"Do I look to you as though I'll feel like joining you?"

"I can't make that decision . . . and I'm late."

"Do you think you could try to make an effort not to be so phony? It isn't necessary. I don't ever join you and Furio. You'd hate it if I did. *I'd* hate it. He'd stab himself. I don't want any goddamned dinner, and if you don't the fuck know that by now . . . Oh, for Christ's sake!"

"Forgive me. I was being polite."

"Well, *fuck* being polite. Play with Furio and leave me the fuck alone. I'm not bothering anybody, am I? Am I bothering you?"

He turned to glance at her, not lifting his head, but twisting it uncomfortably on the pillow. It had meant to be a quick glance, but he stayed that way, looking her up and down. She was wearing green pants, and a new velvet blazer, over a white shirt. She sensed by his expression that he had been surprised by how good she looked.

"I'm going to the dressmaker," she said, "and then I have a few errands, and the market. I'll be back before six. Furio's coming at seven."

"I don't care where you're going. Why do you give me your agenda? Do you have a lover?"

"You know I don't have a lover," she said. "I've got to go."

As she turned to leave, he said, "You could use a good fuck."

She kept going, slamming the door behind her.

Crossing town, driving the Mercedes through Beverly Hills to Olympic Boulevard, she tried to reason away the feeling of anxiety that had returned when she left his room. It was fear. She had felt it earlier as a chill. Now it was a knot, tied tight in her middle.

Deep breathing was supposed to help that. She inhaled, then held her breath for the count of five, the way Harvey had taught her, then exhaled. "Slowly," Harvey's voice said in her head, "don't hyperventilate."

The air was unusually clear for May, a month that always brought humidity and heavy smog. An unseasonable desert wind had appeared during the night and had made the day crystal clear. The sun was bright and warm but not hot, because the winds had shifted and were coming now from the ocean. It was the kind of day she loved Southern California for, the "kind of weather we used to have all the time," the natives said. She told herself to look at the good day and to enjoy it. But she couldn't. She found, instead, that she resented all the days that were not good. Today was like the weather in the South of France and the Italian Riviera, only there you could depend upon it. Here you could depend upon days of hazy sameness, weather that was non-weather. It hadn't rained in months. Even when it did, there was no excitement to it, no lavender misty days of rain to go walking in, no sudden gathering of black clouds and abrupt thunderstorms. You were never caught in the rain. It crept in, without surprise or drama, and lingered dolefully for a day or two. In winter, the weather turned mildly cold, just enough to make you uncomfortable, but never a bracing kind of cold, never exhilarating, and never bringing snow. She missed that most of all. Unless you went to the mountains to ski, you never saw snow. She had always felt that a city was at its most beautiful when it was blanketed in a heavy snow, most alive when the street had been cleared and traffic began to move again. She even missed the way snow aged into slush, turning gray and brown, and missed the sound that tires made riding over it.

It had never been her plan to stay for any length of time in Southern California. She had assumed the Beverly Hills house would be their home base, and that they would spend most of their time living abroad in Europe, Asia, Africa, South America, wherever Randy's work dictated. People who made films lived not in one place, but in the entire world. It had seemed to her the most ideal way to live, because one could look forward to a new place to go tomorrow.

It was not the familiarity of Randy's behavior that upset her. There was serenity in repetition. She was frightened by what she had recognized earlier in the day, that the episodes had become more frequent, his behavior more destructive. He was drinking more. He was more desperate. Everything was *more*, and for the first time since their marriage, she recognized the possibility that it might not be fixable, at least not in time to keep him from skidding out of control.

Six months ago, even at his worst, he would never have told her she could use a good fuck. It would have humiliated him. At some point, he had decided to give up pride, to indulge himself in its loss, because he wanted to have accusations hurled at him. He needed the catharsis of a fight. From the beginning, he had been a master at provoking insult, but the provocations were mild compared to the things he had been saying lately.

In those early fights, before she had learned to avoid them, she had discovered he reveled in drawing her fire; his insults were like blows, and he meant to beat her into submission. Today, he challenged her to say what he had been wanting to hear for a long time—that he was a rotten lover, that his hatred for women was more than she could tolerate. He liked to hear accusations from the gut, he liked to reduce her to a point of ugliness; he wanted the words to spew out of her with contempt. The few times he had succeeded in mining the full measure of her retaliation, he had looked pleased and smiled, as though he marveled at the degree of her cruelty. The smile, she learned, was the sign that he was fulfilled; it was his way of thanking her for showing her true colors.

He sought abuse for the enjoyment of it. With that discovery, she had made up her mind to resist his provocations. She could not have devised a more cruel form of retaliation.

Until this moment, she had not fully understood the degree of Furio's concern about her dipping into her Swiss bank account. She had regarded it as a practical necessity, pleased to have some resources to help tide them over, because there had never been any question in her mind that Randy would work again. It was only a matter of time. Delays were common in the film business, and you endured them. You waited them out. Feast always followed famine. But she had not considered the possibility that Randy might never work again, because she had not, until now, let herself see the degree of his disintegration. Furio must have seen it. And so had everyone else. Natalie asking pointedly, "How's Randy?" And Harvey Parkes asked the same question the same way. Harvey accepted her lies, because he believed whatever he was told. But he believed it only for the moment, and next week he'd ask the uncomfortable question again. You didn't have to be a genius to see what was happening.

She wondered if there was a lot of talk. Nobody, with the exception of Furio, knew how critical their financial condition was. It would never occur to any of them, not even to Natalie, that there might be no money at all.

Group A people were never broke. Like everyone else, they suffered occasional losses. There were setbacks. There were times when you spent less, when the tax payment had wiped you out and you couldn't afford to buy one single thing, until next month. But you never saw the end of your money, and you didn't know the kind of people who went broke.

Though Randy hadn't worked "lately," it was assumed that he had income from other sources. Didn't everybody have investments in stocks and real estate? It was known that actors received residual payments, royalties on work done in the past. Randy's residual checks, in fact, had been their one supply of income. They had been able to scrape along, until now; the returns diminished with the passing of time.

They lived on an amount of money so minimal, it would have created a scandal if anyone ever found out. But probably nobody would believe it.

The house was no expense at all. It was owned by one of the major studios, and was on loan to Randy, a contract arrangement made years ago with the studio.

Elena knew endless ways to stretch money. She knew how to bargain and trade and acquire services without spending money. Her deal with Harvey Parkes was representative of arrangements she made with art galleries, boutiques, florists, restaurants, auto leasing companies—with anyone who could benefit from the value of her sponsorship.

Her dinner parties were often given at La Boîte, the number one status restaurant in the city. It had earned its rating because Elena gave her parties there. She was solely responsible—with a little help from her friends in the press—for the unique success of La Boîte. In gratitude, and by prearranged understanding, her parties, whether at La Boîte or at home, were catered at no cost.

Though Elena was admired for the way she dressed, she had learned how to spend very little money on clothing. Furio, who had exquisite taste, advised and helped her. Randy, when he was successful, had acquired a wardrobe of fine tailored suits and jackets and trousers that he wore only to parties and other social events. During the day, around town, he wore Levi's and western shirts. Lately, at home, he lived in his terrycloth robe.

The bulk of their money this past year had come from royalties on a TV commercial Randy had consented to make two years ago, after a year of no film offers. It was an important commercial, done with taste, for a life insurance company. Randy took it against his better judgment, saying that it would mark the end of his career, that it would remind all filmmakers that only out-of-work actors worked in commercials. Randy's agent at the time had used the persuasion that Henry Fonda had done commercials, without loss to his dignity, pride, status, or bank account.

Six months later, when Randy was still without a picture, the agent approached him with an offer for another commercial. Randy accused the agent of being determined to destroy him, and told him to get Henry Fonda.

At that time, he was still fighting for position, relying on pride, bluff, and arrogance. He couldn't afford the risk of appearing in television dramas, because it would undermine his value as a star in films. He couldn't afford to accept the few films he was offered, because the scripts and the parts were rotten. He was not ready to take a supporting role, because that would mean the end of his career as a star; he'd be just another actor for producers to reject, while they got almost anybody else for a fraction of his price. He'd been offered one of the leads in the road company of a successful Broadway play, but that would guarantee the end of his career as a film star. That was like wearing a sign, announcing you were a has-been.

At a point of discouragement, he let the agent persuade him to star in the pilot for a television series. Really big stars didn't make pilots, they got guarantees of series on the air; but Randy rationalized that there were exceptions. Rock Hudson had done a TV movie which was a pilot for "McMillan & Wife." Besides, the project the agent offered was, for television, a quality project and an expensive production.

While payment for the pilot was no more than adequate, he had the satisfaction of winning the battle for top money, plus substantial escalations, bonuses and other benefits, all pending on the sale of the pilot. There was no question about its selling. The agent had inside information about a secret deal between the production company and the television network. This was presold. In support of his rumor, the agent pointed out that no studio invested that kind of money in a pilot today, unless somebody knew for sure there was a buyer waiting in the wings.

The pilot turned out to be very successful. Everybody at the studio was high on it. The network loved it. Nobody ever knew exactly why it didn't sell.

Randy told Elena that he would listen to nobody from now on, that he would for once in his goddamned life listen to himself. Because he had discussed the pilot with her before taking it, and because she had finally encouraged him to do it, he told her never again to gang up on him with some asshole agent and pressure him into taking a piece of crap against his better judgment. He had also pointed out to her that since she came into his life, with her mastermind ideas for making his star shine brighter, and her clever takeover of Hollywood society, his career had gone down the sewer, and he was swimming in a sea of shit.

Fortunately, his anger was not focused entirely upon her. His agent, Gil Levin, who was young, tough and reputed to be "going places," took him to lunch and let him know he had a greater enemy.

Gil told him he was drinking too much and beginning to look bloated. He told him it was okay if Randy was prepared to make a graceful transition to character parts, but he thought it would be a shame at his age. Look at his contemporaries: Paul, Marlon, Brynner, Kirk, and Heston. There had been a period when Marlon had let himself go to fat, and the offers had begun to fall away—and that was *Marlon* who, Gil pointed out, "Let's face it, you are not, much as I respect you as a talent and a viable commodity at the box office."

Not only was he not Marlon or Paul or Kirk or Brynner or Heston—he was not, as Gil and he both knew, in their league. Gil might more correctly have said, "Look at Whitman or Stack." But he was an asshole and so, in his pushy way, he was employing flattery. He was too dense to perceive what went instantly through Randy's mind: if Marlon, or Paul or Brynner or Kirk or Heston, had gained a hundred pounds of beer belly and had fallen down drunk at the Academy Awards, Gil would have kissed his ass and told him that he was a beautiful person.

Still, having the word laid on him was traumatic enough. So Harvey Parkes was found, and for a few months Randy endured Harvey's out-calls three grim midmornings a week. Randy didn't fire Gil for six months. It took all that time for his rage to surface.

When Gil moved out of the agency, at age twenty-nine, to produce his first film, Randy followed its pre-production progress in the trades, and picked up clues that argued in favor of its certain failure. When the picture opened to respectful reviews and, in its first two weeks in New York, threatened to do big business, Randy's rage became submerged under a poisonous depression. But the picture turned out not to "have legs" and failed to become a blockbuster.

"It's a bomb," Randy said, refusing to believe the front-page story in *Variety* announcing that Gil had acquired financing on three pictures, one at Warners and two at Paramount. The one at Warners was from a bestselling novel about a washed-up detective. Randy's new agency represented Freddie Dietz, a moderately talented but bankable director who wanted to do the picture and had responded favorably when the agency suggested including Randy in the package to star as the detective.

All studios had been interested and for three weeks, while the agency kept the deal open to lure the highest bidder, Randy enjoyed the heady pleasure of being involved in the best game in town: letting the studios fight over you. Until then, he had given up hope that anything like that would ever happen to him again. He felt worthy, after years of feeling unwanted. He became expansive. He envisioned his new career, his second life. It made such perfect sense. The minor star of action, western, mystery, and war pictures was now to emerge as a serious talent—a major star.

As a minor star, he had been typecast, never allowed to grow. Handsome enough for better parts in better films, he never got them because the better directors accused him of lacking depth. But now, as the world would soon see, age and bitterness had given him a new, harder look, perceived by Freddie Dietz. And it was finally going to happen, because of the sheer luck of finding the right actor for the right part. Chemistry. And if the part earned him an Academy Award nomination, as Dietz and the agency predicted it would, he was ready for that as well. His time had come, just when he had begun to think his time had passed.

The *Variety* story on Gil Levin reported that Freddie Dietz would direct the private detective film, and that Gil, getting advance word that George C. Scott's next picture had been postponed and that he was suddenly available, was en route to Europe to discuss signing him for the lead. They never came to terms, but Randy had been forgotten. There was nothing he could do to Gil. He couldn't fire him, so he fired the new agency, and went with Oscar Berthel.

The story had appeared in *Variety* last spring; it marked the beginning of an acute depression and a prolonged drunk that lasted through all the Easter holiday parties. Looking back, Elena realized now he had never pulled out of it. It was not that his depressions were occurring with greater frequency, as she had thought; it was that they never ended.

Maybe Oscar Berthel would come through with something, as he had promised. Oscar had power and influence. He had been in the business since the thirties, and he was one of the few important agents who had kept his small office and remained independent. Most of the others, along with the stars they represented, had been absorbed by the powerful corporate agencies that had emerged in the fifties to swallow up the industry like so many great white sharks. Oscar had survived because he represented three enduring top box-office male stars, who remained loyal to him. He had few other clients, and rarely took a new one. He was in his sixties and had no interest in exploring new horizons. It had been a surprise, and a stroke of good luck, when he agreed to represent Randy.

Oscar had been around long enough to remember that Randy was, after all, a star, and deserved respect. "I'm interested," he said. "Let me see what I can do. Let me try." He hadn't made the promises Randy now accused him of not keeping. Randy had taken that step in his own mind, encouraged, at the time of signing, to be optimistic. He had told her, "Oscar says he'd like to try. Well, Oscar Berthel doesn't have to try. He knows he can do something, or he wouldn't bother."

But Oscar had meant exactly what he said, and nothing more. He was trying. The few times Elena had been with Oscar at parties, she had observed how diplomatically he handled Randy. He had listened to Randy's grievances about past experiences with agents, and picked up on Randy's adamant refusal to consider television or non-starring roles in films. He never said or even implied that it was difficult to find Randy a job. He made a point of reporting on various projects he considered not good enough for Randy.

He told Elena, in confidence, that while he would keep watching for the one right starring part, he felt he could make something happen sooner if he could persuade Randy to take another chance on a pilot for a television series. He talked differently to Randy. "I don't want to consider television," he told him. "CBS called to ask about your availability. I never say no to anybody, and I don't even know what they have in mind. But, frankly, I'm not interested in television for you. I want to see you in the right film, in the part that's perfect for you. If one of the networks came up with something really unusual, with class, I'd tell you about it. At this point, I'll tell you frankly, I'd try to talk you out of it. But I'd feel it was my obligation to tell you about it. After all, Hank Fonda's done one, Jimmy Stewart's done two."

"I don't know that it did such a hell of a lot for Rock Hudson's career," Randy said. "Fonda and Jimmy Stewart are old men, for Christ's sake."

"As I said," replied Oscar, "I'm not looking for television for you, not at this point in time."

"I like his attitude," Elena said, when Randy reported that conversation to her.

"He's full of shit," Randy said. "He thinks if he keeps massaging my prostate, I'll say yes to anything."

Elena had evolved a theory to explain, at least to herself, why Randy had not made the successful, graceful transition from the kind of leading roles he played when he was younger to starring parts that would suit him now. There was no shortage of vehicles for male stars in their late forties.

The problem was that time had not treated him well. He hadn't lost his looks—though he would, if he kept drinking. He was still handsome. But age had erased the quality he had in his youth and had not replaced it with something else. When he was younger, though audiences and critics never detected it, his homosexuality had worked for him. He had a rangy, rawboned build, and callow but good American farm-boy features. He looked right in western clothes, on a horse, or in army uniform. With his looks, he had a quality of shyness that came across as reticence. It was somehow provocative. His face was boyish, but he had a surly, slightly mean expression that made him appealing. In his movements, one sensed a manly grace, but only because he was a boy. When he reached his middle-thirties, his manly grace disappeared and its place was taken by a softness and passivity. His eyes conveyed nothing. He seemed empty.

7

They were going to have scampi, with *spaghetti aglio e olio,* and a simple *insalata* of garden lettuce with vinegar and French olive oil. Furio had brought everything, including the Valpolicella, which they were sipping now, in the kitchen, while he prepared the shrimp and the lettuce and garlic. He had introduced her to that meal in Rome, because he loved its combination of aromas, tastes, and textures. When she tried it, Elena concurred, and afterwards it became a kind of ritual, one of the special, private pleasures they shared. In their travels through Italy and France, he would order it in restaurants, always giving explicit, patient instructions to the chef, so that it was usually very good, but never as delicate as when Furio fixed it for the two of them. He had brought fresh pears and a soft cheese for dessert, and Elena had stopped at Bailey's on her way home and bought him the meringues he loved to have afterwards, with espresso.

They were going to have dinner in the den, on the coffee table in front of the fire; Elena was fixing trays to take in. She had dressed to please him, in a long black skirt and a black bodice with a V-neck and long sleeves, and a string of pearls.

"After dinner," she said, "I'll model my new dress for you."

"You have it?"

"I picked it up today. Lili didn't want me to take it, because she's not satisfied with something back here that only she will ever be aware of, but I told her I wanted your opinion and I'd bring it back."

"I hope you will."

"Of course I will."

"If Lili says it's important . . ."

"It's important."

"Are you happy with it?" he asked. They had picked out the fabric together, and he had gone with her to the first fitting, offering his suggestions modestly. As always, they were followed to the letter.

"I'm mad about it," she said. "I wore my bargain blazer, and she had a few things to say about that."

He laughed. "I'll bet she did."

"She liked it at first look, but when she examined its insides, she was disapproving. She wants to reline it."

"Let her."

"It's not worth it."

"Why not?" he asked.

"Do you think it is? You weren't very enthusiastic about it."

"If I wasn't enthusiastic, I would have argued with you."

"You did."

"But I gave in. I agreed with you."

"Not wholeheartedly."

"Until you put it on. You did something for it."

"You're riding me."

He smiled. "A little. But I meant what I said."

Elena's green velvet blazer was her special triumph. She bought it at the May Company for thirty-nine dollars—with Furio's consent. They shopped together about once a week, sometimes twice, making the rounds of the department stores and shops in Beverly Hills and the boutiques in West Hollywood and on the Sunset Strip. Every so often, perhaps once a month, she lured him—though he hated it—into an excursion with her to Ohrbach's and the May Company, at the frontier of South Wilshire, where they rapidly went through the racks of sportswear, usually finding nothing, occasionally picking up something that worked, like a cotton shirt or a sweater to wear with blue jeans. Elena was always sure that somewhere, hidden among the thousands of garments on the hundreds of racks, treasures were buried and would be rewarded to whoever had the persistence, patience, and cunning to dig for them. Furio could never convince her that it was a futile, soul-crunching, exhausting pastime, that the few purchases she made were always token bargains, harmless but not worth the struggle.

"You have the idea," he argued, "that you are going to find something for five dollars that you can wear to lunch at La Boîte, and that it will look like five hundred dollars and fool everybody."

"Wouldn't that be marvelous!" she said.

"Elena, it does not exist."

But she was sure it did—if you really looked, if you weren't prejudiced the way he was.

"But it is not worth the time. Besides, what are you looking for and what would you find that you need?"

"I don't know," she said. "I can't explain it, but it thrills me."

"I think it thrills you because you would die if you were ever caught."

She *was* caught, not long after he said that to her. She suspected all along that she was not the only one from the A Group who sneaked off to the May Company's sportswear department, but she never imagined that it would turn out to be Mrs. Barry Springfield, arm-deep in a rack of jumpers, who explained immediately that she was shopping for a birthday present for her maid. A likely story, when everybody knew her maid wore last year's Norells.

"I buy my Levi's here," Elena said.

"Why don't you buy them at The Gap in Beverly Hills?" Mrs. Barry Springfield asked.

"Sometimes I do," Elena said.

"Well, I can't wear Levi's," Mrs. Springfield said crossly, and they parted.

On her last trip there with Furio, Elena had spotted the velvet blazer in maroon and black, and it looked hideous, with its plastic imitation brass buttons. Furio had encouraged her to wear blazers with pants and a silk shirt or cotton blouse, and she had collected a number of them over the years, in different colors and fabrics. It was a classic look, and very right for her.

She had moved away from the rack of hideous blazers, when Furio called her back. He had caught sight of a sleeve, in green, and had taken if from the rack. It was the same blazer, but the color, surely by accident in the dyeing, had turned out to be dark and subtle, catching lights and looking like old velvet.

The cut was simple, single-breasted, with natural shoulders, and the velvet was thin, with less body than it appeared to have.

"Try it," he said.

"It'll be skimpy," she said, but by some miracle it had been amply cut.

She modeled it in front of the mirror, squinting at it and wondering why it didn't look bad. The color was beautiful. Furio circled around her, examining it from all angles. He told her to draw it in an inch at the waist, and when she did, she saw in the mirror that it had acquired style.

"Buy it," he said.

"Really?"

"Yes."

"Doesn't it look cheap?"

"If it looked cheap, would I tell you to buy it?"

They replaced the buttons—and moved them over an inch to bring the waist in—with ones of soft leather in the same green, so there was no interruption, nothing to disturb the simplicity. "It doesn't pretend to be elegant," he said, "and it goes with jeans."

At The Gap, she lucked into a pair of thin-wale velveted corduroy jeans in the same green, a half-toned removed, so it looked right without being deliberately matched. Worn with the blazer and one of her silk Giorgio shirts—and simple gold jewelry—the result was startling, and everyone wanted to know where she had found it.

"Furio found the jacket in San Francisco," she said. "Isn't it lovely? And these are just fourteen-dollar Levi's."

She was envied for her ability to wear Levi's, a youth-status-symbol, like blue jeans when they were authentic and not tricked up by boutique tailors with patches or sequins or other busy variations on the theme.

To lunches at La Boîte and to other afternoon affairs, Elena wore Chanel-derived suits, and for dinner parties and to formal affairs, classic-cut dresses with full-length skirts and long sleeves, all of imported silks and fine woolens she watched for regularly at the fabric shops around La Cienega Boulevard, all tailored for her to Furio's specifications by Lili, a brilliantly gifted half-Russian, half-German seamstress he had discovered through a friend who worked as a fabric cutter at Western Costume.

There was no point in pretending that her clothes were expensive, so she didn't try. (In Europe, Furio had told her to avoid the high-fashion couturiers. "It shows only that a woman's husband has money. The emphasis is on money. When you hang ridiculously expensive cloth on yourself, you are less you. You become an advertisement for a tailor, and just one of a small army of women, without individuality.") She gave Furio the credit, because that removed any suggestion she shopped for bargains, and she was envied because she had her own designer. "I'd be lost without him," she said. "I'd wear jeans and socks. I have no real interest in clothes. I like to be comfortable."

She spent money on accessories—shoes and handbags—and coats because you couldn't cheat there. Gold chains and bracelets and rings. She had expensive jewels—diamonds and emeralds, because green was her color—all given to her, with love and in adoration, by the prince and the several wealthy lovers who had preceded him. She wore her precious jewels with discretion, choosing only one piece—a ring, a pin, a bracelet, a necklace—to wear at a time. Often she wore no jewelry. She couldn't afford the little pins and other pieces of costly costume jewelry—from Kenneth J. Lane, of course—that the others kept acquiring, and so she established as part of her style the look of wearing only gold jewelry in volume or better pieces, one at a time, one beautiful emerald pin, a diamond ring or a bracelet over the sleeve of her dress.

She laughed good-naturedly when she made the best-dressed lists, and said it was a delightful compliment, but to Furio. For two reasons. For the advice he'd given her and because it was he who had first introduced her to Eleanor Lambert. Eleanor Lambert lived in an antique-laden apartment on Manhattan's upper Fifth Avenue. It was Eleanor who drew up the lists of best-dressed nominees each year. Miss Lambert was the Contessa of couturiers and of Seventh Avenue. She controlled the international fashion world.

"Did Lili admire your bargain pants?" Furio asked.

"She had nothing to say. She doesn't quite understand about Levi's."

"She's jealous because she can't wear them."

Elena could wear Levi's, because she was slim-hipped, and because her tensions worked for her, and because she was thirty-two, a good fifteen years younger than the mean-average age of most of her peers, the formidable ladies—not known for their social generosity—who had accepted her into their exclusive circle. It was a testament to her considerable charm, and her not inconsiderable guile and ruthless determination, that they did so in spite of her looks. She was allowed to get away with being attractive, just as she was allowed to get away with wearing Levi's, because she was able to make those women feel at ease and not threatened. Though she charmed their husbands, it was implicit that her loyalty was to their wives. Her beauty, unlike theirs, was permitted imperfections. Furio had taught her that simplicity was the key to style. He had encouraged her to be casual and natural in her dress and makeup, explaining that her imperfections enhanced her beauty and were the prerequisite for what is termed "natural beauty." He taught her that nothing was more sterile than perfection. While others spent hours, as often as every day, in salons having their hair and nails done, their faces and bodies massaged, having wax applied to remove hairs from their arms and legs, chins and upper lips, Elena went only for manicures. Occasionally, for parties, she had her hair done, but never styled in a way she couldn't comb out.

"When you have your hair styled," Furio told her, "you look like everybody else whose hair is in fashion. Never be in fashion. Always be yourself. There's nobody like you."

She was the only woman in her circle who had not been to a plastic surgeon. They went not only to preserve youthfulness, but to correct imperfections. Noses were trimmed, eyelids were cut, skin was peeled, with the result that too many had too much of the same doe-eyed look, the same flat-planed noses, the same unflawed, denuded skin. Paula Dexter, after her divorce, disappeared for two months and returned with a new, slightly more pronounced chin. You could detect the work only by the small tuck underneath, barely discernible, but you finally noticed it when you wondered why she always sat through an evening with her finger there, like Shirley Temple about to curtsy. Anne Hague had a similar habit. She held her forefinger to the tip of her nose, pushing it up. She had the idea that otherwise her nose would gradually fall and return to its original condition.

Elbows were done, and hands. A pioneer patient, Harriet Bowen, had begun when she was in her late twenties, altering whatever displeased her, catching every line as it appeared. Now, at seventy-two, there was not an inch of her body, including toes, buttocks, vagina and labia majora, knees, elbows, hairline and ears, which had not been re-sculpted, skin-grafted, drawn tight and polished. She wore clothes designed to cover the telltale scars that no miracle of surgery could remove completely. She never went into the sun, not even a hazy sun; nor was the sun permitted into rooms where she was. She never showered, took baths or touched water without wearing gloves, for water was irritating and drying to delicate new skin; she arduously cleansed and stroked her body every morning and evening with cotton dipped in baby oil.

"Are we ready?" Furio asked.

Elena had just returned from the den, where she had lighted the candles and turned on the phonograph. Earlier, she had chosen the records . . . Mozart, whom Furio had taught her to appreciate and then to treasure, and a Henry Mancini album that gave the sweet and easy sounds reminiscent of the music they used to dance to in Europe.

"Whenever you say," she said.

"Then we're ready."

Everything had been prepared, and now timing was important for the cooking of the pasta and the fast broiling of the scampi. He turned up the flame under the pot of water that had been kept simmering. The row of shrimp, pale pink showing through the thin orange shells, was in the casserole, ready to go into the preheated broiler.

Elena stood beside him at the stove, and together they watched the water come to a boil. She prepared to hand him the pasta, a little at a time. It was one of the small jobs she referred to as her "butlering," when he cooked, an unnecessary assistance, but a gesture of sharing, a way of being together. He smiled to see her there beside him, taking her part like a good child.

When he had arrived this evening, she explained that she needed to talk to him about Randy. "But not now," she said. "Later, when we're fixing dinner . . . or later . . ."

But later she kept avoiding the topic, because it was unpleasant and she didn't want to spoil their being together. The wine had helped to ease her worry, and Furio, always aware of her feelings, made no mention of Randy. By tacit agreement, they were postponing it. Instead, she had told him the news of Marina's break-up with Rick Navarro, and of her scheme for inveigling Natalie to bring Marina in substitution.

Just as the water came to a boil the phone rang. Elena looked at it and said, "I can let the service pick it up."

"Take it," Furio said, knowing she was eager to get Natalie's call.

"I'll be quick," she said, and hurried to the phone. It was Natalie.

"Darling," Elena said, "we're just starting dinner. Can I call you back? I'm dying to hear . . . "

"I can't talk either," Natalie said, her voice tense and muffled, as though her lips were pressed to the mouthpiece, "and I'll call you later, if I can ever get this one to go to sleep. . . . Just one quick question, while I have a second . . . Christ, I'm *exhausted!* She hasn't let me *breathe.* Thank God she had to go to the bathroom. . . . "

Elena looked at Furio, gesturing to let him know Natalie was going on, but that it would be just a moment. He smiled and whispered to her to take her time, then turned the flame down to simmer under the pot of boiling water.

" . . . where she is sitting on the john, watching me, because she is terrified to let me out of her sight, oh God. . . . Do you have the picture? It's a long shot, through two doorways. She keeps having cramps, but nothing happens . . . naturally, because she hasn't eaten, and won't. I've tried to tell her it's like the dry-heaves, there's nothing in there to come out. But she hears nothing. One thing I'll say for her, she does have beautiful boobs. . . . "

"Tell me quickly," Elena interrupted, "how bad is she? Is she basically all right . . . or destroyed, or what? Is it definitely over?"

"It's definitely over. She is basically a lunatic. She is not destroyed. One forgets, she's strong . . . there is something of the cow in her, you know. She is going to destroy *me*, however, if she doesn't stop talking at me, and she has only just *begun!*" In a desperate whisper, she added, "I don't know how I am going to get through the night. I'm ready to collapse."

"Can't you give her a pill?"

"You're joking."

"To put her to sleep, I mean."

"Darling, please. They don't make that pill. She's taken every pill they make."

"Why did he leave? What happened?"

"Do you have four hours?"

"Give me the general idea."

"The general idea is that he's a madman. I'll tell you the psychopathia sexualis part later. Otherwise, he told her that she sang flat and moved like a truckdriver and he told her that she looked like a glass of shit. Does that answer your question? No."

"What does that mean?"

"I can't help you, dear, I've never seen a glass of shit. Look, we'll talk later. Just one question: is it okay, because I wouldn't mention it to her without checking with you, even though I know it's okay . . . about your party . . . I mean, if it seems helpful, can I say you want her?"

Elena almost gasped. She glanced at Furio, her eyes wide, astounded by the speed with which her scheme had materialized. The thrill of success, coming so suddenly, affected her physically; for a moment she was speechless.

Quickly she said, "Darling . . . " Then, pausing to give herself time to recover, she said, "Don't be in such a hurry. Don't rush her. Give her time. She needs your *friendship*, not a social life."

"I think it's vital," Natalie said irritably, as though what Elena had suggested on the phone that afternoon was now her own idea, "for her to get out in public. If she locks herself away, there'll be rumors about pills and suicide attempts and God knows what."

"But give her *time*, darling," Elena said.

"Let me be the judge of that, dear. I'm not an idiot. She doesn't know it yet, but she needs something to look forward to, and this is something I can use. Unless you object. Do you object?"

"Of course not. But I don't think she'll want to come. It's not her kind of group."

Furio grinned and lifted his arms high and made a gesture of silent applause.

"Fuck what she wants," Natalie said. "She'll do what I tell her to do." Then she began to point out what Elena had already determined, the benefits Elena would gain by having Marina attend the party . . . and then she stopped, and said, "Why am I *selling* you? I'm handing you a prize!"

"Darling," Elena said, "do *whatever* . . . of course. I adore her, and I'd be delighted. But only if it helps you to help *her*. If I *needed* her for the party, I don't have to tell you, I'd plead with you. But I have Victor Kroll, so though I love her, I don't need her." She gave just enough emphasis to the words "Victor Kroll."

"That's ridiculous," Natalie said. "She's not going to upstage Victor Kroll. They're not in competition, for God's sake."

"No, dear, you misunderstood my point. I told you I would be delighted. My point about Victor Kroll was only to tell you to do whatever is best for *Marina,* not for me. That was my only point about Victor Kroll."

"Then I can say you asked me to invite her?"

"Please, by all means."

"Fine. I have to go. I'll try to call you later," Natalie said, and then she clicked off quickly.

"I *love* it!" Elena said, coming away from the phone.

Furio got the wine bottle, filled their glasses, and they drank a toast to her success.

For Elena, there was nothing in life to match the exhilaration of success. No matter that the accomplishment was comparatively trivial. The thrill of *winning* was what counted. It represented not only success, but also a sense of power. It was like Kip Nathan's tennis game. She had always understood, where others were baffled, why it was so important for Kip to win at tennis. He devoted long hours of his weekends to the game, choosing his partners and opponents with the strategy of a general. He didn't "play" the game; he worked at it, with the same intensity and concentration he gave to the movies he produced. He played for stakes, and he loved to receive the money when he won, and hated to part with it when he lost.

Those who were secure enough in the industry, who did not have to depend upon his power, either refused to play with him or fought with a vengeance to beat him. Others were grateful for the opportunity to let him win, buying his affection and hoping that would bring favors in business. David Kellogg, his assistant, had been hired by Kip on the strength of his lesser credentials on the court, on a kind of non-athletic scholarship. Just as other executives did not want competition in the office, Kip abhorred rivals in his backyard. Some, of course, were less fortunate than Kellogg. They received only affection, and waited endlessly for favors that never came, because they hadn't David's ability or his charisma. There were jokes made about Kip's greed for money. He'd heard the jokes, and could not have cared less. He even enjoyed them, because they were created around the fact of his winning. Elena knew what few people understood—that the money meant nothing to him in terms of what it could buy; it was his trophy, evidence he could hold in his hand to show he had won.

8

Being with Furio, sharing her small triumph about Marina and also the pleasure of their meal, the music and candlelight and warmth of the fire, Elena felt her anxiety about Randy gradually fade. Only the edges of it remained, and because she didn't want to spoil the evening, she chose to decide that the problem with Randy was not really so different than it had been yesterday, or last week, or a month ago. His depression would lift, his mood would pass. She told herself she had over-reacted and that the faint edge of anxiety still hovered.

"Furio," she said, "let's not talk about Randy tonight. There's nothing new, anyway. Tell me about the show. What are you designing?"

"All kinds of beautiful things Robert Fryer will make me change."

He looked at her for a moment. Soft-spoken and graceful, he gave the impression of being passive, but he was very strong. She found it curious, and interesting, that he was so strong and discreet in his homosexuality, where Randy, ambivalent in his attempts to control and express it, was so weak.

Furio was endlessly patient and unusually kind, especially to women. Over the years, at parties and gatherings they attended together, she had observed him giving all of his attention to the girl most-boring-on-sight, the one everybody else studiously and self-protectively avoided. Elena would listen as the girl poured out her heart to him.

Later, alone with Elena, reviewing the evening, Furio would comment about the girl. "You know, poor child, she is too very sensitive." He would be sincerely concerned, searching to find a solution. "If she would only not wear stripes," he would say, "and if she could learn to bring her voice down out of her nose, and if somebody could tell her not to wear her hair in bangs—because it gives her a little face and, you see, poor thing, she needs her forehead—she could be rather pleasing in her own way. She would like herself better and life would be easier for her."

Furio was rarely with the group of gays who clustered apart at parties, like wives. And Elena had never seen him on the make. He was the only homosexual she had known who didn't cruise everything that went by.

In company, he loved to talk to women, especially to the ones who were active in life and who used their intelligence without aggression. He found most straight men boring, because they talked business or sports even more compulsively than usual, he felt, when they were in the presence of a homosexual. And most homosexuals he considered equally boring. "They are *terrible* in groups," he once told her. "You must avoid them in groups. Alone, one or two, there can be an exotic quality, an animal attractiveness, even to a woman, because they are so aware of their sexuality. But in a group, they confuse each other, their—how do you say?—façades fall apart. The nellies become nervous and wave their arms, and the butches forget and begin to giggle. The trouble is they're not free to be themselves, because they're aware of the disapproval of the straights, and so either they freeze or they feel challenged and decide to rebel. Actually, in groups of their own, when they are free to relax and be themselves, they're much better."

Elena was sitting on the white rug in front of the fire. Furio sat on the leather hassock, and that reminded Elena to tell him her new Harvey Parkes story, about Mel Ferrer. The phonograph was playing Mancini's "Moon River," and Elena closed her eyes and let her body sway to the sound.

"How we used to dance," she said. "Nobody dances anymore."

"Oh, they do," Furio said.

"I mean people we know. I guess you outgrow it."

She had not danced, not even once, since her marriage to Randy. In fact, the last time had been in Rome, with Furio, before they went to the film festival at Cannes, where she met Randy. Almost exactly three years ago, the first week in May. She and Randy were married a few weeks later, at the end of the month. Their third anniversary was approaching, an event she had not considered until this moment.

"Would you like to dance?" Furio asked.

They did—on the narrow strip of black slate floor between the white rug and the fireplace, with barely enough room to move. She closed her eyes and let her cheek rest on his shoulder. The feeling was surprisingly familiar, as though three years had never passed, and she realized she had not experienced this feeling of warmth and closeness to any person in all that time.

She opened her eyes and saw, over Furio's shoulder, Randy coming into the room. Her instant reaction, before she had time to think, was guilt. And her second reaction was surprise, because Randy was shaved and dressed, carrying a jacket, apparently on his way out.

"*Caught* in the act," Randy said, meaning it lightly, an actor's joke.

Furio was surprised but recovered quickly. "I knew it would happen, sooner or later," he said, smiling.

Though they had stopped dancing, she and Furio were still standing in their embrace. All three understood the innocence of the situation, but the moment was awkward. Furio helped it by easing her away from him and going over to Randy to shake hands.

"*Come stai*, Randy?"

"*Così-così . . . e tu?*"

"*Abbastanza bene, grazie.*"

Elena was at the coffee table, getting a cigarette. Randy came over to get one and to take a light from her match. It didn't work, because he was very drunk, and she had to light another.

"*Grazie,*" he said, managing by innuendo to sound provocative rather than grateful.

"You're going out?" Elena asked.

"I'm going over to Tommy and Duke's," he said. "Duke's screening a movie for some friends." Tommy LeMay was a cultured, highly respected producer in the industry, who made expensive, distinguished films. Duke was his kept-boy. It would have been more accurate if Randy had said he was going over to Duke's, because Elena knew that Tommy was currently in Europe. She also knew that if Duke was screening a movie for some "friends," it would be a homosexual porno film, as prelude to a night of sexual play. Or, just as likely, there would not be a film at all. "When LeMay's away, Duke can play," was a familiar joke to the industry's homosexual contingent.

"Furio," Randy said, "I'd 'preciate getting your opinion, seriously now, on a little *dispute* Elena and I have been having, hm?"

He glanced at Elena. Her impulse was to stop him, but she sensed that it would be safer, and less disturbing, not to interfere.

"I don't mean to *impose,*" he went on, "but Elena and I have a little . . . *marital* problem, hm? And you've known us for a long time . . . I mean, after all, you introduced us, and we don't have any secrets from you, Furio. I'm sure we tell you everything. So maybe you can help shed a little light on this situation."

"I don't know if I can," Furio said. "But I will try."

"Good," Randy said. "Good. Now this is the problem—well, *one* of the problems—in our marriage. See, I happen to dig cocks . . . and Elena doesn't. Hm?"

It was as bad as she had feared, and it was going to get worse. "Randy . . . " she said.

"Now, I'm not addressing myself to you at this moment," Randy said, turning to her, "so if you don't *mind* letting me finish . . . Oh, am I embarrassing anybody? Furio?"

"Do you embarrass me? No. Perhaps Elena."

"*Nothing* embarrasses Elena. She's not exactly a virgin. She happens to be a very tough broad . . . and I am not saying anything to you that we have not discussed between ourselves." He looked at her for compliance. "Hm?"

She didn't reply. She folded her arms and sat back in the corner of the sofa. Since Furio was willing, she would let it happen. She had, as Randy implied, endured this particular discussion numerous times when he was drunk, always deploring it and never dreaming he would demean both of them by involving a third person. But maybe it was just as well that Furio hear and see for himself the evidence of Randy's disintegration.

"Now," Randy said to Furio, "don't you think, in your considered and objective opinion, that it is *abnormal* for a woman not to dig cock?"

Furio smiled. "How can I answer that question?"

"Okay, okay," Randy said. "I see your point, I see your

point. Let me put it this way. I dig cock, right? We accept that. I mean, you accept that, Furio, you understand that. Elena accepted that, she understood. I mean it was perfectly understood, right from the word go, everything right out there in the open. I leveled with her. But *she* didn't level with me. And that is our problem."

He paused, and Furio said, "I don't quite see."

"I'll clarify it for you. A marriage is an institution based upon the proposition that two people share a common interest. I mean, for the purposes of this discussion, that is a viable definition of a marriage. Okay? I dig cock. Elena, when she entered into this union, gave me to *believe* that she dug cock. Okay? Two people. Both dig cock. There you have a common interest, hm? Okay, dissolve and it's three years later, and now she tells me that she does not dig cock. And I maintain that a woman who does not dig cock is not a normal woman. I maintain that she is therefore a dyke."

She saw Furio's look of bewilderment, but she had no intention of being drawn into the further madness of what he was really talking about. She would explain it to Furio later. For the moment, Randy's only motive was to provoke and to humiliate.

It was true that she had married him knowing that he liked to swing both ways. He considered himself to be bisexual. But in the beginning, he had been discreet about his liaisons, not mentioning them. Gradually, under the pretense of wanting to be more open about that side of his life, he began to use his homosexuality aggressively, to torment her.

He would, for example, show her a photograph—from a collection of pornography he had previously kept private—of a male model exposing an erection. She was supposed to admire it with him. This was called "sharing." She told him she found it offensive. He couldn't understand that. Why was it any more offensive than the perfectly acceptable situation where men, for example, admired nude photographs of women with big breasts? She would try to stop the discussion, but he would persist tirelessly, until she finally left the room.

The last time he had tried to show her a set of photographs, she refused to look at them. He accused her of being inhibited. "If I showed you a picture of a guy with all his clothes on, and said he's handsome, isn't he?, you'd look at it and give me your opinion. You wouldn't run screaming out of the room like a virgin or a dyke, saying you weren't interested in men. So why can't you look at the picture of a guy with his clothes off?"

She tried, finally, to reason with him, saying that she would like to be able to share his enjoyment with him, but she couldn't. She tried to explain that she could accept his homosexuality as an abstraction, but she preferred not to see or hear vivid details. "I'd rather not think about that," she said. "Do I have to?"

He baited her to the point where she admitted it was repulsive to her. He leapt upon that, yelling at her and demanding that she admit that *he* was repulsive to her, that the image of him making it with a guy—and he described "making it" in graphic terms—disgusted her, until she screamed her agreement, that yes, it did.

Later, when he was sober, he apologized and said it had been a cruel thing to do to her, and cruel also to himself to demean himself in her eyes, to give her that picture of himself.

And that was the whole point of his conflict. He despised his homosexuality, and at those times when he hated himself most, he was driven to force her to hate him for it. She could accept his homosexuality, but not the self-hating way he used it.

Elena looked at Furio, aware of how difficult this must be for him. Unlike most homosexuals she had known, he never talked lightly about sex, and he was discreet to the point of being secretive about his affairs. He always lived alone, never with a lover or a "friend." It was only after she had known him for a long time that she had learned to perceive—from a casual reference or by a quick phone call he made to confirm or break a date—that an affair was in progress, or had ended, or was beginning.

They did talk about her affairs, in the years before she met Randy, because she needed to confide and always sought Furio's advice. But, matching her discretion to his, she spared him the details of sexual intimacies. Furio would talk freely about sex when it was not personalized to invade anyone's privacy, but found it uncomfortable to use the "in" terminology for sexual organs and acts because, he said, they sounded either ugly or hostile and seemed therefore inappropriate. She had been relieved when he told her that, because it had always embarrassed her to use those words.

"Can't you say *'tits'?!"* Randy once screamed at her. "They're not *'breasts'* . . . like on doves . . . they're *tits! Tits,* for Christ's sake!" She didn't like them to be called *tits,* and she didn't like them to be called *boobs,* either. Natalie loved to call them boobs. Natalie's vocabulary was matched only by Henry Miller's. And by Randy. And by Nancy O'Brien, Kip's wife, who despised Henry Miller for being the arch-male-chauvinist-pig-of-the-century while she adopted his style.

Randy had stopped pretending to wait for Furio's response to the "problem" he had invented. He didn't expect answers. It was a game. He was using Furio's presence, taking advantage of his civility, to see how far he could go and find out how much Elena would tolerate.

Randy had decided to pour himself a drink for the road, and now he gestured with the glass while he paced and expounded. Like almost everything he did, it was an actor's performance. Drunk, he was letting himself act the part; it was "in character" for him to be aggressive.

"Elena's very tricky," he said to Furio. "Did you know that? I didn't know that. I was hoodwinked. True, I kid you not. I mean here's a broad who's been around, you might say, not exactly pure as the driven snow. And it turns out she's a fuckin' *bigot.* Explain that to me, if you can. You're her mentor. *Whence* this puritanical streak where she comes on like Victoria Vagina, holier than thou? And trickier. Hm? I have been trying to open Elena's eyes to the news that sex-u-ality is in . . . hetero, homo, bi, or any otherwise. She doesn't know that they're letting everybody out of the closet. Out into the sunshine and clean fresh air. The little tight-assed broads who used to keep their legs crossed are creaming all over the centerfolds in *Playgirl* and *Viva.* There's a goddamn sexual revolution going on, but Mary Poppins doesn't know about it. She's deaf. But not so dumb. Would you say guilty? Because she knows she'd fuck anything to get what she wanted? And has? Man, woman, child, dog, faggot, you name it?"

Elena saw Furio's face redden and his tolerant smile disappear. Randy saw it too and over-reacted with a look of surprise.

"Who—excuse me, *whom*—have I offended?" he said. "Womanhood? Have I offended womanhood? Did I say womanhood? Did I say something we don't already know, calling it by some other name, not so sweet? If I've offended, I retract the offense. I'm the first to admit that she had a moderately rotten life with me. *I* admit it, but she doesn't. Do you see her dilemma? She hates her life with me, but how can she give it up? Because you can't be the hostess with the mostest, if divorced. What price glory, hm? Without me, this shell of me, her whole game is blown, her jig's up. Her *gig*, too. Her jig and her gig. Without her gig, see, she's just another actor without a part."

He looked at her, showing a smile of cold satisfaction. So that was his point—to expose what they all knew, and had known from the beginning—that she used him as he did her. But why, aside from the excuse of his drunkenness and his defensive need to destroy, was he making his point? It was a threat, she realized, and he had managed to score though he would probably apologize later when he was sober. She felt threatened, because he never before mentioned the idea of divorce.

Still looking at her, the cold smile fixed in place, he said, cryptically, "People who play in porno movies shouldn't throw shit."

She felt the blood leave her head, felt a numbness in her lips and hands. She sat motionless, as she heard him making mock apology to Furio for having intruded on their evening. She saw him leave, taking his drink with him, wondering why it didn't spill when he was walking uphill.

She brought her hand up to her face and covered her eyes, closing them. From far away came the sound of the Mercedes starting up. Moments later, she opened her eyes in response to Furio's voice, soft beside her, asking if she was all right.

He was deeply concerned and, beneath that, very angry. He wanted to know how long this sort of thing had been going on. She told him that it had been more and more this way, that these episodes were becoming more frequent and worse.

"Do you only endure it? Do you never answer?"

"There's no point. He's drunk."

"You don't have to endure it."

"Usually, I walk away. If necessary, I run. This time was different. You were here."

"Why don't you tell him not to talk to you that way?"

"He'd love it. Anything I tell him invites more. He doesn't know what he's saying. It's better to walk away."

"It's not better to be violated so ruthlessly. Are you a masochist? I don't understand you."

"I'm not a masochist," she snapped, surprised at the anger she felt.

"You're afraid he'll leave you, the way he threatens?"

"No. It had never crossed my mind. Was it a threat? Did it sound that way to you?"

"Are you so afraid?" He seemed puzzled. And disappointed.

"I put up with it," she said, forcing her mind away from her panic, "because I understand why he does it, why he hates himself, why he drinks. It would all be different if he had a job, if there was even some hope about a part. But I don't *enjoy* his abuse. It's not my idea of a good time."

"I think perhaps you are too understanding. Are you never entitled to think of yourself? Can you not make a demand?"

"I don't need to. If he's ruthless, so am I, in my own way. I married him without feeling, opportunistically. Isn't that ruthless?"

"No. The understanding was mutual. But now you have learned all the ways in which he is weak, and you consider him."

"I consider myself first."

"Do you?"

"I'm very selfish. You think I care about him? How could I?"

"I wonder. Because he is your sick child . . . ?"

"You know me better than that. I've never been anybody's mother."

"I'm not so sure. What about your Italian prince? In a way you were a mother to Cesare."

"Never. He *had* a mother, as we both know."

"But you were, as now, very understanding. He was weak and you were strong."

After a while, she said, "Yes, I do care about Randy, but not out of any feeling of love. I want to help his career, and

I want him to be successful again . . . but for *me*. I detest his failure, because it's mine, too."

"So for your own ego and your pride, you would like the marriage to be successful."

"If he had a job, if he could get a good part, he'd like himself better . . . and he'd be the way he used to be."

"Oh, and how was that? A loving husband?"

"Civil, that's all."

"Admit it: if you could have your way, you would try to transform him sexually."

"I tried that."

"You'll try again. You'll never give up, until you give him up."

"This time you're wrong, Furio. I've gotten very hard. I accept reality."

"You say that, and at this very moment, you are thinking: he will find that wonderful part, he will like himself better, he will be proud to be a man, and he will turn to me and be my lover."

He was absolutely right. That had been her secret thought all along, and even now, against the overwhelming evidence of Randy's homosexual obsession, the thought persisted. She resented her failure.

"You couldn't be more wrong," she said, "and, Furio, I feel we're having a quarrel and that you detest me."

"Cara," he said. "I am only trying to wake you up."

"You think it's hopeless."

"Can it be any other way?"

"I don't *know,"* she said. "Last year when he almost had that picture, he came to life and was different again. You know? Who can say what success could do for him?"

"I can. No amount of success will solve his problem. He cannot accept his homosexuality, and that is why he hates himself."

"He's, anyway, bisexual."

"Elena, he is a faggot. Believe me, I know. I think, so do you. Can you accept that?"

"No."

9

She didn't argue when Furio made an excuse to leave earlier than usual. It was the first time, in all the years she had known him and loved him, that their evening did not extend into the small hours of the morning. But she wanted him to go. Though she had always felt she would be happy to spend eternity with Furio, sharing every moment and experience of her life, she couldn't escape the humiliation she felt at the scene Randy had caused. And she couldn't escape from its intrusion on their evening.

At the door, Furio put his arm around her. "If I upset you . . ."

"No, please, Furio," she interrupted.

"I don't like to see you look so unhappy."

"You know, I'm really just tired," she said.

"I will phone you."

She nodded. He kissed her on the cheek and gave her a hug.

"Ciao," he said. As he turned to go, he added, "Tomorrow things will look not so bad."

"I know."

"There's nothing you cannot fix. There's nothing to be afraid of. You know?"

"That's right," she said.

She closed the door quickly, shutting away the fear, and went into the den.

As she gathered the glasses and the few dishes that still remained, she tried to think about the party, about Natalie, Marina . . . but her mind refused. Randy's threat to divorce her, and memories of those two lost years in Germany—was it two?—kept reappearing.

She brought the things into the kitchen, then went upstairs to change her clothes before doing the dishes. She looked at herself in the mirrored doors of the closet and tried to reconcile the image she saw with the memory of the frightened girl who, thirteen years before, had escaped alone into West Berlin. It was difficult to understand where that girl had found the courage. But she had.

Tedium had been as much an incentive as ambition. One could not know the dreariness of those days behind the Wall unless one had suffered them. East Germans were not allowed to dance; she remembered being told by a girl friend who had gotten permission to visit Moscow that dancing was permitted there. Perhaps that was why Elena so loved to dance. Perhaps that was why she had missed it so, during her three years of marriage. Her recollections of East Berlin became as vivid as her face in the mirrors. The young girls and boys, the old women and men, who had walked the shabby, blacked-out streets where hardly a car intruded. Automobiles were a luxury reserved for Communist bureaucrats and for the daily tourist trade from the West. Some of the residents had chosen to stroll along the dingy, rubble-strewn avenues, grim reminders of Nazi grandeurs proscribed by the Communard, reliquaries of burnished buildings leveled but never restored. Their eyes were glazed as they shuffled across the wide streets where Hitler's *Sturmabteilung* had strutted; their eyes avoided those of fellow-pedestrians in ragged clothes, the men in frayed coats, the women in tattered shawls. Elena remembered equating starved children with ravenous animals. Children and dogs and cats roamed the streets, their tongues swollen, their stomachs distended, their spines a succession of rings. She had seen such misery nowhere else.

She knew that if she had had to choose all over again, she would still chance death over bondage, and boredom. Nothing was more stultifying than boredom, not even now, unless it was ugliness. To Elena, they were one and the same. Bored was ugly. Ugly was bored. That is why she liked to surround herself only with "beautiful" people: "To be depressed I don't need." But Randy depressed her, purposely, as he had tonight, because he scorned women and all they represented.

As she dabbed cold water, then cold cream, on her face, she trembled. Furio was the only man she had told about the porno movies. How had Randy learned about them? Why had she made them? To escape the oppressiveness of

Die Blaue Katze and the mashers who felt her up for the price of a bottle? For the money, the urgencies of survival? With it all, Elena had felt compassion and even fondness for Wally Swoboda, that strange, determined, weird little man.

She knew very little about herself at the age of nineteen. She knew, or at least thought, she wanted to be an actress. That gave her a purpose—something to say and somebody to be, even though it was only an illusion. She knew that she was puzzled about the lack of remorse she felt over having left Karl. But she experienced a feeling of guilt, less for leaving him than for pretending to have loved him.

It was easier to think about Helmut, because there had been no deception in their relationship. They had made an agreement and kept it. Sex was easier that way, somehow more free, and toward the end even pleasurable. She didn't love him, but she had eventually found a satisfaction in his enjoyment.

Beyond those feelings, that small knowledge of what love and sex might be, neither Karl nor Helmut was important to her. She couldn't relate to either of them, because she didn't know who she was, or what her values were, or what she wanted or was willing to give.

After her arrival in West Berlin, she only knew the importance of survival. Later, she discovered that she lived in a world run by men, where women were accepted and only considered sexually—or as mother-images, nonsexually, given roles to play in which they would be adored and feared. Either way, women were used.

So she learned about life from people she met. She didn't choose her teachers, but accepted them where she found them, whoever they happened to be. It didn't seem to matter, because at that impressionable age she was acutely aware that everybody, no matter how lacking in education, knew more than she did.

She hid her self-doubt, and most people were fooled. It had always been in her nature to act self-assured. In school, she had been criticized for being too quick to say "I know" whenever she was told something she hadn't known. She couldn't help it, and she couldn't explain that she considered it an embarrassment not to know. She had the ability to learn instantly, and the moment she was given a piece of information that made sense to her, she absorbed and recorded the knowledge. When she said "I know," she really meant, "Now I know."

And so, as an actress, she had started young. She had continued with Helmut, playing a part, pretending that she liked him. The same had been true when, as a B-girl in West Berlin, she manipulated strangers. There was satisfaction in the power she had over men.

She had continued to test her power, playing a teasing game with that second Karl, her co-star in Wally's film, when his prick had grown huge in her mouth, tasting the emission he could no longer contain. Her unwillingness to release Karl's throbbing cock symbolized for Elena, as the sex act had ever since, a "getting-even"—a woman's trouncing of man in a world that was ruled by man in every other way. Increasingly. Despite, or maybe because of, the Women's Libbers, the Nancy O'Brien Nathans who were bearing down so hard on the opposite sex. Or was it, as Natalie would have put it, on the same sex?

"It's here that we get them, and don't forget it," Natalie had told her one afternoon, pointing to her crotch. "It's the cunt that conquers the world. Forget Trevelyan. That's been going on for centuries, before and since Eve, or Cleopatra."

"I thought you were more turned on to sucking, darling," Elena countered.

Natalie laughed. "That's part of it. Keep the cock in its place. If we don't turn the knob for them with our cunt-mouths, their boyfriends will. But beware," Nat added, "every swallow is ninety calories. *They* get thin, while we get fat."

"I never thought of that," said Elena.

"The answer is to wear a diaphragm, or rush to the john and spit it out."

What Furio couldn't know was that Elena was innocent of Randy's vile charge earlier that night. Far from being indifferent to cock, to not "digging" it, as Randy put it, Elena regarded the penis as a pleasurable entity in the bedroom. True, she could not admire the lewd photos or male nude centerfolds of erections or flaccid tools that Randy so often showed her; there was something too impersonal and clinical about such photographs. It was Randy who had the problem, for he was the only man she'd ever known who refused to let her caress his prick. Apparently, that territory was reserved for the boys. During their early infrequent sessions of lovemaking, Elena had tried, in an effort to please him. "Cut that out," Randy shouted. "I've never been able to stand that." Similarly, when her fingers sought for his anus, he rebelled. "I have piles, damnit," he told her crudely. The truth was, he had an anal fixation; he took suppositories or enemas almost every day of his life.

As she slipped a robe over her Lucie Ann nightgown, Elena saw that it was almost 2 A.M. She wondered whether this very minute Duke and his gay friends were going at Randy's precious cock and his so-exclusive asshole. No matter. She went downstairs and gathered up the remains of dinner, stacking the dishes and glasses in the sink. She had the urge to rinse them and put them into the dishwasher, but she was afraid that Randy would return. She couldn't face another confrontation.

She turned off the lamps, leaving only the night-light by the front door and one over the stairs. She noticed that the phonograph was still playing, softly, and she re-entered the den. Elena stood there for a few moments, listening. This was neither Mozart nor Mancini, but Cole Porter. It was the song that was playing the night she and Randy had met at the bistro in Cannes, the song they had adopted as their own during their brief courtship. The lyric struck her now as ironic and inappropriate:

> I love the looks of you, the lure of you,
> The sweet of you, the pure of you,
> The eyes, the arms, the mouth of you,
> The East, West, North and the South of you . . .

Quickly, she snapped it off, but she could not check the despondency that rose within her like a wave of nausea. "The East, West, North and—the South of you." The lyric haunted Elena, like the dirge for someone she had loved and longed for. But the words, if not their meaning, evaporated as she mounted the stairs.

10

Elena ran into Ted Buckley at Pickwick's, while the clerk was wrapping the new Harry Waller novel. "I didn't know this place specialized in legal textbooks," she said.

"If it did, you wouldn't find me within a hundred miles of it." Ted put the book he was holding on the counter. It was the Harry Abrams volume on Roy Lichtenstein. "Now why couldn't I have been smart enough to take up painting like this guy? Then I'd be dealing with dots today, instead of dissolutions."

"Is that a house charge?" the saleswoman asked Elena.

"Yes. Mrs. Randall Brent. Nine-eleven North Maple." The woman went to look it up in her Rolodex.

"Guess who's going through the stacks of Erotic Art?" Ted said.

"Henry Miller," Elena said.

"Better than that. Barry Springfield, Pasadena's gift to dirty young women."

Now that was a bit of gossip Natalie would love. Elena stored it away.

"Who can blame him, when he's married to Haughty Helen? I caught him examining discombobulated genitals and boy, you can bet he was flustered. He told me he's trying to find a present for Helen's birthday."

"He'd do better at Norman Norell's," said Elena.

"He'd do better at Schwab's. They have colored vibrators. Would you believe they have them in black?"

"Don't you believe in equality? Or the fantasies of women?"

He laughed, and kissed her on the cheek.

Ted was Hollywood's top attorney and one of America's most powerful men. He controlled every union in the United States. He could organize a dummy corporation in Transylvania with as much finesse as he could orchestrate a property settlement during a messy divorce. When Elena had first met him in Rome a decade before, Ted was considered the most handsome man in Hollywood except for Cary Grant. He had squired and bedded the stars of the Golden Era—although on Hollywood's private and cruel information exchanges he never had high marks for performance. Now nearly sixty, Buckley was still good-looking, in a pre-lunchtime gin-on-the-rocks sort of way. The years of dissipation showed in the puffy skin beneath his eyes and on his jowls. He was undeniably charming. If, since his second divorce, he escorted starlets rather than stars, it was only by choice. Most female stars of today were well over thirty. Ted Buckley, at fifty-seven, had the seventeen-year-itch.

"I didn't know you were interested in modern art," said Elena.

"I wasn't until I met you, my love. So how about it? Eleven o'clock, my place? You've always presented a challenge to me, you know."

"You're impossible, darling. What you mean is I'm the only woman in town you haven't slept with. Believe me, it's tempting, but I'm too much of a courtesan for you."

"Ah, yes, I remember Mama in Italy. I remember you with your American correspondent, that mattress-back with the baggy pants who always looked as though he'd just crawled out of your bed. You know how jealous I was."

Elena flirted a bit, as she had learned to do in her B-girl days. "But, darling, of course. You tried. Remember the dozens of roses? I loved them. And the chauffeured cars that picked me up to bring me to those 'friendly' lunches at the Excelsior. You were constantly raving about your rooms and asking to show them to me. Your rooms—and *your* mattress."

"Don't look now," he said. "Barry is sneaking out."

"You nasty man," she said. "You ruined his book-buying spree, and on the one day he escaped from Pasadena."

"Let him go back to his Convair jets," said Ted.

"And the—what did you call them?"

"The vibrators? You've never used one, Elena?"

She didn't know why, but she was embarrassed. She was aware that her face was flushed. Women in Europe would be ashamed to admit they had used a vibrator. Women in

Hollywood were ashamed to admit they had not. The clerk returned with her book.

"Just remember I'm always available, Mistress Mattress." Ted grinned. He kissed her, this time on the mouth. She noticed the smell of slightly stale, malted barley on his breath.

"Darling, what would I do without you?" She meant it, but in a subtler way than he offered, and they both knew it. Once, only once, she had come close to going to bed with him in Rome. She'd even gone so far as to tour his suite with him. Ted had been duly flattered, even though she had made a nervous, hasty exit. He had been her confidant ever since. She gave him a peck on the lips and walked to the parking lot, wondering once again why she seemed to have such a minimal sexual drive.

She was thinking of Ted, and of Barry Springfield, as she fought the five o'clock traffic home.

Elena found Randy's note on the table in the hall. "Dear Wife," it said. "An old buddy of mine from before our blissful days in Cannes showed up. I'm going to show him the spots, and I don't mean the spots on your bathroom or kitchen sinks. Don't wait up for me. Your loving Randall."

She felt relieved because she hadn't been looking forward to another night of Randy's abuse. She suspected that one of his homosexual lovers had gotten him out on the town, but she didn't care. She would have urged Randy on if Francis, The Talking Mule, had shown up. She fixed a tray for herself, a frozen chicken pie, some leftover meringue from the dinner with Furio, and tea. Once settled in bed, she opened *Rogue's Gallery*. To her surprise, she read all through the night; the novel had everything—narrative, action, delineation of character, suspense, a point of view. Mostly, she reflected, it had a hero who was ideal for Randall Brent.

Anti-hero was more like it, Elena decided. Donald Bellamy was one of the best-drawn fictional characters in years. Innately a schemer, he was what medical science defined as a psychopath, a scoundrel who manufactured charm when he saw potential gain as Detroit manufactured cars. Bellamy was the leader of a gang of convicts, all of whom were prison escapees. A crippled mobster, he was the only man who had escaped from Alcatraz. The other characters were a motley lot. One man had eluded the notorious safeguards and prison guards at Sing Sing: another, like Papillon, had made his getaway from Devil's Island; still another had broken away from the prison in Monterrey, Mexico, and crossed the border to the U.S. at Nuevo Laredo, Texas. They shared a common bond, one woman whom each had known and loved in his way. And they shared a single goal: to pull the ultimate heist, to invade the impregnable fortress of Fort Knox. As preposterous and larger-than-life as it was, the story worked. The author clearly knew his characters and plotted with devious brilliance. If properly executed, *Rogue's Gallery* would be a bigger hit than *The Godfather*.

Elena had to get the part for Randy. She knew from experience that the agent, the packager, was the key. She had tried, with Gil Levin, to push her husband into the starring role of a movie based on a play by Leonard Gershe. She had failed when Levin drew up the package to present to the studio. Considering Randy a has-been, he had decided to better his chances to sell the project by offering another, better-known client for the lead. Levin clinched the sale by delivering Gershe himself for the screenplay, along with a hot young director and a sexy, formidable female star. He had managed to sign them all as clients beforehand, of course.

Elena could not let that happen again. She had to find out who Harry Waller's agent was. Adam Baker might have the option on the novel, but it was Waller's agent who would put the package together. Elena had to convince him, by any possible means, that Randall Brent was right for the part. Randy might have to give up a few points of percentage or some of his salary to the agent, but in today's market he had no bargaining power. Power in Hollywood was contained in the package. Computers and agents ran the industry.

Elena looked at the clock. It was almost 8 A.M. When she finally fell asleep, she didn't wake up until noon.

Randy was in the kitchen, again in his terrycloth bathrobe, again nursing his wounds with a screwdriver. Whatever adventures he'd had the night before had not improved his temper. "I not only married a Communist cunt," he said, "I married a lazy Communist cunt." He sneered at her unnecessarily. Randy's sneer was in his language, as always. The physical sneer was redundant, a mere italic to his syntax. Elena ignored him, pouring herself a cup of coffee.

"What were you doing all night? I saw the light. I suppose you were playing with yourself. I 'spose I can't blame you. You don't get fucked any other way."

"If you really want to know," Elena said softly, "I was reading Harry Waller's novel. The one Grace St. George recommended for you."

"Anything Grace St. George recommends, you can shove," he said. But Randy betrayed curiosity by a slight, unconscious forward move of his head. "Okay, how was it?" he asked, when she maintained her stubborn silence. "The book, I mean, not the masturbation."

Elena knew that if she praised *Rogue's Gallery*, Randy would hate it. Indian wrestling wasn't a pastime, it was a ritual. "It's so-so, I guess. Not exactly Herman Wouk, but probably good for forty-five weeks on someone's bestseller list. I'm going up to dress. I'll put the book in your room, in case you have time to read it."

"Now, what kind of a stupid remark is that? Does it look to you as though I'm rushing to Warner's to make a five o'clock call? You know goddamn well I have time. You haven't heard Sheinberg or Calley or Wells fighting over me, have you? All I have is time."

The outburst was calculated to detain, but Elena kept walking at her normal pace until she reached the asylum of her room. She heard the telephone ring from Randy's quarters; she had forgotten to switch it back on when she got up. It was Grace St. George. Elena sighed audibly, even though she'd intended to call Grace herself to set up a lunch with Adam Baker.

"Hel–lo," said Grace, in that obsequious, drawling manner she had. It reminded Elena of Act Two from Puccini's *Turandot*, deadeningly dull and trying to hold you, as you squirmed in your seat. "Elena, dear, how are you?"

Forget the amenities, Elena thought. You know I'm alive, or I wouldn't be on the phone. "I'm lousy," she wanted to say. "I was fine until you called me." Someday, she vowed inwardly, she would say it. But now, for the first time, she needed poor Grace St. George. Perhaps more than Grace St. George needed her.

"Have you heard about it, dear?" Grace was saying.

"Heard about what?" Elena responded unthinkingly.

"You mean you didn't read Clare Ballen this morning?" Grace said slowly, like a miser ladling turkey soup from his cauldron.

"Darling Grace, I haven't had time to breathe this morning. In fact, I'm just rushing out to meet my dressmaker. I'm late and you know, no, you don't know, how Lili is. If I miss this fitting I won't have a thing to wear for two months. Now, if you can tell me quickly, what earthquaking revelation did Ballen make?"

"My dear, it's unbelievable. Would you believe Marina Vaughan . . ." Grace paused for effect.

"Oh, darling, I know all *about* Marina. You mean the break-up with Rick?"

"Well, that's what Ballen reported. But that much was in the stars. It's a very bad month for Aries, you know, dear, especially in conjunction with Gemini. Marina's an Aries and Rick's a Gemini. I could have predicted it." Elena winced. Poor Grace was on the astrology bit again; if Elena allowed it, Grace would be telling her on what day Marina would have her period. On what day, for the next ten years.

"Really, Grace, I have to finish dressing. So if that's all . . ."

"That's not nearly all. Do you know who spent the night with Marina, comforting her? Natalie Kaufman. Jack had to go to the Matthaus' dinner alone, and he told Carol how Natalie had rushed to Marina's side." Poor Grace's fawning voice became her bitchiest. "Just picture it, dear. Marina with all those drugs and the booze, and Natalie back with her helpless protégée. I had to know. So I drove over myself this morning, supposedly to deliver a copy of a 'free' item I'd given Army Archerd on Marina's next project. That Mexican girl wouldn't let me see Marina, but I dragged it out of her. She admitted Marina was up all night—well, most of the night—with 'La Señora' Kaufman, and that they were both in bed. In the *same* bed. Sleeping together. Now, what do you think of that?"

"I think it's filthy gossip," was what Elena wanted to say. What business was it of Grace's, or anyone but Jack, if Natalie swung both ways? "My bath is running over," Elena said. "I'll call you back in fifteen minutes."

"Just one more second, dear," said the galling woman. "I

think you should meet Adam. You know, he's the producer who has the option on Harry Waller's novel. I wouldn't even suggest taking up your time, but this part is so perfect for Randy. Oh, I know you're not looking. I know he gets dozens of scripts every week, but this one is different . . ."

Elena smiled in the emptiness of the room. She had hooked poor Grace. The instinct, which seldom failed except with Randy, had told Elena that Grace would push her new client harder if she, Elena, showed indifference. That was Elena's footwork, prancing, evasive, never aggressive, until she knew she could make it the final round. Her Italian gangster had taught her that. Machiavelli, he said, had demonstrated the tactic. Never maim. Never strike, until you know you can kill. But poor Grace was no challenger to the title, because poor Grace was a nitwit. Elena felt like Muhammad Ali scoring a knockout punch against a featherweight.

"Darling, all right, if you absolutely insist," Elena said. "I haven't read the book yet, but if you say it's good—well, who's the agent?"

"He's the best. Warren Ambrose."

"In that case, why don't you ask this Mr.—what's his name?—he can meet me for lunch tomorrow. How about The Bistro? Do you think he can make it?" Elena stressed the "he." She didn't want Grace St. George to make it.

"My dear, I know he can. He has a morning meeting with an old friend, but that will only last an hour."

"One o'clock, at The Bistro," Elena said. She was not about to listen to Baker's appointment calendar for the bicentennial year. "Tomorrow. I'll reserve a table for two, in my name." She tossed in the "two" as insurance. There was a strong possibility that Grace had missed the point and would turn up with her client. You could never be sure with a featherweight whether he was listening to the count.

This time, she was sure. "Don't bother, dear," Grace said. "You have so much to do. I'll make the reservation for two, in Adam Baker's name."

11

Early the next day, purposely early, Elena arrived at the restaurant. She was radiant; she had dressed with care. For over an hour she sat at her dressing table, applying her makeup impeccably, and studying each feature with the concentration that alone could achieve the "natural," no-makeup look. Ordinarily she did this only for formal dinners or sittings with the photographers of *Vogue, Town & Country*, and *Harper's Bazaar*, magazines that hailed her as a beauty and Hollywood's foremost hostess.

But today she wanted to look her best. She wanted to give the impression of idle rich. She even discarded Furio's rule that she wear just one or two important pieces of jewelry at a time. She chose cautiously, though: a beige Ultrasuède Halston shirtdress (the Halston was three years old, but timeless), her gold-and-emerald Bulgari pin, matching bracelet, and bullion-bar emerald solitaire ring.

All the jewelry had been part of the settlement she received from the prince's family, for relinquishing the Prince. Dear Cesare, she thought, as she fastened the clip to reveal just enough of her firm, ballerina breasts. Her tits, as Randy would say. She decided that they would be the focus of her luncheon companion's attention today. Experience told her that any adventurer had to be impressed by her youthful pectorals. The evidence told her that Baker was an adventurer.

No earrings, she thought. They'd simply distract from the daringly unzipped neckline of the shirtdress.

When Elena entered The Bistro, owner-host Kurt Niklas placed his hands on her shoulders and greeted her with the usual kiss.

"If you were a permanent ornament," he said, "we'd get rid of the rest." He gestured toward the late nineteenth-century posters of the Moulin Rouge and the art nouveau panels of flowers on mirror. Billy Wilder's art designer had adapted The Bistro's decor from Wilder's *Irma La Douce* and Paris' famed Grand Véfour. Billy had been one of sixty initial investors in the restaurant, along with Greg Bautzer, Jack Lemmon, Sam Spiegel, Merle Oberon Wolders, and Frank Sinatra.

The Bistro had caught on at once. But for reasons known only to God and restaurant bookkeepers, the angels kept complaining to Kurt they weren't getting a good return on their money. Finally, Kurt, disgusted, consulted with Sidney Korshak, another founder. "Tell every one of them that if they aren't satisfied," Korshak said, "I'll personally buy back their shares." Korshak was a man of his word. The controlling interest in The Bistro now belonged to Sidney and Kurt.

Korshak, a potent Chicago lawyer, was the gentlest, most faithful of friends. "He's the only man I've ever known in my life," said his friend David Janssen, "who never asks for a favor. He's always doing favors for others." Elena had learned that was true: he was one of her pets.

Sidney used The Bistro as an office from noon until three whenever he was in town. His was the Number One table, which occupied the corner on the left of the room. In the manner of Number One tables everywhere, it commanded a view of the door and of everyone who entered. Hollywood-types, particularly actors, didn't necessarily know that. Stars tended to cluster in the second tier of Manhattan's "21"; it enveloped the bar, and was the noisiest. To be sure, the third tier was, like the far side of the dance floor at El Morocco, Siberia; it was strictly for the rubber-neckers. But only zealous students of the Jet Set, like Elena, realized that "21's" best downstairs table was in the first tier, the one facing you on the right, in the corner, as you entered the room. The log of pseudo-society had been structured on such frivolous bits of information.

The Bistro's Jimmy Murphy led Elena to the Number Two table: Grace St. George had for once done her homework and mentioned Elena's name. She noticed that Korshak wasn't at his accustomed table. Apparently, Sidney was out of town.

Elena nodded to Warren Ambrose, who was sharing table Number One with a couple of men she did not recognize. She couldn't interrupt him now. The men had to be important. Warren didn't waste lunches, or minutes, unless a big deal was involved. He had confessed to a national news magazine that he once traveled tourist from Hollywood to New York and spotted a very important producer on the same plane. The producer, of course, was flying first class.

"I blew a tremendous deal, God knows how much," Ambrose had said. "This guy would have been a captive audience for six hours. I'd have made a million. Instead, I was trying to save a lousy hundred bucks." Ambrose never traveled anything again but first class. He was so first class, in fact, that water never touched his lips: rumor had it he even brushed his teeth in champagne.

Warren had been born and raised in the East, the son of a famous Yale footballer. He had been graduated from Yale himself, then attended Harvard Law for two years. But when a friend of his father's offered to take Warren into his literary agency at a salary of $200 a week—double the going rate for novitiate lawyers—he quit law school.

Ambrose moved on to set up his own agency, taking with him two clients, both bestselling writers. He had established several beachheads with lunches at Manhattan's Voisin and "21," mixed nightly with the artistic, theatrical and new society Jet Set at parties. His client list soon included top figures in show business. Warren lunched regularly with such glamorous women as Dorothy Rodgers and Nedda Logan until, through them as well as their husbands, Richard and Josh, he signed many of Broadway's most talented, most easily saleable celebrities.

Some years later Ambrose merged with one of the smaller talent agencies on both coasts. Eventually, he bought out his partners. Now he controlled the biggest agency in the word with the single exception of ICM.

As a manipulator of big names and bigger deals he was equaled only by Irving Lazar, but Lazar's was a personal, one-man operation. Warren ran what amounted to a commissary peopled by dozens of yes-men and boys-on-the make. His staffers took on the minor deals. Warren assumed responsibility for the first and most famous, who did not necessarily coincide. They might be clients, government VIPs, high-echelon businessmen or the few remaining rich ornaments of the royal family trees of Europe. Ambrose, in short, was a snob. But as he himself once put it to Elena:

"I pull it off better than anyone. All that counts, as Christ, Metternich, Winston Churchill, Evelyn Waugh and P. G. Wodehouse taught us, is pulling it off. Richard Nixon taught us even better, by *not* pulling it off."

Typically, lifelong Democrat Ambrose had made a strong bid for Nixon's memoirs (business had no relation to ideology, in Warren's lexicon) but Warren lost out to Irving Lazar. Warren brushed off Lazar's *coup* at the time by telling his friends, "I wonder if Richard Nixon knows that Lazar used to be Frank Sinatra's roommate."

Elena tried to anticipate Warren's reaction when he saw her lunching with the man who held the option to Waller's novel. She took a sip of her Bloody Mary and, as she lit a cigarette, she smiled across the room at Doris Stein and at the back of Kitty LeRoy, with whom Doris was sitting.

Elena recalled a funny story she'd heard about Mervyn LeRoy. It had happened just before last year's Academy Awards. Both LeRoy and Mike Frankovich had offices in the same building on Sunset Boulevard. As they were crossing the lobby for lunch, they ran into Ali MacGraw. In a highly-publicized, bitterly-fought romance, Miss MacGraw had left her husband, Paramount's then studio chief Robert Evans, for Steve McQueen. Evans' studio had won an overwhelming majority of the Oscar nominations that counted: like everything else in Hollywood, the Oscars were categorized by A and B. Who wanted the Oscar for Best Score? Best Picture added a million dollars to the box-office gross. Best Actor or Best Actress, half a million. Beyond that, forget it. From Best Director on down, the Awards meant nothing to a movie's box office. The previous year the stakes race had seemed to be close. It involved two Paramount pictures, Francis Coppola's *Godfather II* and Evans' first independent production, *Chinatown*. Eventually, Evans' *Chinatown* lost. But it, like *Godfather II*, had received an impressive eleven Academy nominations.

LeRoy said to Ali, "Aren't you proud that your boy got so many nominations?" Ali said "Yes," and hurried away.

Frankovich turned to LeRoy. " 'Your boy'?" He laughed. "They're divorced. She married McQueen."

"Oh, yes. I forgot," said Mervyn.

"Excuse me, Mrs. Brent," said Jimmy Murphy, as he pulled out the table. Adam Baker slid in beside her on the banquette. She noted his Turnbull & Asser shirt and Gucci loafers. "So this is the famous Elena Brent, the maker and breaker of creaky social bones on both coasts," he said.

"You make me sound like a munitions factory."

"A pretty munitions factory. A knockout, in fact. Grace never told me that Hollywood's Number One hostess was sexy as well as hazardous."

"You are making fun of me," she said, "with that Number One hostess remark. I don't think I like that."

"Look, Elena, if I can call you Elena, I admit I don't dig all this social stuff. I don't understand these people out here who run their lives by sleeping on Supercale, which has three more threads to the inch, or judge their friends by whether they've met Irving Wallace. I know Irving Wallace, and Mailer, and Breslin, and Waller. But it's like Tom Wolfe said, 'I'm a Boho.' Bohemian. A guy from the sticks of Nebraska. I got out just a little faster than Henry Fonda and Johnny Carson, and just a little slower than Fred Astaire, whose mother took him on tour when he was seven."

"You needn't feel sorry for yourself," she said. "I grew up in East Berlin. Do you know how a woman, or a girl, escapes? She sleeps her way over the Wall." Her eyes narrowed. "That isn't pleasant."

"It can be," he said. Then, seeing the sadness in her eyes, he added, "Forgive me. Listen, I've gotta level. I thought you were just a celebrity-fucker, like so many others I've met. Let's have a drink, another for you." He flagged the headwaiter. "Why don't we have some cracked crab along with it." It was no question; it was an order.

"Tell me about Nebraska," she said. She reached for a cigarette, and he lit it with a Cartier lighter.

"If California, to paraphrase someone, is a great place for lemons, Nebraska's for cornballs. My father was a telephone lineman, and we were poor. I wanted to go to Princeton, but my rich uncle refused to pay my way. I went to the state university instead. One summer I worked in stock. That means cleaning the cans and painting the playhouse. But I was lucky. John Kellner, the director, spotted me. He must have liked the way I wielded the Jonny Mop, or something. Anyway, he gave me a part in the Broadway production of the play. To say that I was a flop as an actor is to understate it. My understudy took over the morning after the notices came out."

"And you gave up acting?"

"I not only gave up acting, I decided I'd never be fired again, that I would do the firing. I figured if I couldn't act, I could handle actors, so I got a job with William Morris. The super-agency. The ITT of the flesh-peddling trade."

"And in no time," Elena said, "you were peddler Number One."

"I was hand-holder Number One. I got fed up having to coddle all their dinosaur clients. Waller was one of the dinosaurs, but he didn't take to coddling. We became buddies, which means we got drunk together every night. We broke every nose in every bar within a twenty-mile radius of Jilly's.

"I wasn't exactly welcomed by all the snooty accounts. There's a story you may have heard about me; if not, you'll undoubtedly hear it. It involved Freeman-Patman, who had five shows on the air at the time."

Elena knew them well; they were now the most successful producing team on television.

"William Morris handled them and tried to shift me to their account, so their agent could take on someone new. This Golden Boy who had six shows. The Golden Boy wanted nothing to do with me.

"So someone called Freeman and asked if he'd take me as his agent instead of Teddy Miller who'd been handling them. At first Freeman said that Miller had been his agent for years, and he wasn't about to give him up. Then Freeman put it on the line: he said, 'Baker's a prick.' 'We know he's a prick,' said the guy from Morris, 'but he's *our* prick.' "

Elena laughed. This man had charm, and he also had guts. Anyone who had the sense of humor to tell that story on himself had guts. And there was nothing pretentious about him. Elena felt, in Adam, a kindred spirit. Adam Baker might be a prick, but he was her kind of prick.

Over the cracked crab, she learned that the first play Adam had produced was the work of a neophyte pal of Waller's. It lasted for three forgettable performances.

"I escaped to London just ahead of the creditors," he said. "I got into what you would call the A Group and managed to produce another bomb by what you would call 'an aging literary lion.' It got sensational reviews and did no business. This time I was just ahead of the audiences, who fled like long-distance runners from Chelsea's Royal

Court. I flew to Paris and roamed Montmartre like a lot of heelers before me." He resembled Steve McQueen, she reflected, McQueen with a slightly receding hairline, except that Adam's eyes were brown, not blue. He was blond and tanned. Elena could imagine him racing a mini-car recklessly through the traffic on the Champs-Elysées. But while McQueen would be taking slugs from an open can of beer he clasped between his legs, Adam would prefer to be drinking from a silver flask filled with Chivas Regal. He was the sort of man who could ridicule the boys in the naked male centerfolds with the guys and discuss the City Center benefit for the American Ballet Theatre with the ladies. Adam was well informed, a man who believed in keeping up.

They were on the entrée, cheese soufflé, and her wily luncheon partner still hadn't mentioned *Rogue's Gallery*. She perceived that this dilettante-Boho was playing the guard to her forward, trying to force her to take the offense. She accepted the challenge.

"Darling," she asked, "how did you ever get the option from Waller? I read the novel the other night. It's such a great book."

"It could only have happened with Waller." Adam started describing a series of epic pub crawls he'd had with Waller in London during time-outs from his sessions with Belgravia's A Group.

"One night we were at this great bar in London, Les Ambassadeurs," he said. "There was this chick—really beautiful. They always are. And Waller's always there. The only trouble was this chick had a guy with her. Needless to say, that didn't bother Waller. He waded in and there was pushing and shoving and punching and bloodied noses. The guy disappeared, but the dish stayed on.

"After a few more drinks Waller said to me, 'I'm taking this chick to the flat.' He'd borrowed the flat from a friend, and we were both staying there. He was really pissed. I told him, 'You're never gonna get anyplace. It's a dry run. You can't get it up.' He said, 'I sure as hell can. You wanna bet?' I said, 'Sure I'll bet.' He said, 'Whaddya wanna bet?' I told him, 'I'll bet you the movie rights to *Gallery*.' Waller was almost on his ass. He was leaning all over the bar. He spilled his drink and shouted for another. 'Okay, sure,' he said. 'What do I get if I win?' I said, 'You know I got no money. Listen, if you can make it, you can kiss my ass.' Waller loved that.

"The three of us no sooner got to the flat than Waller passed out."

"What happened with the 'chick,' as you call her?" Elena said.

Adam grinned with that frankness Elena found disconcerting. "The flat had two bedrooms, see?"

"That's enough," said Elena.

"I thought so." He noticed her face was flushed and dropped his eyes a few inches to smile at her cautiously half-displayed breasts. "I like that dress," he told her. "Enticing. It makes a guy want to play with the zipper. No, leave it alone. It's at perfect half-mast."

"You were telling me about the option," she said.

"So I was. There's not much to tell. When Waller woke up next morning and found us in bed, he raised the screwdriver he was holding and said, 'Congratulations, buddy.' He was never one to welch on a bet. He called Warren Ambrose long distance and told him to draw up the papers for the option."

Baker told her he used the time while the contract was being prepared to embark on a rather prolonged affair in Paris with Susan McConnell, the Superstar. The celebrated beauty was famous for landing any man she went after, but Adam refused to drop anchor. One day she arrived at his hotel, The Elysée, with several suitcases and announced she was leaving her husband, Superstar Philip Burgess. Adam refused to marry her, and they quarreled. Hours later, Adam returned to find her almost unconscious, an empty bottle of Carbrital beside her on the bed. But Susan had taken the usual precaution. She had phoned the hotel operator to tell her what she had done. The manager arrived just seconds after Adam.

"You didn't leave her then?" asked Elena.

"I couldn't stay with her then," he said. "I made sure she got to the hospital, left the hotel, and sent her three dozen roses with a note on the way to Orly."

"Is that the way she and Burgess broke up?"

"It is. She's quite a woman, but she's also a pain in the ass. I guess he'd had it."

The divorce of the internationally famous acting team had been highly publicized. It was attributed to her dissolution in drink and his in drugs. The yellow journals had also carried stories about an over-riding sexual indifference to one another. Before his dependence on drugs Burgess had, as Natalie put it, "laid everything but the living room rug," including Marina Vaughan, who was Susan McConnell's professional rival. It occurred to Elena that this anecdote, which she would relate with diligence to Natalie, would further bolster Marina's interest in attending her party. Susan McConnell's recent lover was certain to reactivate Marina's libido; Marina lived and breathed and slept in Susan's image. She even overdid the makeup on her eyes like her darker-haired, darker-skinned rival. Insiders knew that Marina was so competitive she had to have every man Susan slept with—and then some.

Elena had no doubt that Adam was telling the truth, if only because he so deftly detailed his story. Besides, he never referred to Susan as "Sue." The show business coterie knew that you never called Philip Burgess "Phil" and you never called Susan "Sue." The same was true of Elizabeth Taylor and Richard Burton. The unknowing members of the press might be guilty of transgressions like "Sue and Phil" or "Liz and Dick," but there were no abbreviations in certain celebrity lives.

It was rather more a matter of usage with Harry Waller's name. No one ever referred to America's most controversial living writer as "Harry." In the familiar parlance of Hollywood, Capote was "Truman," Vidal was "Gore," Breslin was "Jimmy," Wallace was "Irving" (even if there was an Irving Stone)—but Waller was inevitably "Waller." Just as Harvey Parkes was "harveyparkes," one word. On such minutiae was status determined in a city where such opposite types as Doris Day and Milton Berle could be found each afternoon at the same delicatessen. That was Beverly Hills' In hangout for the Toothpick Society. Had Harvey Parkes bumped into them at Nate 'n' Al's, he would have called those celebrated habitués "Miss Day" and "Mr. Berle." He might be the A Group's exercise man, but Harvey was strictly "B" in terms of social intercourse.

Adam Baker mocked the A's, but his mockery included a grudging acknowledgment of their strength. He had learned to insinuate himself into any company. His disdain for the A's enabled him to tolerate them, to master their body English and act out their mores. His attitude was that of a witty, slightly roguish second cousin come to visit. A cynical relative who could occupy the guest room knowing that, although the room was prettier than others, there were better places to sleep. Adam would put up with either Valerian Rybar or Mica Ertegun, but he would not differentiate between them. In fact, he had once described them both as "outrageous designers who make every room in the house look like a dandified bathroom." Adam, Elena realized, was making a living from what she made a way of life.

Determinedly, she brought the subject back to *Rogue's Gallery*. "Where do you stand on the book? Have you got a studio or a distributor for the movie?"

"Not yet. I guess I've been too busy introducing kicky Superstar ladies to the Left Bank."

"Have you got a director?" Elena persisted. "Have you got a star?"

"Give me time," he said. "I'm just beginning."

"Then all you've got is a book. Or rather, an option on a book, which could run out?"

"And will," he laughed, "unless I find another beautiful hooker and make the same bet with Waller."

Elena resented his coyness. "What are you doing here? You're trying to get the project underway?"

"Why else would I spend my time in the land of the lemons?"

"That means," Elena said, "that you are trying to meet the right people. How do you intend to meet the people you need?"

"I'm not sure yet. I'm pretty aggressive, but this is a damned tough town."

Elena had to make sure she had him. If he wanted to use her as a conduit to get to the VIPs, he was going to have to admit it. If he wanted an invitation to her party, as he certainly did, he was going to have to sweat for it. She wanted something, too. She wanted Randall Brent to play Donald Bellamy, and unless Randy's chances were more than excellent, Adam could hitchhike his way back to Omaha. "Who do you want for the lead?" she said.

"That depends. A lot of people could play it. Burt Lancaster, maybe. I liked his power in *Gantry*. Even Chuck Heston, if people could take him as a hood instead of God. There's a young guy I saw in New York and liked—I forget his name. He's too young, but I think he could do it, with the right makeup." He's baiting me, Elena thought. Maybe he wasn't her kind of prick after all. "I've even considered your husband," he said. "I admire his style. I think he could be much bigger, very big, with a knockout story like this and the right direction."

"Randy would be magnificent," she said. "I kept seeing him as Bellamy as I read the book. You're right. He's gotten bad scripts until now and low-budget pictures. Darling, you must remember Cannes, when the critics went crazy over Randy in *Sagebrush*."

"I never saw that one."

"It ran out of competition, got raves, and didn't even earn ten cents in this country."

"Too bad. I'd like to look at some of his work again. I remember one picture; the picture wasn't very good, but there was this kitchen scene I remember. Brent knocked the brains out of the bad guy, whoever he was, and then the girl and Brent defied her father and left together and made it in his shack."

"That was *The Shortest Way To Kill,*" she said.

"Listen, do you think you can arrange for me to see him?" He might have been talking about a stranger instead of her husband. His eyes were caressing hers, dark brown into green, like timber in a gully. Good Lord, thought Elena, what do I see in this man?

"I might arrange that," she told him.

Adam took a sip of his brandy. "You really like *Rogue's Gallery?*"

"I think it will keep you in Gucci bracelets for the rest of your life," she said. She added carefully, "If you get the right package."

"I have the best packager in the business," he said.

"Darling, Ambrose is the best," said Elena. "Warren's a very good friend. In fact, he's coming to dinner on Friday night." She felt heady enough to drain her espresso. She was pleased that Ambrose was Waller's agent, instead of Lazar. Swifty was a close friend, but Swifty wasn't one to confuse a friendship with movie-star charisma. Swifty didn't handle actors but, to protect his property, he would have recommended Clint Eastwood for Donald Bellamy. Ambrose was tough, but there were ways of getting to him. Through Alice, his wife. Through Ted Buckley, his lawyer.

Through Kip Nathan, who bought a lot of talent from him. "Adam plays excellent tennis," Grace had told her. That should appeal to Kip, whose avocation it was.

Adam had called for the check, and he signed it. "I'd like to see some of Randy's old films, and I'd like to talk to him."

Elena put her hand over his before she stood up. Clearly, he understood the terms of the deal. It was a simple trade. The Bellamy role for Randy in exchange for Elena's ability to introduce him to the "right" people, the people who could get *Rogue's Gallery* made. Many similar trades had taken place in this room.

"You'll talk to Randy," she said. "You'll talk to some other people, too. You'll talk to everyone who can help you make your picture. Just come to my party on Friday. You'll meet them all."

Before she had reached The Bistro parking lot, Elena started to draft her campaign for Adam Baker. She would give him the power of an incumbent in the politics of the New Hollywood. According to Ballen, Elena turned Z's into A's by the merest nod. Mr. Baker, she reflected, was a man on the make who didn't know he had made it.

12

"Listen, how are you?" said Rex Reed. The unmistakable accents of Baton Rouge trailed over the long-distance wire.

"Darling." Elena was pleased. She truly liked Rex.

She was a press collector as well as a people collector. She had been known to associate even with lower-echelon journalists, because their methods of operation, their power was endlessly fascinating. Raised in East Berlin, a city without a free press, Elena recognized the homage that was paid to the media in the West.

Elena had never developed any skills with the written word. She coveted writing talent as other women coveted merchandise in boutiques—because they didn't own it.

She saw a parallel between her devotion to status, people, and party-giving and the columnist's predilection for reportage. Suzy, her friend, was clever, but in a snickering way. Rex was special. He was corrosive, vitriolic, dead set on molding any chance rumor into his particular kind of gossip. Rex was an outright pessimist. Elena loved humor, and so she loved Rex. She had never met a funny optimist. "Rex, my love, you must fly out. I've been meaning to call you. I'm giving this little party for Victor Kroll and Marina Vaughan. Next Friday."

"Elena, I am coming out there. I don't know. I might. Johnny Carson keeps insisting he wants me to do his show before he goes away. And it's great exposure."

"You sound like a publicist. Grace St. George," said Elena.

"How can you mention that horrible woman?" asked Rex. "She has those terrible lunches for all her secret women clients at The Bistro, and they look like a meeting of the Mattachine society."

"You don't mean Grace is queer?" said Elena.

"Well, I don't exactly see her as Brigitte Bardot. How is

Randy?" Rex knew more about her problems with Randy than anyone except Furio.

"Randy is fine," she lied, because Randy was in the room. "Now tell me what's happening in New York."

"I had my own screening of *Day of the Locust*. Even Jerry Hellman didn't know. Dyan Cannon was there and she said 'How did you get this film? Hellman won't even let his brother see it.' I think it's a masterpiece. A lot of people didn't like it. Someone said, 'It's such a lousy story.' If you don't like the story, blame it on Nathanael West. We all know he was a schlepper. This movie is an artistic achievement. It has the most beautiful imagery of any film I've ever seen. But you know New York. It's instant opinion here."

"Of course," said Elena. "Who was there?"

"Sidney Lumet, who pointed out that if Paramount likes a picture, you can tell by the food. He said that when they screened *Orient Express* they served soggy quiche. At this one we had fresh shrimp, and filet, and chocolate mousse. Woody Allen came, and Angela." Lansbury. There was no other Angela in Reed's semantical jargon, as there was no other Melina than Mercouri. Aside from these women and several others, Rex used last names when dropping them. That habit pegged New Yorkers for Californians like the Crazy P brand on cattle. The family name was an easterner's snob concession to the Hollywood dolts who might otherwise mix identities. The five-boroughs contingent had to be sure that the celluloid smart set was suitably impressed.

Rex continued his verbal semaphore. "Shirley MacLaine and Pete Hamill, Nora Ephron, Richard Dreyfuss—you know, he played Duddy Kravitz—and Bill Atherton. He's in the film and will be a big star. He steals it. Faye Dunaway, Betty Comden and Adolph Green, Irene Selznick, Stephen Sondheim, Geraldine Stutz—she's the president of Bendel's. . . . "

Doesn't he think I read *Women's Wear Daily?* Elena reflected. Doesn't he know I make it my business to lunch with fashion store presidents like Gerry and Norman Wechsler whenever I'm in New York or San Francisco? How does he think I get my clothes?

"Fantastic," Elena said. "Darling, are you writing another book?"

"Another collection, maybe. Ellis Amburn called me

with a fabulous offer to do a book, but do you know what it was *on?* Asking five hundred famous people how they lost their virginity. If I have any clout, I'm going to save it. I'm not going to waste it on *that*. Can you imagine anyone in Hollywood answering a question like that? I'd be a laughingstock. Anyway, Elena, I just wanted to tell you I may come to the coast. If I do, I'll let you know."

"What day are you taping Johnny?" she said.

"On Thursday. I could stay over at Richard and Jean's. Are they invited to your party?" Richard and Jean were Richard Brooks and Jean Simmons.

"Darling, Jean's still in London with *Eine Kleine Nachtmusik,* and Richard can never get a baby-sitter. Besides, he hates parties. His idea of an exciting weekend is to screen three movies in three nights. I think he eats film for nourishment."

"God, what a diet. I've seen more bad movies lately than hustlers on Seventh Avenue. Well, look, Elena, this is costing a fortune. Why don't I call you on Monday? I'll know by then."

"All right, darling. But do plan to come. I want you to meet Victor Kroll."

Randy laughed sarcastically from the sofa. "What a phony cunt," he muttered.

"I wouldn't be there to meet him," said Rex. "I'd be there because of you. Goodbye, Elena."

"Goodbye."

"You were speaking of books," said Randy. His disposition was improving. He'd bothered to dress, if only in jeans and a sweater. "Hey, lady. You may be a pet of the social set. You may be Rex Reed's and Ballen's *A* hostess. But one thing you're not is a critic. I mean that Waller novel. It's a gem. The best thing he's ever done. How was your tryst with that guy who has the option? Will you sell your body for me? I want that part."

"It went fairly well," said Elena. She had to be careful; this might be a trap. Besides, she hadn't forgotten Adam Baker's rugged features and slightly tousled hair. Nor his wrists, which were bony. Elena had always gone for men's wrists. Bony wrists represented, for her, whose own wrists were square like her peasant mother's, aristocratic breeding. "Warren is handling the package."

"Then you'll have to sell your body to Ambrose. Damnit. He has all those Big Name actors. What would he want with me?"

"The point is that Baker, who holds the option, wants you."

"Did he say that?"

"He said he is a fan, and wants to review your old films, and meet you. Why else would he have bothered to lunch with me?"

"For your beautiful beaver," he said. "By the way, do you still trim the hair on your beaver? A husband is curious about those things. Where are you going?"

"I thought I'd start dinner," she said.

"No, relax. I'll make us a drink. You know, you look pretty smashing today. I might even put on the phonograph, light the fire, and pretend you're Furio." When Randy joked about his sexual preferences, his spirits were good. She knew better than to answer that one, though.

"Can you still make the best Orange Passion in the world?"

"Try to beat me," he said, from the bar. That was a vodka martini with just a touch of orange juice and peel, set aflame. They'd discovered it at a tiny bistro in Cap Ferrat. He selected an orange from the fruit in the bowl and cut it in half. "Do you think I should call Berthel?" he asked.

"I think you should fire Berthel," Elena said. She was taking a chance, but it was calculated. "Randy, Oscar doesn't deserve you. He hasn't made a deal for you in twelve months."

"You have something there," he said. "Nobody can deny. Oscar never passed spelling. He doesn't read. He couldn't find a property if Pickfair blew him down in a hurricane. But baby, I'm stuck with him. Where else do I go?"

She had to make him think it was his idea. "Lots of places," she said. "Any place. Since you like the novel, and the role, and Baker wants you for it—well, let's not let Oscar hear about it. You know as well as I do that he'd be pushing to get Paul Newman, and ten percent of the salary and ten percent of Paul's ten percent gross."

"Not to mention one hundred percent of Joanne Woodward." He handed her a glass, and sat down with the other. "But if Warren is putting this together, shouldn't Oscar give him a call?"

"Warren won't accept Oscar's call. Warren and Alice will be at our party on Friday."

"So you just might seat Warren next to you?"

"I just might seat Alice next to you."

"Tricky Charlie," he said. But he said it appreciatively, with a smile. "Look, would Warren take me on? I mean, if he's making this deal, that would be my best insurance, wouldn't it?"

"Your insurance, Randy, is your charm. When you choose to turn it on, no woman, not even straight Alice, can resist."

"Straight Alice, who keeps those damn feminine hygiene cloths on the dressing table in her guest bathroom. What are they called?"

"Bidettes," she said.

"My God, it's like she thinks the dames haven't douched before coming to dinner. Or maybe she does it in case they fuck between courses."

Elena laughed. "Randy, you've got a square dinner partner. So use it. Use her hang-ups. Use Ban and Mitchum's; use three deodorants. Use Listerine. Use Fabergé Brut For Men."

"She'd prefer your perfume by Paco Rabanne," he said.

Not Alice, please, thought Elena. You're not making Alice a Lesbian, too. Elena had read about the New Sexuality, which was bisexuality. Liberationists and artistic elitists like Shirley MacLaine and Vidal called it "nature's natural state." If bisexuality was so normal, Elena wondered, why did bisexuals try to make everyone else bisexual? Or homosexual. She hadn't forgotten Furio's observation on Randy. "Elena, he is a faggot. Believe me." I can compete with a woman, Elena thought, but not with a man. Like any woman, Elena knew that there are three things you cannot upstage: a child, an animal, and a faggot.

She wasn't much of a cook so on Fridays she always left something out for Fannie, the maid, to prepare. Tonight they had turkey. Randy was uncustomarily cheerful, his depression clearly over. Hyped by a few more Orange Passions and wine, he decided to take a sauna. She showered, put on her yellow terry cloth wrapper, and telephoned Natalie. "How's Marina?" she said.

"How am *I?*" said Natalie. "Youth is resilient. She'll be fucking around in no time, and I'll be in Camarillo." That was a vision—Natalie in a state mental institution, bullying orderlies, analysts, and inmates alike. "What's so funny?" said Natalie. "I tell you she's done a transference. Her traumas are mine. Why do youth and senility burden the middle-aged? All we want is a peaceful menopause. And then safe cock."

Nat was too young for menopause. And with Jack she had safe cock. He had had a vasectomy years ago. He'd had it, like many New Hollywood men, so he could screw around indiscriminately and avoid paternity suits. Natalie knew but didn't care. At least she said she didn't. Natalie had admitted to Elena she used to steam open Jack's mail and reseal it before he came home from the studio. She'd see a bill for a Tiffany bracelet and then, weeks later, tell Jack, "That broad of yours has a pretty big mouth. She's been explaining that eighteen-carat bracelet to everyone she meets." Then Natalie listened with satisfaction outside his closed door as Jack called his current mistress and screamed at her over the telephone. "He thinks he's never known a dame who doesn't draw up his fucking habits on a chart," she told Elena. "But how did you like Grace's latest dummy, the one you had lunch with?"

It was the question Elena anticipated. It launched her campaign for Adam Baker.

"Darling, he isn't a dummy. I don't know how Grace got hold of him, but I assure you it was by mistake."

"He's worth getting hold of, then? How big is it?"

"Natalie, let's forget sex. Although he as much as told me it was his long affair with Susan McConnell that broke up the Burgess marriage." Elena wanted to raise Nat's interest in Adam; she had decided that Adam would be Marina's escort to the party.

"How did he get away from McConnell? Whatever she fucks, she marries."

"Darling, he's different. You'll see. I've asked him to my party. He's too young for Susan. She only marries her fathers."

"Her father-fuckers, you mean. So describe Grace's Little Prince. Is he handsome? Does he wear a toupee?"

"He'll need one in a few years. Right now I'd describe it as a high forehead. He's good-looking in a rugged way.

Like McQueen. But intelligent. Blond. Brown eyes. About six feet tall."

"You sound like a casting director. Which brings me back to my earlier question. How big is it?"

"Darling, you are too much."

"Can't you guess?"

"Can't you?"

"I mean if he's been Susan's lover, and all that masculine, he must have had a small hard-on, didn't he? It didn't swell?"

"I didn't look under the table, Natalie."

"Pity. Under the table can be fun."

"We discussed this book, I told you."

Natalie sighed. "*Rogue's Gallery*. I bought it today. Grace said it might be interesting for Jack."

Elena swallowed her rage. Stupid Grace. Phony Grace. Poor Grace. Always working. "I doubt it, darling. You see, it's this sprawling novel on several levels, with con-men and intrigue and social significance. It's not exactly a situation comedy for TV."

Natalie noted the change in Elena's voice. It was edgy, tight. So that was to be the game? The Waller novel was fine for Randall Brent, who peed in a sandbox and had the acting ability of a cat, but wrong for Jack, because he directed comedy on TV? At least Jack Kaufman has a job, was what Natalie wanted to say.

"Well, I suppose I'll read it," said Natalie. "Since you say this super-stud will be at your party, what can I lose? Listen, if he's as good as he sounds, he'd be a diversion for Marina. She needs a new fuck."

"Oh, no," Elena drawled carefully. "I'm asking Victor Kroll to bring Marina. That is, if you still think she is up to a party."

"I've told you she is," said Natalie sharply. "Tomorrow we're going to Giorgio's to choose her dress. Victor Kroll. I must tell you, Elena, that's good publicity. And won't that be something to put Rick Navarro back into acid rock. Or acid. Whatever he takes. Can you see his face when he picks up the paper and there's Marina with Victor Kroll?"

"I certainly can," said Elena. "Darling, that's just the point."

"There will be photographers?" she asked. "You have arranged that?"

"Darling, have you ever seen one of my parties without photographers?"

The New Hollywood paparazzi would line the sidewalk outside the house, because Elena had taken Jody Jacobs to lunch to be certain she mentioned the dinner in the Los Angeles *Times*. Elena intended to supplement that by calling Sylvia Norris to tell her the cast and the arrival time. Sylvia got such tips because she reciprocated. She passed them along to reporters and other photographers. Maple Drive would be as crowded on Friday as Grauman's Chinese on premiere night. Elena would see to that. Although there would be no photographers in the house. *Harper's Bazaar*'s Nancy Dinsmore was invited to the party; Nancy had asked Elena if she could bring a photographer. Nancy got the obligatory no. One never allowed photographers inside. That was strictly B.

Even without Victor Kroll, Elena assured herself, the dinner dance would have ample coverage by the press. The biggest headlines, of course, would happen when Randy got the most important part of the decade. Elena's party was no longer a party. It was a plot.

13

The story broke on the TV late-night news on Wednesday, two days before the party. Next morning, the *Chronicle* gave Victor Kroll its banner headline: KROLL FLYING TO GENEVA FOR ECONOMIC TALKS. The story went on to say that Kroll's meeting with several heads of state "was set up a month ago, but withheld because of the gravity of the economic crisis. Mr. Kroll revealed his plans in a press conference called at 7 P.M."

Elena could not have arranged the timing better. Her phone started ringing early Thursday—everyone wanted to know if the dinner-dance had been canceled.

"But of course not," she told her callers sweetly. "Victor phoned me from Washington days ago, but he swore me to secrecy. You know how mysterious he is about his missions. I told him the party would be a disaster without him, but everyone understood. He sounded exhausted and disappointed when I said I'd arranged for him to escort Marina Vaughan. You know how he loves sexy actresses."

Only Mickey Ziffren questioned that statement. Mickey was the wife of California's former Democratic National Committeeman and the sharpest woman Elena knew. "Victor is far too intelligent for those little starlets," she said. "I think they're his monkey bars, his playground away from world crises."

"That's perfect," Elena conceded. "I once asked Victor why he dates actresses. He said, 'Because I'm not about to marry any of them.' "

Kroll had been smart enough not to marry Nancy O'Brien Nathan, although they had a liaison for more than two years. He met her when she came to Washington to interview him for an *Esquire* profile. Kroll was impressed by her patrician beauty and by her awareness. As a politican fixed in future recountings of history, Victor Kroll was understandably intent on exerting his potency elsewhere, on manipulating the lives of those in his circle. Nancy possessed a vast supply of information which, if it remained uncoded, would turn to misinformation. In short, she presented a double challenge, a challenge that was at once intellectual and emotional. And Nancy was badly in need of Kroll's guidance. Besides, she was intricate enough, he decided, to deserve formulation. A child's spinning top is, after all, no toy for a statesman.

Typically, it was Kip Nathan's secretary, not Nancy, who called to check on whether the party was on. "I swear Pacific Telephone would fold," Randy said, "if it weren't for you and your crony-bolognas. When is Rex picking you up?"

"At eight, right after he tapes the Carson show. Are you sure you don't want to join us? You like Dom's."

"No thanks. I have to make myself pretty for Alice tomorrow. Besides, a vacation will do you good. You've been patient with me, Elena. I want you to know I know that. Rex always perks you up."

Randy had perked her up by calling her "Elena." When he was acrimonious, he never used her first name. He addressed her as "you" or with one of his four-letter words or with numerous other coined slurs.

"Thank you," she said. "I want you to know, Randy, it was very considerate of you to suggest we eat out. You're right. I burn my fingers cooking the night before a party."

"Have you done the seating?"

"I'm about to. I didn't have all the names until an hour ago. Ted has had four weeks to decide who he's bringing. And I still had to call him to insist on the name of his date. He's a pain in the ass."

"A powerful pain in the ass, though. So all you ladies put up with him. You'll be lucky if he doesn't throw whatever chick he's bringing out before dawn and turn up with another."

"Or alone," said Elena. "He's done that, too. Which will totally ruin my seating. Can you imagine? Rex didn't let me know he was coming till yesterday, and I had to invite an extra woman for him—this late. Then Rex had the nerve to suggest I ask Doris. Doris *Day*." She sounded as though she'd been bitten by something.

"I like Doris Day," Randy said.

"So do animals. But darling, you don't invite Doris to a party if you want an answer while you're still alive. It's ulcer-time. She doesn't say yes and she doesn't say no. She says maybe. My God, I prefer a quick no."

"Except from Ballen, you do."

"Randy, Clare is our friend. She's coming for drinks, and she'll write about it, although I told her she didn't have to. She has to cover the benefit for the Neighbors of Watts tomorrow."

"You have to admit, Elena, you didn't jump for joy about that."

"My point is, why oh why can't Doris Day give an answer? I will not invite her. I told Rex. If Edie Wasserman can answer, and Lucy, and Carol Burnett, in an hour, what makes Doris so special?"

"She has a soda fountain and fifty dogs to feed," he said.

"Edie has Lew to feed."

"He's skinny. He doesn't eat much."

"Okay, my darling. I'm going to do the seating right now." Elena took her guest list and settled herself at the desk with a ream of paper.

Randy poured himself a drink. It was five-thirty, and he felt he deserved it. He'd been on the wagon for days. Besides, he knew what was coming. Endless comments. When Elena drew up her seating plan, she sounded like Hope delivering a monologue. Elena was more amusing than Hope. Randy could have left the room, but he enjoyed it. If you're married to Hollywood's top hostess, you may as well take what she can give. Who knows? thought Randy. Someday, I may want to give a party myself.

He sat on his favorite chair and put his feet on the leather gout-stool. He stroked the gout-stool's enormous back; it was made in the image of a rhinoceros.

"Forty-eight people," Elena was saying. "Six tables of eight. You and I will take the tables in the hallway and by the kitchen. That way, people won't be insulted; they may not be with the host and hostess, but they'll have better tables. Now." She drew six circles in the exact position the tables would be. George, La Boîte's owner, had come by today to check the placement. "This is *not* a bad guest list," she said. As though she'd never seen it before, Randy mused, much less studied it for four weeks, day and night, like a student cramming for a physics final.

"Do you know," said Elena, as if he didn't, "that we have both Gene Kelly and Fred Astaire?" In the quasi-Burke's Peerage of Hollywood, Randy knew, either one in attendance made the party straight A. It didn't matter, with Kelly and Astaire, if the rest of the group was made up of trash collectors, chimney sweeps and plumbers. The party was A.

"Which one do you think I should put next to Alice?" Elena said. Randy took a sip of his drink. He knew from experience it was a rhetorical question. No one told Elena how to seat. On the contrary, she was apt to seat her friends' parties for them. "I think Gene," she said, almost immediately. "We give Alice both you and Gene, Gene gets Natalie Wagner, she gets Prentis Hale, he gets Carol on his other side." Elena meant Carol Matthau, Walter's wife. Carol was a close friend of Prentis and of Denise Minnelli Hale's; Carol constituted half of what Elena considered the requisite "fun couple" for any party. "Fantastic," Elena said. "We put Adam Baker next to Carol, Marina on his other side, with you on Marina's right." She straightened, lit a cigarette, and considered what she had wrought. Randy's table. Table "1," which would not be so designated at the party. The number, nestled in the centerpiece, would be something innocuous, like "4"; Elena's own table would be "6," the sixth out of six. All of this was calculated to salve the egos of those at the other four tables.

A party, in the New Hollywood, was a stratagem and an artifice. Elena, as the tactician, chose her belligerents with respect to the battle, not with regard for seniority. Otherwise, she would not have put Randy between Marina Vaughan and Alice Ambrose. Alice was at Randy's right not because she outranked such A's as the Edies, both Goetz and Wasserman. Alice was at Randy's right because the host and hostess needed Warren Ambrose. Alice drew Gene Kelly for the very same reason: Gene was a Superstar, certain to please and charm her.

Elena placed her cigarette in the ashtray and went back to work. That's her work, Randy noted silently. In a crisis econony, my wife's lifework is tending to seating lists for millionaires. The party was complimentary, of course, as were all the Brents' parties catered by La Boîte. It was strictly a matter of mini-finance. Elena's business brought the restaurant, free, thousands of dollars worth of publicity.

Still, Randy marveled at how Elena accomplished the bargain.

Ballen, at lunch, had recently told him, "Can you imagine, one of my escorts actually thought I get lunches free at the Polo Lounge. Because I do almost all my profile interviews there. Well, I have an expense account. I go there because it's close to home. I've never gotten so much as an apple from the Polo, or any other place in town. The *Chronicle* wouldn't permit it, even if the restaurants offered." The point, Randy thought at the time, was that they hadn't offered. Ballen, and the late Jackie Susann, had made the bar of the Beverly Hills Hotel a household word. Maybe you had to ask. He was sure that Elena had struck the deal with La Boîte at the time it opened to the competition of Chasen's, The Bistro, Perino's and others. But Randall Brent didn't care to know the details. He knew he was broke and they were destitute. Their mansion was all facade and no cash. It was strictly a Potemkin villa.

"What will you do with the Kaufmans?" he said, going back to the game. "Surely your best friend, Rattley Natalie, has to be at one of our tables."

"With Alice next to you and Warren next to me? And Natalie wanting Jack, that never-has-been, to direct *Rogue's Gallery?* Darling, never. I'll give them each someone important to make them happy. But they will be miles away from the Ambroses. Even though Natalie is sure to corner him both before and after dinner.

"Since Alice is on your right," she said, "I'll put Warren on my left. We can't be obvious. The party isn't for them. But who on my right? My God, we have Billy." She meant Wilder. "Lew. Paul." (Ziffren, of course.) "Greg." (Peck. Who else?) "Norton." (Simon, who owned, among other things, Hunt Foods and Jennifer Jones, his wife.) "But there's Kip. He's a pain in the ass. He cares where he's seated. He seldom goes out. And he cares where he's seated."

"Kip wins," Randy said, amused.

"Kip wins," she said. "Darling, what else can I do? Oh, I'm going to be so bored. I must have Ted and his hooker, I guess. He's another pain about seating." Besides, she thought, I might need him. For Randy, with Warren. "Why does a hostess always get the most boring table?"

"That, as you long ago figured out, my dear, is what

makes a good hostess." He didn't add, "And a scheming wife."

She lit another cigarette. Table "2," which was otherwise known as Table "6," was complete. She took a few drags, then bent forward and finished the seating in minutes. Randy's suggestions were, inevitably, ignored. "If you want Nancy Nathan to have a good time," he said, "why not give her Billy?"

"That's like giving MacArthur to Patton," she said. "They'd kill each other. Billy has Mickey and Janet De Cordova. Nancy's doing better than she deserves. She's between Paul Ziffren, who's brilliant enough to be gentle, and Walter, who's funny enough to laugh it off."

"You can't do that to Walter," said Randy, identifying with Matthau. "That female chauvinist Black Shirt? You'll destroy his humor forever."

"Walter will be all right. He has Mary," she said, referring to Mary Lazar.

"What have you done with the Kaufmans?" he said.

"Much too much. Jack has Jennifer." Elena meant Jennifer Jones Simon. "If you can believe that. But I gave her Lew Wasserman. That should make up for it. Jack has Ruth Gordon, too, although he's never seen a play or a feature movie, much less read a book."

"That sounds like shitty casting to me."

"Randy, you don't understand. Ruth has to be there because she has to be next to Rex. He insists."

"Okay. And what, my dear, have you done with Natalie Kaufman? You mentioned Wagner."

"She has David and Gar."

"You can't mean it. Elena, you're out of your gourd. Poor David," he said. They meant David Janssen. "She'll bore them both to death."

"Darling, don't you trust me? David has Edie," she said. She meant Wasserman, not Goetz. It was getting confusing. Edie Wasserman always wanted to sit next to David. Randy remembered that from one of Elena's nursery-school instructions on party-giving. "And Gar has Mary on his right." Irving Lazar was Kanin's agent. Dear Elena. She knew what she was doing.

Elena rose from the desk and handed him the diagram. It was, he had to admit, nearly perfect. If not superb. Then his eyes caught Table "3," which would undoubtedly be called Table "1." "You can't stick Fred Astaire and Ray Stark with Grace St. George," he said.

"Would you prefer to be stuck with her? Fred is a Superstar. He gives class to the table, and won't be intimidated, even by Grace. I must admit I didn't know what to do with poor Grace. She's so terrible. I'd take ten Doris Days over one of her. Or even Doris' empty chair. But you know we had to have her. Anyway, I've made up for Grace," she said. "I've given Fred Felicia." She pointed to Astaire's left, where she'd penciled in Felicia Lemmon. "She's beautiful and bright. I've given Ray Veronique." She meant Peck, who was stunning, he thought, and, for a woman, intelligent. "That's a table of talkers," said Elena. "R.J. Wagner. Dani. Janssen. If Lucy and Gary had made it, I'd put him beside Grace. He'd drown her out." He'd drown her, thought Randy. I would. "Short of Gary, who's better than Ray? He even manages to get along with Barbra." She meant Striesand. "Ray is always up."

"Even Ray couldn't get it up for Barbra, or Grace St. George," he said. "Oh, Jesus, why try to reason with women?" He felt like a man who'd looked on a jigsaw puzzle, bare. Everything fitted, but he didn't know how. Randy walked to the bar. "I'm going to have another," he said. "Will you join me?"

"No, thanks," she said. "I'd better take my bath."

Only then did he look at the clock. It was 6:45. They had spent over an hour discussing Elena's seating chart. We might have spent three hours, he thought. At least with Elena you knew the time was wasted profitably.

Elena's passion for the hostess game was amazing. She knew who liked gazpacho and who despised turtle soup. She knew the foibles, the politics, the prejudices, and the eccentricities of everyone in or out of the industry circle. Apart from her careful calculations, supplied or affirmed by the gossip mill, Elena had an instinct for chemistry that was unerring in everything but her mating with Randy.

The party would be a smash. Fred Astaire might even ask Grace St. George to dance. Randy smiled at his joke. Astaire never danced at parties; he hated social dancing.

Randy took a long swallow of his Beefeater's on-the-rocks. He suddenly envied Jack Bean, Lucille Ball, and Gary Morton because they were out of town.

14

"A-one-a, a-two-a, a-five-a, a-seven-a." Harvey Parkes was doing his imitation of Lawrence Welk. He knelt on the exercise mat in the guest cottage, gripping Nancy O'Brien Nathan's spindly ankles. Nancy was doing sit-ups.

"Shit," she said. "Why do you have to skip numbers? I lose the count."

"You're not supposed to be counting. I am," said Harvey. "Now *breathe*. You're turning blue, Mrs. Nathan. Okay, that's good. Now the bench." By the time Harvey folded over the exercise mat, she was propped on the padded slant board, well into the leg extensions she knew came next. Nancy was more skillful at Harvey's exercises than any of his female clients except Polly Bergen. Polly was the best. But Polly had worked with Harvey Parkes for years.

Nancy had only been using Harvey on and off since her marriage to Kip, into the early months of her pregnancy and again for the last eight weeks. Nancy took exercise and beauty routines more seriously than many an actress. Actresses depend on their looks for their living. Nancy depended on her looks for her life. The time she didn't devote to beauty was spent crusading for Women's Lib, leaving only the dinner hour and an occasional screening at home for Kip. Kip didn't like to go out, which fit in nicely with Nancy's schedule.

Harvey came to her four days a week. She filled in with Ron Fletcher's gymnasium in Beverly Hills, supplementing Harvey's contraction exercises with Ron's machines. Harvey didn't know that, of course. He was niggardly about his clients and envious of his competitors, be they Fletcher or private exercise man Marvin Hart, or fat farms like Deborah Mazzanti's Golden Door or Dallas' Greenhouse. If Harvey ever learned that Nancy went to Fletcher, he would drop her, as he had many others. On the other hand, if Harvey's clients dropped him, as did Natalie Wood and Bob Wagner, Harvey spoke disparagingly about them. Harvey Parkes was a character from the pages of Hawthorne. Possessive, puritanical, he expected his clients to be solely, inextricably bound to him. Hollywood women cheated more easily on their husbands than they did on Harvey Parkes.

Nancy, who was equally tenacious, rejected attempts at possession by anyone else. She was as proud of her duplicity with Harvey as she was of the scrawny body and the patrician face on which she spent so much time and effort. She took natural vitamins. She took Dexamyl every morning to cut her appetite. She picked at her food. She didn't drink. She had facials and steam baths in Beverly Hills at Aida Thibiant's. Aida had special steam cabinets she had imported from France; Aida called them "Biozone" baths. Anywhere else the term would have been considered an affectation; in Hollywood, Biozone was accepted as different, and different, in Hollywood terminology, translated as compelling. Aida's salon was a favorite of such as Mary Tyler Moore, Cher Allman, Candice Bergen, and Ali MacGraw.

"Come here," said Nancy. She'd finished five sets of extensions. "I told you we have to hurry, Harvey. I've got to get dressed."

"That party of Mrs. Brent's," he said. "I've never had so many cancelations. Nobody had any time today. You could rest for a minute, Mrs. Nathan."

"I could also look like Totie Fields," she said.

"Not you. But you could look like Cher. If you don't eat something soon, you'll look like Cher"

"What's wrong with Cher?"

"She has no behind. When you get too thin, it collapses. You have no behind."

"Who wants a behind?" said Nancy. "Only dancers are assmen. Haven't you noticed that?"

"I like a behind, and I'm not a dancer," Harvey said.

Nancy often wondered about his relations with his female clients. Through the years, he boasted, he had seen and massaged more beautiful bodies than anyone. When Nancy asked him if he'd had affairs with the women he worked on, Harvey admitted to several: "But that was a long time ago, when I was young. I was a stud. I learned you can't mix business with pleasure, Mrs. Nathan." Harvey still looked like a stud in a Mr. America kind of way.

I'm horny, thought Nancy, forcing herself to stop staring at his muscular frame. I'm bloody horny. No wonder, she thought. Kip hasn't touched me for eleven days.

"Feet together, knees apart," Harvey was saying. He grasped her inner thighs with his hands, and she pressed against them. That was to firm the outer thigh. "Please *breathe,*" he said. "You're going to suffocate some day, and they'll blame it on me."

"Non-breathing. You can call that the Nancy Nathan," she panted, working hard. "As opposed to the Jennifer Jones and Kirk Douglas." Harvey had a habit of naming his exercises after his clients. The Jennifer Jones was the one in which you lay flat on your stomach with Harvey's hands on your lower buttocks; you tightened the muscles and released them. That was the one for assmen, or dancers. That was supposed to eliminate the sagging behind, which Harvey called "saddle bags" and Nancy called "the chessboard"—the checkerboard lines and pouches that occur at the base of the buttocks. Harvey's Kirk Douglas was only for senior students. It was tough, if not obscene. You lay on your back, legs raised, while Harvey put all the weight of his body against your knees. You pushed him away; he came down on you again. That routine, with its forward and backward thrusts, resembled Position Three in sexual intercourse. "I've lost a lot of clients because their husbands came into the room while I was doing this one," Harvey told Nancy.

The intercom rang. Two buzzes; for her. "Go to hell," Nancy said. It buzzed again. Harvey picked up the phone. "It's Mr. Nathan. He says the hairdresser's here, and you have to take your shower."

"Damnit," said Nancy. "Okay. But tell Kip to go ahead. Cliff can do him first. I'll be there in five minutes." She got up from the bench and moved deliberately in front of the window, where Harvey could see her body against the failing sunlight. She was wearing a yellow leotard. Nancy always wore white or pastel Danskins, the better to show off her body. The boyish body she cared for as other, more feminine, women cared for their children. The body she loved to display to all in anything—undersized T-shirts worn braless, short-shorts, bikinis. Exhibitionism, after all, is the twin to vanity.

Harvey stayed by the telephone, his eyes skimming her body because he knew she wanted him to. He smiled approvingly. Harvey faked the obedient servant for his clients. "We've come a long way in two months," he said. "You look terrific, you know. Mary Benny was telling me that today." She really did look good, he thought, if you like pottery and Modigliani-type women. Harvey preferred his women with curves. Jill St. John. Raquel Welch. They were both former clients. Nancy O'Brien had never excited him physically. Even Audrey Hepburn had never turned him on.

Nancy pulled the curtains on the remaining windows. She turned and faced him, standing still, like a fashion model posing against backlighting. Jesus Christ, Harvey thought. She might just as well be naked. Harvey inhaled deeply, then exhaled, unconsciously pursing his Reagan-like mouth. Nancy moved languidly towards him. Harvey tried not to breathe harder. (*Breathe,* Mrs. Nathan.) She stretched. He saw the flat breasts, the navel, the triangle just below and between her wiry hipbones pushing hard against the pale yellow leotard He saw her nipples puckering; normally small, they became even tighter, tiny dark knobs. He wet his lips, and he felt the swelling in his groin as she slowly, intentionally lowered her eyes to his porous, onionskin trousers.

"I'll see you on Monday at four," he said. Then he headed for the bathroom, presumably to change his shirt, as he always did.

"I'll walk you to the car," said Nancy. "I'll wait."

She sprawled across the bed, elated, listening to the water running in the guest bathroom. Harvey Parkes is washing his cock with cold water, she thought, because I excited him. Harvey Parkes is an idiot, but Harvey's not easily aroused. Nancy knew because she had tried to seduce him before, unsuccessfully. She could still hear the water running, the tearing of toilet paper, the Kleenex being pulled out of the holder. Nancy became annoyed, as well as elated. Annoyed because Harvey was taking so long.

Kip would be furious if she wasn't ready on time. Kip can go to hell, she thought. Kip cared more about that fucking studio of his, he cared more about every producer, director, and writer than he did about her. He certainly didn't care about sex. Whenever they did it, Kip had both ears attuned to the phone, listening for a call from the bilious chairman in New York, the company's president, or the star of his latest picture. And when they did it, which wasn't often, Nancy couldn't reach orgasm. Like him, she was waiting for the goddamn phone to ring.

She thought about Harvey tending his Mr. America cock in the bathroom, and she felt a surge of wetness between her legs. As absurd as he was, she had to have him. She had to have him now, in this goddamn house that Kip built, a house Kip wouldn't let her change in any detail, this goddamn glass and plastic house in which even the stuffy butler treated her as an intruder, as merely the last of his master's various wives. "Wife," said Nancy. She spat it out like some other four-letter word. "Wife" had once suggested control and command to her, the manipulation of household and business, of servants and sycophants. Harvey Parkes represented to Nancy what Kip was not—a victim, an underling, animal-like, subservient to his passions. Harvey Parkes, with his silly, flattering hard-on, represented to Nancy her dominance over the male. She had tested him today, and today she had won.

Harvey, the afternoon's loser, emerged from the bathroom at last. He was holding his "working" polo shirt and wearing the LaCoste in which he arrived. He tried not to look at her. He picked up the attaché case, unzipped it, and put his shirt inside.

Nancy parted her legs just slightly. She tightened the muscles below her buttocks, as Harvey Parkes had taught her to do, and glanced with satisfaction at the protuberance of the mound below her flat stomach. "Harvey, darling," she said. "I wish we'd had time for just a short massage. I ache all over." He was pretending to search for his car keys which were, as always, on the coffee table in front of the sofa. "Come here," Nancy said. He stiffened and walked to her, keeping his distance from the bed. "Just do my shoulders." She stretched again and yawned. She raised her arms on the pillows and tensed. Her legs formed an open V, although the dampness in her crotch made her want to pull them together and rub herself. Her flat boys' breasts and her pubic hairs were pressing relentlessly at the transparent exercise suit. Harvey stared at her triangle. He saw that it almost matched the thick auburn mane on her head. The pubic hairs were darker, their color and texture unmistakable. He felt the throbbing of his expanding cock, then the warmth and the wet. Jesus Christ, he thought, I've come in my pants.

"Sit down," said Nancy, "on the bed." He moved closer, looking down at her. "You know, the sunlight feels almost as strong as your hands when you massage me." She ran her fingers over her body, tracing it, touching every forbidden part, the parts that Harvey had learned to avoid while massaging his women. With her thumbs on her crotch and her palms on her thighs, she shoved her legs even further apart. The mound became more perceptible, seeming to protest its captivity under the Danskins. Harvey saw the longish orange hairs that curled down on her inner thighs beneath the body suit of her leotard. They were shrouded only by the single wispy thickness of tights. He felt his cock revive. It was growing bigger and hotter, forcing itself against his wet shorts and damp trousers. He noticed that Nancy was staring at his prick, as if mesmerized.

"You'll have to turn over if you want me to do your shoulders," Harvey said. His voice was hoarse and emerged like a whisper.

Nancy sat up, her head on a level with his erection. She stretched out her arms, her hands on his buttocks, and drew him closer, pressing her face against his distended prick. She felt the tremors passing through his body. She began to unzip his fly. Harvey was breathing heavily now, so loudly he couldn't conceal his excitement. (*Breathe, Mrs. Nathan.*)

"You have to get dressed," he said. "And I'm late for my last appointment." As he said it he pushed her hand away gently, reluctantly, zipping up his fly, as if to pretend that she had never touched him.

"You told me *I* was your last appointment, remember?" Her voice was thick. She stood up and embraced him, thrusting her pelvis into his, touching his cock, then enveloping it with her thighs.

"But your hairdresser . . ."

"He can wait . . ."

"What about Mr. Nathan?"

"Fuck Mr. Nathan. No. Fuck *me*. Mr. Nathan is so concerned with Mr. Nathan," she said, "that Cliff will have to spend at least an hour blowing his hair straight." She pulled him down on the bed, all two hundred pounds of him, effortlessly. "Lie on top of me," she said. She wanted his weight. She wanted to feel his cock against her hot cunt. "Take it out," she said. "Take out your fucking big prick." My God, she was wet.

He rolled over beside her. She propped her head on her arm and watched him fumbling, first with his belt, the Hermès belt he had boasted Victoria Principal gave him for Christmas, then with his zipper, then with his pants. She found the overlap in his jockey shorts, parted it and seized his cock. It was long and thin and hardly the tool you'd expect of Mr. America. She examined it with her fingers, running them over it, working her hands around and up and down, creating accordion rhythms on the skin. Nancy O'Brien was a tease. Natalie had been right. Nancy wouldn't give head, but she liked nothing better, during foreplay, than making her lovers think she was going to.

She slid down and put her mouth so close to his cock that he felt the heat of her breath against it. Suck me, he thought, please suck me. Another man would have said it, but Harvey Parkes was not another man. Harvey was first and last an employee. He felt the heat of her breath lower down, on his balls. She was kneading the testicles through the baggy scrotum. She caressed first one, then the other, reflecting that Harvey's balls were unusually thick, unlike his cock. His cock began throbbing more and more; his need became unbearable. "My cock," he said. "Take my cock." She ran her fingers lightly, provocatively, along the underside and over the tip, where she felt the stickiness and saw the white drops. She slid her hands to the base of his cock and touched the damp of the shorts from which it protruded. She laughed aloud, a tiny, triumphant laugh. Mr. America, Harvey Parkes, had come in his pants. She had made him come. She had made him shoot it out, just contemplating the body and cunt of Nancy O'Brien.

"Did you lock the door?" he said.

"Of course."

"But the windows . . ."

Christ, she thought, I wish he didn't sound so much like a lackey. "Pull the curtains, then." She would have enjoyed it, in fact, if Kip had walked in and seen them fucking. One of her fantasies was to fuck in public. Just the thought of fucking in public started her cunt-lips throbbing. She struggled out of the body suit while Harvey Parkes was drawing the curtains. Harvey grabbed her and put his enormous hand down the front of her tights, encircling her mound. Then he parted the crease and rubbed her, feeling the wetness of her twat. He caught her frantically, pulling off her tights, exposing the thick orange hairs that were damply entangled now. He knelt and pressed his lips against them, then opened his mouth and sucked the patches of hair. Nancy wanted his tongue inside her. Use your tongue, she thought. Stick your tongue in my pussy, and I'll come. I'm almost there. Instead, he let her go. He was flushed, but his manner was deferential. "Take off your clothes, for God's sake," she said.

Now he was straddling her, as she lay on the bed. "Not so fast." He had forced her legs apart and was trying to insert his cock. Harvey leaned forward and cupped the quarter-moon creases of her supine breasts. "Not that," she said. "Suck." He licked the nipples in a cursory way. "Bite them," she said. Too late. He had mounted her, forcing her legs so wide apart that he could see the stiffened clitoris, even as he pushed his pulsating cock inside her. Nancy raised her legs and wrapped them around his neck, needing to feel his narrow prick against the ravenous, fleshy walls of her cunt. She felt nothing. His body was moving faster and faster, his cock insistent, expanding, contracting, a linear volcano about to erupt. He came in seconds, as Nancy knew he would. Too soon. The sexologists called it premature ejaculation. Nancy O'Brien called it self-indulgence, the meanness of the male chauvinist pig. She turned away so he wouldn't see the degree of her frustration.

His arm encircled her body from behind, his hands glided over her feverish skin, trailing down and down, across her schoolboy stomach, into the seaweed-tangle of orange hair, caressing her bulging triangle, violating the slit below. Massaging her stiffened clitoris tenderly, thrusting three fingers into her twat, filling her cunt and continuing to play with her cock manqué, his thumb moving over the rigid surface, rubbing the tip. She rolled on her back and raised her buttocks, humping his hand with her pussy, feeling his fingers deeper, feeling his thumb stroke the base and the sides of her throbbing clitoris. "Come," he said.

She felt the contractions, the spurt that surged from her

cunt and covered his fingers, dripping onto the bedspread, drenching her, drenching everything. "Jesus, I'm coming," she said, both loving and hating it, wanting it, wanting it not to be over, shaken by spasms, knowing the spasms would end. Living one minute (*Breathe,* Mrs. Nathan) and dying the next.

Kip slammed down the receiver angrily. He looked at the manuscripts piled before him on the table beside the pool. He had to finish two more before his weekend meetings with the writers. Damn her, he thought. Damn that bitch. Damn her exercise sessions and damn her aggressive, sacrosanct, skeleton body. Damn her for not being ready to dress. Not that that was unusual; it was par for the course. Let Kip dress first. Let Kip wait an hour while she plucked her eyebrows, squeezed the whiteheads, applied shade after shade of makeup to her beautiful face.

He would dress first as he always did, to keep up the front, to pacify the ever-obliging Cliff Williams, hairstylist Superstar. Then Kip would wait patiently, downing too many scotches neat, pacing the living room, too upset to concentrate on his screenplays.

Damn her, he thought. He turned his tanned face to the sun, resentfully, knowing he had to leave its invigorating warmth, knowing that Cliff was waiting. Kip followed the sun—to Palm Springs, to Acapulco, to Montego Bay, to the French Riviera. The sun was his restorative in the midnight life of office politics, the slashing of long-distance knives from New York, the cuts of switchblades at weekly story meetings. Before their marriage Nancy had been a willing, even delightful companion along his trail of aridity or humidity. That, he reflected, was understandable. Nancy was forever on a crusade. Her goal in those days was Kip, if only to spite Victor Kroll, who had been only too willing to dump her after she served for two years as his mistress.

Kroll set Nancy up in an apartment while he was married. She had jumped at the chance, coolly phoning her lover, a leading painter of the Hard Edge school of the sixties, instructing him to pack and send her belongings. Victor's divorce had no political side effects; in fact, it enhanced his reputation as the most eligible bachelor in Washington. He rather enjoyed the glamour, and tired of Nancy as much for the bevy of girls who were suddenly in his realm, as for her increasing mania for Women's Lib and other politically embarrassing causes. By the time Kip showed interest in Nancy, the statesman was happy to pass her off to his Hollywood pal.

Kip had to admit that he had been totally taken by Nancy O'Brien. Looking back, he could not blame Victor for failing to clue him in to Nancy's faults. Kip remembered telling Ted Buckley, his friend and lawyer, after their brief two-month courtship, "Yes, I'm going to marry her. She's the only woman I've ever known who doesn't want anything from me." How naive can you be? Kip thought.

Dear Nancy. Nancy who deballed you, who made you feel like a eunuch, who turned you from man into woman. Nancy, who never gave of herself when you fucked her, but wanted it all: the foreplay, the missionary position, the hours of frigging her when you were exhausted. The recriminations because she had not come. Nancy is frigid, he thought, a frigid nymphomaniac. He smiled at the redundancy. Kip had married a Jewish Princess, except that she was not Jewish.

He recalled a story she had told him. Nancy had gone to Dalton, a progressive school for girls on Manhattan's Upper East Side. She was the only gentile in her class. "How clever your parents were to change their name to O'Brien," a fellow-student told her one day. "That name is so Irish no one would ever suspect you're Jewish." Nancy considered that one of her most amusing stories. She had the sensitivity of a mercenary. Kip considered her what he called a professional liberal—a crusader in public who privately cracked the whip on minorities, be it her husband, her lovers, or even servants who couldn't answer back.

Nancy refused to acknowledge that values were oddly reversed in the West. The movie industry had been founded and run by Jews. In Beverly Hills or Hollywood gentiles were nowhere. At best they were tokens within a company. In Beverly Hills all was angled for Judaism. The public schools closed down on Jewish holidays. The gentiles were probably lucky just to get Easter and Christmas off. Nancy's latest crusade was to enter the Nathans' daughter, Elizabeth, who was only four months old, in a private denominational school. Over my dead body, Kip thought. Elizabeth will attend the public schools, which are highly rated. She's one-half Jewish, and she will mingle with Jews.

Nancy O'Brien, Women's Libber, Crusader For Causes, anti-Semite, anti-black, deserved her lot. She had made her choice. She had married a Jew.

Kip entered the house reluctantly, leaving the sunlight behind, to shower and dress. Since their marriage, Nancy agreed only grudgingly and infrequently to accompany her husband to the desert, the Caribbean, and the Mediterranean resorts. On occasion Kip had to bribe her, and Nancy's bribes were major. They could be devastating.

One example was an early crusade in which she urged Kip to finance a quickie film on Women's Lib. The message movie was a disaster from treatment through script to execution, enough to topple Fox and Warners together, enough to topple their joint disaster-film-of-all-time, *The Towering Inferno*. Nancy's project cost Kip's studio five million dollars. It grossed $500,000. That movie, Kip knew, could have cost him his job and his career. One more such indulgence to his bride, and he might well plunge from the Hollywood tightrope, the fine line that separates genius and geriatrics.

Nancy was taking a bath, although she usually showered at night. She needed a douche. For cleanliness, not for safety. Nancy was on The Pill. She had decided, after the birth of their daughter, that she would never have another child. She had never wanted children. "I'm not the *hausfrau* type," she told her best girl friend years before. As far as she was concerned, she was right. Elizabeth was a mistake. For years Nancy had been using a diaphragm. She had had three abortions; she knew the diaphragm wasn't safe. But this time, five months into their failing marriage, Nancy told Kip that she was pregnant, and he insisted she have the baby.

Kip had wanted Elizabeth, and he adored her. Nancy found herself one inch thicker around the waist, unable to cope with a child who cried almost constantly, and jealous of the time and attention Kip lavished on their daughter. Childbirth merely reinforced Nancy's resentment of men and her conviction that women, although superior, were subservient. Nancy vowed that she would never be subjugated again.

If she got her kicks, and a certain satisfaction of late, by exciting more men, it wasn't her fault. It was Kip's. He made her feel inadequate, as few other men ever had. Even Victor Kroll had taken time out from his government business to frig, if not to fuck, her. On those occasions when Victor was too exhausted for sex, he'd come while fingering Nancy. Sex, to both of them, was an outlet for tension. Sex, to both of them, was an exercise. It wasn't romantic, except at first. It was a release, enjoyable, like Iranian caviar or a hot bath.

She and Kip had been married now for sixteen months, but after two weeks of marriage, the infatuation was over. She had tried. She flaunted herself before Kip. She sat nude at her dressing table—Kip ignored her. One of her earlier lovers, a prototype of Don Juan, had been married four times but cheated on every one of his wives. "Your wife," he told Nancy, "can be the most beautiful creature in the world. Grace Kelly. Garbo. But if she's your wife, she won't have any sex appeal." Nancy concluded that he was right; as soon as her lover got his fourth divorce, she left him. Nancy didn't want to be a sexless wife.

The highest stakes were money and power. The way to either, for women, was via sex or intellect. Sex is a game, thought Nancy. So is intellect. Nancy and Kip were more alike than she knew. Kip played tennis for money, but Kip didn't care about money. He cared about winning. So did Nancy. Men who expected her to be intellectual were treated to her sexiest manner; those who expected her to be sexy were icily subjected to her intellect. "She is a double agent between Women's Lib and Male Chauvinism," one of Nancy's bruised suitors observed.

Nancy was closer to Cliff Williams, her hairdresser, than she was to her husband or child. She was in the forefront of any revolution; that included Gay Liberation. Cliff was a faggot, and he admitted it. Cliff was also the most "In" hairstylist in town. Like Kenneth (who was listed in Earl Blackwell's *Celebrity Register* without a last name), Cliff had refused to appear on Johnny Carson's show because he was warned that Johnny might kill him. Carson was known in network circles as lethal, but it took a special kind of courage not to do his show.

Nancy apologized to Cliff for being late as she entered the upstairs sitting room. "That's all right," he said. "I combed Ted Buckley before I came to you." Ted Buckley had a steady appointment with Cliff every night and every morning. He wouldn't leave for the office until Cliff combed and teased his hair to hide the bald spots. If the slightest breeze disrupted the combing, Ted called Cliff to his office before he emerged for his early and liquid lunch. He was, by now, a virtual alcoholic.

"Who is he bringing to the party?" Nancy asked.

Cliff smiled conspiratorially. "I've never seen her before, but her clothes were all over the place. I did her hair."

"After Ted undid it," said Nancy. "Is she pretty?"

"Until she opens her mouth. She has terrible teeth."

Nancy was pleased, which came as a revelation to her. In her present, obstreperous mood, she had been wondering how to make Kip jealous. Cliff had hit it: Ted. He might be a drunkard, but he was single, powerful, and a multimillionaire.

Through his mob connections, he had gained control of two of Hollywood's major studios. And put his front men in. He had recently sold his interest in a Las Vagas hotel for $20 million. He had never appealed to Nancy, who knew him too well as her husband's attorney and confidant. But tonight she wondered, why not? If Nancy could seduce Victor Kroll when he was at the pinnacle of his power, she could surely seduce Ted Buckley. Ted was no longer at the pinnacle of his sexual power, as every woman knew. He could be had.

Cliff started to set her hair in hot curlers. "What are you wearing tonight?" he asked. "Do you want your hair up or down?" Nancy had intended to wear a prim, high-necked Oscar. She changed her mind.

"The while silk jersey Halston," she said. "It plunges all the way to here, and it's clinging."

"You look very sexy in that." Cliff approved. He lived vicariously through his clients, as did Harvey Parkes.

"What was Buckley's girl wearing?" she said.

"Some kind of *schmahta*." That was a trendy Yiddish word she had taught him, picked up in the days before Victor and Kip, when Nancy was living with the struggling artist. She bought all her clothes from cheap shops in Greenwich Village; she'd never heard of Halston or Oscar de la Renta.

"Leave the rollers in," said Cliff. "Why don't you do your makeup now?"

"That means an hour," said Kip. He stood on the threshold, impeccably tanned and dashing, in his dinner jacket. "Elizabeth had to go to sleep. Nana said she couldn't keep her up any longer to kiss you goodnight."

"Nana wouldn't let her kiss me if I crawled on my hands and knees," said Nancy. "Nana hates me. Nana is cheating the IRS. She's one of those goddamn overaged, overpaid nurses who demands cash because she's already collecting social security. In addition to which she turns our children into Beverly Hills brats. The psychiatrists call it smother-love."

"What are you wearing tonight?" said Kip. It was a diversion to avoid the governess argument. He couldn't have cared less what she hung on that sçarecrow body of hers. Until she told him. Kip hated the Halston.

"Are you sure that's proper?" he said. Kip hated the Halston because it was almost as revealing as Nancy's yellow leotard.

"Anything Mrs. Kip Nathan wears is proper," she said. Her sarcasm wasn't lost on Kip, or Cliff.

15

"We've lost the Mike Nichols movie," Elena said.

"How do you mean, we've lost it?" Randy, wearing his blue-jean Safari suit, was about to leave the house. He could not take the last-minute preparations for one of Elena's parties.

"Rex has seen it. He told me last night at Dom's. He went to Mike's private screening in New York."

"Rex has seen everything. Let him see it again. If he's going to act like a goddamn social butterfly, let him suffer for it."

"Rex hated it," said Elena, without conviction. "He says it's terrible."

"Rex thinks everything's terrible, unless it stars his goddamn Angela. Give me a shitty paperback, I'll make a potboiler starring Angela in two days, and Rex will say it's better than *Gone With the Wind*."

"Randy, you know how insistent he is. Besides, he *is* our guest."

"He's one of fifty guests, for Christ's sake. That hardly gives him the majority vote." As well as Randy knew her she still startled him at times. How could she be willing to scrap the movie? She had taken the trouble to call Nichols personally at his farm in Connecticut to get a print. Nichols was one of a handful of producer-directors who had the caché to refuse to let prints of his films get out to the private screening rooms of the Bel-Air Circuit.

There was an etiquette on the film exchanges of Hollywood. Most creators who guarded their prints discovered it cost them points at the studios, future favors, or even jobs. Nichols was an exception because he was hot and most of his films were highly profitable. Neither profitable nor hot was to be mistaken, necessarily, for "good." The adage.

"You're only as good as your last picture," was meaningless in a town where promotion passed for proficiency.

The Nichols comedy had not been screened at all in Los Angeles. That very fact made this "The Picture to See," "The Most Eagerly Awaited Movie in Town." Had Elena gotten it after its release she would have scored an incredible coup. Having gotten it now, she had performed a miracle. Knowing Elena's innate compulsion to better the best, outdo the doers, vanquish the unvanquishable, Randy could not comprehend her willingness to relinquish 115 minutes of virtually unattainable celluloid.

"I've been talking to Kip," she said. "Rex gave me a list of the movies he hasn't seen, but Kip says none of them are finished. He offered us one of his own that he hasn't shown to anyone."

"I don't blame him. It must be Nancy O'Brien's latest apology for having three balls."

"It's a science-fiction thing," said Elena. "Something about red ants who take over the world. Kip says it's a documentary that took two years to make. He says it's like David Wolper's."

"The closest Kip ever came to Wolper was staying ten floors above him at the Plaza Hotel. Now listen, Elena, nobody wants to see some lousy, fucking thing about ants. You hang onto that Nichols print, or I'll break your goddamn ass. Showing some goddamn ants instead of Nichols is like substituting a junkie like Marina Vaughan for Victor Kroll. You may bamboozle people into thinking that nymphomaniac dyke and Kroll are one and the same. But they ain't, and you know it."

A man from the cleaning crew entered, saying the Abbey Rents truck was there. "Go to it," said Randy, relieved. It was astonishing how Elena exhausted him on the minor, obvious decisions, while she pulled off the major contrivances by herself. "I'll be back when they've all cleared out."

"Where are you going?" she said. Not because she cared, but because he expected her to ask.

"I'm going to The Daisy," he said. "I'm going to watch the girls and the boys pass by in their asstight shorts and their airtight pants. Take your choice." The Daisy was owned by Jack Hansen, who made his fortune in Jax, the specialty stores that sold women's sportsclothes. At night

The Daisy was a private club for members only, "private" meaning that anyone with a thousand dollars or any hooker without any dollars could join. By day The Daisy's sidewalk cafe, which had an overview of Beverly Hills' Rodeo Drive, served as a kind of pub for actors, agents, and just plain oglers. The restaurant was the Los Angeles version of Paris' Café de la Paix—if you sat there long enough, as the saying went, you were bound to meet everyone you ever knew.

The men from Abbey Rents had already placed two of the tables in the dining room, which the cleaning crew had cleared that morning. Elena supervised as they moved her own table and chairs, her sideboard and breakfront into the garage. She told the head Abbey man where to put the other rentals. "You didn't forget the mirror-tops?" she said, but she didn't hear his reply. She was thinking of Randy and his pals at The Daisy. She was hoping that Randy would not drink. He had been on the wagon for days, except for a cocktail or two before dinner. That, for Randy, was abstinence. She pushed the worry away. She was grateful that Randy was out instead of acting, as he sometimes did, like a backdoor major domo.

Elena phoned Marcia Lehr, who did the placecards in script, as well as the favors and decorations for her parties. She gave Marcia the name of Ted Buckley's date. Marcia invariably left one placecard blank and wrote in the name of Ted's "Girl of the Hour," at the last minute. "How did you get it out of him so early?" Marcia said. "This one must be something extra, if he knows he won't change by tonight. But I'll bring an extra placecard, just in case. I'll see you at three. Harry's sending the flowers at one."

Harry was Harry Finley of Flower Fashions in Beverly Hills. Elena had an arrangement with him. Throughout the year, when people sent her flowers, Harry withheld them, calling Elena to tell her what had been ordered so she could send a thank-you note. Whenever she gave a party, Harry provided Elena with flowers free. He and his partner, Fred Gibbons, also filled the house with plants all year. The arrangement was more than just, thought Elena. By using them, she gave Flower Fashions promotion they could not buy.

This was the most ambitious party Elena had ever attempted at home. Normally, she invited her guests to cocktails at the house before dinner at La Boîte. That served a double purpose. It was personal, more so than having everyone meet at the restaurant. Most importantly, it was less expensive. People who drank at the Brents' drank less when they got to La Boîte. Elena had turned necessity into established custom: the Brents gave dinners at restaurants, preceded by cocktails at home. In the insecure sanctums of the New Hollywood society, Elena's stratagem worked.

Still, she had broken the rules. Basically an A dinner took place at home; it was cooked and served by one's own staff. There were exceptions, but they were few. Lew and Edie Wasserman. Paul and Mickey Ziffren. Each of these couples had servants equipped to deal with the zillion amenities called for in the strictly A party. Each got away with substituting outside caterers, because each had millions of dollars reinforced by style. They weren't exceptions to the rule; they made the rules. Lew was Board Chairman of MCA, the conglomerate that owned Universal, savings and loans, ran the tours of the nation's capital, leased the concessions in Yosemite Park. Paul was the most renowned attorney practicing in Los Angeles, if not in California. The Wassermans' parties were catered by Chasen's, the Ziffrens' by Mrs. Shields, who was semi-retired and worked for no one else. Their dinners were a matter of style and of preference, clearly not a privation. Elena, on the other hand, was an anomaly. She might not have a staff, but she had such skill that her parties were widely accepted and highly acclaimed. Elena reigned, a bar sinister, in the New Hollywood.

From the beginning, Randy had advised her to hold this party at La Boîte. But Elena was trying to prove a point, a "phony" point, Randy called it. Elena wanted to demonstrate that the Brents were well-off. She had learned very quickly in life that façade was everything. Her earliest worlds were those of the opera and of the theater; they were façades. The drama took place against painted, juxtaposed flats. The flats were alike—the design made the difference. Illusion was all, reality nothing. And Elena Brent had never read one line of William Shakespeare.

There were allied purposes for the dinner. Elena wanted to prove herself the top hostess in the New Hollywood, finally, incontrovertibly, and she wanted Randy to get that ever-elusive Big Break. This had to be the best, the most fun, party ever.

There were rules for each type of A party, regulations as unofficial and rigid as precedent laid down in English law. You gave a party in a restaurant like The Bistro, Perino's, or La Boîte, with or without an orchestra. You gave a dinner party at home, and you devoted the evening either to talk, with or without a combo in the background, or to a movie in your projection room. Elena, who could spot an ash about to drop on the carpet at fifty paces, had recently noticed that party guests had split up, some preferring to see the movie, others to talk in another room. The A Group, Elena decided, was getting bored. Unchanneled extravagance for the rich was humdrum, tedium.

That was the "handle," as Randy would say, for this gala of galas. Elena was giving her guests alternatives. They could talk, they could watch a movie, or they could dance. Heretical, to be sure, but if it worked Elena knew that she would become the most-talked-about hostess in town. The alternatives cost her little. La Boîte provided the food and the service free; the Brents supplied their own liquor, in any case. Kip was contributing the projectionist; he would write it off. As production chief for Pacific Pictures, Kip was entitled to a projectionist seven nights a week. The only additional charge to Elena would be the orchestra. She weighed that expense as carefully as she did a pair of $40 slacks from Ohrbach's. The potential gain, she concluded, outmeasured the added expense. No one would offer Randall Brent a job if they thought he needed one. In Elena's crowd, necessity was the mother not of invention, but of façade.

Harry Finley delivered the flowers personally, the oranges and yellows Elena liked to set off the beiges of the living room, the pinks and reds for the den, the all-white centerpieces for the tables. She and Marcia Lehr had settled on what Marcia called "a Sun Valley decor"—pale blue tablecloths covered with mirrors, reflections of silvers and whites. "Like moonlight on snow," said Marcia.

Finley gave Elena his usual scoop, which was almost invariably a non-scoop. If one were drifting off to sleep, it would hardly open one's eyes. "We're doing Sinatra's opening at Caesar's Palace," Harry said. In some ways, Harry reminded Elena of Harvey Parkes. Anyone else in Hollywood would have called it "Caesar's." Still, she would pass that along to the press, for what it was worth to them, or to Harry. "He gave us a budget of sixty thousand dollars just for the decorations for the private supper. And," Harry added, underlining the word, "Sinatra pays his bills on time. Do you know how many thousands of dollars my other 'Big Star' customers owe me? I wish I had more like Sinatra."

No wonder, Elena thought. She remembered reading some years ago, when Sinatra was in his studdish prime, that the floral bills for his girls alone totaled more than $50,000 a year.

She was helping Marcia set up the dinner tables when Kip's secretary called. Carol said that a print of Pacific's sci-fi film, *Community Future*, was on the way. The phone call reminded Elena to check the projectionist's room for the Nichols movie. She intended to let her guests decide which film they wanted to see. She had no doubt they would vote for Nichols over the Hymenoptera (a classification easy to recall for scatological reasons). That would precipitate a scene with Rex: "Elena, I stayed here just for your party, but I have to fill my column," he would say. "I have to see a new movie." Elena would offer him, instead, Marina Vaughan's first public appearance since her split with Rick Navarro. "Darling, you know this is news," Elena would say. "Corner her. Write a profile on her, one of the ones you do so well."

It was after six by the time she surveyed the house to be sure that everything was in order. Monogrammed matches in every ashtray. Guest towels in every bathroom. Varying brands of cigarettes in Revere bowls throughout the house. She checked the Baccarat crystal dishes, filling them with fresh candy and nuts. She asked the bartenders whether the liquor she ordered had arrived.

Thank God for La Boîte, Elena thought, as she finally settled into her bath. The men from La Boîte moved into a house with precision, bringing dishes, glasses, ashtrays, silver—and left it immaculate. They behaved as though the house belonged to them. It may belong to them soon, she thought. If I don't pull off tonight and *Rogue's Gallery*, it may belong to anyone. Randy's former studio had agreed he could use the house on a lifetime basis, but deals were canceled faster in the New Hollywood than insurance policies after a beneficiary made a claim. Randy was now a bad risk. And Elena knew, although Furio would not tell her, that the balance in her Swiss bank account was dwindling fast. She could not keep up the maintenance on the house, the once-a-week maid, the gardener, repairs, not even by supplementing her own money with Randy's residual checks. She could not pay for the dinner-dances, the discounted designer gowns. She could not even afford the grocery bills. She could not keep up the façade.

Stepping out of the tub, Elena shuddered. Tonight, she thought. Tonight is all. She felt apprehension flooding over her, clinging to her, as surely as her bath oil. It was Carnation, by Mary Chess, a luxury which Elena could no longer afford.

16

"This," said Ted Buckley, pointing to one of the photographs on the Brents' piano, "is the only picture of me anywhere in the world." He grinned approvingly at Elena. "That's true, you know. There are no others. Not even my daughter has one."

"But why?" said Iris Gordon, Ted's date. She was one of the last of the studio contract players. She was at Universal, although she had never made a picture there. She had just been loaned to Pacific to make her movie debut, a bit part in one of Kip Nathan's upcoming films. "Why aren't there any pictures of you?" she repeated. "Is that why you wouldn't let them take a picture of us outside? I mean, how is a girl going to get anywhere without publicity?"

Ted was well-oiled, but showing it only slightly. He looked like a sober actor playing drunk. "I'll show you how to go places, baby," he said. "Including where to go. Meaning on me." He leered at the breasts that were all but out of her purple, spaghetti-strap sheath. Only Ted Buckley's women dressed like that for A parties. Ted had inherited all the dummies the day Kip Nathan married Nancy.

Nancy Dinsmore, the West Coast editor of *Harper's Bazaar*, was scrutinizing the only photo of Ted extant. "Where was this taken?" Nancy asked.

"At Santa Anita." Ted controlled Santa Anita, as well as every other racetrack in the country, through the labor unions. The track's official photographer had sent Elena the picture with Ted's permission, since obviously he had approval of stills. Ted guarded his photos more carefully than actors and actresses do.

"Elena," said Nancy. "Do me a favor. Can our photographer take you with some of your guests?"

"Darling, of course," said Elena. Nancy was as chic as

ever in a tailored black Saint Laurent. Elena wondered how she managed to dress so well on a reporter's salary, even if, as she assumed, Nancy bought wholesale. "Is there someone in particular you'd like me with?"

"Anyone. Why don't you choose?"

The room was jammed with *Bazaar*-type VIPs. Elena could see herself in the "Parties" section of the magazine's August issue. She was also sure to make *Women's Wear Daily*, since Karin Winner was there. Karin wasn't invited to dinner this time, so she was outside the house. Karin was astute enough to feature Elena anyway, because if she didn't she'd never be asked to another party at the Brents'. Besides, in the parasitical jungle of Hollywood, Elena was news. Unlike the wives of her guests, she didn't have to pay Grace St. George to get mentioned.

"I think we missed the Pecks coming in," said Nancy. "And Fred Astaire. Would you mind asking Fred to pose with you?"

For a picture in *Bazaar*, Elena would have asked Henry Kissinger to re-enact the evacuation of Vietnam. She ushered Astaire outside so fast that Nancy had no time to tell her photographer to get the shot. Some photographers needed guidance; the man with Nancy happened to specialize in socialite-types from Pasadena. He wouldn't have known Astaire if Fred had produced Ginger Rogers and restaged *The Barkleys of Broadway*. *Women's Wear* got the photograph, and the *Chronicle* and the *Examiner*, and both the New York and Los Angeles *Times*, and Nate Cutler, and Sylvia Norris, and all the other free-lancers for the news and fan magazines. So did Kelly Lange, the pretty local reporter for NBC. Kelly was there with a camera crew, because NBC was planning a special on home entertaining in the New Hollywood. Nancy got to her man and started signaling to Elena as Astaire was re-entering the house.

"Fred, darling," said Elena, taking his arm. "Just one more, for a personal friend." Astaire was normally, in fact almost abnormally, press-shy. But Fred was also a gentleman, and Elena was his hostess. He let her draw him back to the driveway, and a dozen shutters clicked. Elena was only concerned with one: she looked straight at the Nikon that belonged to the man from *Bazaar*, and she heard it click three times.

"Would you like me with someone else?" Elena asked Nancy when Astaire had gone.

"I can't say a backup would do any harm."

Elena understood the media business through years of study. She had given the world of communications the same attention she gave the trivia gathered from her friends. Gossip and news were both the stuff of dissemination. Elena had learned to anticipate the editor in Chicago, Cleveland, New York, Detroit, Philadelphia, and Washington. She knew that certain picture editors chose a print because it was sharper and more defined than the others, because of its social or political impact, some for its sexiness, some because the people looked great, and more because the people looked ugly. Elena didn't discount eccentricities. A certain editor might detest Fred Astaire; another might call him "yesterday's news" and toss the photo composite into the wastebasket. Outcomes had to be weighed against unpredictables. Reporters earned their livings by drumming up stories and photos. Elena survived by providing them.

"How about the Lemmons?" asked Nancy. The boy from Valet Parking was taking their car. Elena kissed Felicia and Jack, insinuating herself between them. A cardinal rule of photo-grabbing was to position yourself in the middle. Picture editors, when they ran short of space, had to crop the people on either end. Unless the photo ran as a single, in which case the editor could choose any one of the three, Elena was in.

"Will you stand between the two ladies?" asked Karin Winner's photographer. What a bastard, Elena thought. Jack obliged. Elena smiled, but she fidgeted inwardly. Jack was a Superstar and his wife was a star. Triple cuts were rarely used in magazines and newspapers. A photo of Jack with his hostess instead of his wife was unlikely. I hope they use the one of me and Astaire, Elena thought. She gave Astaire a fifty-fifty chance against the Lemmons, which was as much as Jimmy the Greek, Las Vegas' famous oddsmaker, would have done. Such were the vagaries of the press.

"My Go-d-d-d," said Rex Reed, his voice a blast that would have stifled a fully amplified concert by Elton John. Silence fell over the groups around Rex's, a silence that keened for information. "Why is it that it's always the people with the most horrible bodies, the ones you don't want to see, who take off their *clothes?*" said Rex. "I mean, *look* at that woman. I'd like to give her my coat to cover herself with. " The laughter was general, not so much at what Rex said as at the way he said it.

"Rex, she can hear you," said Alice Ambrose. "Poor Grace."

Poor Grace didn't hear him, because she was pumping away, like something hydraulic, at the end of the room. "George Hamilton's so handsome," Grace was saying. "Jack, you should get him for a series."

"George *Ham*ilton?" Natalie said. "Jack should put George in a box and seal it. Or somebody should. George Hamilton goes to Acapulco, and George puts matches between his toes so he'll get an even tan. God forbid George Hamilton's skin should be lighter than Sidney Poitier's."

"Dear, you're being unfair," said Grace. "George, right now, is at the peak of his career."

"It's time he peaked," said Natalie.

"Listen, his horoscope told me that he would marry Alana, just as it tells me now George is ready for a comedy series on TV."

"Well, I won't deny he's a comic," said Natalie. She, like Rex Reed, found it hard to take her eyes away from Grace's transparent beige chiffon party pants. Grace dressed like sixty going on twenty-five. Her shriveled arms and trunk were only partly concealed from public view by a sprinkling of ruffles. Her face was corrugated like that of a tennis player who's taken too much sun in her lifetime; her dyed-black hair was straight and short like a man's. She looked like a former physical education teacher endeavoring to be in a bassinet.

Natalie wanted to walk away and leave her with Jack. But Jack was ahead of her. He was chatting with Janet and Freddie De Cordova and Kip Nathan by the bar.

"Now you know *Town & Country* wouldn't have chosen Alana for its cover and the Hamilton house for that special spread on California last year," said Grace, "unless they were beautiful people."

Oh God, she never gives up on a subject, thought Natalie. Nancy Nathan, of all people, saved her. "Did I hear you mention *Town & Country?*" she said. She made the magazine title sound like the latest fatal disease.

"Why, yes, dear," said Grace, oblivious to the scathing tone.

"*Town & Country*," said Nancy O'Brien Nathan, crusader, "will not print the name of a Jew. It's a goddamned bigoted glossy brochure for the WASPs and the *Social Register*."

"The *Social Register* has some Jews in it," Natalie said, defensively.

"*Not* the *Social Register* of the 1930s," Nancy said. She walked away. She had spotted Ted Buckley in the den. Jesus, thought Natalie Kaufman, I'm gonna be stuck with this astrological ghoul all night.

"By the way, I'm giving a lunch at The Bistro on Tuesday for Helen Springfield," said Grace. Helen was one of Grace's "secret" clients, of course. Grace had been handling her for two years. In that time Mrs. Springfield, of the Norells, had not made the Ten Best Dressed List nor the society pages, except as her husabnd's wife.

"The lunch," said Grace naggingly, "will be small. Just eight or ten women, dear. Of course you must come."

Of course you can go straight to hell, thought Nat. "Sorry, I'm busy on Tuesday," said Natalie, desperate now to escape. Nat was seldom desperate for anything, because she cared neither how nor whom she offended. "Excuse me, Grace, I have to speak to Norton," she said.

Norton Simon, thought Grace. Then, aloud, abstractedly, "What I wouldn't give for a client like Norton Simon." No one heard her. Poor Grace, in her flimsy ruffles and ripoffs of Kenneth J. Lane's costume jewelry, was standing alone.

Elena, like all A hostesses, spent the hour or so before dinner mingling with guests who wouldn't be at her table. Clearly those friends who would not have a chance to talk to you during dinner deserved your attention before and after. Just as clearly, tonight was special. Tonight involved business. Elena had assigned Adam Baker to Randy's table, not hers. Had Adam been there, she would have accosted him about *Rogue's Gallery*—tactfully, of course—and she would have been abiding by the rules. But Adam was very late, which was undoubtedly on account of Marina. Marina was always late. Which was partly due to a Superstar's arrogant timing (Marina *must* make an entrance), partly due to her dislike of big parties (Marina found the Establishment tedious), and mostly due to her insecurity (Marina often changed clothes three times before leaving the house). In defiance of convention Elena sought out Warren Ambrose, the man who could insist that Randy star in *Rogue's Gallery;* he handled the author and thus, in the last analysis, the property and the packaging. Warren was standing with Alice and with Kip, who was seated to Elena's right at dinner. By approaching Kip and Warren she was committing a double gaffe. No matter, she thought, time is vital.

"Who do you rent your plants from?" Warren asked. Only in the New Hollywood would someone say, "Who do you rent your plants from?" instead of, "Who do you buy your plants from?" People in Hollywood rented their plants the way people elsewhere rented apartments. Before their divorce, Polly Bergen and Freddie Fields had rented all their indoor and outdoor plants. The rental men tended them: if one yellow spot sppeared on a leaf, they replaced the plant. Even now producer Fields, the former boss and top agent of ICM, maintained that renting his plants had been less expensive than paying a gardener. Apparently agents had a thing about leasing their foliage. The Ambroses also rented their plants.

"We don't rent them," Elena said. "We get them from Harry Finley."

"I think they're prettier than ours," Warren said to Alice. His tone was accusing.

"They're beautiful," said Alice politely. Everyone knew that the Ambroses' rented plants were more sumptuous than the Brents', or anyone else's in town. "I tried Flower Fashions," Alice said, "but I just couldn't get along with them. It's a matter of personality, I guess."

"Well," said Warren, "then change your personality." He smiled as he said it; still, Elena and Kip felt Alice's humiliation. Warren had a habit of embarrassing his wife. Those who knew them, loved her. Alice was self-effacing, the A Group's most tolerant wife. You didn't have to be Nancy O'Brien Nathan or Betty Friedan to favor her over him.

"Listen," said Kip to Warren, "when are you going to find me a great original property?" When Kip was trying to change the subject, he went to one of three: business, women, or tennis.

"Why do you want an original screenplay? Everything is original. I have a marvelous book. The new novel by Harry Waller. It's going to be a tremendous bestseller. It will make a fantastic movie." Whenever Warren talked business, he spoke in superlatives. Warren rolled adjectives around his nouns as though they were endpapers. He was a super agent by virtue of his enthusiasm. If he did not believe in a client or a property, no one and nothing could persuade him to take it on. If he did believe in him or it, no one and nothing could dissuade him. He prided himself in selling only the best, for the highest price. Buyers understood that about Warren Ambrose. That is why they paid him the highest prices.

Kip was unmistakably interested in Waller's novel. How fortunate, thought Elena. Warren had introduced the project; she could simply follow through.

"How come you haven't sent me the book?" said Kip.

"I sent you the galleys months ago," said Warren, irritably. "I can only suppose that you sent it along to one of your readers, those guys who haven't read anything through since the Hardy Boys, and they gave you a negative report. Which you shredded or tossed in your 'No' box for filing."

"What's the title?"

"Rogue's Gallery."

"I like that. I like the sound of it."

"So does every other studio chief in town. And they've read it."

"I read it last week," said Elena. "Darling, it's fascinating. It's a couldn't-put-down."

"Where did you get it?" said Kip. "Will you lend it to me? Remind me to take it when I go home tonight."

"That won't be necessary," Warren said. "If you're curious, I'll send you a copy by messenger first thing tomorrow. By the way, the fellow that owns the option on the book is coming. He *is* still coming, Elena?"

She nodded. "With Marina Vaughan." She could have said "With Jackie Onassis," and neither man would have blinked.

"I thought *you* handled Waller. Since when does Waller give options? Who is this guy?"

"His name is Adam Baker. How do I know how he got

it? Waller asked me to give it to him. They're pals. Elena may know more. She had lunch with Baker last week."

"Grace asked me to," said Elena, sweetly.

"Since when do you do anything Grace suggests?" Kip said. "There's more than that. Come on, level."

"Darling, I told you I simply adored the book. I wanted to meet this man. Besides, he had this steaming love affair with Susan McConnell that broke up her marriage. Now wouldn't a man like that be intriguing to any woman?"

"Any woman but you, Elena. If you wanted a man, you wouldn't have to arrange a blind date. This town is full of studs. For you, even I'll turn stud."

She smiled. Good old Kip. "All right, darling. I'll tell you my secret. Adam Baker thinks Randy could play the lead in the Waller novel." She saw the disbelief on their faces and hurried on. "So do I. The part was written for him. He'd be fantastic. Now, I don't want you to say a word until you've read it. Warren, I don't want to hear anything now. Just think about Randy as Donald Bellamy. Anyway, that's not what I wanted to talk about. I need your advice. You know as well as I do that Randy needs a new agent."

"You don't want his advice," Kip said. "You want Warren. Warren's the agent for Randy. He'll put him at the top. And Warren, you could do a lot worse. Randy may be difficult, but he's talented." Dear Kip, thought Elena, he knows that Randy can't touch the lifts on the shoes of Ambrose's stars. But he also knows that I need his help. Kip never failed to advance the cause of a friend, or to take advantage of an enemy. He was the Godfather—young and tanned and dashing—but the Godfather.

"I'll leave you to work your magic on each other," Kip said. "But I warn you, Warren, it's not an equal match. Elena's better looking."

Elena was indeed at her dazzling best. She was wearing her pink Luis Estevez, the one that was cut just low enough to elicit the stares of men and the envy of women. Luis had explained that the color was hers, not pale enough to suggest a sophisticate feigning innocence, not harsh enough to be vulgar. It was just the right shade to implement Elena's fair skin and green eyes. Tonight she had chosen her gown as carefully as she had chosen the menu, and on the same principle. Don't try something new and untested, like Mrs.

Barry Springfield, in her brand new Norell by Gus Tassell. Elena didn't dress for the other women in her set; pathetic Wally Swoboda, with his mothball coat, had taught her to dress for men.

Her hair was drawn back and caught in a chignon that, as Furio liked to tell her, "advertises the elegant nakedness of your face." She had spent the ninety minutes before her dressing table wisely, blending shade upon shade of makeup, applying translucent skin tone over it all to give the impression that she had just stepped from her bath. The only perceptible evidence of her labors was the mascara, shadow, and pencil around her eyes. Elena was proud of her eyes. Furio, in the minutest exaggeration, told her she was the only woman in Hollywood who could attain the doe-like, faddish, Sophia Loren eyes without the help of a plastic surgeon.

"Darling," said Natalie, breaking in. "You're absolutely monopolizing Alice and Warren." Tactful Natalie, thought Elena. Soon she'll be asking Warren to let her husband direct the next Kubrick picture instead of Kubrick. Well, let her and Jack put in their bid for *Rogue's Gallery*. Warren was too shrewd to take a TV director when he could get virtually anyone: Friedkin, Frankenheimer, Kubrick himself. "The flowers from Victor Kroll are very impressive," Natalie continued. "But darling, wasn't it gauche to leave his card beside them? I mean, I thought it just a bit obvious. Besides, who knows if it *was* his card? I mean, for all we know, my dear, you sent them to yourself."

"That never occurred to me," said Elena. "You see, I'm not as clever as you are. Who else would have thought of that?" She had long ago learned that the only way to handle Natalie was by matching insult with insult. Natalie couldn't stand a put-down.

Elena had been impressed by the flowers from Victor Kroll. Indeed, she had tossed the card on the table intentionally. After all, she reasoned, she'd promised Kroll to her guests and reneged; she owed them a certain vicarious assurance.

"Since Natalie thinks I'm monopolizing you," Elena told the Ambroses, "I'll see to the other guests. Besides," and her eyes hit Natalie's like the dart its target, "I have to say hello to Marina." Whatever else you could say about her,

Marina *did* have Superstar timing. She and Adam Baker had just arrived. Elena fled.

"Bring me another," said Nancy Nathan.

"Perrier water on the rocks, coming up," said the waiter. Nancy scowled. She hated presumptuous waiters as much as she hated men. How dare he announce to the room what she drank, or didn't drink?

"Make mine a double," Ted Buckley said, as he handed over his glass. "And not Perrier on the rocks, my good man." He was mocking her.

Nancy moved closer. "Why haven't I ever gotten to know you? You're Kip's best friend, you're very attractive, and yet you've never even asked me to lunch. You're also a legend. You've replaced Howard Hughes. You can't imagine the stories they tell about you back East."

"I'd like to hear them. Besides, it's not every day a lovely lady asks me to lunch. It's a date. You name it."

"Tomorrow?" she said.

"I have to play golf tomorrow. How about Monday? The Polo Lounge? My car will pick you up at twelve-thirty."

She laughed. "That's one of the legends, you know. The Rolls-Royce that picks up the broads. Next day, the broad receives two dozen American beauties. Or don't you send flowers to married broads?"

"That, my love, depends on the broad. I'd say you deserve at least three dozen roses."

"I'll drink to that," she said. She edged closer, raising her glass and brushing his arm with one of her boyish breasts. She pressed it against him, taunting him mutely for just another second.

Nancy moved back. His eyes swept over her boldly, coming to rest on the knots of her nipples, visible through the thin white jersey of her gown. Then he was staring into the folds of her wraparound halter, discovering her pointed mini-trilons.

My God, what a bitch, he thought. What a tease. Ted recognized a seduction when he saw one. He thought he had seen them all—there were only as many variations on Circe as there were on complaints in the courts of Blackstone. Law was his occupation, but women were his preoccupation. He'd made a lifetime study of both. But he couldn't believe Nancy Nathan, although she was apparently serious in her role of enchantress. Before tonight Ted would have taken an oath that not even Nancy O'Brien, female chauvinist pig, would be rotten enough to fuck her husband's best friend.

"Hey, take it easy," he said, as he handed her the glass from the waiter's tray. "Old man, weak heart."

"Young woman, tight twat," she whispered.

My God, thought Ted, she has the dirtiest mouth since Natalie Kaufman's. "I'll drink to that one," he said. If she really meant to betray Kip, he wanted to know. He'd kill her; not literally, of course, but effectively. They clicked glasses again and he stared at the tiny bulbs of her breasts with their flat, constricted nipples, feigning appreciation rather than feeling it. Maybe that's what attracted Kip to Nancy, Ted thought. No silicone.

Iris, Ted's date, was the Superstarlet of the Silicone Set. Before and after the mini-skirt craze, she specialized in mini-minis, trotting around the Universal lot in thigh-high skirts and short shorts that exposed far more than MCA boss Lew Wasserman would have approved of, had he seen her. Inevitably, one day he did. He stopped his sand-colored Bentley convertible, the classic car that Edie now drove, and asked Iris her name. He told her that if she wanted to keep her job she had better come to the studio "Properly dressed." Lew had similarly chewed out an office boy for not wearing a tie. The office boy had to comply; he worked in the black-glassed tower where Wasserman and the other executives had their offices. Iris, however, would not be intimidated. Within a few days, Miss Gordon reverted to her slashes and skimps, although she stayed away from the tower and its environs. Lew had given Iris several disapproving looks tonight, but she merely smiled back at The Boss. Her contract said nothing about her evenings.

Not that Iris' evenings couldn't be bought. She was a "starlet" in the Old Hollywood sense of "call girl." Whenever important visitors—moviemen, bankers, TV executives, magazine editors—came to town, they were provided with pretty contractees who were willing to play for a night, or a week of nights. Even in the old days, the starlets didn't come cheap. Harry Cohn's PR man had once dipped into Columbia's stables for an editor from *Newsweek* who was writing a cover story on one of Columbia's biggest female stars. The editor worked by day; at night, he dated the starlet. After five nights, Cohn asked him if he was having fun with the girl. The editor was a cube, a married man with a family back in Ossining. "She's terrific," he said. "You know, I think she likes me. I think I might even make it with her tonight." "Jesus Christ," Cohn screamed later at his Vice President for publicity, "we're paying that whore $150 a night, and he hasn't even fucked her yet."

Iris was one of the holdovers from that particular era of entertainment. She could be bought and had been, although her inflation-economy price was $250 a night. She had also been known to do it free with anyone who could help her. Iris would have slept with a cheetah if she thought the animal could advance her career. Around the Hollywood circuit Miss Gordon was called "the American open."

Iris had had a brief fling with Kip Nathan shortly before he married Nancy. Alice Ambrose's favorite story concerned their affair. Alice had been at CIA, her beauty salon in Beverly Hills, when Iris walked in in bare feet. She was wearing sawed-off jeans and a T-shirt two sizes too small with the decal, "Iris Fucks." Her long dark hair was soaking wet. "Do you have my Fermodyl?" she had asked Guy Lawson. Guy handed Iris the boxes from the shelf. They contained two dozen vials of the conditioner, which retailed at $5.00 a vial. Iris picked up the boxes and started to leave. "Are you going to pay for those?" Guy asked. "Just charge it to Pacific Pictures," said Iris. "She must be one of Kip Nathan's girls if she's billing Pacific," said Alice. "Funny, I thought I'd met all of Kip's women. What a messy creature. Kip must keep that one at home." Guy laughed, "If you had that one, wouldn't you keep it at home?"

Since Ted hadn't left her at home tonight, Miss Gordon was the carnal object of Barry Springfield's attention. Iris was telling Barry about her acting class and a course she was taking in cinema at U.S.C. Barry pretended to listen, but his eyes never left her juglike breasts. He was distracting to watch, like certain actors who address themselves to the actress's cleavage rather than to her face. Barry's wife, Helen, was standing nearby. Barry reminded Helen of David Brooks, who blissfully serenaded the boobs of Marion Bell in the original Broadway production of *Brigadoon*.

Except that Barry was almost as small as a Scotsman's kilt. So he had to look up, not down, at Iris' boobs.

The Springfields represented the generation of Los Angeles socialites whose ancestry qualified them for membership in the super-elite Wilshire Country Club. The second-most-social enclave, the Los Angeles Country Club, was founded by people who'd been rebuffed by Wilshire. Both of the clubs spurned Hollywood-types, although less than a handful of actors had managed to make the roster of the Los Angeles Country Club. They included Robert Stack, whose California-socialite parents had long been members, and Fred Astaire, for reasons no one could figure out. The Springfields, like their young-socialite peers, lived in San Marino, which was the principality of the suburb of Pasadena. San Marino, with its ivory castles and emerald lawns, was strictly non-Hollywood, consisting of third- or fourth-generation Angelenos like Otis Chandler, the publisher of the Los Angeles *Times*. There were few exceptions to the non-show-business populace of Pasadena. Writer and ex-LAPD Detective Sergeant Joe Wambaugh was one. The most notable show-business types were the Dennis Stanfills; Dennis just happened to be the Board Chairman and President of Twentieth Century-Fox. Stanfill was essentially a financial wizard and a longtime San Marino resident. He had moved from the L.A. *Times* to the movie company and now commuted each day from his million-dollar mansion to the studio in Century City.

The Springfields had no connection with the industry, but surely that wasn't their worst offense. Most people found them intolerable because they were bores. Along with humerous outer-directed millionaires from San Marino, the Springfields were impassioned intruders on the New Hollywood scene. Grace St. George was Helen's passage over the borders that separated Hollywood's beautiful statesmen from its dismal lobbyers. There was a kind of West Los Angeles Wall that confined the stars, the movie and television executives, writers, directors, producers, and assorted VIPs who moved among them—the governor, senators, mayor, judges, doctors, lawyers, agents, business managers—all of whom huddled together in the overweening community that was Hollywood.

Helen Springfield's angry glances weren't lost on anyone in her group. Only her small bald husband was too engaged to notice them. Barry, the ardent aero-executive, was explaining the technical aspects of aircraft engineering to Iris Gordon's boobs.

"Randy." Marina fairly shouted at him as she made her way through the crowd, pausing only for a dutiful hello to one of her friends. She stood on tiptoe to kiss her host on the cheek. "You're such a dear to have me," she said. "I've missed you all so. Randy, have you met Adam? Adam Baker, Randy Brent." Marina's voice was higher-pitched and sweeter in conversation than that to which her fans were accustomed. With or without a microphone, she belted a song like Ethel Merman, Judy Garland, or Liza Minnelli.

Physically, Marina didn't resemble any of them. She was more like her mother, Bobbie Shaw. Tiny and thin as a waif, she had long, streaked hair. Marina was blessed by the lumber-yard-brown of her hair, because the nebulous color lent itself to streaking in a single process at Elizabeth Arden's no more than every three months. Other actresses fussed about foreign colorists or learned to bleach their own hair on location, attaching mirrors to the back of their heads in an arduous operation. Marina had no such problems.

Tonight she looked wispy and more feminine than usual in the full-length Thea Porter chiffon that she and Natalie had selected at Giorgio's. At first she had rejected the gown, telling her maid, Teresa, to hang it back among the hundreds of outfits in the adjoining bedroom she had turned into a closet. She had picked an ankle-length skirt with an overblouse and the latest, trendiest contoured boots instead. Marina was frowning at her reflection in the floor-to-ceiling mirrors of her dressing room when Adam arrived. She told Teresa to give him a drink and say she'd be right down. Suddenly she hated the way she looked. This *was* an establishment party, as Natalie had endlessly reminded her, and she wasn't used to Establishment parties. Marina preferred funky parties. She liked to wear jeans, three-quarter skirts, or mini-skirts with boots. What she minded was dressing up, whether in the flowery, preening haute couture that characterized Bianca Jagger, or in the elaborate, stately terms of a Rosalind Russell. She didn't want to stand out as a *gamine* at the party, so she changed to the formal print while Adam waited patiently in the living room.

They were the last to arrive. Marina asked for white wine; Adam ordered a vodka martini on the rocks.

"I'll have a refill," Randy said. He was drinking club soda. After his recent binge, he'd been almost as abstemious as Nancy Nathan. He'd lost four pounds in three days, and he knew how well he looked. Even Warren had noticed. "You've lost a lot of weight," he had said. "You look better than you have in years." I should just look good enough to play Donald Bellamy, Randy thought.

"Marina, you're so beautiful tonight," said Elena, joining them.

If you like a strawberry phosphate, Randy wanted to say, but he let it go. That belonged to Thornton Wilder and *Our Town.*

"I like your Renoir and Monet. They're very nice," said Adam.

"Very shitty is what you mean," said Randy. "A bad Monet, a bad Renoir. Have you noticed that every wall in Hollywood's covered with bad Impressionism and bad Neo-Impressionism? When you get west of Palm Springs, they're all outbidding each other for the worst of the dead and therefore acceptable artists."

Adam laughed. "Okay, I was being polite. When you put it so bluntly, I have to agree with you. I've seen a lot of bad art and a lot of dark restaurants. You can't see what you're eating, which may have its advantages. Come to think of it, that might work with the paintings. Light them badly, so you wouldn't see what you're seeing. I'm into Pop and contemporary stuff, myself. Andy Warhol and Jasper Johns. I can't afford them, except for their graphics. But these people can. Why do they accumulate the worst of the masters instead of the best of our time?"

"I'll tell you," said Marina. "It's insecurity. You could hang Andy Warhol himself on that wall, and no one in this room would know who he was."

"Jane Robinson, who built Eddie's second collection with him, told me, 'Always buy at the artist's peak, and you'll always make money,' " said Randy. "She got over six million dollars for just a part of it when Eddie died. Since then, she's been adding on to it."

"Much to the chagrin of our mutual business manager,

Marvin Freedman," Marina said. "She told me he gives her daily lectures on budgets. Then she goes to the bank, takes another loan of $85,000, and puts it down on another Chagall."

"You have to see her collection, Adam," said Randy. "It's a must for newcomers—like the grounds of the Bel-Air Hotel."

"How about that?" said Adam. "I was here one day, and Grace insisted on driving me to the Bel-Air. We got out of the car and all I saw was this low building flocked with palm trees and bougainvillea, a quaint little bridge, and a lake with a swan. It was like an illustration for a children's book. Pretty, but I mean, a tourist attraction?"

"It has more attractions than that. Each room or suite has a separate back entrance. No one can see the girls and the guys come and go. So it's one of the natives' favorite hangouts, as well as tourists'. Usually married natives. Where are you staying, Adam?"

"The Beverly Hills."

"That's closer in," said Randy.

"Yes." Adam grinned. "And more convenient, they also tell me. It has a great pharmacy, a newsstand, and a coffee shop. What a town. I saw Paul Newman, Mark Goodson, Art Carney, and Irving Mansfield in the coffee shop in one day."

"Have you ever heard the paging at the pool?" Marina said. " 'Mr. Charlton Heston, calling Mr. Heston'—or 'Miss Norma Shearer,' telephone, please.' 'Miss Liza Minnelli.' It's hysterical. They say it's all phony, of course, to impress the tourists."

"Well, it's pretty impressive," said Adam, with a nod of his head and a hardly perceptible flourish of his hand. Taking in the house and the people, he thought in terms of certain cities that boasted a kind of ostentatious obsolescence. Vienna, with its street of palaces standing side-by-side, around the corner from sidewalk cafes where old men sat for hours, sipping coffee and reading their local gazettes, seemingly oblivious to spacewalks, summit meetings, and wars. The seven-layer *Doborsch Torte* excellence of the food. The fat women still waltzing to Johann Strauss in hotel dining rooms. Why, Adam had always wondered, did the middle or lower-middle classes seem to think that the fatter their families were the more prosperous they appeared? The upper classes knew better. Gloria Vanderbilt was a collage of bones. The guests at Elena's. Mickey Ziffren and Paul. Lew Wasserman. Nancy Nathan. Adam remembered a Fred Astaire quote he'd read in Ballen's column: "If you want to lose weight, eat one half of what people serve you. They always serve far too much."

Still, there was the fatty tissue of Viennese peasants here. The tension of surfeit. Pre-Columbian figures set on reproduction tables, buffed to the mirror-image level of TV commercials. The geometrics of Rockford crystal glasses reflecting on unpatterned Baccarat candy dishes. Antique cameos hanging on modern gold chains. Overlaps of Harry Winston on Buccellati. The nouveau riche, thought Adam, combined the complacencies of the Old World with the naïveté of the young. There was something of the schoolgirl about it. Her boyfriend gives her a fresh camellia, and she rushes home to press it into her book of mementos. To wither and brown, but hopefully last for a lifetime. The older he got, Adam had to admit to himself, the more he was fascinated by the intricacies of bad taste.

"There are other collections you have to see," Elena was saying. "Ray Stark's. His Henry Moores alone I'd die for. Fran and Ray are here tonight. They're tastemakers in every sense. And Edie Goetz's collection is fabulous—she's the daughter of Louis B. Mayer, you know. And then there is Martha Hyer's and Hal Wallis' collection—it's better than seeing the Pasadena Museum."

"Don't forget Irving's," said Randy. "I mean Irving Lazar. Sorry. I'm sure you're not up to our first-name-dropping yet."

"The only first names you can't drop in Hollywood," said Marina, "are Irving and Sidney."

"There's Sidney Korshak. What other Sidney is there?" Elena said.

"Sydney Chaplin."

"Who talks about him?"

"You were saying. . . ."

"Oh yes, Lazar—he has some beauties, as well as the best private pornographic collection west of Hugh Hefner. By masters like Gustave Klimpt and Egon Schiele. Now, about the Renoir and Monet monstrosities, I want you to know I didn't spend money for them. Jesus, that stupid I'm not. Bill Fineman, that crafty old bastard, gave them to me as gifts. As bonuses, instead of money. Fuck the salary and percentage." Randy was referring to the Old Hollywood tightwad studio chief for whom he had worked in the early fifties.

"Lately," said Marina, "they give away cars. Paramount sent me my Ferrari after my special won the Emmy."

"Listen," said Adam. "The Ferraris and Lincolns and the Mercedes are less negotiable than the bad Utrillos. My God. The Mercedes is the Ford of Hollywood. From the way you people buy them, you'd imagine we were on the German side during World War II. I've never seen so many Kraut cars, at fifteen to thirty thousand skins, in my life."

"That's a status thing," said Elena, "that's lost its status. Like those Elsa Peretti diamonds-by-the-yard that Natalie's wearing." Who the hell is Elsa Peretti, thought Adam. "Hollywood, like anyplace else, has its fads," Elena continued. "Only here they don't last as long as anyplace else. The studios used to get Lincolns or Cadillacs, but mostly Lincolns, for using tie-ins in pictures. So every executive drove a Lincoln. Then they became so common that nobody wanted to drive them. Years ago, Clare Ballen printed that press agents always drove Lincolns, and Warren Cowan turned in his Lincoln that very day for a Cadillac."

Adam was amused, "So what happened? Cowan got a Mercedes, and they were out?"

"No, the TV people latched on to the Mercedes and it was out." She pronounced "TV" as Randy did: the word came out like "arsenic."

"Okay, so what's 'In' in automobiles?" asked Marina.

"Darling, now it's economy cars," said Elena. "Hank Fonda drives a souped-up Mazda, of all things. And Jimmy Stewart likes the Volvo. Does that tell you something?"

"That Shirlee Fonda spends too much money on clothes," said Marina, "or maybe that Paramount can shove my Ferrari."

"They can shove it in my direction," said Adam. "My God, what a town. Jimmy Stewart of the long legs in a Volvo!"

"Jimmy says it's comfortable, plenty of leg room," Elena said. "There is. I've been in it."

"The car, I hope, not the legs," said Randy. Even sober,

he was reverting to form. There was a moment of tension.

"Elena could do worse," Marina said, "than Stewart's legs."

"Listen," said Adam. "I never know what to say when I meet a star. But I mean this, Randy. I'm a fan from way back. Talk about Stewart and Fonda; you were my personal hero, western-style."

"Thanks," Randy said. He said it so simply Elena knew that he meant it. She hadn't seen such pleasure in Randy's eyes since Cannes three years before, when he closed the festival as its star of stars with *Sagebrush*. Elena had had a few qualms about her lunch with Adam at The Bistro, because of his cat-and-mouse game with her. Even now, she found it odd that Baker did not bring up the property. But Randy's reaction to Adam's professed admiration of him was reassuring. Randy's judgments of others, when they involved himself, were generally as precise as a metronome.

"Darling," said Natalie, closing in on Marina. "You look ravishing. And who is this latest stud, my dear? He's divine."

Marina looked suddenly, accountably, weary. Reticence had never been one of Natalie's virtues. "Adam," said Marina, "this is Natalie Kaufman. She's one of my dearest friends."

"I've heard so much about you," said Natalie, rushing in. "I trust it's all bad. I'm charmed." He was smiling the characteristic half-smile that was almost a tic to the others, but Elena took it as an intentional signal, like that of a seaman tapping out "Mayday" in distress.

"Have you seen that two-dollar whore who has Barry in tow?" asked Natalie.

"You're as confused as Sinatra, darling," Elena said. "They cost more than two dollars now."

"In that case, she's overpaid," said Natalie. Nat had never been one to extract the hook and throw an undersized catch back into the water. "She looks like she was dressed by the wardrobe woman for the Playboy Club."

"Who's that?" asked Adam. "Not the wardrobe woman. The chick."

"Her name is Iris Gordon, my dear, and you mustn't judge the party by her. She came with Ted, but before the night is out, she'll come with Barry. He's been ogling her tits as though they were the entrée."

"Oh, Nat," said Marina. Marina had done it all, but she didn't approve of obscenities outside of the bedroom, or bathroom, or pool, or wherever she happened to do it.

Elena, sensing Marina's discomfort, thought the time was propitious to serve her own ends. "May I borrow you for a minute?" she asked the girl. "There's someone here who's dying to meet you."

"Right on the nose, Elena," said Adam. "Save the innocents. Women and children go first, except on the French line." He managed to sound as though he were used to traveling back and forth on the *France*.

"Darling," Elena said to her main attraction. "I want you to say hello to Clare Ballen before she leaves. She can't stay for dinner. And you must meet Rex Reed. He worships you. Rex begged me to ask you for an interview, but even though he's a very close friend I made no promises. Darling, it's up to you. This is social. I told Rex. Still, you might consider it. Rex is most amusing, darling, and he's syndicated." Any other hostess would have allowed Rex Reed or Clare Ballen to make the approach to her Superstar, but Elena was taking no chances. She followed the simplistic rule of successful publicists: "Clients come and go, but the press is here to stay." There were more Marinas than widely-syndicated columnists.

"Whatever you say, Elena." Marina, the international idol, was even more vulnerable than the cliques and clans who found her irresistible, the millions who thought she was made of steel and stood in line for her concerts or movies, the tasteful or the merely trendy who became entrapped by her talent. Marina needed guidance, Elena thought. She cried out for direction. Maybe, Elena thought, what Marina needs is Adam Baker.

Even as she conceived the idea, she shuddered. Elena had never experienced a passion so close to jealousy.

17

The dinner was a sensation, even by Elena's standards. The key, for her, was that people lingered over their empty coffee cups and brandy snifters, reluctant to leave their tables, caught up in a conversational interchange whose noisy articulation reminded her of the honking of horns on the freeways at rush hour.

But if her guests were enjoying themselves, Elena was not. She was too nervous. She had noticed earlier that, almost as soon as she and Marina left them, Randy and Adam separated to talk to others. Adam had, in fact, been blatantly using her guests. He had an eye. He gravitated to those who would be most useful to him. Board Chairman Wasserman. Studio chief Nathan. Agents Lazar and Ambrose. Elena had broken away from the Pecks and led Adam, literally, over to Randy.

"I thought you had some business to talk about," she said bluntly. She gave Adam a look that left no doubt about what she meant. "I thought we struck a bargain," she told him. After she walked away, she saw them exchange a few sentences, laughing together. Then they parted. Adam stood talking to the Starks and the Prentis Hales until Armand announced dinner.

All through the meal, she kept watching Randy's table. Adam, who was sitting one chair away from Randy, talked determinedly to everyone else. Elena's edginess turned to anger. He *is* a prick, she thought. He had managed to use her as his entrée to her powerful friends, and he had no apparent intention of using her husband in his movie.

Randy stood up, tapped his glass with a spoon to get attention, and took a vote on the movie. As he had predicted, everyone except Rex Reed rejected Kip Nathan's movie. Including Kip Nathan.

As usual, Irving Lazar was the most outspoken. He was

outrageous and therefore fun. "I'm not going to see some damn picture about some bloody ants," he said, in full hearing of Kip. "I came here to see Mike Nichols, and that's what I'm going to see."

Rex Reed was pettish. "You don't have to fill a newspaper three times a week," he said. "All you have to do is deposit your ten percent of Irwin Shaw."

Kip ended the argument by saying he'd have some people in for dinner the following week and show Reed *Community Future*. If Kip had not been a studio chief, Elena thought, he could have been ambassador to Israel. He could have been Henry Kissinger. Lazar, on his part, reflected that Kip would have made one hell of an agent. An agent almost as good as himself.

Like Elena, Kip had a gift for conciliation, except on home ground. During dinner, Kip had built a case for Randy as Warren's potentially brightest new client that would have astonished any superior court judge. Elena found it unsettling that neither Adam nor Warren had mentioned Randy in terms of *Rogue's Gallery*. She had introduced the subject to Warren during dinner, as well as before. He avoided it. In her exhilaration, she put it aside. Her party plan was working better than anything since the New Deal.

Roughly one third of her guests stayed behind to talk and dance. The others, including Elena's certified A draws, dancers Kelly and Astaire, went on to see the film. Rex had latched onto Marina faster than Kelly scuttled a parapet in any of his movies—but with far less emotion. Typically, Rex elected to see the Nichols movie a second time, although he kept repeating it was bad. Adam told Marina he had to speak to the Brents in private and said he would join her later. Marina not only accompanied Rex to the screening room, she made an appointment with him for an interview the next day.

"Can I speak to you?" Adam said.

"I don't think we have anything more to say," said Elena. "Unless it's that you're a liar. You fooled me at lunch, you know. That was quite a performance. You ought to go back to acting."

"Elena, please," he said. "I meant it at lunch. That's what I've been trying to tell you all night. It's important." She let him draw her into the downstairs guest room. "You know I wanted Randy for Bellamy; well, I wanted Randy to test, at least."

"That's what you said at lunch."

"And I meant it. Listen, Elena, it's Waller. He just doesn't like your husband. He says he won't have him."

"Since when has an author any say about casting?"

"When he owns the property. Damn it, Elena, my option expires in less than a month. Waller refuses to renew if I mention the name 'Randall Brent' again. I've argued, I've pleaded, I've licked his goddamn boots. But he won't budge. I just can't turn the bastard around."

"What's his phone number?"

"That won't help. Waller's sadistic. A woman-hater. A boozer. An all-out son-of-à-bitch. And I need that option."

She gave him a pen and a slip of paper. He wrote down the number, one on New York's West Side. "Don't tell Randy," she said.

"Do you think I'm a sadist, too? Elena, I like you. More than that, I dig you. Believe me, I tried. . . ."

"I know," she said. She saw the truth in his face. She felt suddenly dead, a corpse. Her party, her house, a burial ground. She blinked involuntarily at the sting of mascara and tears.

He drew her to him. "Screw Waller," he said. "He's a shit. He's a buddy of mine, so I should know. When he's made up his mind, he's intractable." He pulled her face up to his and tried to kiss her. She beat him away with her fists.

"Forgive me," he said. "I'll keep trying. I'll do whatever I can. I didn't know how much this part meant to you. I guess the pass was inopportune. But damnit, for all your guile, you're a little girl." She remembered her father back in the early days, in East Berlin. She remembered her mother. Whenever she fell and hurt herself, her mother would scream that she was awkward and send her to her room. Her father would sometimes seek her out, find her crying, and wipe the wound with peroxide. There were no bandages in the house because they were poor. She thought of their poverty, and then she thought of Randy.

"Excuse me," she said. She ran up the stairs and dialed Harry Waller long distance, person-to-person.

The man who answered the phone asked who it was. "Mr. Waller's not here," he told the operator.

"Is there any place I can reach him? It's urgent," she said. The man claimed he didn't know where Waller was. He must know, thought Elena. Waller had three ex-wives and five children. He must have made it a practice to leave a number in case of emergency. "Operator, please ask if they know when he'll be back." Elena heard a click as the phone on the other coast went dead.

What was Adam's word for Waller? Intractable. Warren, Elena thought. As Waller's agent, Warren must know how to find him. She ran into the bathroom and dabbed her face with cold water. Then, without even pausing to straighten her makeup, Elena hurried downstairs.

"My dear, Antonini's impossible," Grace was saying to Prentis Hale. "He's a Taurus. That explains it in part. But he must have something terrible rising. The combination—oh, I guess it's also because he's Italian. A hoodlum." Anyone else but Grace would have said "a hood," not "a hoodlum." Poor Grace. "My dear," she continued, "Tony treats his women like chattel. I know. Have you heard about Carnegie Hall?" The question, like all posed by Grace, was academic. "I heard it from someone who was right on the spot. After Tony finished his concert, he was hearded out the back door by those bodyguard-mobsters of his. They were pushing their way through the crowds. When they got to the car, he started shouting, 'Where the hell is that broad?' He meant Jane."

"He should have lost her," said Natalie.

"Finally, Jane appeared. 'Where the hell have you been?' screamed Antonini. 'Look, don't scream at me, Tony. I could take a taxi.' "

"That hooker should take a taxi into the Hudson River," said Natalie.

"Well, do you know what Antonini did? He went into his imitation of Bogey. '*Take* a taxi, baby,' he said. And he slammed the door in her face."

"I love it," said Natalie.

"I don't believe it," said Edie Goetz. "Tony is one of the greatest gentlemen I've ever met."

"Tony is a gent with the ladies, but he's a rat with broads," said Natalie. "Jane's a hooker. Antonini's okay."

"He's a prince," said Edie Wasserman. "He's also the greatest singer of our time." That ended the controversy.

Edie had the final word on any subject in both the Old and the New Hollywoods. If she didn't want to hear any more about Tony Antonini's peccadilloes, that was that. At least until she left the room.

"I thought you went to the movie, dear," said Grace in her fawning way.

"I did, but I can't stand people talking back to the screen," said Edie. "Neither can Lew. I won't let anyone say a word when I'm running a movie at home."

"Elena doesn't either," said Dani Janssen. "Or she wouldn't allow it if she were there."

"Where is she?" asked Edie. "We have to leave. Lew has an early meeting."

"I haven't seen her or Randy since dinner," said Dani.

"They're probably hiding out to avoid the latest gruesome twosome," said Natalie. "Barry Boring and Iris whatever-her-name-is. Iris Irksome. They're carrying on right in front of that climbing wife of his. It's a scandal."

"Now, dear," said Grace, who felt she ought to defend her clients. "Helen Springfield isn't a climber. She's descended from one of the oldest families in California. . . ."

"Jesus God, don't give us her family tree," said Natalie. "She's a goddamn hanger-on, and you know it. Still, I feel sorry for her, sitting there in the screening room while her husband is feeling that little tramp up in front of everybody. That'll teach the Princess of Pasadena to crash a party."

"She didn't crash. Elena likes her," said Grace.

"Listen, he's all but screwing that hooker. It's like the main attraction. Rex Reed will call Ballen, and it will be all over the papers tomorrow. If you're so loyal to your secret clients, you'll get Helen out of there."

"Why didn't you do that, dear?"

"I did. I walked out after looking in."

"I'll bet you did," said Grace. "I'll bet you've looked in on every room in this house. You're the bugle of Beverly Hills, if you don't mind my saying so."

"I certainly do mind," said Natalie. "I mind mostly when it comes from a tacky press agent whose own clients won't admit they're her customers. Incidentally, is that a wig you're wearing, darling? I don't think black dye is flattering at your age."

"You still have the manners of a nightclub singer," Grace said.

Lew and Edie Wasserman missed the bickering. They had slipped out of the room and the house because of Lew's breakfast meeting, because they were wise, or because they were intuitive. Whatever the reason, their departure spared them the midnight unpleasantness that ensued.

Adam found Marina sitting with Rex in the screening room. "Hey, watch this," she whispered. "No, I don't mean the screen. I mean Iris and Barry, in front of us."

Iris' head was on Barry's shoulder, his arm around her. One of his hands was inside her sheath. It was stroking her only sheltered tit. The strap of her dress was down on the side where she leaned against him, her silicone breast erupting from the ruffles of his shirt, clearly visible in the reflected arclight from the screen.

Helen Springfield had long since left. Barry shifted, cupping the beach ball of her naked breast between his hands. He listed toward her and licked the enormous nipple, slipping his hand between her legs and down, then up beneath the disheveled dress.

"My God," said Adam. "How long has this been going on?"

"All night," Marina said. "Where were you?" She snuggled close to him, and he felt her long fingernails tapping his thigh.

"I was talking to Elena," he said.

"I'll bet you were." He locked his legs together, but Marina was not deterred. She was wiggling her imprisoned hand, attempting to stroke his balls.

"I want to suck you," she said. "Let's go."

"Now what would Mike Nichols say about that?"

"He'd love it. He made *Carnal Knowledge,* didn't he?"

"He'd love it if he were here beside you instead of me," Adam said. He reached down and removed her hand. She clasped it over his and placed it on his lap. He tried to concentrate on the screen.

"Just look at them now," she said. Iris' feet were on the table in front of the love couch. Her legs were parted, and Barry's fingers were working away. Marina felt the surge of Adam's cock as it expanded. He pushed her from him.

"Come on, Mr. Hard-On," she said. "I want to suck your cock."

"Marina, the Brents . . ."

"Where are they? They're probably fucking each other."

Adam tried to will away the heat in his loins. My God, Rex Reed was listening to her. Didn't she care?

"Are you coming?" She giggled at the pun. "I made a joke, didn't I? Come on, or I'll drag you out of here."

He had no choice. If he stayed, she would keep insisting until everyone heard her. He followed her through the projectionist's booth at the back of the room and upstairs. She led him to the bathroom and opened the door of the sauna. As he closed the door behind them, he noticed there wasn't a lock.

"Here, help me," she said. She turned, and he unzipped her dress. It fell to the floor. She was wearing nothing underneath. "Now let me do you," she said. She tackled his belt and fly with expertise, then pulled off his trousers and shorts in one motion. She dropped to the floor and took his flagpole cock in her famous mouth. He sank down on the bench, and he let her eat him until he could stand it no longer. He could almost taste his own fuck in his throat.

"Stop," he said. Somewhat to his chagrin, she obeyed.

"What's the matter?"

"The matter is if you keep it up I'll come. I guess I'm peculiar, but I like my women satisfied."

Her pale eyes looked up at him. "Didn't you like it? The way I sucked you?"

"Of course I like it. I love it. That's hardly the point."

"That's the only point," she said. "I like it, too. You can't imagine how many fags I've converted this way."

"Jesus, this ain't a fag, little girl. You can get the hell back to your doll's house."

"Please, Adam, I'm sorry. I didn't mean that. I just meant I love sucking. I love the whole scene. I guess I shouldn't have mentioned the fag thing."

"I've heard all those stories and more." Marina was internationally famous for grabbing gay johns at parties, taking them into a bathroom, and sucking them off. She usually chose the guest bathroom, as if she wanted to be discovered. There were numerous stories, all of them funny and most of them true, about how people had to wait for hours to go to the bathroom when Marina was at a party.

In Cincinnati Marina had also been caught with a woman. That was during one of her concert tours. Her manager, the man she used for years before Rick Navarro took over, had kept the incident out of the press, although it was all the talk of Cincinnati's Indian Hill. Only one story appeared: it was blind, an item in a fan magazine, and it named the hostess who interrupted the Superstar and the lady. Neither Marina nor her companion had been identified.

Once more Marina was kissing his lob. "Have you ever done it in a sauna?" Marina asked. "It's even more exciting when it's hot."

"And more debilitating, I'll bet." He laughed. "Thank God we haven't got time to warm it up. It takes an hour to reach two hundred degrees." He pulled his stiffened cock from her mouth. "I'm there already, baby." He cupped her breasts and raised her, kissing her roughly, sliding his tongue along hers. The girl had imagination. She liked fucking in saunas. That was why she had chosen the upstairs bath instead of the powder room. Her tongue was playing with his, and her lips were trembling. He was stroking her demitasse breasts with firm hands.

He pushed her down on the floor, on the rug that lay between the slatted wood benches. He bent over her, his tongue tracing the shallow channel that ran between her breasts, exploring her navel, sampling the slit in the tawny forest of her pubescence.

"Oh, God," she said.

He pushed her legs apart with his hands, and she lay before him, spread-eagled. He mounted her. "I'm going to plug you, you bitch." His cock was enormous.

She felt a twinge of pain as he entered her, plugging her totally, as he had promised. Then there was only ecstasy, a daydreaming vacuum of mind, a whirling weightlessness as she watched his waxen cock moving in and out and touching her, feeling her everywhere. Then the mounting and the ascension, the rising as a balloon, the passing through insubstantial clouds to giddy ether.

"Don't take it away," she screamed. "I love it. Keep fucking me."

"That's right," he said softly. "That's right, you bitch, talk to me. Tell me you like my cock in your cunt. You love my cock plugging you, don't you?"

"I love it, I love—I can't stand it, I love your plugging," she said. "I love your gigantic, beautiful prick, your hairy cock. I want it to plug me forever."

It happened to both of them simultaneously. Marina uttered short, loud screams as she came, but Adam was silent. Marina knew he was coming by the hot rush of his fuck and by the tortuous cessation, slowly, slowly, of the insistent muscle inside her.

She lay on her side, her arms encircling his body, her cunt not wanting to let him go, her legs entwined around one of his. She wanted it now, again, at once. She wanted another orgasm. I'm insatiable, thought Marina. That was part of the legend about Marina Vaughan. She was insatiable. Now as his cock became flaccid, slipping out of her tremulous cunt, she fondled it with her hand. When it didn't respond, she knelt between his legs and took it into her mouth, working gently, bending over him, until his belly was covered with the damp wisps of her hair. Her face was steaming with perspiration. She teased him, letting his cock slip out of her mouth. Her tongue moved up through the bristling square of his pubis. She disregarded the limpid prick, exploring the parentheses that demarked his loins.

He felt the urgency of awakening. Groping the tangles of her hair, he looked down at his cock. It listed at an angle of forty-five degrees. His desire was uncontainable; his need was to have her take him. To be raped was presumably a female fantasy. Jesus, Adam thought, it's also a man's. She was still ignoring his rigid cock. Her tongue was at his balls. Her index finger was in his anus.

He grabbed her roughly, and pushed her head down on his cock. "Suck me, you bitch."

His prick exploded, as if to accommodate the tunnel of her mouth. It forced itself deeper and deeper into her throat. She retched silently, agonizing, as in a dry vomit. At last, when she thought she could stand it no longer, he came, the thickness of sperm assaulting her palate. She backed away to swallow it. One third of his cock, still stiff, was blanketed in her mouth.

"Hold me, you bitch," he said. "Don't let me go."

She felt it grow again, contorting. She did not move. She was propped on her arms, exhausted, but wanting it, cherishing his lob. It was smaller now, but hard. She felt the contractions, ever more insistent, inside her cunt. She felt the vacancy there, the urge for invasion.

"Lie on top of me. Fuck me," he said. His cock was too soft now; she had to massage it before she put it in. This time she established the rhythms, moaning noisily, never letting go of his joint at the base, commanding its movements. She was hot. She was wet. She wondered why any woman needed the help of a lubricant.

Gasping, screaming, rocking sideways and back and forth, she came. She kept his prick inside her until she felt yet another surge of his fuck. She came. He had come three times, she twice. And Marina wanted to come again.

Michel was second in command of catering after Armand at La Boîte. He was emptying ashtrays in the master bathroom when he heard them. Michel had a sense of everything in its time and place. So Michel had come upstairs to collect the dirty glasses and neaten up. But Michel was also a busybody. His curiosity could be compared to that of spies, tacticians, government agents, investigative reporters, domestics—and caterers.

Michel's keen ear became even keener as he pressed his head against the door of the unlockable sauna and listened. What he heard were the unmistakable strains of the private, not public, voice of Marina Vaughan, Superstar. The refrain was not unfamiliar: Michel had heard it at parties, behind bathroom doors, for years.

He resisted the temptation to open the door of the sauna, aware that he could have pretended he entered by accident. Michel was nosy but, within the limits of his calling, he was discreet. By exploring the house, by eliminating the guests he knew so well, Michel determined Marina's partner was her escort, the stranger known as Adam Baker. Having crammed for the final exam, so to speak, he returned to the kitchen. *"Ah, mes amis,"* he said, *"voulez-vous savoir qui est dans le sauna, et qu'est-ce qu'il se passe?"*

Had Grace St. George ever lost her trade, she could have taken up the profession of caterer. Grace, whose habit it was to go anywhere, naturally wandered into the kitchen. Grace was promptly, precisely indoctrinated by the servants. Adam and Marina were screwing.

Minutes later, the news was all over the house. "My boy doesn't lose any time," Grace said proudly. "My dear, at this very moment he's in the bathroom upstairs, making out with Marina."

"He's fucking her, you mean. For God's sake, say what you mean," said Natalie. Grace blushed. Like all indelicate people, she deplored profanity. Natalie was of two dispositions on hearing the news. On the one hand, she was pleased that her master plan to bring Adam and Marina together had worked. The affair was sure to increase Jack's chances to get *Rogue's Gallery*. On the other hand, Nat felt threatened as she had been by Rick Navarro. Rick, who had removed Marina so effectively from her obsessive whip hand.

That must not happen again. She would prevent that, somehow.

Meanwhile, she let her imagination travel vicariously to the lovers upstairs. She knew Marina's body so well. She wondered whether Adam was sucking that small, responsive mound. She saw the gyrations of their bodies, his cock moving in and out of her, rubbing the downy hedge of her snatch. She thought of his pecker, and she thought of Marina going down on him, of Marina girding its outsize corpulence, tasting the fuck that she, Natalie, could not provide in their Lesbian sessions. Then Natalie Kaufman, who never could keep a secret, set out to find Elena.

"I couldn't understand it," Dani Janssen was telling Jack Kaufman, "I always got the Number One table at The Bistro, while other, far more important people, like Greg Bautzer or Cleveland Amory were at banquettes. One day I asked Kurt if Sidney was in town. He said, 'Mrs. Janssen, if Mr. Korshak were here, you wouldn't be sitting where you are.'

"Then I had lunch there with Joanne Carson one day. Again I got this big table for just the two of us. I told Joanne I couldn't understand it. As we were leaving, I handed Kurt a twenty-dollar bill. And Joanne said, 'My God, no wonder you get the best table. You're crazy. You don't tip a headwaiter twenty dollars.' "

Jack's warm brown eyes showed amusement. Whatever his shortcomings as a director, he had an attentiveness that appealed to ladies. Besides, he was good-looking, in a vacuous way. He reminded Dani of a macho Ty Power. "So what did Joanne advise you to tip?"

"She said you give the headwaiter a dollar."

"My God, if you give the headwaiter only a dollar," Jack said, "then what does she tip the parking attendant? Twenty-five cents?"

As everyone who watches "The Tonight Show" knows, Johnny Carson paid his second wife something like $100,-000 a year in alimony. Joanne could have bought and sold The Bistro ten million times over. But the New Hollywood had its *droit de seigneur*: the richer the donor, the lower the tip. Joanne got the Number One table, in fact, without tipping at all.

"I don't know any better," Dani said. "David always tips fifty dollars to get a table at the Hollywood Turf Club." David Janssen was known to be one of the biggest spenders in Hollywood, if not the biggest among the stars in his income bracket. Like Sinatra, he was uniquely extravagant for an entertainer.

Actors were generally chintzier than Second-Hand Rose. That was perhaps understandable. They were used to being courted. They were kings in the caste system. Their agents and press agents picked up the tabs, although, ironically, the actors were paying for it. Either through the sizeable monthly retainer they paid or because the press agent billed his client separately later on. Nonetheless, the Superstar moved in a fantasy offscreen as well as on—a world of luxury in which secretaries, airline tickets, house seats, ringside tables, or cars and drivers appeared as quickly as the snap of a light switch. Dani, the garrulous blonde who was fondly known as "The Mouth," had either been lucky or discriminating. She was divorced from Italian singer Buddy Greco whose generosities, during their marriage, were extraordinary. Now she was married to David, whose generosity was even greater. Janssen was one-quarter Jewish. In this era of the Arab and the Japanese, Dani, the charmer, was fond of saying: "Never get involved with any man unless he's Italian or Jewish."

Jack had left the movie because he'd wanted to corner Adam Baker or Warren Ambrose about the Waller project; he hadn't been able to find them. Jack's eyes searched the tented patio; he saw Dani. Bernie Richards' orchestra was playing "Our Love Is Here to Stay"; Jack asked Dani to dance.

"Have you seen that bomb of a musical Sandy Meyers made with his girl?" Dani asked. "*Parade of 1976?*"

"She parades like O. J. Simpson," Jack said. "No acting, no singing, no dancing. That dame is the singing, dancing Bella Darvi."

"You know what happened to her? She was arrested for loitering on the screen."

"Now he's using her in his next for United Artists. She'll run the poor bastard into the ground."

The music changed to a waltz, and they sat down. Alice Ambrose and David joined them. "How was the movie?" Dani said.

"Pretty good," said David. From him, that meant "excellent." David was a tough critic and prone to understatement.

"It's hilarious. The funniest film I've seen in years," said Alice.

"I wish I'd made it." Billy Wilder was arguing with Rex Reed. Nobody argued with Billy, except Rex Reed.

"I think it's a piece of horseshit," Rex said. "It has no plot, for God's sake."

"Young man, whoever you are," said Billy, "it seems to me you were telling me earlier that you thought *Day of the Locust* was a masterpiece." Billy turned and walked away.

Rex joined the others.

"Where is Marina?" said Alice.

"Haven't you heard?" Reed said, his annoyance evaporated. Rex liked nothing better than a bit of gossip, unless it was spreading the gossip. He could see by their faces they hadn't heard. "My Gawd," he said. "It's all over the house. She and that Baker fellow are fucking. Listen, she begged him. Like mother, like daughter. The minute he came in the screening room. She kept telling him she wanted to suck his cock."

Alice reddened.

"Well that's what she *said*," Rex added, defensively.

"So you mean they went home?" asked Dani.

"Since when do you have to go home to suck cock?" asked David.

"One of the waiters found them upstairs," Rex said. "He just walked in on them." So had the story grown. "She's famous for jerking guys off at parties, just like Bobbie Shaw was."

"Damnit," said Natalie, who had come up to the table. "You've heard."

"It's true, then?" said Jack.

"It's true. They're up there eating each other. You'd think they hadn't had dinner."

"Natalie." Alice blushed again.

"For God's sake, Alice, they're not playing patty-cake. Anyway, any guy with a dong like that . . . "

"And how would you know?" Jack said.

"He fucked Philip Burgess right out of dear little Susan's cooze," said Natalie. "I would say that Susan, after six marriages and a few hundred affairs, is an expert."

"I'd say she'll do it with *any*thing," said Rex. "My God, that woman's a lawn mower."

"That reminds me," said Natalie. "Where is Elena?"

"I haven't seen her for half an hour," said Dani. "She was looking for Warren."

Audrey Wilder had been a singer with Tommy Dorsey's band before she married Billy. Audrey had taken the mike with Bernie Richards' group and was performing, by demand, when it happened. Armand answered the doorbell and hesitated, blocking the entrance to the hall. With his cultivated cognizance of the *à propos,* Armand knew that the caller was no initiate to Elena's cabal. The man who stood before him was unshaven, although he looked barely old enough to shave. He was wearing filthy sneakers, worn jeans, and a sagging T-shirt. A hippie, Armand concluded, with the instant snobbery that is unique among servants of the upper class.

Rick Navarro pushed Armand aside and staggered into the entryway, all but felling the Pecks. He was patently into drugs or drink, or both. "Marina," he snarled. "Where is that bitch Marina?" It was more of an animal outcry than a question; no one answered. Navarro steadied himself against the grandfather clock and stared dazedly at the guests. With his chalky complexion and acned skin he resembled a virulent, teenage clown.

Greg Peck, with his usual presence, stepped forward. "Take it easy, son," he said.

Navarro shoved him back, but had to regain his balance by leaning against the wall. "Who the hell are you? You mind your own goddamn business. Marina's my business, that bitch. I'm Navarro, Rick Navarro." Most of Elena's friends would no more have known him by sight than they would have Andy Warhol. But everyone knew Navarro by reputation. The rock 'n' roll empire he built and controlled had made him a music mogul and millionaire before he was twenty-five. He was also the evil producer-manager and sadistic ex-lover of Marina Vaughan. Everyone present except Navarro knew that Marina was still upstairs, undoubtedly still in the arms of Adam Baker.

Alice Ambrose was standing beside Jack Kaufman. "Shall I try to warn her?" she asked.

"For God's sake, no. Stay out of it, Alice. He's waiting for that. He'll follow you."

"Jesus, can't anyone do something?" Alice said.

"I'll break her apart," said Navarro. He took a few inebriated steps and reeled into the virginal chiffon gown and the wizened body of Grace St. George. Rick seized her ancient arms so hard that her flesh turned white in the wake of his hands. "Where is she?"

Poor Grace was visibly terrified. "Now, dear . . . " she tried.

"Goddamnit, I asked you a question."

"Well, I think she just went to the powder room, dear." Navarro had chosen well; of all Elena's guests, only Grace was so blundering as to tell the truth.

"Why didn't she say Marina left?" asked Alice nervously.

Navarro hurled open the door of the bathroom and slammed it. "Try again," he said menacingly.

Alice knew what was coming. She wanted to throttle poor Grace, but she hadn't a chance. "I meant—I meant maybe the one upstairs."

Tanked as he was, Navarro took the steps two at a time. He bounded through the bedroom and crashed the full weight of his body against the bathroom door and he turned the knob. He leaned against the splintered door for a second, staring at the two bodies in intimate outline behind the glass-enclosed shower. Marina stood on tiptoe, kissing Adam's neck, her fingers buried in the golden hairs of his chest. Adam's arm was around her waist; he was soaping her back with a sponge.

Adam's reaction was instantaneous. He pushed Marina against the tiles behind him, shielding her nakedness with his own. "What the hell?" he said.

Navarro gaped, a bilious expression on his face, but he didn't move.

"My God," Marina said. "Be careful. It's Rick."

Adam stepped out of the shower, sliding by Navarro, slamming the door. "Get the fuck out of here, little boy, or you may get hurt. Don't you know it isn't polite to barge in on ladies?"

"You rotten shit. That happens to be my lady. I should say my whore. I'll break you apart." He lunged forward drunkenly, missing his adversary, who sent him reeling across the room with a punch to the jaw. Navarro came at Adam again, an amateurish antagonist for the brawling companion of novelist Harry Waller. Adam put him away with a blow to the stomach. What Navarro lacked in technique and sobriety, he made up in guts. He grabbed the toilet, raising himself to his feet, falling backwards again toward the sink.

Navarro groped for a weapon; he had a choice of two—a glass or a bottle of cologne. He smashed the Paco Rabanne on the basin and aimed the jagged remnants at Baker.

Adam raised his arms to fend off the blow, but this time Navarro hit the mark, drawing a bloody gash across Baker's cheek. Then Navarro kicked him, hard, on the balls. Adam fell to his knees in agony, shielding his groin. Marina sprang out of the shower, naked and graceful as a cheetah. She wailed—it was the wail of something primeval, untamed—and grabbed a towel as she ran to Adam. As she wiped the blood from his face, she saw the contortions of pain. Adam looked suddenly old.

"Get out," she screamed at Rick. "You get the hell out of here, you bastard." Then she knew terror as Adam began to stir, to rise for another encounter. She clutched him, his naked body swaying against her own, the girlish contours of her back and ass a shield between him and Navarro. Gene Kelly and Ted ran into the bathroom. Thank God, Marina thought. Together, they dragged Navarro into the bedroom. Marina put all her weight on Adam's shoulders, sinking, with him, to her knees. She dabbed the cut on his cheek with the towel. The blood ran down his body and traced a line across her breasts.

Marina was unconscious of the melee in the bedroom and of her nakedness as she moved once again to the sink and ran cold water on the towel.

"A bathrobe," Grace shouted from the doorway. "Where's your bathrobe?"

Elena seized a towel and threw it around Marina. Then she brought her a dressing gown and closed the bathroom door. Adam started to laugh, abruptly and unaccountably.

"What is it?" Marina said.

"It's my favorite story about Waller. He was at this party in Paris, lusting after Danielle Roualt, the French actress. Waller took her into the kitchen and started screwing her on the butcher's block. Someone walked in while they were going at it, but they never lost a beat. All the actress said to the guy who walked in was, 'For God's sake, throw a towel over my face.' "

Marina smiled and kissed him. "You know, I think I'd like Waller," she said.

He ripped off the towel and patted her on the ass. "I know he'd like you," said Adam. "But forget it, baby. This is mine."

Randy scratched. He took a ball from the pocket and put it on the spot. He had been playing pool since dinner, his sober body too restive to watch a film. Warren was trouncing him badly, but Randy was pleased to be the loser. He was intent on charming the powers that handled *Rogue's Gallery*. Never kill the king before he has knighted you. That was one of Elena's precepts.

The meal had gone even better than Randy anticipated. Adam hadn't talked to him much, but Randy overheard him citing details of scenes from a number of his movies. Adam had told Marina how much he liked Randy as the boozing aerialist in *Big Top*. Then there was Alice Ambrose, who sat on Randy's right. She had paid as much attention to Randy as she had to Gene Kelly, who could hold forth on any subject. Randy was on an alien high, the kind of trip that neither Dexedrine nor liquor had ever aroused in him. I'm a goddamn ascetic, he thought, as he sipped his club soda on the rocks. He was an elated ascetic.

Before he met Elena, when his career was at its peak, Randy had behaved like a shit to everybody. He knew that people had not forgotten. Randy attributed his decline as a star to his transgressions against the buyers of talent while he was on top. Psychiatrists termed it an ego-saving device.

Randy preferred the self-image of "reprobate" to "has-been."

He interpreted Warren's curious silence favorably, choosing to think that it signified deliberation. He assumed that Warren's narrow-eyed glances between his shots meant the agent was weighing him as a possible client, or even as a potential Bellamy in the Waller movie. He regarded Warren's quiet tension, his fidgeting during the intervals between play, as a tic instead of anxiety. Warren kept chalking the tip of his cue, chalking over and over as he sized up a shot. Everyone knew about Warren's fastidiousness. He was simply treating the chalk as he would a deodorant.

Warren sank the eight ball and won another game. "How about a drink?" he asked. "How does somebody get a drink around here?"

Randy ignored the handsome young bartender, making it himself.

"There's something I've got to tell you," said Warren. He sat on the couch and searched the table, placing his glass meticulously in the center of an ashtray. "Damn it, Randy, this is a lot of bullshit as far as I'm concerned, but it's something you've got to know. This business is lousy at times."

"I know that. I suppose it's better than hustling." Randy felt suddenly skittish, like someone who needs a cigarette after sex.

"It's about the Waller property." Just then Elena appeared in the doorway. She froze, unseen by either of them. "Look, Baker wants you—at least he was insisting on a test—and I think that's only fair. But Waller insists you're wrong for the part. It has nothing to do with you as an actor. The guy is convinced you're wrong for his fucking character."

"He told you that?"

"He's told me that now for a week. He's no different than any bloody writer I've ever known. They work for a year on a book, and all of a sudden they think they're the cat's pajamas on casting. They have a bestseller and all at once they're producers, directors, cameramen, gaffers, and costume designers. Did you know that Capote insisted that Richard Brooks use unknown boys to play the leads in *In Cold Blood?* Richard agreed, but that's not the point; Truman behaved as though Richard can't cast except for a marlin. Ray Stark got *The Sunshine Boys* from Doc Simon because he promised to use Jack Albertson in the movie."

"Stark didn't use Albertson."

"Stark owned the option outright. No strings. In Waller's case, he says that if Baker insists on using you, he won't renew the option. Waller's a damn good writer and he's my client, but I'll say this: once he's set his mind to something, that's it."

"I see," said Randy. As he walked to the bar to take his first drink of the evening, he spotted Elena. She was still glued to the threshold like something wooden. "My God," Randy said. "What have we here? The hostess with the mostest is honoring us with her presence. She's deep-sixed the Establishment crowd. And how is your A and B seating working in the screening room?"

"Randy, don't," she pleaded. She watched him select the biggest glass he could find, a ten-inch highball. He filled it to the brim with Jack Daniel's.

"*Salut*," he said, raising his glass in a caricature of Marcel Marceau. "Here's to my wife, who gives the best party, if not the best head, in Hollywood." Randy drained one-third of his drink at a swallow.

"I'll second that," said Warren. As an intrepid troubleshooter, he was trying to be conciliatory. "Elena, this is the greatest party I've been to in years. It's a knack. Alice has it, and you have it."

"Thank you," Elena said. She wanted to add, "The knack for what? For moving through life like a loser, like somebody tearing up his win tickets just so others will trample on them as they leave the Directors Room at Santa Anita?" Why was her world the filthy boards of a stadium strewn with boxes and popcorn and empty beer cups after a football game? It seemed to Elena her destiny was to root for the Rams and to see them lose by the point-after-touchdown. If she had placed a bet on the Pittsburgh Steelers this year at the Super Bowl, the Minnesota Vikings would have won.

Randy was leaning toward the bartender. He whispered something, and both of them laughed. Randy moved closer, embracing the boy, his arm enveloping his shoulders. The scene, for Elena, was *déjà vu*. Supplication. Sublimation. Desperation once more for Randall Brent.

"Let's go find Alice," said Warren. "My truant wife." He

and Elena left together. But Warren was no longer playing the mediator. Randy had forced the issue, as people are prone to do in a divorce; Warren had to take sides. "Why do you take that shit?" he asked. "You know Randall Brent is washed up. He's a nothing."

"You don't understand," said Elena. " 'That shit,' as you put it, is my life. I bet on him, Warren. I bet on him calculatingly, trusting his track record. He's my life. If he gets a break, it will make all the difference in my marriage. This isn't self-sacrifice. It's selfish. What I'm doing for him, I'm doing for myself. Warren," she paused. "Do you really believe there's no chance for *Rogue's Gallery?*"

"I really believe there's no chance for Randy, Elena."

She turned, to hide the tears.

Natalie stopped her before she could reach the stairs and the sanctity of her bedroom. "Darling," she said. "I've never seen anything like it. You predicted it. Marina and Adam. They've hit it off, if that's what you call it. Adam's been fucking her in the sauna. Jack tells me Rick Navarro arrived and found them, and cut Adam to ribbons. . . ."

"Natalie, please, not now," said Elena, wondering vaguely how Natalie had missed out on all the commotion Navarro's invasion had caused. Elena almost ran through the hallway, her eyes on the floor, her brain imploring God that no one would stop her. But her prayer, like the party itself, was fruitless.

The entrance hall was jammed with departing guests, and a few were bent on conforming to the amenities.

"I'm so sorry about that rude man," said Veronique Peck.

"It can't be helped," said Greg. "That boy was surely on something. It happens," he added, in his virile bassoon of a voice, "even at the best of parties. Thanks, Elena. The dinner was great. And the movie was the funniest I've seen in years." Greg usually didn't deal in superlatives. How nice, thought Elena. I've missed a good movie.

Billy Wilder was talking to Edie Goetz nearby. "Nichols is a major talent," she heard him say.

Audrey, Billy's wife, came over to say goodnight as the visitors parted like the Biblical waters for Moses: Ted and Gene were leading a dazed Rick Navarro out of the house. Iris, Ted's date, was nowhere in sight, nor was Barry

Springfield. They had probably left together. Thank God for that, thought Elena.

At last she escaped by sheer will and by rudeness, but not before noticing Adam with Marina. Adam was staring at her, a vague articulation of empathy in his eyes. He started to follow her as she bounded up the stairs, almost blinded by tears, but Kip beat him to it.

Kip took her gently by the shoulders and turned her around. "Elena, is everything all right?"

"Nothing's right," she said. She began to sob.

"Not here." He guided her into the bedroom and closed the door. "Now tell me. Everything."

She told him.

"I'll meet with Ted first thing on Monday," he said. "We'll discuss it. Don't worry, Elena. I know how badly Randy needs a job. We'll work something out, I promise."

Elena kissed Kip on the cheek. "I thought I understood people," she said, "but I don't understand you. You're my very best friend. You came to me when I was in trouble, and Kip, you're not asking for anything."

"Just your love," said Kip. "I love you, Elena."

"What would I do without you?" she said.

"You'll never have to do without me." He was very handsome, in fact very beautiful, at that moment, but Kip looked sad. And then he added, as if he'd been reading her mind, "Elena, that's no shit."

Adam had been waiting at the foot of the stairs. "I'll see you next Sunday at two," Kip said. He referred to a tennis match they had arranged that evening.

"Two o'clock sharp," said Adam. His mind was not on the sport, but on Elena. How could he explain away the events of tonight? As Nancy and Kip departed, Adam walked upstairs and knocked on the door.

Elena had never before abandoned her guests if only because, by the rules, A hostesses did not behave that way. But tonight was different—for one thing, she didn't care. Let them all go to hell, she thought. Or to heaven. At least they have a choice, which is more than I had in East Berlin, and more than I seem to have in East Beverly Hills.

Her clothes were a messy pile on the bedroom floor. She was dousing her swollen eyes with cold water in the bathroom where the fight had occurred not an hour before. Someone, probably Armand, had cleaned it up. There wasn't a trace of blood, although she found a sliver of glass from the spray bottle Rick had smashed. She picked it up and threw it into the basket. Then she heard a tap on the door. She assumed it was nosy Natalie.

"Who's there?" she asked.

"It's Adam."

She opened the door just a crack. "What the hell are you doing here?" She was conscious that she was wearing only a nightgown.

"Elena, please let me in. I have to talk to you."

"I think I told you earlier, even before your sexual demonstration, that we have nothing to talk about."

"But we do. Elena, please."

She stepped aside, permitting him to enter. His eyes seemed to burn a hole through the nylon of her gown like the spark from a cigarette. She walked to the closet and selected a robe. Unconcerned about sex from her early days, she was even more nonchalant about nudity. That was her legacy from the porno films she had made in Berlin. Still, this stranger embarrassed her. He had only to peruse her body, as he had a moment ago, and she could hardly contain her excitement. She despised him for it.

She walked to the table beside her bed and lit a cigarette. "All right, what is it?"

"Elena," he said, "I couldn't leave without apologizing for what you call my 'sexual demonstration.' I can't explain it. I guess when a man gets to a certain point, he really can't help himself. Unless he's a man who likes closets and masturbation."

"If that's what you came to say, forget it. What you do in saunas is strictly your business."

"I want you to understand that fucking in saunas is not my bag. It may be hers. I don't know. But I won't lay it off on her. She wanted to fuck. So did I. But it's not Marina, it's you I really want. I'm capable of being aggressive, as well as being taken."

She crossed her legs in an effort to stop the insistent urge of the muscles between. "I told you before. Forget it. You're old enough to know what you're doing. And you've been doing it, using my friends all night to put your picture together."

He crossed the room and sat on the hassock in front of her chair. She moved her legs to accommodate him. "Elena, I'm sorry I can't do anything for your husband."

"He hardly needs you." She shifted, her wrapper parted, and she saw him follow the motion. As he talked, he continued to contemplate the sheerness of her nightgown and the rise between her legs. My God, she thought, he's just fucked Marina. I know he can't still be hot. He's playing with me. In spite of that, she felt a rush of wetness between her legs. She considered retrieving the half of the robe that lay on the floor, but she let it go. She wouldn't give the bastard the satisfaction of covering up.

"Elena, maybe Randy doesn't need me," he said. "You're the one I'm interested in."

"I'm accounted for," she said bitterly. "And apparently so are you."

He placed his hand on her thigh, just below the hem of her gown, but he didn't venture further. She didn't move. To reject the advance would be to acknowledge the chemistry of his touch. "I can tell you don't believe me," he said, "but if there's anything I can do for Randy, I will. And it's you I want to do it for, not him."

His palm, still motionless, cauterized her skin. She drew her legs to her chest and grasped them, conscious that her gown fell back as she did, aware that Adam didn't miss the split second of revelation. Even when she was fully dressed, he made her feel naked. "I think you should leave," she said.

"I'm afraid if I leave I'll never see you again, and I must," he said, touching the Band-Aid that only partially covered the jagged scar on his cheek. She saw him react to the pain. "Elena, I'm going to prove that I care for you. You can fight it, but I'm going to make you understand. What happened tonight with Marina was just an incident. Like one of Waller's brawls. It's just what happens with you and me that matters."

My God, she thought, he is an opportunist. What wouldn't he say to stay "in" with her and her friends? "I'm sure Marina is waiting for you. You'd better go."

"I'll call you tomorrow."

"Don't bother." Her voice was frozen, a gesture of dismissal conveying the infinity of an Ice Age.

She closed and locked the door behind him. She usually locked the door against Randy. Tonight she had locked the door against Adam. This time, she realized, was different. Elena wasn't afraid of intruders. She was afraid of herself.

BOOK TWO

THE AFFAIR

1

"Under the spreading chestnut tree, I sold you and you sold me."

Those bitter lines of parody were used by George Orwell to sum up the condition of the world in *1984*, when faithlessness had become a daily habit and the exploitation of people a public virtue. They happened to be the favorite lines of Warren Ambrose, the full-time head of Hollywood's second major talent agency and part-time dispenser of midnight philosophy. Warren liked to quote them, usually with variations. In his more mordant moods the lines would emerge as: "Under the spreading chestnut tree, I screwed you and you screwed me." When he was being a bit more temperate and subtle, it was merely: "I used you and you used me."

No one could pronounce the word "used" in quite the same loving, lingering, menacing tones as Ambrose—like a snake charmer's flute that was slightly off-key. He was eloquent on the subject. "Hell, people *use* each other all the time," he would say. "It's primal politics, and it begins with our first scream. Children use their parents; parents use their children. Teachers use their pupils and vice versa. Politicians, statesmen, soldiers, saints, poets, philosophers—they all use each other and their followers, or should I say clients? Businessmen and admen and agents like me, we just do it a little more openly, with the price tag in almost full view. And do you know who uses each other most savagely of all? Lovers! Loving is using."

Over his third Camus brandy (he long ago switched from Remy Martin, prompting a bitchy friend to remark, "He likes the existentialist sound."), Warren would develop his theories. "What's wrong with it? People exist to be used. We think of being useless as death." Every now and then a newcomer to Warren's circle would rise to the bait and argue against such sophistry. A Boston lawyer once grew quite excited about people not being objects or property and ended with what he thought was a devastating thrust: "Haven't you heard, the Dred Scott decision has been overturned?"

"Not out here, baby," Warren replied, without a second's hesitation. "For that matter, not in Washington, either, or in Detroit, or at the Vatican, or at the Harvard Law School. People are objects and we use them. Out here, I like to think, the trappings surrounding the transaction are a little more attractive. But we're all users."

Warren did much of his using during the day, but basically he was a night person. Like a musician, Ambrose played better in artificial light: he was used to it. He dealt in darkness, regarding houses, his own or anyone else's, as boardrooms in which to negotiate business. Whether he gave a party or went to one, he assumed squatter's rights. If anyone left his parties before 2 A.M., he considered the night a fizzle.

Because he was a carouser he spent his mornings in bed, arriving at his office after one o'clock. He kept all the tools of the trade on or around his four poster: *Publishers Weekly*, outlines, manuscripts, book reviews, magazines, movie-TV and TV-movie sales, daily and weekly *Variety*. Warren's three push-button telephones each had a thirteen-foot cord ("I lost four feet when the company went from seventeen feet to thirteen," he complained). He had settled more deals on those mindless instruments in a day than Henry Kissinger had in all his travels. Ambrose had eight lines, a couple of which were hookups to his agency in Beverly Hills. Another instrument was a Watts line, enabling him to phone any place in the world for fifteen cents. Nonetheless, Warren's out-of-office phone bills totaled $55,000 a year.

Diane, his personal secretary, worked in an adjoining oak-paneled room, which was a cross between a newspaper morgue and a library; it was somewhat cluttered with filing cabinets, a Xerox machine, and floor-to-ceiling books. Almost all were first editions, and almost all were signed by their authors. The books overflowed into every room of the house. Warren had the best collection of autographed volumes west of George Cukor, who, as someone who knew

Bernard Shaw and Somerset Maugham, was the envy of every bibliophile in the world.

The English Tudor-style house in Bel-Air, which Alice called "The Agents Colony," was set up for Warren's quirks as well as for his professional needs. On this particular morning, Warren was giving Paramount's chairman, Barry Diller, a tour of his coliseum-sized bathroom. Diller, who had an executive meeting at eleven o'clock, was edgy and anxious to get to business. But Warren, the night person, liked to procrastinate.

"I'll bet you've never seen a silver bidet," he said. That's for sure, Barry thought. "Bidets were invented for men, not women. They had them in the early days of the Roman Empire for the infantrymen returning from the wars. I haven't had a hemorrhoid problem since I installed this. Get a bidet and your ass will be as soft as a baby's." Barry smiled. Warren sounded like a commercial for Preparation H and Johnson's Baby Oil.

"That's *won*-derful," said the chairman of the board of one of Hollywood's seven major studios. "It's *won*-derful. I must get one." His sarcasm was lost on Ambrose. Jesus, Barry thought, what people have to put up with to buy a movie property.

Warren was now expounding on another of his indulgences, the Jacuzzi which was adjacent to the sunken marble bathtub. This, in the rarest demonstration of philanthropy, he insisted on sharing with visitors. Warren's Jacuzzi romps were famous; they acted as a deterrent to strangers and anyone not in the Ambroses' slam-dunk milieu. Guests arriving for dinner, male and female, were urged to strip for the communal bath. "It's great for circulation," Warren would say, unconscious of his double entendre. Alice was innately modest, but she had been programmed through the years to take part in the ritual during which their butler, Thomas, served cocktails. Those who waived the Jacuzzi rites were marked as poor sports and never invited back. Those who took part were offered one of a vast assortment of kaftans which Warren kept on hand for informal dining.

Barry had heard all about what were known as the "Ambrose Aquacades." Kip Nathan described them kindly one night as "part and parcel of Warren's fetish for fastidiousness."

"Nonsense," said Natalie. "Those gang gropes are his substitute for fucking. Surely you don't think he'd have bodily contact with anyone?"

"What do you think he does with Alice?" Elena said.

"Whatever he does with Alice, he does it with a sheet between them, a sanitized sheet. He takes his own linens along when he travels, for Christ's sake. Who'd trust the Connaught? Still, I wouldn't miss one of his parties on my life. It's like going to temple to count the noses. Going to Warren's is counting the dongs."

"And the muffs," Jack said. "Don't forget the beautiful, furry muffs."

"Which Alice tells the ladies to wipe, oh so carefully, with those paper douche rags."

"So that's why they're always out on the counter," Randy said.

"Of course. Would Warren allow a germ or a sperm to stop up his Jacuzzi jets? What I love to watch is the johns whose dongs are so stiff they don't dare to get out until everyone's gone. I once sneaked back and saw Ted with a prick like a candlestick. A small one, naturally."

"Nat," said Elena. "Please."

"Don't be silly. We all know about Ted's deficiencies. It's no golf club, I'll tell you."

"You mean his fucking handicap," Randy said.

"Tell me, Jack, have you ever gotten a hard-on in that Jacuzzi?"

"You put it so delicately, dear. Since you ask, there have been moments."

"You bastard. Just by seeing the snatch, or by frigging them under the water, or by jerking off?"

"Whichever." He displayed the smile that women couldn't resist. "I do it, whichever, while you are so busy sizing up the cocks and the furburgers. You do size up the furburgers too, my dear, don't you?"

Natalie flinched. Jack had had too many drinks. He had never before publicly hinted at her bisexuality.

"You'll have to try the Jacuzzi sometime," Warren Ambrose was saying to Barry. "As a matter of fact, we're giving a party next week for the Baron and Baroness of Lansbury. Alice will call you."

"I'll be in New York next week," Barry Diller said quickly. He was somewhat relieved. "Now, about the

Grigsby script. . . ." Diller was offering $600,000 for Henry Grigsby's latest original screenplay. That was the highest price on record. Fox had paid $400,000 for *Butch Cassidy* and $450,000 for *Lucky Lady*.

"We'll sell on one condition," said Warren.

"I'm offering you a bloody fortune," said Barry, "a price that any agent would give his eyetooth for, and you tell me you'll *take* it on a condition. What is it?"

"You've gotta give it to Stanley Goldstone."

"That two-bit hack? You can't be serious. Stark barred him from the set on his last two pictures. Since when do you decide who produces? Why Goldstone?"

"Goldstone's my client," Warren said simply.

"So's Grigsby, who'd like the six hundred thou. Goldstone is not the right guy for this project. You have a hot script, but that doesn't mean you're entitled to twenty percent, instead of ten."

Warren picked up an argument as another man would his attaché case. "Now listen, Barry, what the fuck difference does it make to you? Take Goldstone. Bar him from the goddamn set just like Ray did. You hire a good line producer, you know it won't matter. You gotta pay somebody something. No other agent's gonna get that producer percentage while I have the property. You're smart enough to know this picture is next year's blockbuster. Nothing's coming out of your pocket. Zanuck/Brown and Universal would buy it in a minute, Goldstone included. Take it or leave it."

Barry, the tough young businessman, knew he was being taken. But he wanted that screenplay. "Okay, but I'll tell you something, Warren. I'm the one who's going to make a blockbuster out of this lousy script. I'm the one who's going to get it the rewrites it needs—three rewrites if necessary. Paramount will make it a hit. You know as well as I do that a property's only as good as the people who make it, cast it, sweat over it, and promote it."

They shook hands. "Alice will call you when you get back. There's something we're giving two weeks from now for somebody, I forget who, upstairs at The Bistro. Black tie."

Barry grinned. "Is Goldstone invited?" he said, sardonically.

"Never. Don't be ridiculous, Bar. You know Goldstone isn't into the A Group."

For $600,000, Barry thought as he took the wheel of his canary-yellow Corvette, I don't even get a Jacuzzi. But he hadn't done badly. Goldstone's record of late wasn't good, and Paramount wouldn't have to pay him much. Meanwhile, Diller had landed the story of the year.

Warren's half-smile became a smirk as he buzzed for Diane. Thank God I handle good writers and bad producers, Warren thought, and not the other way around. In the New Hollywood the property was the star. Take *Jaws.* Take *French Connection.* Take *Love Story.* Take *The Godfather.* The films made the stars. Richard Dreyfuss came out asking $500,000 a picture after *Jaws,* and Roy Scheider got a cover on *People* magazine. Gene Hackman emerged from obscurity because of *French Connection.* Ryan O'Neal got *Paper Moon* and the Kubrick movie after *Love Story.* Al Pacino was an accomplished actor who couldn't get arrested until he appeared in *The Godfather.* No. The New Hollywood stars were not stars in the old sense. Nor were the producers and directors. C. B. DeMille had been a star. As had David Selznick, Ernst Lubitsch, Frank Capra.

"Get me Goldstone," Warren told Diane on the intercom. "And what about that call to Randall Brent?"

"Mrs. Brent said he's out. I left a message. And Mr. Sands is here, Mr. Ambrose."

"Screw Mr. Sands. Let him wait." It was Warren's conviction that any agent worth the power he played with never received a client on time. "Get me Goldstone. Then call Nathan's office to confirm the meeting at three."

Goldstone was disbelieving and then elated to hear the news. He had no illusions about his track record. One of his last five medium-budget features had just made back its money; two others had bombed. Only the Rastar films, which he had nothing to do with, were successful. Goldstone could not imagine how Ambrose had gotten him the assignment; as a producer Goldstone was no David Brown or Dick Zanuck. Because of the price the studio paid, he realized this would be a high-budget investment. Paramount would stop at nothing to make it a hit. In the New Hollywood there was no smell; there were only computers. Given material by a top writer and high stakes in terms of financial backing which in turn assured preferential marketing (that is, favored promotion and bookings over other studio projects), almost no one could miss. Goldstone, who had four personal fouls against him, was in the key court.

"Now listen," said Warren. "Stay out of this. Let me make the deal with Sylbert." Dick Sylbert was Paramount's studio chief. "You gotta get a percentage of the gross."

"On this one, I'll take the net."

"Stanley, I don't care if you never go near the locations. Neither should you. The less you do the better. It's the money that matters. I'll take care of it." Warren hung up abruptly, as was his habit. He never said goodbye on the telephone, nor did he give any indication he was about to terminate the discussion. Nor did he listen to others. Like so many people mesmerized by their own voices, he had to have all the words, including the last.

Diane buzzed him. "I confirmed the appointment with Mr. Nathan. Shall I bring in Mr. Sands?" She said it hopefully, feeling sorry for the odd-looking little man who had already leafed three times through a year-old copy of the *New York Review of Books*.

Warren had forgotten that Walter Sands was waiting. Warren had lapses. "Make a note for me to call Grigsby in Chicago. He *is* still there?"

"At the Blackstone. He'll be back tomorrow."

"I want to reach him today. He's probably at lunch. I'll try him later. By the way, I just sold his script for six hundred thousand bucks."

"Wow."

"Right-o," said Warren. Over the years, the agent had picked up vocal mannerisms from famous people he'd known and admired. This particular jargon was mock-Noel Coward. It was louder and far more grating than Warren's adaptation of Christopher Isherwood, who had retained his English accent although he'd lived in Santa Monica for thirty years. Warren had also perfected the Ivy League idiom of Vidal and Plimpton. He could fake the high-pitched Southern drawl of Tennessee Williams, or the lisp of Ned Rorem. With Harry Waller, he affected the four-letter words and abbreviations of the underworld. He imitated only the rich and famous: it was Warren's peculiar skill at name-dropping.

"I'll see Mr. Sands," he told Diane in his Coward voice.

Sands was a new client who had accumulated millions as a producer of hard-core pornographic films. Warren had shown a few in his screening room; he had been impressed. He became even more enthusiastic after reading an article in *Rolling Stone* that called Sands "The King of Smut." Since Warren's cilia rose like a peacock's hackles on seeing someone dubbed the king of anything, he ordered one of his lieutenants to find the producer and sign him.

Ambrose had been carefully briefed by his assistant. Walter Sands, né Wally Swoboda, was born in Czechoslovakia. He escaped to West Berlin, churning out cheap porno movies that enabled him, eventually, to come to America. Swoboda changed his name to Sands and settled in San Francisco, where he met and married a wealthy dowager. With her inheritance, he produced a dozen dirty movies under almost as many pseudonyms.

Sands had moved to Hollywood seeking respectability. He wanted to get with a major studio as "a first-class producer." He had signed with Ambrose because he headed the most respected of talent agencies. Warren, on the other hand, intended to try to talk Sands into staying with hard-core porno; it was becoming an increasingly lucrative field.

The agent's initial chore, as Sands entered his bedroom-office, was to suppress a laugh. Sands was decked out like a ten-year-old boy on Halloween. He wore a tan suit with multicolored embroidery on the lapels, a matching embroidered vest, a flowered shirt, and a blowfish tie. He approached the seating arrangement by the window slowly. Warren's large paw engulfed Walter's like a vise. "Sit here," said Ambrose, indicating the chair that faced the window. Like a nasty attorney taking a deposition, Warren placed a potentially unruly party in the glare of the sun. To any man but Warren Ambrose, the ruse would have seemed unsporting, since Walter Sands had a blink, in or out of the sunlight. Warren smiled, secure in his advantage. He had hit a lob to a midget in the forecourt.

"I like your work," he said. "In fact, I envy you. It must be terrific, making your living by posing pussy. I like watching guys come on with girls and girls coming on with guys and guys coming on with guys. I gotta tell you, at heart I've always been a voyeur."

"Then shake hands," said Wally. "I suppose that's how I

got started. I got turned on by watching. When I was a kid, I drilled a hole in the wall between my bathroom and my parents' bedroom. I'd crouch there for hours just waiting and listening. Then they'd go at it, and that's how I got my Ph.D."

"Did you ever get caught?"

Sands blinked at the light. "No, never. It was a very small hole. You'd think they'd have found it, but my mother wasn't adventurous. Not even during the sex act. She'd lie there, flat on her back, and my father would beg her to take his prick in her mouth but she wouldn't. So then he would rub it over her face and her breasts and massage it to get it up, and then he'd just stick it into her, smash it into her cunt, and come very fast." His eyes were blinking more rapidly now, remembering. "I don't think my mother liked it," he said. "I don't think she ever came."

"But you liked it?" Warren stared at the albino man, enthralled by his recital.

"I loved it. I'd jack off, and then I'd grab a hunk of toilet paper and wipe up the floor. I was afraid to flush the toilet, afraid they'd find out what I was doing. I had my first piece of ass with the girl who came to clean every week. I never could get anywhere with her; I was short and ugly. Girls paid no attention to me. You know how I excited her? I showed her the peephole, and invited her back after work to watch with me. My father did it every Wednesday and Saturday nights, like clockwork. Sometimes more."

"So what happened?" said Warren. He was getting horny, listening to Sands.

"So what happened is she got so excited lying there she put her arm around me and pulled her skirt to her thighs. She had nothing on underneath. I twiddled her and she was sticky. We did it right there on the bathroom floor. Then, you know what? She asked me to pay her. Somehow I liked that. I told her I'd pay her if I could stick the bill in her cunt. That made her go off like a rocket, and we did it again. I was taking a leak, and she was holding my cock, and I realized that fucking is special when people do it for money. You can make them dance to your tune. It gives you a feeling of superiority. I won't say I don't like fucking when it's free, but . . ."

"I understand." Warren pulled his robe tighter and retied it, the better to hide his hard-on.

"I'll miss making people fuck for me, going legitimate. As you said, it's not the same when you watch it on the screen. Those were real fuck films I did, live action. I never faked it like some people do."

"What if a guy couldn't get it up for a scene?"

"I'd make him play with himself, or make the girls play with him, or the other guys. Whatever excited him. Sometimes I'd substitute for him. We'd use cock-shots of me." Sands flushed. "I know what you're thinking. I'm small, but I've got a big joint."

"How could you control yourself, watching them fuck?"

"Sometimes I couldn't. Sometimes I'd get so hot I'd pull out my cock and jack off or do it right there with one of my actresses. You get pretty hot posing pussy, as you say, parting a girl's legs and lips so the camera gets split beaver, or showing guys what to do with their cocks and their tongues. Sometimes I got it off just thinking about what they'd do for pay."

Ambrose understood the visual aspect of arousal. He had an array of dirty books and pictures which even Alice didn't know about. Nothing elated him more than sneaking a look at the naked women and men who shared his Jacuzzi during cocktail hour. Cock-tail, he thought, was appropriate, and he smiled at the pun. Why not cunt-tail? Maybe it proved that men had invented the English language. Warren was a voyeur, but an active voyeur. He got his biggest sexual kicks from mass encounters. They were clandestine, of course. The meticulous agent of the A Group met one night a week with like-minded participants at a rented apartment in West Hollywood. Alice didn't know about the gatherings. "Sweet Alice," as everyone called his wife, was the daughter of an Oklahoma clergyman. Alice would not have approved. Even dirty movies disgusted her. When Warren showed one, she made an excuse to their guests and fled to her room.

Walter Sands was an unmistakable candidate for Warren's orgies. Collective intercourse was an acquired taste, and initiates were scarce. Even in the New Hollywood with its purported sexual freedom.

"As you may know," Sands was saying, "money I've got. Money I'm willing to spend. I'm rotten with money. Your job is to get me, to *buy* me, if necessary, a decent position with a movie company."

Warren stroked the poll of gray hair at the nape of his neck. "What I've been trying to tell you," he said, "is you've got a good thing. Why give it up? Why let go of the pussy that laid the golden egg?" The agent chuckled at his joke. "You've made millions because you're the best, which is why we signed you. We take only the best in every field. And the market for porn is growing. You want to be one of those duds producing G-rated movies that don't make a dime? Baby, they want to be *you.* I wouldn't take one of them on as a client for a million times what you've got in the bank."

"It's no good. I've already done it. I don't need outsiders telling me what it's like. When I started, I dreamed of making the ultimate porno film—not the 'ultimate movie' they're talking about now, snuff movies where people really get killed. I have no taste for S and M. Sado-masochists give me the creeps. I once wanted to create the greatest sex extravaganza ever. I've come close. And I know I'm the best. That's why I want to move on."

"Human nature." Warren scoffed. "Human nature gives me a pain. You're a man, you think being a woman is better. You got curly hair, you want straight. You got money, you'd give it all up for a date with Natalie Wood. You can buy any newspaper, you'd rather be in the society columns."

"That's it exactly." Sands was exuberant. His eyes blinked strenuously at the sun, which threw pink streaks on his platinum hair.

"All right. I get the message. I'll see what I can do."

"You know something?" Sands said. "When I had no security, money was my goal. I thought people only did things for money. Fucking, working, stealing. Now that I have the money, I still believe that."

"You poor bastard, I think you really do," Warren said. He felt a revulsion for the man. "Just remember money can't buy you everything."

"Who says? I have my health, and that's it. If I didn't, I could afford the best doctors."

"Don't worry, Walter. You're on my client list. Since you insist, I'll make you the most respectable goddamn social producer in town. But just remember this, one thing I can't make you is talented. I've seen them come and go. That's why I thank God I'm an agent. You have a talent for sex films, but you may not have talent for anything else. And even if you do, your talent will run out someday. You'll be finished. As for me, I'll find somebody new with talent. That's why agents have taken over every major studio in this town. You come and go, but it's us, the agents, who last. We're survivors."

"You're pricks," said Walter.

"Sure we're pricks. That's why people perform at my parties. I'm using them, sure, like they're using me. To get jobs. You want to come to my parties?"

Sands was blinking painfully now, the crows' feet furling around his eyes. "You want prints of my fuck films?" he said.

Warren smiled. The man was a freak, but he wasn't stupid. "We understand one another. I have a suggestion. You want to be on the society page and in the gossip columns? Hire a press agent. I don't plant; I just sell."

"Who do you recommend?"

"That depends. For your movies, or for the social scene? *Women's Wear*, Manners, *People*?"

"Let's start with *Women's Wear*."

This time Ambrose grinned. The mavericks were predictable. "In the East, Earl Blackwell. Out here, Grace St. George. She's stupid as hell, I warn you, so don't admit she's on your payroll. That in itself will put you on the 'Climber-Unacceptable' list."

"Then why should I hire her?"

"Because she has done people favors. She's sucked them off. She operates like a hooker or pimp. She gets second-rate stars to host parties for second-rate royalty, and the other way around. She'll get you a blow job or an invitation to any party. She's dumb, but she knows where the bodies are buried, and Grace is not above exhuming them. She's also not above blackmail. That's why her clients, or non-clients, ask her to parties. They entertain her at their houses in Acapulco, the Hamptons, the French Riviera—you name it. St. George is a super-user, Sands. A conniving, two-bit profiteer. But she'll get you wherever you want to go."

Sands' chin jutted up like the beak on an ancient galley. "What's her number?"

"Diane will give it to you." Ambrose buzzed. "Give Mr. Sands Grace St. George's number on his way out. And try to get me Grigsby in Chicago. I think he'll be pleased to learn he's more than half a million skins in the black."

The man who believed that people did things only for money was plainly impressed by the figure. His lips parted slightly while Warren was talking. He tugged at his printed vest as he left, presumably to cover the paunch that signaled his first-generation prosperity.

Having lost the argument for pornography, Ambrose knew where to go. He intended to stick Pacific with Walter Sands in a triple play. Kip Nathan wanted *Overwrought,* the mystery novel by Everett Loring. Kip would get it if he put Sands on his company payroll and topped the offers from Fox and Columbia for Waller's sure bestseller, *Rogue's Gallery.* Since Kip wanted Randall Brent (God knows why, thought Ambrose), the agent was going to sign him; that way, he'd collect another ten percent. The conversion was simpler than dollars into francs.

Ambrose smiled contentedly, smoothing his monogrammed robe. He fingered his erection, which had shriveled only slightly since Sands' graphic account of the making of fuck films, as he called them. Warren decided to masturbate, which was easier than getting Alice aroused.

He buzzed Diane. "Have you gotten through to Grigsby yet?"

"He's still out, Mr. Ambrose. I left a message."

Warren went to the bathroom and stripped so as not to soil his pajamas, or robe. After satisfying himself, he washed and crawled back into bed, where he reviewed the events of the morning. He had done well in his packaging, even on the personal side. Grace St. George was one of the regular recruiters for Warren's orgies. He paid her a small retainer and let her attend them. Knobby old hag that she was, she was useful as a participant. Warren hadn't lied when he'd said, "She'll get you a blow job." He had simply understated the case. Grace would give you a blow job herself. She'd give you a finger job, or whatever you wanted. Yes, Warren thought, she was useful. Even to the extent that Grace, not Warren, would introduce "The King of Smut" into Ambrose's bacchanals.

He hoped that Grace would also introduce Sands to a conservative tailor—John Galupo, who dressed David Janssen and Fred Astaire; Harry Cherry, who dressed Gene Kelly; Dick Dorso, who also dressed Kelly on occasion, plus Paul Newman, Walter Matthau, Steve McQueen, NBC's David Tebet, MGM's Daniel Melnick and ex-CBS man Jim Aubrey (Dorso just happened to be an ex-CBS man himself). Richard Crenna, who spent more on clothes than any man (or woman) in town, preferred Eric Ross and Dick Carroll. Carroll was a disillusioned press agent when he started his haberdashery; Arte Johnson once worked as a salesman there. Elegant and conservative, Carroll was Hollywood's answer to Brooks Brothers. That meant Carroll was out of the running, or rather a million lengths away from the flamboyant tastes of both Walter Sands and Grace St. George.

2

Kip left the house while Nancy was still asleep (As usual, he thought), stopping only to kiss Elizabeth, who reached up to him vainly from her crib. He had no time to play with his daughter; he didn't even stop for coffee because he was late. He had had a bad night, waking up almost every hour. Finally, at 5 A.M., he had taken another Seconal and dozed off until nine. Kip was in agony; his back was out again. He refused to attribute the relapse to the three sets of tennis he'd played the day before, although he knew his doctor would have. If he called Dr. Abraham, he would have to put up with the chronic chiding which, to Kip, was worse than the pain. Tom would order him not to play tennis, and Kip had never been one to follow orders. That, he reflected as he waved at the studio's gateman, was the crux of his problem with Nancy. Why hadn't he seen it in time, the Tinkerbell poison within the bright Tinkerbell wand? I didn't see it, he thought, because I'm myopic, if not when I'm on a tennis court, when I'm on a woman.

Carol followed him into his office and watched him collapse on the couch. "Mr. Nathan, let me call the doctor," she said.

"No. Get me a pain pill. I'll be all right."

"You'll be all right when you cancel weekends. It's tennis that does it. Every Monday you're like this." Shrugging her disapproval, she went to the medicine chest in his bathroom and returned with the pill.

"What time is the story conference?"

"Right now. Whenever you're ready. But I think you should know Mike Richards has been acting up again. He stormed the office and said you should call him the minute you arrived."

"Richards is a pain in the ass," said Kip. "As opposed to a pain in the *sacroiliac*. What is it today?" Mike Richards was starring in an adventure film that was shooting on the lot.

"It's the same. He says he can't work with Erica Marshall. He says she was twenty minutes late and then demanded that her makeup be redone. She held up the first take, and he claims she okayed some stills that made her look great and him look terrible."

"Does Richards have approval of stills?"

"I checked his contract. No."

"Good girl," Kip said. Carol, unlike most other secretaries he'd had, thought ahead. She anticipated his queries. "Get that conceited excuse for a centerfold up here, and fast."

If Richards was wielding a hatchet, Kip was an armed guerrilla. The movie had only been shooting for three days. Richards could still be replaced. His demands, if they continued, would cost Pacific more than reshooting the footage it had. "Whatever you came to say, I don't want to hear it," Kip told him. "In fact, if I hear one more complaint, you can leave. You can leave this office right now and disappear. I've seen the dailies. Erica Marshall happens to be the best thing in the film."

Richards' gaunt face, with its splinter eyes, grew tight. "Are you saying that I'm no good? If so, you can shove your goddamn picture. *And* that ugly cunt you call an actress."

"I'm saying Miss Marshall is good, and she stays. I'm saying I couldn't find an actress you'd get along with. That's what I'm saying. No actor in this damn town, or any other, is worth the hassle you've caused in a week of rehearsal and three days' shooting. It's nothing personal, Mike."

"Nothing personal?"

"Personality conflict, as they say in the trades. How would you feel if your kid threw a tantrum because you were five minutes late coming home? Erica comes across on the screen. She may have her personal problems, but name someone who doesn't. Mike, you're a pro. You must understand what I mean."

Mike understood. If he walked off now, Kip Nathan would put out the word that he was ousted for being difficult. The industry, despite its vicissitudes or because of them, was a fraternity. "Okay, but I don't have to like the bitch, do I?"

"You don't have to marry the woman. You're just reading lines to her."

"There are a few I'd like to read her."

"From what I hear you've already done that," Kip said. He suddenly winced in pain.

"What's a matter? Your back out again?" Kip's thoracic vertebrae were legend at Pacific.

As Richards left, Kip poured some water from the thermos beside him. He took a deep breath and let out an audible sigh; his doctor called it "Reichian breathing." It was supposed to release one's tensions. Kip knew that Richards' real gripe was not his co-star, but rather his deal on the movie. Erica Marshall, who had found the property, had a percentage of the box-office gross. Richards was working on a straight salary. The amount of money up front wasn't good for a star, not even a fledgling star, but Richards had wanted the role so badly he had tested for it, as had many other young actors.

Ted, as Mike's lawyer, had represented him—and, for once, Kip outsmarted his friend. Knowing that Ted was a virtual alcoholic, Mike had flown to New York to have an excuse to call him at 6 A.M. Los Angeles time to negotiate the deal for him. Kip knew that Buckley would be soused by 10 A.M. and blind by 6, so he put him off all day. Kip finally met Ted after work at the Polo Lounge and transacted a very bad deal for the actor, one highly favorable to Pacific. "You son of a bitch," Ted told Kip later. "You got me."

"Even Buckley can lose one case," Kip replied. Since then, they had referred to the incident, in a private joke, as "The Richards Attachment."

Worrying over Mike Richards' obstreperousness, Kip recalled statements by two of Hollywood's top directors. "All actors are cattle," Alfred Hitchcock had said. Billy Wilder, after winding up *Some Like It Hot*, had made his famous remark about Marilyn Monroe: "I'll never use that woman again," said Billy, "until I need her."

Carol appeared at the door. "Are you all right, Mr. Nathan?"

"Fair to middling," said Kip. "I was better before that

hopped-up Adonis came in." He saw the question behind her eyes. "Yes, he's still on the picture. He says he'll behave."

"Good luck," Carol said. "Do you want the story conference now?"

At the meeting David Kellogg, who was Kip's executive assistant and reader, suggested an alternate script to *Overwrought* for Randall Brent. It was an original screenplay by a veteran scenarist who had been on the Hollywood blacklist in the late 1940s. The story, as Kellogg described it, was "one of those CIA numbers" in which Randy would play a double agent. In Kip's opinion, the public was satiated with the government scandal business, most notably because of such movies as Robert Redford's *The Candidate* and *Three Days of the Condor*. Redford was getting typed, Kip thought. The New Hollywood was regressing to the Old. Instinctively, he preferred the escapist genre of *Overwrought;* nonetheless, he promised David he would take the script home and read it that night.

When Warren presented his terms at their three o'clock conference, Kip learned that he was boxed in by the agent. If he wanted *Rogue's Gallery,* which he did, he had no options. Ambrose was not one to dicker; he presented his package like a Broadway scalper who has fixed his price for the last two tickets to the hottest show. Kip was convinced the Waller novel was a natural. He wanted the property Ambrose controlled as avidly as he resented the agent's insistence he hire Walter Sands.

"I don't need another producer, certainly not a smut producer, on my payroll," Kip told him. "Pacific isn't a massage parlor. Haven't you heard? Sex shops are out of style. The cops keep closing them down."

"They open again with a different name," Warren said. "Listen, Sands is a plus for Pacific. He has the talent; I'll vouch for that. He wants to get out of the smut market, as you call it. He was the best in his business. Besides, he knows what the public wants. He has the common touch."

"I'll buy that," Kip said.

His sarcasm was lost on Warren, who was imperturbable. He rose from his chair and walked to the mirrored bar to examine himself. What he saw seemed to please him; he smiled. He straightened his tie and smoothed his nape-hairs, which always reminded Kip of the fringes on an awning. Then Ambrose approached the couch and stood over Kip, all six feet of him.

"That's the deal. You can take it or leave it, as Harry Cohn would have said. I'll give you till Monday. I have to let Ladd and Jaffe know." Ladd and Jaffe were Fox's and Columbia's respective studio chiefs.

"For the price you're asking Pacific, Ladd and Jaffe can wait until Peckinpah makes a comedy," said Kip. He admired the agent's chutzpah. He was the buyer, Ambrose the seller, but Ambrose had the complacency of an angler holding a bucktail lure. He had managed to reverse their roles. "I'll call you," Kip said. "You know, you're a bastard, Ambrose."

Warren was unruffled. "Bastard is a synonym for agent," he smiled, and added, "or studio chief."

Kip buzzed for Carol as Warren left. "Get me a Percodan," he said.

"Not another, Mr. Nathan?"

"Another. What time is it? Four-fifteen. Late enough for some booze. You can bring me two fingers of J&B. neat."

She obeyed him, grudgingly. Carol was a teetotaler. She would have been in the forefront of any movement to reinstate Prohibition.

"No phone calls, Carol, except for emergencies," he said. "I'd like to nap. But wake me at six. Tell Grossman I want to see him when he winds up for the day." Grossman was the director on the Mike Richards picture. "I wonder how Mike's been behaving."

"Haven't you heard? He threw an ashtray at Grossman, walked off the set to his trailer, and wouldn't come out until the assistant director assured him they'd shoot around the portrait and get a new one."

"What portrait?"

"The portrait of him in the beach house scene. He didn't like it."

"Jesus," said Kip. "Was he drinking again?"

"I don't know, Mr. Nathan. Probably."

"Before you go Carol, get me another drink," Kip said. He said it firmly; after seven years with an otherwise perfect secretary, he recognized their unspoken argument over liquor.

She started to leave, then turned back at the door. "May I ask you a question, Mr. Nathan?"

"Anything. But I may not answer." Lorne Greene had said wisely, in a speech to the Hollywood Women's Press Club, that "there are no embarrassing questions, only embarrassing answers." Kip never forgot that observation, which had made him a favorite with reporters. He might refuse to answer a question, but he had never lied to the press.

"I suppose this is silly. It's something I've wondered about since I came to Hollywood," Carol said. "If I had to choose—well, I think I'd rather be a director than an executive. A director has so much creative control, and if he has a hit, he gets both the credit and the money. What I mean is, why did you choose to be an executive, not a director?"

"It's very simple, Carol. I didn't want to deal with actors."

3

Kip had asked Ted to come by at eleven, an hour before the day's tennis began. As the lawyer for and the power behind Pacific Pictures, only Ted could convince George Cohen to accept the steep deal that Ambrose insisted upon. Hollywood was a market largely run and rigged by agents. At the outset, Kip had been George Cohen's darling; under the burgeoning pressures inherent in running a studio, the favorite son lost favor. Kip was enervated by the president's phone calls; they were pointless and they came at any hour, day or night. After his marriage to Nancy, Kip became ever more conscious, through her nagging demands for attention, that he had to establish an order of precedence. Nancy scoffed at his long post-midnight talks with the boss in New York as "absurd." Eventually she persuaded him to silence every phone in the house, except the ones in the kitchen and servants' quarters.

Kip's initial determination to make their marriage work was reinforced when Nancy produced his second child. His teenage son by another marriage lived in St. Louis with his mother and stepfather. Kip seldom saw him. Compulsive as he was in business, Kip was unaware that his job and those he depended upon, like Ted, would always come first. He had deceived himself into thinking his family took precedence over his career. In reality, no studio chief could have racked up his list of accomplishments without making personal sacrifices. Kip Nathan had the best record of any studio chief in town, but now he had the uneasy feeling he'd lost control. The president's demands and eccentricities had nothing to do with the quality of the product. They related to pretty starlets and the price of Pacific stock in a tumbling market. Ted, who had convinced George Cohen to hire Kip, had become the troubleshooter between them.

Kip had always been at odds with the company's president. A gambler, a man who bet as much as $500 on a single game of tennis, Kip would wager $10 million of company money on a first screenplay cast with unknowns. While Cohen respected Kip for his winning streak, he wasn't a man for taking risks. The battle lines had been drawn from the beginning.

Kip's back was still out. Ted found him lying on a poolside chaise. "Hey," he said, "you're not looking bad for an invalid. I'm sorry. I was detained. A labor mess in Detroit."

"And a chick in Grosse Point, no doubt." Kip smiled.

"But of course."

"So you leave at five?"

"Four-thirty."

"You need some fortification." Kip started to prop himself up to reach the intercom on the phone, then grew pale and fell back on the chaise. "Will you buzz for Peter? Tell him to bring us a pitcher of Bullshots, and tell him I need a Percodan."

"I'll have a Bloody Mary, if you don't mind. I've already had three this morning. . . ." Ted held up three fingers.

"Then order a pitcher of each," Kip said. "I'm expecting a mob today."

"So what else is new? I'm glad I took up golf."

"By the way, Nancy said she enjoyed that lunch. It was nice of you to take her."

"I thought it was time I bought her a lunch. You don't mind?"

"Be my guest."

"All the way?"

"Have I ever said no to you, Ted?"

"You're safe. I had to fly East that afternoon."

"I know I'm safe, my friend. So are you. My beautiful, brainy wife is a cockteaser. She lies on her back and expects you to plug her. I guess that's because she's so scrawny. I once read somewhere that fashion models can't do it because they're too weak."

"Well, you ought to know about models." Ted said it to mask his embarrassment. Kip had often been graphic about his sexual episodes with one-nighters but never, in their long friendship, had he commented on his wives.

"I wouldn't have thought Miz Nancy was to your taste,"

said Kip. "I mean, you've never exactly spread your houndstooth for her. Besides, she never goes to lunch. God forbid she should gain one-tenth of a pound."

"Well, she didn't eat much."

"She doesn't," Kip said. "She doesn't eat at all. Now why am I telling you that? Catharsis. It's a husband's problem. My problem."

Peter arrived with the drinks, and Ted drained his glass in a motion. "Too bad," he said, sounding nervous. "Now how about this movie for Brent? Have you got it?"

"I have and I haven't. That bastard Ambrose is holding me up. If I want this goddamn mystery, I'm supposed to pay a premium for the Waller novel. On top of that, he's trying to stick me with a porno producer who wants to go straight."

Ted refilled his glass from the pitcher beside them. He grinned. "Cheer up. At least you'll get stuck by somebody. After what you said about Nancy, I'd say you need it."

"Don't think I haven't thought of that, and everything else. It's lucky I learned to masturbate. But back to business. What Pacific needs is another producer, right?"

"How much for the mystery?"

"That comes cheap. I can get it for $50,000. But Ambrose is making it up on the Waller book. He's asking $400,000 with escalations and points for Waller."

"It sounds like a shotgun deal."

"It is. I happen to know that Warren's highest bid is $300,000 outright, from Stanfill."

"You want this B mystery movie for Brent?"

"I want *Gallery,*" Kip said. "It's a shoo-in. Besides, I want to help Elena. You know all the favors she's done for me—getting rid of all those dames who wouldn't let go of me, inviting them to her parties, and passing them on to other suckers."

"Then accept the deal."

"Will the president go for it?"

"Cohen will go for it. Take it from me. I put him in; I can get him out. Believe me, selling Cohen to the Board was harder than selling this turkey you seem to think is right for Brent."

"He's not easy. How do you cast a broken-down boozer who hasn't worked in years? As Rebecca of Sunnybrook Farm? Look, Ted, he needs the job. They need the money.

Besides, if we keep the budget around a million, we can't lose."

"What's it called?" Ted asked, as he poured another drink.

"*Overwrought*. It's by a guy they're calling the new Ross Macdonald."

"I read that. I read it on a plane. You're not casting Randy as the detective?"

"Never. He's wrong. Too old. Too weak. But how about the ladies' man who turns out to be the murderer?"

"Not bad," said Ted.

The telephone rang. "Make it three," Kip said. "The court will be busy till then." He hung up. "The tennis callers started two hours ago. Compared to scheduling tennis, running a studio is a cinch. I have too many people coming, as usual, but how can you say no to a white Anglo-Saxon in Beverly Hills?"

"How's the back?" Ted asked.

"It's better. The Percodan is beginning to work."

"You're not going to play today?" Ted asked the question mechanically.

Kip's reply was as sure as the single word that fits a Double-Crostic. "Sure I am. It's okay. Harvey Parkes is coming to give me a rubdown before the screening tonight. I asked him to be here at two, in case the other players want him. How's that for super-A at a tennis party?"

"Harvey Parkes is massaging women openly? Iris told me he swore her to secrecy on that one. He says it's illegal to massage the opposite sex in Beverly Hills, or L.A., or something."

"He has to be a nut. Have you seen those signs along Santa Monica Boulevard, 'Temple of Oral Gratification: Either Sex Welcome'?"

Ted laughed. "I admit I've been tempted. Those places open and close like Iris Gordon's snatch."

"Since you brought it up, what happened the other night with her and Barry Springfield?"

"Who knows? I was busy throwing that rock guy out of Elena's. They probably went to the Bel-Air Sands motel. When I looked for her, I was told they'd left together."

"Sorry," said Kip.

"Good riddance," said Ted. "I was afraid she'd be hard to unload. Even through Elena."

"Well, I can tell you one thing. Considering his height, he had to go up on her."

Ted laughed. "So Harvey Parkes is stroking women. Iris told me she was at a party and Edie Goetz, who was standing with the Governor, called across the room, 'Doesn't Harvey give the best massage you've ever had?' "

"So what did Iris do?"

"The next time Harvey mentioned that the massages were secret, she told him, 'Don't talk to me. Talk to Edie Goetz.' "

"At the money he's charging today, he'd better massage the women," Kip said. "I also have Cliff standing by to comb the ladies."

"I'm glad you're rich," said Ted, and they laughed. They both knew that Kip lived light-years beyond his income. He had inherited over $2 million from his family, who were wealthy toy manufacturers in the East, but he had unwisely invested the money in glamour stocks. Even more unwisely, he had bought them on margin. When the market plunged, he had had to cover. He mortgaged his house. Since then, to keep going, he had taken a sizable loan from Al Hart, the founder of the City National Bank, with Ted as co-signer. Hart was the man who had opened his vaults at night to provide his friend Frank Sinatra with the $500,000 ransom when Frank, Jr., was kidnapped. "The rich are different than us" was as true in the days of Gerald Ford as in the days of Fitzgerald.

The phone rang again. "Jesus, tennis is a calling card," Kip said, before answering. He was right. In the New Hollywood, on the weekends, people who didn't even play the game dropped by to drink or to gossip. Single women considered a match a potential matchmate with men. Junior executives came to ingratiate themselves with superiors. Status-seekers arrived in quest of a party invitation or a glimpse of Chuck Heston. Others of the tennis elite had nothing better to do on a Saturday or a Sunday. Only a handful enjoyed the game or wanted the exercise. The sport was so compelling that realtor Stan Herman and others told their clients they could not get them prime rates for their properties unless they added a tennis court. Mansions with acres of land, estates with bathhouses, swimming pools, Malibu villas with hundreds of feet of beach frontage had high tabs, but went begging. They were either unsal-

able or glutting the market, a million dollars a doz
was In and swimming was Out.

Kip tried to lean over, but grimaced in pain.
the phone to Ted, who replaced it on the cradl
the new producer in town," Kip said cynic
guy who's hustling *Rogue's Gallery.*
thirty."

"My God, I'm glad I'm a
don't know how you kee of half of

"I don't know ho 're married
give him a peck his
her husband d it's not
breakfa is? It's bad
siste w put on your
at I'm balls around. Not
he left.
e nursery. "That damn
ver stops crying."
over the dresser and scanned
tight. I'll get him, so why be up-
ley, she thought, unable to shake
rebuff. Then she remembered Harvey
kes would be there today. Harvey
ch, but he was accommodating.

g, Kip had underestimated the turnout for ten-
court was so busy that he had played only one set
noon. Inevitably, because he chose his partners with
care, he had won.

Nancy, who didn't like to lose any more than her husband, decided against the competition. She chose a table with an umbrella to shield her bikini-bared skin from the sun.

"What are you reading?" attorney Greg Bautzer asked her.

"I'm briefing myself, as you might say, on the competition." She showed him the picture on the back of the dust jacket. "She's kind of butch, don't you think? But this reads like a bitch. It's called *Down With the Masters*. Her theory being that boobs are better than balls."

"There's nothing new about that," said the handsome man who had been Howard Hughes' personal lawyer. "I've worked on that premise all my life." Greg was as cavalier

off the tennis court as he was a militant on it. He was one of the men who aimed his most powerful shots at his female opponent in mixed doubles. At the end of a match, he jumped the net and embraced the women. On or off the court, he was a lady-killer. Anti-feminist females loved him.

Nancy, the feminist, hardly acknowledged him, just as she was ignoring the others who were waiting for a game. They included John Tunney, who had arrived with Linda and Sy Weintraub; Gene Kelly, who was talking to Bob Wagner; Tom Mankiewicz and Richard Brooks; Natalie and Jack Kaufman; Gladyce and David Begelman; Charlton Heston and Anne Douglas. Anne, who had played on the Belgian women's tennis team, was so good she drove her husband, Kirk, to the golf course.

Kip was playing host, as he always did, to his Sunday visitors. He was trying to avoid a game with Dick Zanuck, who kept himself in top physical shape, and usually won when they gambled together for outrageous stakes. At the moment Kip was talking to Dick and Adrian Aron, while keeping an eye on the court where Adrian's fiancé, Pierre Groleau, was playing. Pierre was an absentee restaurateur who started Manhattan's Hippopotamus and Hollywood's Ma Maison. Pierre was a fulltime tennis player: he rounded up every private court available and behaved as though he owned the place. One popular story had it that Pierre invited his friends to play at Jerry Weintraub's house, then asked Gene Kelly, between sets, "Who is Jerry Weintraub?" Weintraub managed John Denver and Frank Sinatra.

"Who are those chicks?" Kip said to Adrian, indicating two girls by the swimming pool.

"If you don't know, how should I?" she replied. "But I checked. Their names are Lucy and Alice. They're tennis groupies, I guess."

"Hmm, not bad," said Dick, who was nothing if not a man with an eye for form. "And who's the brunette over there?"

"Pat Lukas," said Kip. "She's in television. She's the hottest female writer in town after Fay Kanin."

"That says something for Women's Lib," said Dick. "Your wife should meet her."

"My wife has met her. They're planning a screenplay together."

Kip turned his attention to the game. Pierre and Dick Crenna were teamed against Adam Baker and David Kellogg. Adam was playing an excellent game. Kip noted that he was as close to a pro as any he'd seen since Pancho Gonzalez took part in a charity tournament on his court. Adam and David were winning, four to one, against their opponents, although Pierre's returns were so reliable that he was called "The Backboard" along the tennis circuit. Pierre was steady. Sometimes his ground strokes were less than potent, but in the end he wore one down, invoking a kind of passive resistance that would have pleased Gandhi.

Adam had no perceptible weaknesses. Several times he had served an ace, his placements were deft, and his two-handed backhand might have derived from Jimmy Connors. Kip was determined to take Adam on as a partner.

The game was still going on when Elena arrived. "What the hell are *you* doing here?" Kip asked. "You don't play, and you hate to watch tennis."

"Darling, let's say I love watching you. It's your special charm." She was wearing a white cotton shirt, imported French jeans, and espadrilles.

He drew her aside. "Come on, Elena. You're worried about the picture for Randy. Couldn't you wait until tonight? You're expected for dinner and the screening, you know."

"I'm afraid I can't make it, Kip."

"What is it? How do you mean, you can't make it?"

"It's Randy. He's—well, I told you he didn't come home until Monday morning, and he's—he's just not well."

"Elena, say it. He's on a bender. So what? Let him be. I expect you tonight. It's a damned good science fiction movie. I've never screened it before, and you need the diversion."

"Kip, I can't stand this much longer." She fingered the narrow link chain around her neck. "I've got to tell someone. He spent the whole weekend with that Italian waiter." Kip knew she was nervous because she lapsed into a pronounced foreign accent. She sounded as though she were arriving next week, or still hadn't arrived.

"So what else is new?" he said. "You didn't think you

were marrying Frank Sinatra. I admit I've wondered how you put up with it, but you've handled it beautifully."

"I can't any more. It's me, not Randy, who's changed. It's not so much sex. I can live without that. It's not what I live without. It's what I live *with*."

"I know," he said.

"I think you do." She was silent for a moment, meeting the empathy she sensed in his gaze. "There are the depressions. The accusations. The benders, as you call them. I've had it. I've got to get him a job. I've got to get him on his feet, so I can leave him."

"You can't mean that, Elena. Without him, you're just another single woman. With him, you're Mrs. Randall Brent. Elena Brent. You've built yourself into that. You've worked for it and you deserve it. Stay with him until you get something better. Without him, who are you?"

"I'm Elena Schneider, a displaced person, a refugee who escaped because I had to escape. I'm back there again, Kip, in East Berlin. It's *déjà vu*. I went over one Wall. It's time to go over the Wall again. Help me, Kip."

"You know I'd have called you the minute I had something definite. Well, it's close. I've found a book with a character that's perfect for Randy. It's only a matter of firming the deal."

"Thank God," she said, and she kissed him. "Warren signed Randy this week. Did I tell you?"

"That bastard Ambrose will do anything for another ten percent. He knows I'm dead set on Randy for *Overwrought*. Don't think he didn't try to sell me a client instead. But listen, that's great for Randy and for you. I hate to give it to him, but Warren is still the best. He'd sell his father as Rodney Allen Rippie for a buck." He took her hand. "Now, don't do anything hasty, little Kraut. Would you like a Valium or a drink?"

"No, thanks. I'll manage. The Kaufmans have offered me their beach house, and I'm tempted. What do you think?"

"I think you should jump at it. Get away. You need a rest. By the way, Harvey Parkes is here. In the guest cottage. Why don't you have a massage? A massage would relax you."

"I think I will."

"I heard that," said Natalie. "You could relax her far

better. Considering that cooze you married, I'm sure you're ready to get it on, Kip."

Elena had never seen Kip react so intensely. If eyes could spit, his were spitting at Natalie.

"You're a guest in my house," he said, "so behave like one. I've known you for years, and sometimes you're not very funny. You're vicious. Just hold your tongue or get out." He had never wanted to hit a woman, any woman, before. He had to get away. "Elena," he said, "I'll see you later. If I have to, I'll come pick you up myself."

He took the steps to the tennis court two at a time.

"Now what's the matter with him?" asked Natalie. "Darling, people can't stand the truth. Did you notice he didn't say 'our house'? He said 'my house.' "

"Nat, I don't understand your . . ." Elena wanted to say "meanness," but changed her mind.

"And what did he mean, 'If I have to pick you up'?" Natalie was preparing for Take Two. "Don't tell me. Randy's on the sauce again."

"Honestly, darling, you *are* impossible. Randy is fine. He's reading scripts. I'm tired and I had no intention of coming tonight. . . ."

"I'll bet you hadn't. At least not with Randy."

"Now stop it, Natalie." Instantly, she regretted the flare-up. "Kip insists that I see this movie. The one he's showing for Rex. About the ants."

"I can't wait. We refused it," Natalie said. She wasn't about to admit that the Kaufmans had not been asked. "But you really know who can't wait? Those dummies there by the pool. The black-haired Dahlia and the black-is-beautiful one. They've had their hooks into every man in the place. And imagine sunbathing *naked* in front of strangers? What does she think, she's back in her topless joint? Who are they? I've never seen them before." She didn't stop for an answer. "Just look at the mouth on the white one. It looks as though it's been on a stretcher. She'd go down on anything, darling. The *Titanic*."

"Natalie, can't you behave?" Elena laughed. Then she tried a ploy. "I think they want you for tennis."

"I haven't heard a thing. Now listen, Elena, what are you doing here? You don't play."

"I just explained. I came to tell Kip I couldn't make it

tonight. It was such a beautiful day, I decided to walk . . ."

"You're not on that silly walking rotuine? Norma Shearer, Harriet Deutsch, now you. It's a fad. No wonder the doctors are being accused of malpractice. Incidentally, your discovery Adam Baker is here. He plays one hell of a game, and I don't mean only tennis. Marina tells me he's got a bigger lob than you'll ever see on a court. Just think, it all started in your sauna, so *publicly*. Adam's moved in with her. My dear, they haven't been out of bed until today."

"That's nice," Elena said. She was recalling the fuchsia plant which Adam had sent her after the party. His note said, "Only you." Later, each time he phoned her to ask for a date or profess his love, she cut him off. But her curt refusals, instead of discouraging him, seemed to make him more determined. He's trying to use me, she thought; he's trying to use my connections for his movie. He was probably calling from bed, while Marina nestled against his shoulder. Elena could imagine them laughing together, and then making love. . . .

"The best thing of all," Nat was saying, "is that he has Marina under control. She hasn't taken so much as a Librax. But then with a lob like his, who'd need Librax?"

Thank God I won't have to see him, Elena thought. She was relieved to notice that Adam was rallying on the far side of the court with Kip. "I'm going inside," she said suddenly, determined to get Adam completely out of her sight. "You know I hate tennis."

"I'll come with you."

"That's hardly necessary. You want to play. Besides, I should say hello to Nancy."

"Don't bother. You won't find her. She left for the cottage. She's getting her kicks from Harvey Parkes." Occasionally, the most facetious remark by the most inventive gossip was true. "She went for a rubdown—the only 'down' she's ever gone for. Can you see the calluses Harvey will have on his hands from massaging that skeleton? Incidentally, darling, you can't imagine what Harvey said to me yesterday during our exercise. 'Now I have Dinah Shore. Who else is there for me to get?' When you found Harvey Parkes, Elena, you created a monster."

"God creates monsters. Women encourage them."

"That sounds like a tract by Nancy O'Brien. Although I agree. Men are pigs."

"Natalie, darling, sometimes so are women."

4

Lucy was a tennis voyeur in search of a plastic surgeon. She needed a rhinoplasty which, outside of medical textbooks and in Hollywood circles, was called a nose job. Doris, her chum, had a body that appeared to be, if not the prime exhibit for Anatomy I, constructed of polished mahogany.

"Look at that," said Pat Lukas to Jack Kaufman. "Most women have cellulite. She hasn't got a ripple on her."

"Who are they?" Jack asked. "I've never seen them before."

"You are naïve," said Pat, the TV scenarist who made it her business to know the scene. "They came through Grace St. George. They're hookers. Didn't you know that Grace has a stable, both male and female, of people who pay her ten dollars to get into Kip's weekend tennis meets? These are the latest. Grace got them in by telling Kip they were friends of Warren's. They've never set eyes on Warren Ambrose, but they're somebody's sandwich, that's for sure."

The notion intrigued Jack even more than the news about Grace's fiscally inventive pool of tennis groupies. The girls were carousing like children, ebony-ivory playmates, a mix one seldom saw in the parks surrounding Century City, where the Kaufmans lived. Their apartment, high up in one of twin towers, overlooked Fox on the west and Hillcrest, the *A* Jewish country club for the industry, to the south. That section, as well as the surrounding areas of Holmby, Beverly Hills, and Bel-Air, were not noted for integration, largely because they were too expensive for blacks. There were exceptions, of course, but they were either stars like Diana Ross, Bill Cosby, Sammy Davis, and Ella Fitzgerald, or millionaire music moguls like Berry Gordy.

Jack had noticed the black and white chessmates when

they arrived because they were young and pretty. They were wearing T-shirts and slacks, which they had taken off when they sat down by the Delft-tiled swimming pool; the pool was angled just above the players. The semi-striptease left Lucy naked above the waist. Doris kept on her strapless halter. Both girls wore short-shorts.

They were laughing raucously as they covered one another with Bain de Soleil. Jack watched Lucy kneel on the flagstone surrounding the pool to apply the lotion to her friend. His eyes were riveted to the full, round breasts that had clearly been sculpted by God or nature and not a cosmetic surgeon. They more than compensated for the single fault of the nose on the otherwise pleasing face. Lucy returned his stare with an impertinent wink before she lay down on her stomach and propped herself on her elbows, intentionally, Jack was certain, giving the crowd a profile view of one shiny, sunlit boob. She giggled as Doris held the aerosol can to her back and sprayed. "Ooooo, it's freezing," she said.

"Can I help?" Jack was tired of waiting for the tennis court. More importantly, he knew that Nat was preoccupied with Elena on the terrace above. Jack figured he had twenty minutes at least before his wife returned, and ten more before she showed any interest in where he was. After nine years of marriage, he was a pro at judging Nat's apostasies.

Doris, sitting astride her companion, gazed up at him in mock shyness. He admired her flawless complexion and the sleek umber legs that stretched across Lucy's body, pulling the short-shorts even higher on her upper thighs. "That's the best offer we've had today." She gave him the suntan oil, sprinted to the next chair, and lay down. "Lucy forgot my shoulders," Doris said. She hitched her thumbs inside her halter and lowered it to her midriff, exposing her acorn breasts. The nipples were gleaming black finials. My God, Jack thought, she's beautiful, his eyes tracking her body like a student of art.

"What's your name?" said Doris.

"Jack."

"I know you. Jack Kaufman. You're the director. I'm Doris, and this is Lucy, my girl friend."

"Are you an actress?" Jack used the euphemism consciously.

"I'm trying. So far I've only landed one TV commercial."

"Maybe I can help." Jack thought of Natalie then, and his voice was edgy. He had little time to lose. He noticed that a couple of tennis freaks were staring in their direction. "Listen, you both seem to want an even tan. Like no halters. There's a solarium below the court. How about it?"

Lucy still lay on her stomach, but Doris sat up and fingered the halter that circled her midriff. Jack looked over his shoulder. David Kellogg, who had come off the court, signaled approval, his thumb and forefinger forming a circle.

"Hmm," said Doris. "Copacetic. If Lucy agrees, that is. She's an extra, you know. She starts a movie tomorrow."

Lucy regarded him brashly. "You got a C-note?" she said. She might have been a society matron soliciting tickets for a charity ball.

Jack nodded. The thought of paying excited him. He had not done that since, at eighteen, he and a bunch of boys from Pittsburgh went to a whorehouse in McKeesport. That experience, with a portly prostitute named Emma, had been his initiation to sex.

"Okay," said Lucy. She pulled on her T-shirt, revealing unshaven armpits. Jack thought, incongruously, that Lucy would have turned Salvador Dali on. He remembered a review of the artist's autobiography. His first affair had been with his governess. Dali had been attracted to the patches of hair in her armpits.

Jack led them through the grove that concealed them from the tennis clique. He reached over the gate and unlatched the solarium. He had never used it before but Nancy, shortly after her marriage to Kip, had displayed it to him as the sole token of her occupancy. Nancy had not been permitted to change Kip's bachelor decor in any way, except to add the solarium. Its walls were decked with bougainvillaea, its floors were concrete, and two wooden benches with tables beside them completed the compound. A reflector and several beach towels were stacked on one of the benches. Nancy's only contribution to the Nathan house was ironic, Jack thought; neither he nor anyone else had ever seen her expose her face to the sun.

As Jack moved the benches together and spread the towels on the deck, he felt Lucy staring at him. He turned, and she brought her gaze up from his shapely legs and small-boned physique to his aquiline nose. He felt suddenly sorry for her. He hoped she would find the right plastic surgeon—perhaps with his C-note for a down payment.

Doris had started stripping, placing her halter on the far side of the deck. She was just about to remove her shorts when he stopped her. "Hey," he said. "Wait a minute."

"What's the matter?" Doris asked. "You queer or something? You want to drill us through our pants?"

"Not quite. I want to look at your slices, baby. I like the way the material crawls right into your basket. Isn't that why you buy your shorts too short? So a guy goes crazy seeing the flesh pushing out on either side? Seeing your creases, your butts, and your triangles? Does it tickle you, that cotton pushing into your little cunt? Does it give you a thrill when your panties rub you?"

"Well, sort of, sometimes," said Doris. " 'Specially when you talk dirty like that."

"A man can turn on when he rubs against something. Tell me, is a woman like that?"

"I just told you."

"I want to hear it. Say it."

"Yes. I love to have something rubbing me. Mostly a tongue, or a finger, or a prick. Is that what you want?"

"I'll show you what I want," he said. He reached down and felt her, sensing her hardened knob of clitoris through the thin cotton as her legs grew tense and her lips gripped his manicured fingers. Her hand covered his and held it there, between her legs, and she trembled.

"Are you wet, baby? Are you wet?"

"Oh, God," she said.

"Try me," said Lucy, moving in front of them, hips swaying, fingers and thumbs indenting her crotch. Her bulbous lips were elongated like a pear—a pear, Jack thought, with a gash through the center. These girls were pros. They caught on fast.

He turned his attention to Lucy; Doris emitted a groan as he freed himself on her hand and leg-lock. Pushing Lucy back so she leaned against the bench, Jack seized the fleshy, distended lips between his fingers and cinched them together, running his forefinger into her slash. He felt her lower legs stiffen. As he teased more briskly, her limbs became scissors-like, seizing and parting, propelled by his rhythms. He tried to get into her pants, but they were too tight, so he reached around, unzipping them, as she slipped her fingers into his tennis shorts, plying his testicles gently through his jockstrap. He slipped his hand upward, under her shorts, and explored her bush, which was thick and soft to the touch. He pulled at the longish hairs until Lucy let out a small cry.

"Be quiet," he said. His fingers crept into the crevice, which was tight as a virgin's. "Take off my clothes," he said, as he lowered Lucy's shorts. She stepped out of them, and it was Doris who knelt to unzip his fly as he removed his shirt. Lucy played with his rigid cock while he kissed her breasts and fondled them, one at a time. Suddenly Doris was grazing the small of his back with her own acorn breasts and moving her swollen mound seductively into his buttocks. His desire to suck the dense hairs that formed a black patch on Lucy's suntanned body was overwhelming. "Lie down," he told her, indicating the beach towels on the solarium floor. He knelt between her legs and tasted her slowly, rummaging through the dark forest into the begging flesh underneath.

Doris was kneeling behind him now, plying his testicles, licking his buttocks. His prick was surging, insurgent, demanding, as Doris' tongue went deeper, finding his anus, and circling the rim.

Lucy's muff was streaming with his saliva, her legs moving faster, her patch shifting upward until his tongue found its mark. He gnawed her, taking the speed from her motions, until she screamed out, and then was silent. "Christ," she said, "are you always that good?"

"To paraphrase someone, beauty is in the twat of the beholder." He flinched as he said it, ashamed of the silly response.

Doris was hugging him now from behind, her tongue tracing patterns on his neck, her hands tracing waves on his cock. "Now me," she said. "I want you to put it in." She had removed her shorts, and she circled him, brazenly naked, mounting the bench.

"My God," he said. She hadn't a hair on her shiny dark avocado mound. Doris coincided with Jack's image of whore. Since the night at McKeesport, he'd had the impression that prostitutes shaved their pussys ("Fancy women," his mother whispered, whenever they passed the hookers on Pittsburgh's Wylie Avenue). The nakedness served only to emphasize her slit: it gaped like the eye of a needle. Her baldness was as deliberate as the act of an exhibitionist. To Jack, it was tantalizing. "My God," he repeated.

"You like my body?" said Doris. She perched on the sunbench, legs dangling, arms outstretched.

"I like it. I like your pussy." He didn't move toward her then, but stared at it, mesmerized. His prick was hurting, palpitating, wanting to plug her; but Jack was immersed in his fantasy, his vision of cock convoluting inside the shorn cunt. He thought he understood the sexual deviates who favored pubescent girls. He settled into her arms and brushed the smooth shell with his tongue as she sat there. Then, parting the tawny lips, he buried his face in the aperture.

"That's nice," said Doris, "but wouldn't you like to put it in?"

"This Joe digs cunt," said Lucy, who was stroking her girl friend's breasts. Her voice conveyed excitement and envy. "I dig cunt, too."

"For a hundred dollars," Jack said, "I don't care what you dig. You've had your turn. This is mine."

Lucy, who had been kissing Doris full on the mouth, retreated. Jack lifted Doris' slender ebony legs and placed them on the bench. Then he mounted her, whispering hoarsely, "You want the dildo, baby? Okay. Only this is no dildo. It's real." She wrapped her legs around his shoulders, and he came almost instantly, not wanting to, wanting to prolong it. Lucy was kneeling behind him, thrusting her fingers into his anus. "Jeez," he told her, "if that's what bisexual means, I'll join you."

"Would you like to see what bisexual means?" asked Lucy. Jack wanted to. He had never observed two women making love. Once Natalie and her friends in Tijuana had tried to persuade him to visit a "circus," but he had refused. His adventures in sex had been more numerous than varied. In fact, he had never experienced sex as a "sandwich" before this afternoon. He had never slept with a black girl either, although he had never admitted to that among his male friends. They would have pronounced him a square.

"We're not performing, you understand," Lucy said.

"We're lovers." She stood at the end of the bench and thrust three fingers into Doris' crease—the crease, Jack observed complacently, that all had admired this afternoon but none had invaded, as he had just now. Doris reached up, her pectorals tightening, her acorn breasts pointing backward toward Lucy. She seized Lucy's mound and began massaging her tenderly. Lucy squirmed against her friend's fingers, shutting her eyes in ecstasy. Finally, she took Doris' hand and placed it at the tip of her mini-cock, emitting tiny squeals as her partner brought her to orgasm. Then Lucy lay down on the bench beside Doris, embracing her, sucking her breasts while fondling her lower parts with her hands and fingers until her companion's spasms told her that Doris was fulfilled.

"Do you understand that?" Lucy said, finally.

"Baby, I understand. We're a sandwich, you and Doris and me. Like an Oreo, only in reverse." He dressed, but not before getting their phone number. Then he headed for the bathhouse to shower.

"Where have you been?" asked Natalie sharply, as Jack rejoined the tennis habitués.

"I've been in Tijuana," he said.

"I'll bet you have," said Natalie.

There was no further grilling. Only the confident seek illumination.

The man who opened the Nathans' door to Elena that night was a stranger. He seemed obsolete in the modern setting, like Garbo at the Artists and Models Ball. He jarred with the modern chrome étagères and the bench mark touches, like the Mies coffee tables, which had been provided by the decorator. Elena, whose taste ran to heavy Old World antiques, had never liked them.

The man was not only dressed, he was overdressed. He wore a navy suit, a white shirt and a Countess Mara tie. Men who wore Countess Mara and safe blue suits to screenings along the Bel-Air Circuit were on precarious ground. The Nathans' guest suggested a parvenu who had mistaken a casual dinner for an audience at the Court of St. James.

He motioned her in with the hand that held his drink. The liquor was dark, and the rocks were few; Elena guessed Bourbon. "Peter's still making the hors d'oeuvres. I'm helping out," he said. He was tall with a thin salt-and-pepper mustache, his thick gray hair combed back from a broad, unbalding forehead. His eyes were heavily lidded and too small for his face.

"I'm early," Elena said. She knew it was rude to be early, but Randy had been in so surly a mood she had to escape him. During a brief exchange that afternoon, she hadn't dared tell him Kip might have a movie for him. Randy would have accused her of interfering with his non-existent career.

The stranger set his drink on the mirrored table and hung up her jacket. "Lovely," he said.

Elena took the compliment as intentionally ambiguous. Whatever else he might be, the man was courtly. She was fond of the jacket, which was a gift from her gangster-friend in Rome. He had ordered Furio, who was then his lieutenant, to take her to Balzani, the furrier, on the Via del Corso. Elena preferred a stone marten fingertip coat, but Furio agreed with the owner, Signore Balzani, that the lynx was more flattering to her Nordic complexion. Signore Balzani described it as "next year's fur." He proved to be correct. While marten declined in popularity, lynx became highly fashionable. Recently Duffy Edwards, of Beverly Hills' exclusive Edwards-Lowell, told Elena that lynx was the favorite fur to wear over pantsuits. His Establishment customers—Harriet Deutsch, Bea Korshak, Edie Wasserman, Muriel Slatkin—all had them. Even Dani Janssen, who was indifferent to furs ("Darling, she can afford to be, she has so many," Natalie said), had ordered a lynx to alternate with her red fox.

"I'm Reade Jamieson," said the substitute host, as they entered the den.

"Elena Brent."

"Well." The word conveyed recognition. "I should have known. Kip said you were coming."

She laughed the tinkling laugh that was a grade of flirtation. "What else did he say? Did he fill you in?"

"He didn't have to. I don't know movie stars, but I read the society columns. What will you have?"

"A vodka martini, very dry, if it's not too much trouble."

"That's my specialty." He tended the bar like an expert. "Someday," he said, "I'll make you a real martini. You have to freeze the vodka."

"Really?" Elena said, "I didn't know."

She and Randy kept vodka in the freezer, but she lied because mindlessness to her was a canon for enticing a man. She frequently affected ignorance on such small matters. Women, Elena believed, appealed to men in direct proportion to their vacuousness. The male had an overwhelming compulsion to teach, to mold what he regarded as "the weaker sex." If women were weaker, as legend, science, and the male ego had it, why did Prudential attest to the survival of the least fit? Women, Elena knew, led men in the actuarial tables. Reade Jamieson looked easier standing behind the bar, she reflected, than he would at the watering places of the people she knew. She couldn't imagine him dining at Orsini's, La Caravelle, or Grenouille. He displayed the servility and the arrogance of a rich man's butler, but little of style.

"To your health," he said, and handed her the martini. It was excellent, freezer or no. "We have mutual friends. Bill Paley speaks of you often. John Fairchild, of *Women's Wear*. Elsie Woodward. Judy and Hal Prince. Florence and Harold Rome. Donald Brooks. Tom Guinzberg. Bill Blass. Gloria Vanderbilt Cooper."

"How nice." Elena pegged him as a cube. Eastern socialites spoke of Mrs. Wyatt Cooper in private terms as "Gloria Cooper" or, professionally, as "Gloria Vanderbilt," but not by all three names. Vanderbilt was still in, but "Vanderbilt" used as a middle name was out. Elena had been right in her first assessment of Jamieson. He was on dubious ground. He was tense and unsure of himself, the kind of man who knows the forebears and progeny of everyone in the *Social Register,* the little-old-lady man who hopes his daughter will be tapped by the local Junior League. As a name-dropper, Reade was an untutored Suzy. "You must be a New Yorker," she said. She was angling for a locale. She didn't get it.

"Not quite, although I'm in New York a lot. I just got in two hours ago. I'm still on eastern time." He consulted his Pulsar watch. "Ten-thirty." She took a cigarette, and he lit it. "I'm boring you."

"Not at all." To Elena lies were a fundamental of casual talk. Candor was intolerable, an abandon of self. Randy and Nat, she thought. The showoffs were smartass. Strangers at parties were merely dull; regulars were the transgressors. The ultimate sinners in the corrupt confessionals of the New Hollywood were those who told the truth.

"I'm sorry," Kip said. "Long distance. Business. Nancy will be right out. She just washed her hair." Her hairdresser washed her hair, Elena thought. "I see you've met."

"Can I get you a drink?" asked Reade. He refilled his own.

"Peter will get it." Kip buzzed for his double scotch. "Elena, are you all right?"

She laughed. "You sound like a phonograph record lately. So do I. No, I'm not all right. Except with you."

Reade looked at them quizzically. He wondered whether they were having an affair.

"Relax," said Kip, who caught Reade's reaction. "We're just old friends. We love each other."

The man's ruddy face became ruddier. "I didn't think . . ." he said.

This man is a cube, Elena told herself again. She wondered about his origins. Probably, she decided, he was impoverished Old Society or a distant relation of Nancy's, not Kip's. Jamieson didn't sound like a Jewish name.

The others began to arrive, and she had to explain them to Reade. Anne and Kirk Douglas—Reade recognized Kirk—with Brenda Vaccaro, who had an off-again, on-again romance with Michael, their son. Michael had flown north that afternoon to film his series, "The Streets of San Francisco." Fran and Ray Stark and the Rosses, Nora and Herb, came together. The men were near-Siamese twins since *Funny Girl, Funny Lady,* and *Owl and the Pussycat,* Streisand's big hits. Ray produced; Herb choreographed or directed the movies. As Randy put it, "This is the only time Streisand brought people *together.*"

"Mrs. Ross looks familiar," said Reade. Elena told him that Nora Kaye was a prima ballerina before marrying Herb.

"Now I never knew that," Reade said, "and I'm very into the dance. I'm a sponsor of the Boston Ballet."

Ah, thought Elena, he has artistic pretensions.

Kip introduced him to Ann and Bill Dozier. "He produced 'Batman,' didn't he?" Reade said. "I loved that show. But who is she? Haven't I seen her before?"

"Her maiden name was Ann Rutherford." Just like Gloria Vanderbilt, who married a Cooper, Elena was tempted to add. She decided not to destroy the elation she saw on his face. The cube was clearly impressed by celebrities.

"Hey, thanks for getting me out of that early call tomorrow," Jack Nicholson grinned at Kip.

"Who's his girl?" asked Reade.

"Anjelica Huston. John Huston's daughter—he's the director," Elena said. Reade didn't know it, but he was wired into the best celebrity-spotter in town. Earl Blackwell, who founded the *Celebrity Register,* would have paid a fortune for Elena's counsel.

"There's nothing like being invited to your boss's house for dinner." Jack was starring in Pacific's Big Movie for 1976. He was much in demand after *Chinatown* and *One Flew Over the Cuckoo's Nest;* he was what the industry called "hot" and what Kip Nathan called "torch-time."

Jack had refused Kip's invitation because he had a 6 A.M. call the next day at Pacific.

"Not to worry," Kip told him. "They'll shoot around you. How does one o'clock hit you?"

"It hits me just fine."

Elena was not surprised when Nicholson's friend Warren Beatty entered. Kip was sure to produce at least a pair of the "torchiest" men on the Hollywood scene for Rex Reed and Clare Ballen, who were two of the most influential writers on that scene. Warren's magnetism, both on and offscreen, might begin and end any history of the New Hollywood. The stories about him were legion. Women followed him in their cars when he prowled the Sunset Strip looking for quarry; Warren stopped his Mercedes 450 SLC to pick up any girl who caught his eye. Rex Reed had started the legend by writing an unsympathetic profile of Warren.

"Doesn't Kip know Rex and Warren don't get along?" Anne Douglas asked Elena.

"Darling," Elena said, "it's all right. If Warren accepted a party for Rex, you know he'll act like a gentleman."

Anne was not so sure. With Warren, you never could tell. He was baldly frank, if clever, and above all a desirable guest because he was fluent in the murky protocol of the New Hollywood. He knew how to enliven a lackluster conversation or mood, sometimes tactfully, sometimes not. He was as proficient at charming older, formidable women—for example, a civic leader like Mrs. Norman Chandler—as he was at attacking Henry Kissinger for the Nixon policy on Vietnam. Warren had done just that at a dinner Anne and Kirk gave Kissinger at Hollywood's St. Germain. The other guests, nine of them plus Warren's date, Julie Christie, had listened in horror and fascination. The Douglases were the first people to introduce the Secretary of State, who was then the National Security Advisor, to Hollywood—and to Jill St. John. As the wife of an actor and a close friend of Warren's, Anne was shrewd enough to suspect that Beatty had not forgiven Rex Reed for the portrait. The cliché was authentic: actors tend to forget their good notices, but they memorize every line of the bad ones.

"Who is the pretty girl with Warren Beatty?" Reade asked.

"*His* girl, Michelle Phillips," Elena said.

"I thought he lived with Julie Christie."

"Darling, he's lived with anyone you can name. That was years ago. Warren is, how do you say it? Warren is agile. Still, he stays with his mistresses longer than other men stay with their wives." It was then that Elena saw Adam. He was talking to Nancy. He nodded, and Elena smiled back. Her eyes scanned the room for Marina. She was nowhere in sight. I suppose, Elena thought, with a shudder, she is making out with someone in the bathroom. She took a quick count: there were an equal number of men and women without Marina. Elena remembered Natalie's bulletin during the tennis matches: "My dear, they haven't been out of bed until today." Apparently, Adam was taking a Sunday off.

"Where the hell are the guests of honor?" Kip asked, in his cognac voice. When Kip gave a party, he wanted his guests to arrive on time. He allotted thirty minutes before dinner. Anyone who came late was offered a drink, which was seized by Peter after a sip or two. You had to know your houses and hosts. The Wassermans allowed an hour for drinks with the tacit demand that people be prompt. The Ambroses and the Kaufmans worked on a different schedule. They expected their guests to be late. If one arrived at the appointed hour, he was told that Warren and Alice were taking their evening swim, or that Jack and Natalie were out on an errand.

"Darling, you know Rex is always late," said Elena. "I spoke to him earlier. He and Clare were on their way to Kay Gable's."

"Kay Gable's? She's having a hundred and fifty people. And I'm giving *them* a small dinner. They'll never get away."

"They'll get away. Kay's is tented, yes. But Rex said they're just stopping off. You know what he's like when he gets to a party. He's constantly on the way out, but then Loretta Young arrives and he has to talk to her. He hands the parker his ticket, and Irene Dunne drives up in a limousine. So he has to kiss her and say hello."

"He should say goodbye," Kip said. "Peter is coping with eighteen ducks in the kitchen. *A l'orange*. The *orange* is charcoal. They have to be timed."

"So buy him a timer," quipped Nora Ross.

"Buy Rex a time bomb." Warren Beatty grinned, exposing the Ultra-Brite teeth.

"Listen, Warren, you said you'd behave," said Kip.

"But what else?" Warren said. "Don't I always behave? I'm the perfect gentleman."

"Have you heard the latest story that's going around because of *Shampoo?*" asked Herb Ross. "I overheard a group of teenage girls discussing whether more Hollywood beauties were blonde or brunette. The oldest girl said, 'Only Warren Beatty knows for sure.' "

"That's for sure," said Michelle. "But I'm not sure that crack has anything to do with the movie." She and Warren exchanged fond smiles.

Kip took Adam aside. "We won a thousand on that match today. Half is yours. You earned it. How would you like to be my regular partner? You must have trained at Wimbledon."

"Only off-season. I'm still ranked below amateur."

"Below amateur, seeded Number One."

"Number One is a lesson. After a couple of lucrative matches like that, no one would take us on," said Adam. "How would you like to win with me on the opposite side of the court?"

"I don't understand."

"I'll teach you, baby. You play against me. You play with someone else, but we have signals. Get it? I scratch my leg, I'm going to lob. I adjust my sunglasses, it's a drop shot."

"Where did you learn that action?"

"I've been around," Adam said.

"I'll bet you have," said Nancy. "Kip, the prodigal people are here."

"I'm sorry we're late," said Rex. "But as we were leaving, everyone started arriving, at least the nine hundred who weren't there already. Irene Dunne." Elena and Kip laughed softly. "What's so funny?" Rex asked.

"She got it on the nose," Kip replied. "She guessed Irene Dunne." Both Kip and Elena knew Rex's propensity for older, Golden Age actresses.

"Do you know who was there?" Rex said. "Richard Harris. That slob Richard Harris. I wanted to hit him."

Elena smiled. She knew that Harris had been abusive to

Rex at Jennifer Selznick's because of a vicious review of one of his movies. "Did you hit him, darling?" she said.

"I avoided him. That's why I hate big parties. You can't imagine what it's like to walk into a room and not know who's going to hit you."

"Who can't?" said Clare. She was older than Rex, but still in her thirties, younger than most accredited journalists. She wore her long brown hair in a flip. "I could write a book." She had already written two children's books and had been listed, at twenty-eight, in *Who's Who of American Women.*

"You must mean Guy Green," said Kirk. His eyes sparkled, as only Kirk Douglas' eyes could sparkle.

"Yes indeed. There's mean Guy Green," Clare said.

Kirk was referring to a series of columns in which Ballen revealed the hostilities on the set of Kirk's and Brenda's movie, *Once Is Not Enough.* The actors couldn't stand the English director. When Clare refused to have lunch with Green, he called most of the stars and asked them to refute her accusations against him. The most publicized offense was Green's suggestion that Kirk use makeup to erase the dimple on his chin. When Green asked Brenda to say Clare's columns were false, she phoned Kirk. "What shall I do?" she said. "Do nothing," Douglas advised. "What she's writing is true. He's a prick."

"You know about Howard Koch's party?" Clare asked.

"He told me, but tell the others," said Kirk.

"As a preface, Green called me insisting he knew my sources were Jackie and Irving Mansfield. 'I know they're friends of yours,' he said. 'Mr. Green,' I told him, 'my friends on that movie are Robert Evans, Howard Koch, Kirk Douglas, David Janssen, Brenda Vaccaro, Alexis Smith, Deborah Raffin, Melina Mercouri, George Hamilton, and the Mansfields. You figure it out.' Then Howard decided to give this engagement party for Deborah and Michael Viner. I told him I wouldn't come if Green was there. Howard promised Green wouldn't bother me. I took Ross Claiborne, my publisher, as an escort—or should I say bodyguard? He's tall and very supportive. The poor man didn't know what he was getting into. No sooner had we stepped inside the door than someone came up and said, 'Miss Ballen, this is Mr. Green. He asked to meet you.'"

"What happened?" said Ray Stark.

"Not much. He just smiled and said I was wrong, that the producer and all the actors loved him. But I seem to have done him a favor. One of Green's people told me later that before *Enough* Green couldn't get work, but since my columns appeared, he'd been offered a dozen scripts."

"Proving," Rex said, alluding to the title of one of his books, "that people are crazy here."

"On the theory, Rex, you're familiar with," said Warren. "Publicity, even bad publicity, is better than none."

"Let's be friends," Rex said to Warren.

"We are friends," said Warren, clearing the tension for all except Rex.

"Dinner is served," said Peter.

"May I take my drink to the table?" asked Rex. "I need it."

Elena sat between Kip and Adam at dinner. She tried to focus her attention on Kip, but Adam would not allow it. He directed his conversation to her, and kept repeating, "We must have lunch, Elena. I have to know what's bothering you."

"I have no doubt you'll explain it away, whatever it is," she said, coldly. Then, "How is Marina? Why isn't she here?"

"It could be I didn't ask her. It happens to be, Elena—"

She turned away. She heard Reade, across the table, telling Ann Dozier how much he admired her as Andy Hardy's best girl.

"Do you know," Clare Ballen said, saving the moment for everyone, "what the latest game is?" The table fell silent. "It's called Who Do You Like the Best? You take two terrible people, like Ford and Reagan, and try to decide between them."

"They're not so terrible," Kip said. He was, like his tennis friends Robert Evans and Richard Zanuck, a Republican.

"They're terrible," Nancy said, from the other end of the table. The Lady Crusader was a militant Democrat. Kip suspected that if she had not been when she married him, she would have become one. In Hollywood, bedfellows make strange politics.

"I like that," said Brenda. "Hmm, let's see. Haldeman and Ehrlichman. Who do you like best?"

"Mark Spitz and Norman Brokaw," said Nancy. There was general laughter. Brokaw was Spitz' agent.

"I don't get it," said Reade.

"Blake Edwards and Julie Andrews," said Rex.

"Tony Curtis and Penny," Clare added. "Oh, excuse me, all. Tony Curtis and Leslie. Since she became Mrs. Curtis, she's changed her name to Leslie."

"How fitting," Kip said.

"I know another game," Rex said, plaintively. "Dart boards with faces on them. It's all the thing in New York. Somebody told me Otto Preminger has my photograph on his dart board."

"Considering what you've written about him, you really can't blame him," Bill Dozier said. "Annie, whose face shall we put on our dart board?"

"I have a few ideas," she replied. "We could start with your ten former wives. But we'd need like a thousand dart boards." Bill enjoyed the joke as much as anyone. Reade simply looked baffled.

"My favorite game," said Fran Stark, "is Who Has Class?"

"I couldn't tell you," Reade said, "unless I saw their houses and furniture and the way they entertained."

"That's precisely *not* the point," said Fran. "That is style, which has nothing to do with class."

"I don't see how you can say who has class without knowing how they live," Reade insisted.

"Audrey Hepburn has class," said Nancy. For once you are right, thought Kip.

"Cary Grant," said Clare.

"But not Tony Curtis," said Rex. They laughed.

"Gary Cooper had class," Elena said. "But not Bogart. Bogey had style. A lot of people have style. Very few have class." She was testing the cube, and it worked.

"I don't see how you can say that. You're expressing opinions. Maybe Bogart had class."

"Yes. Maybe he had an excellent houseman," Rex said, sarcastically. "Now, Betty Bacall has class."

"I'll second that one," said Adam.

"I've never been in Miss Bacall's home," Reade said.

Now he'd done it. All eyes turned to Rex, expectantly. "Betty lives in *my* house, The Dakota," he said. "You can take it from me, The Dakota has class. But we're talking about people, not apartment buildings." My God, Rex thought, I bet this joker doesn't even know that Bacall was married to Bogart.

Kip swallowed a Percodan surreptitiously, with his wine. "Why don't we go to the screening room for coffee?" he said. It seemed the only way out.

"My God," said Rex, "has Kip gone stark raving mad? Why do you suppose he would show us such a disaster? We're members of the press, after all." He was speaking to Clare in Elena's den. They had driven her home. She had walked the three blocks to the Nathans' rather than tangle with Randy by asking if he was planning to use the Mercedes.

Elena went upstairs to check on whether Randy was still awake. He was, but he refused to come down. He was watching "The Tonight Show." "That bastard," he said of Johnny Carson. "He's always on vacation. Guest hosts." Randy was plainly drunk. "Go enjoy yourself, my dear, with your personal Fourth Estate. The Elena Brent Press Conference. I'm surprised you haven't got Johnny here too, since he's not on TV."

"What do you think, Elena?" Rex asked. "Could Kip possibly believe that army-of-ants thing is good?" He gave her a brandy.

"Darling, you heard him say so before and after."

"Well, everyone contradicted the man straight after," said Clare. "I mean, no one liked it. No one even pretended to. That's a Hollywood first." People normally feigned approval in front of the moviemaker. "It's all up there on the screen," "You've done it again," and "Intriguing" were more than clichés. They were symptoms of etiquette. Kip had watched the film painfully from the hospital bed he kept in his screening room; he had another bed at Pacific, from which he viewed the dailies.

"The entire night was a farce," Rex said. "I mean, the idea of a bunch of grotesque cartoon ants taking over the world."

"They weren't cartoons," said Clare. "They were real. Kip said they spent two years shooting the movie."

"So much for the cinematographer," Rex said. "He should go back to Disney. And everybody was talking during the movie. I mean, the ants had eaten through everything, through the grass and the cattle and then they were eating their way through the buildings. And didn't you love Nora Ross's remark? She said, 'What do they want?' and Ray Stark called out, 'They want the final cut.' Anne Douglas was so bored she went out and walked around the pool in the rain. When she came back after the movie, she was soaked. Nancy broke out the pot and got stoned. Kip was furious at her. And all I could hear was Jack Nicholson snoring and Elena slapping that fellow Baker's hand." Elena blushed. "Who is he, Elena? In addition to being a sex maniac? I mean he proved that with Marina by staging the Main Event at your party. Everyone knows she's been knocked up more than George Foreman. She's a nympho."

"Dear Rex. And everyone knows I'm not. That's true. So Adam kept trying to hold my hand. That's all." She didn't want to talk about Adam, not to anyone, certainly not to Rex, who knew too much about her misery with Randy.

"I must say you were hilarious, Elena," Clare said. "You chain-smoked like nothing I've ever seen. A cigarette after every slap."

She laughed. "What better way to avoid holding hands than to smoke? A cigarette is a weapon."

"A deadly one, according to the Surgeon General," said Rex, lighting up.

"I find Mr. Baker very attractive," said Clare. "I might even give up smoking if he made a pass at me." She was a trained reporter who served her apprenticeship at *Newsweek* before she joined the *Chronicle,* but she was fishing for gossip, Elena knew. People loved to read gossip even more than they loved to practice it.

"So maybe the picture scared him. Maybe the ants made him nervous," said Elena. The others laughed.

"They made me nervous, for Kip," said Clare. "I advised him not to release it."

"What did he say?" asked Rex.

"He said the wires were out on both coasts for press screenings, but he was very serious. He said he'd consider recalling them. He was stricken, I think, by tonight's reaction."

"I can see the review, a one-liner," said Rex. "The kindest thing to be said about *Community Future* is that it has no future."

"You'd write that, wouldn't you?" Elena said. She was wondering what else her friends in the press had observed that night. At one point, Adam put his hand on her knee and slid his arm around her shoulders. She ducked on the couch, so as not to be seen, and extracted herself. Adam offered to drive her home, not knowing she had no transportation: "You can leave you car here. I'll have it returned in the morning." By whom—Marina?—she thought.

"They could retitle that bomb *Up the Sandbox,*" Clare said. "And let Streisand go after them as she did after me."

"Now that's a story for The Actors Charm School," Rex said. "Tell Elena."

"It also belongs to The Agents Charm School. Sue Mengers was involved."

"What is it with Mengers?" Rex said.

"Can't you tell by her clients? Show me a conniving agent, I'll show you her list of seedy clients. Like goes to like."

"But you made her famous," said Rex. "Nobody ever heard of her until you printed her name."

"So much for my disservice to mankind," Clare said.

"Can you name any agents you like?" Elena smiled. She recalled the game of Who Do You Like the Best?, the one they had played at dinner.

"Of course," said Clare.

"Name one," Elena said.

"Phil Gersh," said Clare. "George Chasin. John Gaines. There. I've given you three."

"There are three?" said Rex.

"There are more. At any rate, *Up the Sandbox* was Streisand's dramatic debut. Sue called and asked me to see it. I wasn't keen to see it. I'd had enough trouble with Streisand already. My rule is simple: if someone's a pain in the ass and wants to be mentioned in your column, don't mention them. If someone's a pain in the ass and doesn't want to be mentioned, mention them constantly."

"I just don't understand actors," said Rex. "You've never written anything bad about Streisand professionally. Not even when she's been lousy."

"That's the irony of it. I've been her biggest booster since she walked on the stage, for two minutes, in *I Can Get It For You Wholesale.* I even told Sinatra to listen to her records. He did, and he sat all the way through *Funny*

Girl—the play, not the movie—and went backstage to congratulate her. Sinatra doesn't go backstage."

"Sinatra doesn't go anywhere," Rex said. "Not for me, he doesn't. I don't understand your loyalty to creeps like him," said Rex, "but I guess that's why we love you, Clare. For your loyalty." Rex was constantly feuding with Sinatra. "Elena, did you read the piece Clare wrote for *New York* magazine on Streisand's shenanigans during the filming of *Funny Girl?*"

"No."

"It was fascinating. Every word was accurate. But Streisand called a meeting, and talked about suing Clare."

"She wouldn't have gotten far," Clare said. "I had my sources—witnesses."

"What about *Up the Sandbox?*" Elena asked.

"I finally saw it at a private screening. Mengers called me at eight o'clock the next morning to ask how I liked it. I said I hated it. 'How did you like Barbra?' she said. I told her Barbra was very good, but I didn't know why she'd chosen such a pretentious piece of junk. Sue asked me to print that Barbra was good. I explained I couldn't do that without saying I hated the movie. 'Just say Barbra was excellent.' I did. I went to Sue's for dinner the day the story appeared. La Streisand was there, of course, with her usual poise and presence. Her date was Ryan O'Neal, as I recall. That was before he switched to his daughter Tatum. At any rate, did Barbra thank me for saying she was good? She attacked me. 'Why did you say *Up the Sandbox* was awful?' she asked. I told her it wasn't that simple, not as simple as 'awful.' I didn't tell her I'd never use the word 'awful' in a critique, because it means 'full of awe.' Who can expect a jawbreaker to be an etymologist?"

"There you have it," said Rex. "I hate actors. There's no way to please them."

"Why try?" Clare said. "We're the worst, though. Writers. People think actors are hams, but writers are the authentic hams."

"Okay," Rex said. "But have you ever heard a reader remark, 'Gee, Julie Andrews is dull'? They say, 'Gee, Clare Ballen's a boring writer.' We break our backs trying to make these slobs interesting."

"I admit I don't know another profession in which they want it all ways. If you love their work, they want you to love them as people. If you love them as people, they want you to love all their work. Art Buchwald writes three times a week. He doesn't expect his friends, or strangers, to like every column he writes. He's terrific. If he hits in two out of five, he's a genius. Erich Remarque once asked me, 'Why do critics treat writers like athletes? They expect us to top our track record every time out.' Remarque was thirty-two when his first novel, *All Quiet on the Western Front,* came out. Margaret Mitchell was thirty-six when *Gone With the Wind* was published. She spent ten years writing it. If the critics are right, Margaret Mitchell was smart to retire. If you believe the critics, Remarque and O'Hara, the brilliant O'Hara, not to mention Faulkner and Hemingway, were wrong. They should have quit on one book."

"You can't compare writers to actors," Rex said. "Actors work by emotion. Writers work by intellect."

"I spent a summer in Westport as an apprentice. I have to agree," said Clare. "One of the plays they did was *Seagulls Over Sorrento.* It ran for thousands of years in London. I told an actor, one of the leads, that his sadomasochistic portrayal was wonderful. All he did was stare at me. Then he said, 'Do I look like a masochist?' He hadn't intellectualized; he was performing by instinct. Suddenly, his performance changed. Charles Bowden, the producer, was a partner in the Playhouse with the Langners. When I told him what I'd done, he was furious. 'Don't you know acting is instinctive?' he said. 'The worst thing you can do to an actor is make him self-conscious by telling him how he's coming across.' *Seagulls* opened on Broadway that fall with that actor and much the same cast. It closed after twelve performances."

"Who was the actor?" Elena asked.

"You know him, Elena. He stars a lot on television," said Clare, "and I'm sure he doesn't remember the incident himself. So I'd rather not give you his name."

"No sources. Okay," she said. She did not say that, from her knowledge of Randy, she agreed about actors. Instead, she said, "You're both being rough on actors."

Generically, show business people and journalists were at odds. Performers dealt in fantasy, reporters in fact. That is, by definition. When the two became confused, there were problems. Writers became inaccurate and actors egomaniacal. Celebrities were as generous to their fellows as they were intolerable to the press. Actors, producers, directors, and scenarists paid a publicist regularly to exploit them, then complained to newsmen that they were being exploited. On occasion, of course, that was true. There were good and bad in both brotherhoods. The consumer, like the insider, was quick enough to spot hypocrisy in either field. Hollywood legend had it that no one could fool the camera. The same was true of reporting; no one could fool with the written word. Those who lasted and those who plummeted, not through petty jealousies, but through the eyes and the minds of the viewer or reader, proved that. No one could fool the linotype, the camera, or the American public.

"There are exceptions," Elena said.

"The exception is all that counts," said Clare. "You know them as well as I do. Better. I couldn't exist as a Hollywood columnist unless there were the exceptions. In general, the Superstars are exceptional."

"Obviously. That's why they're Superstars," said Elena.

"I might add," said Rex, "that this is not an apologia for producers, directors, screenwriters, and all the rest."

"You know our friends there," Clare said. "With exceptions. I like Otto Preminger, even if he has your face on his dart board."

"You even liked *Airport,*" said Rex.

"Along with two hundred million other Americans," she countered. "But I forgive you, darling, because you liked *Bite the Bullet* as much as I did."

"Not to change the subject," said Elena, "but I have a question. Who was that man Reade Jamieson? What does he do?"

"He counts money," said Rex. "*His* money. Kip told me he's one of those guys who invented computers in Cambridge. Kip met him through Victor Kroll. He can get through to everyone from the cheapest hood to the President. He's so loaded with green he sags like a fern."

"But he doesn't know The Dakota."

"He doesn't know *Rosemary's Baby*. Or Mia Farrow. He does know the Burbank Airport. Kip said he arrived in his private jet today. By the way, he was very attracted to you. Are you interested?" Good old Rex. The one and only original swordblade mind.

Elena thought a moment. "There's one thing that interests me, that could even excite me—"

"His money?" Clare said.

"His power," Elena said. "What woman isn't excited by power?" Elena thought of Randy, of his weakness and his dependence upon her; she wondered, briefly, what Reade Jamieson would be like as a husband.

The telephone rang. It was Adam. "I have some people here," she said. "Can you call me tomorrow?"

"Will you talk to me tomorrow?"

"Certainly."

"I consider that statement binding. I'll hold you to it."

Before she rang off, she heard a click. She guessed it was Randy, hanging up. Later, when her guests had left and she'd gone upstairs, she noticed that Randy's light was still burning. She slipped quietly into her room, switched off the lamps and undressed in the dark. She did not need another confrontation. What she needed was out, and fast.

6

The sun was a blinding flash on the horizon, tracked by its own reflection, a path of golden light on the seacaps that resembled the ribbon on a mallard's neck. The bathers had all but deserted the beach. Elena was restless. She tossed a half-smoked cigarette into the sand beyond the terrace and watched it, compulsively, to be sure it went out. Then she turned her attention to a covey of sandpipers pecking away for insects at the water's edge. Their skill at tracking never ceased to amaze her.

She was lighting another cigarette when the doorbell rang. Adam. He was wearing the custom-made jacket and denim pants that Dick Dorso sold for $155 and his printed shirt was unbuttoned far enough to reveal the flat firmness of his chest. He carried an envelope attaché case. "Didn't you bring a sweater?" she said. "It gets chilly."

"It's in the car. I'll get it later." He kissed her fraternally on the cheek. "Hey, this is super."

"But wait until you see the wallpaper in the kitchen. I hate it. Natalie went too far. This is the only place she ever decorated. Their apartment in town was a model. They bought it furnished, right down to the ashtrays."

"Hideous ashtrays, as I recall. What I like about this is the informality." Adam was examining the photos of Jack Kaufman with the stars of his series and specials. They were mixed in with some framed TV awards on the wall behind the Ping-Pong table. "Do you play?" he said, picking up one of the paddles.

"A little. Not well enough to admit it."

"You don't like to lose at anything, do you? Neither do I. That's the book," he said, indicating the Vuitton envelope.

"How is it?"

"It needs work. Kip sees it as campy. I want to do it straight, as a thriller. With comedy situations, but sardonic. A kind of updated *Laura.* Randy's part is the best one in it, the killer, the Waldo Lydecker-Clifton Webb type."

"I like that. Who's writing the screenplay?"

"Pat Lukas. She's never done a movie before, but she's good."

"And besides, she's become a close friend of Nancy's."

He laughed. "Now, where do you get your information? You've been out here for weeks."

"From Natalie. Don't you know the saying, that there are only three wire services in Hollywood—UPI, AP, and N.K.—for Natalie Kaufman."

"And where does Natalie get her information?"

"Darling, she spends all day on the phone. First thing in the morning she calls every doctor to find out who's sick and who isn't: internists, gynecologists, proctologists, surgeons. She knows what millionaire's son is on coke, and who's pushing it. She knows the size diaphragm every woman wears, and who's having a hysterectomy."

"Now that's useful. You mean she knows the dimensions of every doll's snatch?"

"Adam, don't be disgusting."

"I thought I was being practical." He smiled the half-smile which always disconcerted her. "Okay, I'll be charming. Shall I light the fire?"

"Please. I'm not used to the jets. They frighten me."

He showed her how to do it, lighting one of the barbecue matches and placing it on the logs, then turning the key for the gas. She went into the kitchen for the snacks she'd prepared, raw vegetables and Fritos with California dip, which was made with Lipton's Onion Soup mix and sour cream. The dip was a shortcut Jane Scott had taught her. Elena, who hated cooking, was always on the lookout for shortcuts, especially when they came from the wives of reporters who were flattered when you asked for a recipe. Jane was married to Vernon Scott. "I see what you mean about the wallpaper," Adam said. "It's garish, to say the least."

"If you want a drink, there's some vodka in the freezer."

"How about one of my special vodka martinis?"

"You, too?" Elena said. Reade Jamieson's "special martini" had come to mind. She saw the bewilderment on his face. "I mean, everyone seems to make a special martini.

That funny man at Kip's screening who kept tending the bar—"

"He was tending *you,* I noticed. I hated him. I was jealous. You didn't like him?"

"Darling, what was there not to like? He was bland but agreeable."

They watched the sunset together from the deck that led to the beach. The sailboats were gone, and a single fishing boat remained. One man, standing up, had on a red sweater that matched precisely the flaming rays that hovered on the horizon. The wind came up, and Elena shuddered. Adam put his arm around her. "Let's go inside," he said.

They sat by the fire. "Kip's trying us out for the Waller movie—me, Randy, and Jack. This B picture's a screen test for all of us for *Gallery*. Some tryout. I have a twenty-eight-day schedule. My God, that's like a TV movie. Based on a five-day week, that's less than six weeks. Besides, I'm working against a skimpy budget on a stylized mystery whose characters aren't well-drawn. Except, as I said, for Randy's."

"He's got to make it," she said, then added, "You all have to make it."

"Elena, you're not happy with Randy, are you?"

His directness brought tears to her eyes. "That's private," she said.

"Nothing is private, because I love you." She was sobbing. He drew her to him. "That's right, my beautiful darling, cry. I love you all the more for your vulnerability."

She didn't know how long she lay there, her head face down on his lap, on the floor, aware of the knot beneath her, between his legs, that dilated into an arch and then became straight and solid, a pillar. She was deeply affected by his constraint; he made no sexual move, despite his erection. His fingers were gentle, stroking her hair and her back, then strong, as he plied the muscles connecting the neck and the spine. "My darling, you're so tense," he whispered. At last she sat up. He kissed her tenderly, almost reverently, on the mouth. This can't be the man, she thought, of The Bistro and sauna scenes. He's somebody else.

Adam offered her drink. "Take a sip. It's all water now. I'll refresh it."

She followed him into the kitchen and kissed him. "You're very kind," she said.

He took her into his arms. "Not kind. Don't ever mistake me. I'm in love." This time, when their lips came together, Elena's tongue sought Adam's. His response sent tremors of desire through her. They clung to each other hungrily, unashamedly, and mounted the stairs to the bedroom, arm in arm.

He was a prodigious lover, imposing and tender, consuming and being consumed, exerting and exciting her to exertion, investing the act with a reciprocity she had never known.

When they finished Elena lay motionless, staring through the big picture window into the lavender dusk. She remained silent even as Adam, lying beside her, quietly called her name. Her body, the body whose every sense had minutes before come alive, was numb. Her mind was charged with dizzying thoughts—or should she call them fears? Her initial reaction to their lovemaking, physical as it had been, was born of emotion. I must not fall in love with this man, she kept telling herself. *I must not love him.* Elena recalled the thrill when Adam had spoken both those phrases to her that evening, but she was no student of semantics. She was ignorant of the distinction between the terms. It didn't occur to her, until much later, that the two expressions might be a once-in-a-lifetime coincidence, justifying the miracle that had transpired.

When she went to bed with Adam, the Devil's Advocate in her argued that Randy would approve—he had told her to find a lover. She would never tell Randy about the affair. Although they hadn't had sex together for over a year, she knew that he would feel hurt and demeaned. It was not a question of pride, but of possession. From the beginning Randy behaved as though he owned her. He didn't share their life; he supervised hers. He mocked her telephone calls, but he memorized them. He chided her seating lists, but he was gratified by them, as he was with her social success.

If Randy had no sexual appetite for her, he made that clear from the outset. "You're my match," he had said. "Would you like to be my partner?" He understood that sex and love were not in her part of the contract, either.

Measure for measure resulted in a makeshift ethic for them. Elena and Randy were subterfuges, not sparks, for one another's image. If Randy wanted a cover for his homosexuality, Elena wanted a jacket for her autobiography. Randy used her as a front, but she had been using him as a frontispiece.

Adam nuzzled close, his head on her pillow. When she didn't react, he got up and went to the bathroom. Elena was conscious that she did not want to wash. Always before, she had jumped out of bed to clean herself, or bathe, or take a douche. She'd been trained by her Italian gangster-friend to bring back a damp towel; he'd told her he didn't want to soil the bed or the floor. Tonight, Elena relished the smell of Adam's body on hers. She kept recalling the warmth of his emission and the emission he had aroused inside her. She savored the taste of his semen: she was amazed by its purity. Adam had the clean, unmuddled taste of white wine. The flavor varied with every man she had known, but the mean equation was always there, the slight or assaulting sting of bubbles, like ale or charged water. Elena disliked both beer and champagne. She preferred still wine. John Updike had written once, God knows how or why (Perhaps for alliteration? Elena thought) that semen tastes like seaweed. Updike, Elena figured, had gotten his information secondhand. Maybe Updike tasted like seaweed. Adam tasted like vintage Bordeaux, with gardenias.

He returned to bed and she went to the bathroom, but still she neither washed nor brushed her teeth. When she came back to the bedroom, she found him asleep. Elena walked to the window and lit a cigarette. As she gazed at the moonlit waters, she felt his presence behind her—his presence, a force that impelled her like the vortex in the pounding surf beyond. I must not touch him, she thought. I must not let his body touch mine again. I must not reveal the emotions his passion and tenderness raised in me. I understand this man. He's a pirate. He wants to use my friends, my entree, to get his movie produced. He'll do anything—he'll try professions of love, bald sex, crooked tennis (Natalie had clued her in on that)—or Marina. Marina. Adam was screwing Marina, as Natalie put it, because he needed a star for his picture. The notion of Adam and Marina enraged Elena. Natalie said they had broken up the night of Kip's screening. So did Adam. But had they? Fantasies, Elena reflected, were futile. They were, as her friend Capote might put it, un-answered prayers.

She decided to make their dinner. That was, after all, the reason she had invited Adam to Malibu. She would finish the partially cooked lasagna according to Furio's instructions—he had prepared it for them the night before. She would feed Adam, and he would leave.

Elena scooped up her clothes from the chair as she went to the guest room. She did not shower before she dressed, as she had intended to do.

"How do they get my phone number at the beach?" asked Elena, annoyed.

"In one well-chosen word, I'd say Natalie," Adam said. "Hopper and Parsons and Winchell are gone. The only gossip line, from what you told me last night, is the telephone." He was finishing breakfast. Thank God, she thought, for freshly bottled orange juice, Kellogg's Special K, boiled water, timers, eggs, and toasters.

"You catch on fast," she said. "You're fast at all the right things. And slow, to perfection, at others."

"Then you liked it?" he said.

She blushed. "I liked it, yes. All three times. I didn't get any sleep."

"My intention was not to let you sleep. Who was calling?"

"It was Barbara Walters, from New York. She's heard about the picture. I didn't know what to say. I told her to check with you. I can never lie to the press. Why hasn't Kip told Randy about it?"

"Kip just flew back last night from Acapulco. God knows he needed the rest."

"Did Nancy go?"

"Naturally not. Nancy is why he needed the rest. She's a harridan."

Elena poured more coffee for them. "Darling, you don't like Nancy?"

"I don't like women whose freckles represent chicken pox. Nancy is communicable. A disease. She belongs in the isolation ward at Cedars."

"You know," said Elena, "I never thanked you for telling me first. I mean about *Overwrought*. Even Kip didn't call me till later that day."

"He couldn't. He had to know Cohen approved Randy."

"Cohen has approved, hasn't he, Adam? I mean, I just couldn't stand it, after all this, if anyone else got the part." Elena regressed to the dubious foreign accent in moments of agitation. Her elocution was the cue card to her anxiety.

"My love, *mein Schweinehund*, you are a worrier."

"Everybody with an IQ over ten is a worrier," said Elena. "You asked me about my marriage. I'll tell you. Randy has got to get this part. He's got to pull himself together. I say that selfishly, Adam. It's for my sake, as well as his. I can't stay on, and I can't abandon him until he's a hit. Do you understand?"

"Not at all. I think you've been brainwashed by Americans. The great American credo. Failure. Success. That's all they care about. Americans think. Europeans act. They don't give a damn about money or power. They live. They live hand to mouth or Left Bank to Right Bank, but not for your Bank of America. Not for C.D.s that go down when the market goes up. Papa Hemingway called it. He called it a moveable feast. He was writing about the expatriates and the Europeans. They have fun."

"You sound like a displaced person."

"I am. We have that in common, my love. Come here."

She couldn't resist the command. She didn't want to, because it was a command. He was unlike anyone she had ever known. He was masterful. Masculine. Being spoiled, for Elena, did not consist in getting her way. Being spoiled was not getting her way. She was used to winning, with Randy, whether she bickered with him or avoided the bickering. Randy had wanted their party at La Boîte; she gave it at home, and pulled it off. Elena was one of the few remaining women (or maybe one of the silent majority of women) who didn't want to dominate men. She wanted to be dominated. Her strength spelled Randy's weakness. What, she had often thought, was Superman but a corruption of Nietzsche, a parable of the patriarchs of the Old Testament? What were *Moby Dick* or *Jaws* but challenges to the impotent male? "Adam, Randy must make it," she said, as he took her on his lap.

"And me?" He gave her the quizzical smile which enchanted her.

"You've made it. What do you call last night?"

"I call it a preface." He carried her into the living room. "Forget it," he said, as the phone rang.

"I can't. It may be Randy."

"You could have gone to the market."

"You mean the baker." She laughed. "Darling, let me up."

"I give you two minutes," said Adam.

It was Randy, elated. Warren had called to tell him he'd firmed a deal for the movie with Pacific. "I can't talk now. I have to dress and get a haircut. I'm meeting with Kip at four."

Elena sent a smile to Adam. "Darling, I think it's wonderful. Have you read the part?"

"Not yet, but Warren and Kip both say it's terrific. I play—and this won't surprise you, my dear—a killer. As you can well attest, it's tailored for me."

"Nonsense, darling. You sound so well. You sound like the man I married." Adam's scowl wasn't lost on her.

"Will you drive back? This calls for a celebration."

"Darling, of course."

"The Bistro, or Chasen's?"

"Chasen's. I feel like a Hobo steak, and the Number One booth."

"You've got them, my dear. Goodbye. I miss you."

"Yes. I'm so happy for you."

"That's my Elena. It takes so little to make her happy." He had to get in the dig, she thought. The switchblade.

"I'll be in before five. Goodbye."

"You're acting again," Adam said. "The devoted wife."

"You know I have to."

"I know that's shit. Nobody has to do anything they don't want."

"You know what I want?" She walked to him, where he sat lotus-style on the rug. He grabbed one of her ankles and kissed it, pulling her down beside him in the warm sunlight that streamed through the sliding glass doors to the terrace.

"I need you, Elena," Adam said, afterward. "Don't go to town."

"I'll come back," she said. "Tomorrow, next weekend,

whenever I can. Randy needs me now, but I also have needs." She bit his ear playfully. "You've taught me that. I need to be without Randy. I need to think, and be alone."

"Alone," he said, "with me. That goes double."

7

The super-rich, the filthy rich, and the dirty rich commingled at La Costa. Part resort, part health spa, La Costa was eighty miles south of Los Angeles and a twenty-five-minute drive from the Del Mar Race Track. As an aggregate of the international compulsion for leisure-time activities, the compound offered swimming, tennis, golf, opportunities for private gaming—bingo, canasta, bridge, gin rummy—and facilities for rejuvenation, including an optional diet plan. One of its buildings, divided into suites for men and women, contained masseurs, masseuses, Jacuzzis, steam and sauna and facial rooms, as well as a barbershop and a beauty salon. The residents stayed in houses or condominiums, many of them privately owned but available, most of the year, for leasing. La Costa's attractions were clearly as disparate as its clientele, which consisted of Easterners, most of them Families based on Long Island, the men who talked with frogs in their throats and qualified for roles in *Godfathers I, II,* or *III*; anyone west of Fort Lee, New Jersey, and the chubby repeaters, the men and women, usually stars of movies and television series, whose bosses had told them to lose fifteen pounds.

For contrary reasons, on this particular week, both Nancy Nathan and Harry Waller were staying at La Costa. Neither one knew the other was there. The two had been carrying on a well-publicized feud for years—at parties, during interviews, on TV talk shows, and in their own writings. Ms. O'Brien considered Waller Norman Mailer's equal as a leading male chauvinist on the American literary scene. She was violently opposed to Kip's producing *Rogue's Gallery*. She was proposing, instead, another pretentious encyclical, the one she was co-writing with Pat Lukas. Nancy was at La Costa with Pat to polish the script while they took advantage of the reducing program. The concept of weightlessness meant more to most Americans than it did to the astronauts.

Harry Waller belonged to the rowdy, cantankerous, and hard-drinking school of American writers. In his early, brief flirtation with writing for a national news magazine, and in his conviction that he deserved the Pulitzer Prize, Harry was a descendant of John O'Hara. But unlike O'Hara, who proved to be the foremost commentator on one section of the urban American middle-class scene, Waller studied the manners and mores of the outcasts with whom he drank in bars, and the denizens of the underworld who were his Families and friends. Like most progressives, Waller tended to be reactionary regarding the interplay of male and female. Waller was The Upper Hand; his current wife or mistress was his handmaiden. Nancy O'Brien, as Waller once put it on "The Merv Griffin Show," was "mankind's excuse for masturbation."

Waller was in the shower when Cindy, the girl he'd picked up last night in the bar, called out to him. "Who the hell is it?" he said.

"How should I know?" She resumed her cud sound, adding another stick of chewing gum.

Cursing, Waller left a wet footpath on the rug. He sat on the bed beside his naked playmate, and stuck his tongue in her navel. Resting one hand on her stomach, he took the receiver with the other. "What the hell?" he said. Then: "Where are you?"

"I'm in the lobby," said Warren Ambrose petulantly.

"You took long enough. Get your ass up here."

Warren walked the macadam road to the building that housed Waller's condominium. He was irritable. Today was Monday, which meant he was missing his regular orgy—and only because his unruly client had called him the night before, insisting he take the two-hour drive to La Costa for dinner. Warren's expression, caught in the pin-spot lights on either side of the driveway, became a smirk. The situation was ironic. For once, he had given Alice a valid excuse for his absence. Normally, there were fabrications. In the winter months, he claimed he was watching football on telvision at somebody's house; the game and the dinner, during the half, were strictly stag. Alice had no reason to disbelieve him: there were many such groups of sports fans who gathered, ears glued to Howard Cosell, in Hollywood.

In the spring and summer, Warren had to be more inventive—business meetings, billiards, bridge with the boys.

"Harry's shaving," said the girl. She was wearing a see-through shift trimmed with maribou, the kind one finds in the windows of shops at airline terminals or Lili St. Cyr's on Santa Monica Boulevard. Alice had worn one once, ostensibly to entice her husband: he had made her change. It didn't seem suitable for a respected agent's wife, he told her.

"Harry will be right out," the girl said. "You don't mind if I rest? I played two sets of tennis today, and took the Jacuzzi. I'm exhausted."

"Be my guest," said Warren.

The girl removed what there was of the organdie wrapper and slipped into bed. The sheet stopped at her waist. Her breasts were perfectly shaped, like lancet arches seen from the underside. The areolae were dark and wide. Warren sat down, crossing his legs to conceal the tumidity in his groin.

"That's Cindy," said Waller. "Not bad, eh? Listen sugar, why don't you dress? We'll meet you in thirty minutes, in the bar."

"Aw, Harry, I thought I could stay. You said he was a friend."

"Friend is an antonym," Waller explained, "for agent. This is my agent. We have business to discuss."

She stood up, her back to them, dousing a cigarette. Her buttocks were taut as a baby's. "I can't go like this," she said, facing into the room with infant immodesty. Her body was beautiful, tanned all over, emphasizing the broad umber circles that encompassed her nipples and the nightshade of pubic hair below.

"You can go like that for me. How about you, Ambrose?" Waller let out a lecherous grunt.

Ambrose flushed. "Why don't *you* go, Waller, and leave us alone?" He said it lightly, but he meant it. He tried to look away, but his eyes kept going back to the naked girl.

"How much is it worth to you, buddy, pal, agent?"

Cindy pressed her body on Waller's. "I thought you liked me," she said. She buried her face in his hairy chest.

"You're okay," Waller said. "Now be a good girl and go put on some clothes. Not too many. Here, take my robe.

Pretend you're going back to your room from the bloody exercise class, or something. But first"—Waller unsnapped the shaving skirt he was wearing. "First, show our friend how you kiss me goodbye." He shoved her downward, roughly. "Kiss it goodbye," he said.

Waller's tool was enormous, not so much in length as in girth; the girl struggled to get it into her mouth. Warren froze momentarily. He wondered if Waller knew he was a voyeur. No, he decided, recalling the many stories of Waller's exhibitionism. Waller habitually took women in public, at parties. He usually chose an unoccupied room, the library or the guest room, one that was likely to be invaded. He left the door open, on the near-certainty that one or more of the guests would discover him with his latest conquest. Waller had even written that character into one of his novels.

"Hey, baby, you'd better stop. I want to save something for later." He patted her on her behind. "I can pick 'em, can't I?" he said, when she left. "She's even lucky for me. I won two thousand at Del Mar today. I had a pile on the nag that won the stakes, Telly's Pop. It's owned by Telly Savalas, of the lollipops."

"It's co-owned by Howard Koch," said Warren.

"Who's Koch?" He put on his jockey shorts, somewhat to Warren's dismay.

"You wouldn't know. A producer. *The Odd Couple, Plaza Suite, The Last of the Red Hot Lovers.* A talented guy, in terms of producers. He kind of specializes in Neil Simon. He had a horse called Doc Simon that didn't do badly, considering it was lame. Listen, I'll bet if his horse ran today, he's here. You'd like him. Would you like me to try the desk and see if he'd join us for dinner?"

"Ambrose, can't you ever stop being social? We're here to talk business."

"I wasn't aware of that from the sideshow," Warren said.

"You didn't enjoy it?"

"I enjoyed it, as far as it went. I was frustrated, frankly."

"I never thought of that," said Waller. "We'll take care of it, after dinner. Wait till you see the broads in the bar."

Warren didn't pretend disinterest. He was missing his kicks at home, and he was irritated at Waller's impudence. Whatever the "business" his client referred to, his client, not he, should have fought the freeways and met him in Los Angeles. Warren's only reward was the circus he'd witnessed that night. Now Waller was hinting at other compensations. "Okay, let's get down to it. Why am I here?"

Waller pulled a shirt from the drawer and put it on. "Goddamnit, you should ask why *I'm* here," he said. "To drink? I can drink in New York. To play the horses? There's Belmont, and bookies. You know damn well why I'm here. *Rogue's Gallery*, that's why I'm here. I'm not about to renew the option unless I produce." He poured a drink, and handed it to Warren. Then he poured another, neat, and downed it.

"What the hell do you mean, produce? You gave Baker the movie rights."

"I gave Baker an option, that's all, and you know it. He arrives in Oz and goes Hollywood. Randall Brent. Randall Brent for Donald Bellamy? Baker's spaced out. This book is based on people I know, the Hidden Society, you would call it, the bleeding victims, the lepers of the seventies. I work my fucking ass off for over a year, and then you and Baker tell me my hero's a limp-wrist called Randy Brent. My hero's a criminal, sure, but he's tough and he's square. He's a Family man. He's one of the Families. He's crippled, and he's my best buddy. He's Carmine Marzello."

"Cool it, Waller. As I keep telling you, Brent was just a suggestion. He'd have to be tested, like a hundred other guys. You're irrational. What you mean is you want to coproduce the picture. You're telling me now you don't trust the guy you picked up in some bar and gave the option to? Remember you picked him up, I didn't."

"I won't go back on my word, but I have to have control. You say I co-produce, okay. But I'll never lease it to Baker."

"You want to queer the deal? Warren said. "I got you the best goddamn deal since Gutenberg printed the Bible. Didn't you read the letter I sent you?"

"My lawyer read it. He says it's an exercise. Only an exercise, till the option is signed.

"Carol Burnett has been on CBS for nine years, and she's never signed a contract. Believe me, this is sealed and delivered. Hollywood doesn't operate like a cottage industry or a government subsidy. There's such a thing as a gentleman's agreement."

"What you're saying is that the bloody book isn't sold

yet. Number one for ten weeks on all the best-seller lists, and you haven't got it on the dotted line."

"If that's what you want, just sign and return the papers—"

"Without any right to keep these bums in check? I'm glad it's not sold. That's fucking good news. I might add it doesn't say much for you as an agent. Feffer sells Wambaugh just on an outline for four hundred grand, and you can't sell Waller? Ed Doctorow, who no one but Christopher Lehmann-Haupt has heard of, got almost two million bucks in paper, and you can't sell Waller? Doctorow is esoteric, for God's sake."

"Christ, sometimes I think you could do with a bit of esoterica. Listen, Waller, you're talking crap. If I go back to Kip Nathan and say you've decided to co-produce, he'll think I'm an idiot. The only other bids I had were much lower. Besides, I know Pacific will do much better than either Columbia or Fox. Pacific needs a major picture. Pacific needs a quality product."

"That's another thing. Pacific. Kip Nathan can't have much sense if he married that pecker Nancy O'Brien."

"The pecker isn't where the gray matter is. You want the top dollar or don't you?"

"I don't if that chauvinist sow is going to turn my story into a tract. She'll make it a documentary featuring eunuchs and girls who wear chastity belts at the communal pencil sharpener. But of course I want the top dollar. I have three ex-wives and five children to support. That comes expensive, as you damn well know."

"Then let me handle this," Warren said. "Kip wanted something I had, a mystery novel. He wanted something I got, an actor. That's how I got the top dollar for you."

"What actor?"

"What does it matter?"

"I'm curious. I don't know one star whose mortage isn't already held by the Ambrose organization."

"Okay, okay. It's no star. Kip wanted Randall Brent, your pet, for the thriller."

"*Je*sus, Ambrose. Why would anyone want Brent?" He freshened their drinks.

"I'm not a psychiatrist, I'm an agent. All I know is Nathan was hot on the property and on Brent. It's a quickie. It winds up this week. I sold the novel for nothing, to realize more on *Gallery*. I could have given Nathan a dozen better actors—stars—for that money. But who lets principle interfere with business? Brent was, ironically, the key to the sale of *Gallery*, much as you hate him. And that sale cost Pacific a fortune, as I told you."

"You dumped your own client, this mystery writer? You sold him out for me?"

"That's business."

"Ambrose, did anybody ever tell you you're a shit?"

"You have. A thousand times. Now are you gonna get back to that typewriter, or are you gonna queer my deal? You want another agent, I can recommend one."

"I want to co-produce. This book means a lot to me—"

"It's okay with Baker?"

"It'll have to be okay."

"Writers and actors. The writer thinks he knows about casting, the actor wants to rewrite his dialogue. Why did I ever get into this business?"

"I told you, because you're a shit. It's too late to change, Ambrose—your character or your profession."

"I'll talk to Kip. Trust me, Waller."

"The day I trust you's the day I fuck Nancy Nathan. Speaking of which, help me fold this bed back. I don't give a damn what the night maid thinks, but we may find something nice in the bar. Women prefer things neat, unprepared, unexpected—"

Warren didn't understand why the Ins in Hollywood said La Costa was great. By his own meticulous standards, the place was tacky. The condominium "suites" were single rooms—harshly-appointed sitting rooms by day. The bed was king-size, to be sure, and hidden behind one wall. You pressed a button to lower it into the room. Talk about kitsch. The Ultimate Spa had re-invented the Murphy bed.

8

They weaved their way through the indispensable swillers at the bar. "Where the hell is Cindy?" said Waller.

"There she is. She's holding a table."

"Who wants a table?" said Waller. "We're not gonna find a loose doll for you stuck in a corner."

"Waller," said Warren, reluctantly. "We'd better forget the doll. I have to drive back."

"Who says? There are rules? Stay over."

"Alice expects me." He said it weakly, without conviction.

"You're not gonna put it out for Alice. You sleep in separate rooms, for God's sake. You probably cap her once a month, as regular as her monthly."

Waller wasn't far wrong. It was more like once every two months. "Well, I suppose I could call. She knows I hate driving at night."

"Thatta boy. We're gonna get it off tonight. Now what'll you have? I'll get us some booze while you tell that broad to get her ass over here. Look at that lineup of dames at the end of the bar."

The dames, as he called them, had not escaped Warren's eye. He went to the table where Cindy was sitting, observing she'd followed Waller's instruction: "Not too many clothes." She had on a short halter-neck dress that looked modest until you detected the sparsity of it. Two-thirds of her breasts were circumscribed by the material; the rest fell out at the sides. A couple of stags were ogling her from the next table.

"Okay," said Cindy. "I'll go, but let me leave my purse. I have a girl friend I think you'll like. We'll never get another table."

Cindy's friend, as it happened, was a dish. She was tall

and leggy, with a body that moved like a panther's under a thick cotton shift. Her name was Joan. She had hair the color of polished bronze, long and thick. Warren, being bald, was aroused by a woman's hair. He freely confessed to his baldness, admitting he neither shaved his head for effect like Brynner, Preminger, Savalas, and Lazar; nor did he wear a toupee, like Burt Reynolds, Kelly, Sinatra, and George Burns. Warren convinced himself that he had revived the medieval style, the monk's poll, for those with shorn heads. He was vain about his natural state, confident that his hairlessness made him unique. But the quality which he found most attractive in Alice was her plentiful, infant-fine hair.

By the time they were seated for dinner, Waller was smashed. "Since I'm staying, I'd better book a room," said Warren.

"What for? Mine will do. That is, unless you don't dig a *ménage à quatre*." Waller winked at Joan. She blushed.

"I can cut it," said Warren. He was feeling no pain himself. Nor were the girls. They were drinking only white wine, but they were well into the Acapulco gold which Waller carried in his Cartier cigarette case.

"Men-ej a what?" asked Cindy.

Waller copped a feel. Inserting the palm of his hand in the crease that supported her breast, he ran it under her halter top. "Good girl," he said. "She almost made a rhyme. *Ménage à quatre,* men-ej a what? She's a poetess. Think you can publish her, Ambrose?"

"Believe me, I'd like to."

Waller squeezed the tantalizing bulb of Cindy's breast. He adjusted that half of her halter, forcing the silk away, circling the beak of her nipple with his finger. "Now look at that jug," he said. He might have been a guide explaining the wonders of the Prado to a band of tourists. "Ambrose, have you ever seen such a jug?"

Ambrose was on his fifth martini, pacing Waller, but finding it difficult. "I'd like to see Joan's jugs," he said, as he placed his hand on her knee.

"Don't be silly," Joan said, but she didn't resist. Warren, encouraged, reached higher, his fingers massaging her inner thigh. She was naked under the dress. The girl took a toke on the joint, then passed it to Cindy. She remained immobile, indifferent to Warren's lust. He explored the groove between her upper thigh and her box, exhilarated by the hairs that curled over his thumb. "You'd better stop that," Joan whispered, urgently.

"For now," he said. "If you say so."

"It's not that I don't like it," she said.

"Congratulations, Ambrose," said Waller. "You've got the little lady's cunt churning." He flagged the waiter for another round of drinks. "There are more things in heaven and earth, Horatio, than are dreamt of in your philosophy."

"What's that mean?" Cindy said.

"The meaning is incidental, my dear. As Warren knows by his nose for percentages, the play's the thing. Which means the author's the thing. That's Shakespeare. *Hamlet.* Scene Two, Act Two." He lit another joint and handed it to her.

"Hey," said Joan. "That's Mike Richards, the movie star." She said it as though she'd never been west of the Hudson River. Fans were all alike, but in California they were more so.

Warren, who had seen them at the same time, had a sinking sensation in the pit of his stomach. The woman with Richards was Nancy Nathan. "You know, Waller . . . ," Warren began, in an attempt to distract the writer. It was too late. The maître d' ushered Nancy and Mike to a nearby table. Waller was staring at Nancy, hatred in his glazed eyes.

"They have the room next to mine," said Cindy. "I didn't even recognize him." She giggled. "But I never heard such goings-on. They were making love all day long and bumping around and saying the dirtiest things to each other, and when I came back to my room to dress tonight they were standing there in the doorway and she was naked—"

"What else?" said Waller. He was priming for the attack.

"Plenty else," Cindy said. She took a carrot stick and chomped on it.

Waller's impatience was plain on his face. "What else?" he repeated.

Cindy put the carrot down. "Well, he was all dressed, see, like he was going out, but she was completely naked."

"You said that. What were they doing?"

"I saw her from the back at first. She was bending over,

with her hands on the floor. He was licking her—licking her asshole."

"And then?" Waller finished his drink in one gulp.

"Well, I couldn't just stand there watching, even though they didn't seem to notice me. So I went inside, and I looked through the peephole in my door. By then she had turned around, and he was on his knees—"

"You mean he was spooning her?"

"What's spooning?" said Cindy. She looked confused.

"Goddamnit, I mean was he sucking her cunt?"

"Well, yes," she said.

"And then what happened?"

"Nothing. I mean, they kissed, and he left, and she came out in the corridor, without a stitch, to wave goodbye."

"Do you know who she is?" Joan said. It seemed to Warren the most pertinent question of the evening.

"Don't I," said Waller. "That is a filthy cunt bitch named Nancy O'Brien who's married to a guy named Kip Nathan."

"Kip Nathan, the head of Pacific Pictures?" said Cindy. Waller, at last, had struck gold.

"The head of Pacific." Waller sent Ambrose a look that wanted to kill. "The same Pacific to which this birdbrain has sold my novel."

"But why would she cheat on someone as cute and important as Nathan?" Joan said.

"Do you know him?" said Ambrose.

"Not exactly. I met him once in a restaurant, and I've seen his pictures. He's handsome."

"I suppose," said the corpulent writer, "if you like cadavers. Ms. O'Brien does. She deballs them first, then she kills them, and then she fucks them. Or is that redundant?" His voice grew louder and louder, until two couples at neighboring tables were staring with disapproval. As for Nancy, she'd spotted them as she sat down. Warren saw her change places with Richards, so her back was to Waller.

"Listen, Harry," said Warren, consciously using the given name only familiars employed, "let's not have a scene. Why the hell should you care if she's putting horns on Nathan? Just be thankful you're not her husband."

"Her *wife*, you mean. Or do you mean 'his' wife. Fuck it, I've done it all. I've screwed men and women. I've screwed them one at a time, and I've screwed them together. I've stuck apples and oranges. I once dug a hole in the ground, in a trench, and did it with worms crawling over my cock. And you know what? I found it all pleasant, very enjoyable, because it was honest. Nancy O'Brien's not honest. She's neither a prick nor a cunt. She's not even a decent transvestite. What she is is a creep, an asexual in transvestite clothing." He was shouting now, and a pall fell over the restaurant. Everyone strained, in various stages of embarrassment, to hear.

The maître d' approached them. "Mr. Waller," he said, "perhaps you're tired. Perhaps you'd like to order your dinner. We'll send it to your room."

"Perhaps you'd like a shove in the kisser," Waller said. He got up, knocking over his chair. The maître d' stepped back. Waller was laughing wildly. "You're not far off. My friends and I would prefer to eat in our rooms. I find the company here distasteful." He staggered to Nancy's table, steadied himself by spreading his feet, and pointed to her. "Your busboy has got the garbage mixed up," he told the headwaiter, who'd come to the aid of the maître d'. "He put the trash in the dining room instead of the can. You see her? You see it? Well, some people call it white trash, but I'm from the North. I call it black. And I don't mean her skin. That twat is as black as the ace of spades." He smiled sweetly, swaying. "You will excuse the cliché. Her twat is as filthy as her gigolo friend."

Mike Richards was hardly a hero. He was twenty-six, four years younger than Nancy; he had made a second vocation of avoiding the draft. As an actor, he pressed his luck beyond the unwritten precedential bounds. He'd been known to toss ashtrays or glasses or flowerpots on the set, but only when, as the star of a film, he was sure of his margin for misbehavior. Had Waller confined his insults to Nancy Nathan, Mike wouldn't have acted at all. His liaison with Nancy, using Pat Lukas as a beard, was Mike's attempt to get back at Kip for the way he believed he'd been cheated on the Pacific picture.

Richards thought only in terms of his ego. Waller, the drunken son of a bitch, had called him a gigolo. On the one hand, Richards couldn't just take that, in front of all these people; on the other hand, to brawl was to lose. There were two of them, Waller and that bastard Ambrose. Both men were bigger than Mike: he was not about to take Waller *mano a mano.*

Richards grabbed the centerpiece, which was a Japanese lantern, and hurled it at Waller. Ambrose deflected the lamp with his massive arm, and diners scuffled wildly as it hit one of the tables. If it hadn't been for that crummy agent, thought Richards, as both the maîtred d' and Ambrose held Waller back, I'd have hit the shitheel. For all his youth and cowardice, Mike was a crackerjack marksman. He'd had enough practice, aiming at his directors.

Nancy stood up with incongruous dignity. "You fucking cunt," she said quietly. She had learned that ploy from the English. Englishmen, most notably actors like Richard Burton, said, "He's a cunt." They seldom called a man "a prick." On the contrary, Burton would say, "She's a prick." Nancy considered the switch most effective. "You dreary, sadistic, illiterate bum," Nancy said. "I should feel sorry for you. Believe me, I don't." Her rage brought tears to her eyes. I may be the only human being, Warren thought cynically, who ever saw tears in Nancy Nathan's eyes. "You motherfucker." She was screaming now. "Get the hell out of here." She raised her wine glass and tossed the contents straight into Waller's face.

When they reached Waller's room, he went to the bathroom, removed his wine-stained clothes and took a shower. Warren guessed the water was cold. Waller joined them, a towel wrapped around his wide middle, pouring himself a brandy. He was composed. He was markedly joyful. He even appeared sober.

"You are all about to witness the downfall of a bitch," Waller said. "What's Kip Nathan's number?"

"Two seven eight, eighteen hundred," Warren said.

"It sounds like a goddamn hotel number." Waller laughed, and picked up the telephone. "I want to call Beverly Hills, two seven eight, eighteen hundred, person to person, to Mr. Kip Nathan."

"Who shall I say is calling, sir?"

"Mr. François Truffaut."

"But isn't this Mr. Waller's room?"

"This is Mr. Waller. Mr. Truffaut is here. It's okay."

Peter buzzed Kip. "Mr. François Truffaut on the line, sir." He sounded abashed or impressed, Kip didn't know which. "I think I should warn you, Mr. Nathan, he's spreaking in French."

"Then stay on the line. You can translate. I'll take it. François, where are you? Hello?"

"Je suis à La Costa, Keeep," said Waller. "Keep" was his playful salute to the language barrier. *"Si vous êtes interessé, votre femme est inscrite à La Costa, dans la chambre treize. Avec une femme qui s'appelle Pat Lukas. Mais votre femme—elle baise regulièrement avec Monsieur Michael Richards, la vedette de votre film, dans la chambre deux cent trente-huit."*

Waller hung up and started to laugh, uncontrollably.

Ambrose chuckled. "You're a bastard, Harry."

"Drink up," said Waller. "Let's drink to the ex-Mrs. Nathan. And then let's fuck. *'On baise,'* as they say in France."

Warren drove back around noon the next day, his eyes jaundiced from lack of sleep. He smiled with satisfaction as he entered his driveway. He had not missed his Monday night bacchanals, after all.

9

"My God, I thought you'd never get back," Kip Nathan said.

It occurred to Ted Buckley that Kip was a well-preserved forty. His face was drawn like that of a slightly aging matador, except that he was too tense to survive the bullring. That explained why tennis was both his sport and his obsession.

"You're harder to find than Patty Hearst," Kip said.

"But you found me," said Ted. "I flew back as soon as I decently could." When Buckley was on business, and most of his business was equivocal, he was as hard to track as a downhill racer after a snowslide. His most durable mistress once told a friend, "If he says he's in Philadelphia, he's in Poland."

"Did you get my note?" Kip asked.

"With all the 'Urgents,' 'Immediates,' 'Personals and Condifentials' scrawled on the evelope? Yes, I got your note. My driver brought it along to the airport. I assume, since you used a black brush pen, you're determined not to take my advice."

"You assume correctly. I told you, I want a divorce." Kip's memos were as renowned as David Selznick's. When not on the phone, he devoted himself to memos, using different inks to express different moods—red for approval, brown for doubt or reproof, green for money matters. Black meant finality.

"Have you spoken to Nancy?"

"Not yet. I took your counsel that far. Even further. I've hardly spoken to Nancy since she returned from her little excursion."

"As I told you, Kip, you don't know. It may have been innocent. You get a call from some joker using a phony identity, and you jump to conclusions. Now, what are the facts?"

"Okay. It wasn't Truffaut. I knew François wouldn't do that even if it was true, but I checked. He's in the Midi, making a picture. However, my friend, the nut was right. He gave me the room numbers. Richards *was* at La Costa. I called, he answered, and I hung up. I tried Nancy's room and that egghead, Lukas, answered. She told me Nancy had driven to San Diego to see the Shakespeare Festival. The beard wasn't smart enough to say Nancy was taking a bath, for Christ's sake. The Shakespeare Festival doesn't start until summer. Besides, it was three o'clock in the morning."

"Let's suppose this circumstantial evidence holds up. Let's suppose your wife had a one-week fling with Richards. That happens. Kip, I have to ask you something personal. How long has it been since you slept with Nancy?"

"Not long enough, but I see your point. With her it's an animal act. She's the trainer, and I'm the tamed lion. Instead of a flaming hoop, I'm supposed to jump into her muff. Now, how would you like that action?"

"I wouldn't," Ted said. His tone conveyed a lawyer's indictment of Nancy and a man's absolution of Kip. "Have you thought about Elizabeth?"

"I'm thinking of Elizabeth. Do you know how much that fucking so-called mother thinks of her child? I'll tell you. Since she and Lukas haven't been able to peddle their feminist horseshit to a studio, Lukas has set my hammy wife for a lecture tour. She told me last night. I objected. 'Go to hell,' said the lady. 'What about Elizabeth?' I said. 'She can go with you,' Nancy screamed. The baby woke up and started crying. 'You'd better go to her,' I said to Nancy. 'You go to her,' she said. 'I'm going swimming.' And she did. If I didn't know better, I'd say she's a dyke. She spends more time with Pat Lukas than with her daughter."

"She's not a dyke."

"You know?"

"I know."

"Have you slept with her?" Kip asked the question with the curiosity of a sex researcher.

"Never," said Ted. "But not because she hasn't tried."

"You should have told me."

"I thought it was irrelevant."

"Spoken just like a lawyer." Kip's laugh was caustic. "I wonder how many others—never mind. I want you to file, and I want you to give her both barrels. Name Richards as corespondent."

"I can't. The only grounds for dissolution in California are irreconcilable differences and incurable insanity."

"Try the second one, then. It fits."

"Now listen, Kip. I'm going to level. You know I was never exactly enamored of Nancy—I mean as your wife. When she made a play for me, I was so disgusted I wanted to kill her. I wanted to get her out of your life. In a calmer moment, I hoped the marriage might work, for your daughter's sake and for yours. What I'm saying is you've convinced me. I've tried the arguments, you've won the summation. You know I don't go to court, but if it comes to that I'll get you the best goddamn lawyer in town. His name is Arthur Crowley, and he can beat *me*. I'll get you your dissolution, but I won't allow it to hurt the child."

"I want the child, Ted. That's a condition."

"I don't know, Kip. The laws have changed, but not to that extent. It's tough for a woman in California. She hasn't many rights. It's partly a backlash against Women's Lib."

"How suitable. Nancy O'Brien, Champion of Womankind."

"It's partly because the laws for so many years were stringent against the man. But there's still one advantage women have. A woman can be a prostitute, but unless the child finds her in bed with a man, she usually gets the child. She's the mother, and any judge tends to favor the mother, at least until the child's of age to choose—"

"By that time, Elizabeth's life will be ruined."

"I hear you, Kip. I read you loud and strong. But the law is the law, and I'm an attorney. I'm not a child psychologist."

When Ted left, Kip buzzed Carol. "I've got a meeting out of the studio," he said. "I don't know if I'll get back, but I'll check with you later." His secretary looked at him strangely. He always told her his whereabouts when he left the lot, so he could be reached in emergencies.

"If there's something important—" she began.

"If there's something important, tell David."

Kip was a man who followed through on his instincts.

His credo, like that of any gambler, was that your instincts seldom betrayed you. Still, even as he approached his front door, Kip wavered. He hoped his intimations were wildly incorrect.

"Mr. Nathan," said Peter, his voice and his manner communicating not only the expected surprise, but shock. "I had no idea. I'm afraid I haven't prepared any lunch—"

"I'm not hungry," Kip said. "Where is Mrs. Nathan?"

"I beg your pardon, sir?" Peter was playing for time. Although he despised Mrs. Nathan, Peter had a sense of propriety, of meticulousness, of everything in its time and its place.

"Mrs. Nathan is here, is she not?" Kip said.

"I believe so, sir. Yes, she is."

"Where is she?"

"I'm really not certain, sir, but the last time I saw her she was out by the pool."

"Thank you, Peter." Kip sensed his houseman's embarrassment; it matched his own. "I'll find her."

Nancy was not by the pool, nor was she likely to linger there, Kip thought, in the blinding sunlight. Nancy had to guard her complexion. He followed the geranium-fired path to the guest house. The curtains were drawn. This wasn't her day for Harvey Parkes. He wondered, as he approached the door, what he would do if it was locked. It wasn't. It opened easily to his touch. There was not a murmur inside the room. He shuddered, even before he saw them. They were asleep on the coverlet. They had not even bothered to turn it down. Nancy rubbed her eyes with a drowsy movement that woke Mike Richards.

"Get out," Kip told Nancy. "Pack up and get out of my house. As for you," he said to Richards, who was cringing against the headboard, having put the bolster over his private parts, "as for you, I'll talk to you later."

10

Even in its most glorious season, Venice evoked for Elena the cliffs of Gay Head on Martha's Vineyard and the tumultuous chop of the surf against seawalls at Malibu Beach. Venice, its balconies overhanging canals and laden with wash, seemed to represent some housewife's unfailing conviction that, even in the perpetual dampness, the clothes would dry. Venice, with its rococo bridges, tortuous avenues, and chanting kettledrum gondoliers, was an enchanted archipelago. Its desolate waterscape, compelling the outer-directed gaiety of the populace, was invigorating. Elena delighted as much in the complacent preening of the pigeons in the Piazza San Marco as she did in the ethereal flight of the seagulls in New England or California. Randy, who harbored the not uncommon, irrational fear of birds, called them predators. The predators knew their allies—they ate from Elena's hands.

Max von Helsing had not long ago appeared on *Time* magazine's cover under the caption, "The Playboy of the Western World." As if to authenticate the appellation, he was giving the international party of the year. His Bicentennial Ball would be held at the Palazzo Rezzonico, the palace on the Grand Canal where, in the twenties, Linda and Cole Porter entertained at a red and white gala. Earl Blackwell, in the sixties, made it the site of his red, white, and gold spectacular. Von Helsing's theme for his decor and the dress suggested for ladies was, appropriately, red, white, and blue. Invitations were more esteemed by the international jet set than Shakespeare's First Folio is among scholars. Everyone who was no one was uninvited.

The Brents were invited, but they were there through the generosity of Reade Jamieson. Jamieson learned of Elena's marital and financial problems through Kip. When she mentioned the Ball to Reade, he sent her the round-trip tickets which she told Randy came out of her private funds. Reade was not invited.

Reade was unknown, a nonentity in the international jet set, untutored except by academicians. He was a fellow himself. He was one of the remarkable group of university scientists who early saw the potential of the computer revolution and started small businesses in the environs of Cambridge. Jamieson built his enterprise into a major industry. He had been a widower for five years. Elena had done her homework through Kip.

She and Randy and Furio were at lunch when Jamieson called. Elena refused the telephone the maître d' offered, walking through the terrace to the lobby of the hotel. She took the phone from the concierge.

"How's it going?" said Reade. "I miss you."

"We only arrived last night," she said. "You have a full week of loneliness ahead."

"When is the Ball?" His tone betrayed his anxiety.

"It's not until Saturday." Elena was consciously using the event of two centuries to lure him, but the idea of his attending, she thought, must come from him. Natalie informed her that Adam was back with Marina, intent on getting her for *Gallery*. Natalie was arriving in Venice that night. *Overwrought* was finished, but neither Jack nor Adam could leave; they were working on post-production.

"Listen, I seem to have a clear schedule," Reade said. "Can you get me in, if I come? Or should I ask you the other way around? Do you mind if I come?"

"The answer to question number one is yes. I can get you an invitation. Darling, Max is my dearest friend." She was lying, of course. She had met von Helsing through Furio only recently. "For the rest, I'd be delighted to see you."

Randy, who had polished off two bottles of Bardolino, decided to take a nap after lunch. Unlike Elena, he hated Venice (except for Harry's Bar, or anyone else's, she reflected). Randy said it depressed him: his analogy was to Jell-O. "You can do the entire package in twenty minutes," he claimed.

Elena was relieved when he went up to their room. It was Randy, not Venice, she found untenable. With Furio, she walked the narrow pavements hand-in-hand. They settled in the square and ordered espresso. "Furio, darling," she said, "can you do me a favor?"

"For you, Elena, anything."

"Can you get Max to invite Reade Jamieson to the Ball?"

"Ahhh . . . *Ho capito! Il tuo corteggiatore.*"

"My suitor? *Tesoro,* you forget. I am married."

"Elena, I forget nothing. You are not married, as I keep telling you, in the conjugal sense of the word. And you will not be married for long, as you tell me. I approve. I also approve of this very rich man. Very rich is the best."

She took his remark as a slam at Adam, as well as Randy. He knew about their affair. "Never mind the nuptials," she said, more sharply than she intended. "He's arriving on Thursday. Can you get him in?"

"*Cara,* for you I can get Valentino in." They laughed at the switch in legend: some historians wrote that Valentino was gay. Others described him in his popular image of a ladies' man. The Hollywood cognoscenti, or non-cognoscenti, held that Rudy's tool was so enormous he never found a woman who could accommodate him. Furio's dark eyes flashed mischievously. "I will be the best man at your wedding."

"You *are* the best man," Elena said. They laughed again, this time at her mindless incongruity. Furio was the best man in Elena's life, but Furio was gay.

The Brents were staying at the Gritti Palace. Reade registered at the Danieli. In any other man, Elena would have called it discretion; in Reade, she considered it priggish at best. Elena was offended by the Danieli. The Danieli was Eugene Fodor-time: he rated it number one in his guide, above the Gritti. With its atmosphere of tourism, its condescending staff, its reek of new money, Elena had to admit the Danieli suited Reade Jamieson. The Gritti was Ernest Hemingway. The Danieli was Harry Waller. It is also Adam Baker, Elena thought, somewhat sadly.

Reade was duly impressed by her coup, his admittance to Max von Helsing's Bicentennial Ball. Elena and Furio took him to the Lido on Friday afternoon. Randy found the Lido tiresome. To Elena, that Adriatic resort was the ideal retreat in off-season.

When Reade took them to dinner that night, he gave the

first indication that he was less than generous with money. He chose the restaurant, a dingy cafe off the Campo Santa Caterina, with stained tablecloths and—to Randy's dismay—no bar. Reade made much of the fact that Venetians dined there and, by the look of the other patrons, rough men and raucous women, he was correct. They were shabbily dressed and stared rudely at the *forestieri*. Reade ordered the dinner, which consisted almost entirely of fish—an appetizer of eel and, as the entree, a kind of mangled bouillabaisse. Reade and Furio ate the eel. Elena picked at it. Randy shoved it away with distaste. To Elena's surprise, he ate some of the stew. The Brents disliked fish, which hadn't occurred to their host. Reade asked for only a half liter of wine, *vino della casa,* and then discoursed on its excellence. The wine was harsh and bitter, but quickly consumed (to kill the vile taste of the fish, Elena decided). When Reade didn't ask the waiter to refill the bottle, Randy did. Reade went over the check with diligence, adding the figures carefully. Then he presented his Diners Club card. (A write-off, Elena thought cynically. He's making up the cost of the tickets to Venice.)

Elena's friend, Valentino, designed her gown for the ball, a Mandarin-collared fantasy of blue paillettes. Elena reasoned that most of the women, given a choice of red, white, or blue, would select the other, more standout colors. She was, as usual, on the mark in her calculations. For all the royalty, socialites, and stars who were gathered in Venice, she was a favorite. The *paparazzi* trailed her all night.

The Ball did not begin until eleven-thirty, so there were countless private dinners before. Furio took Reade along with him to the Baron and Baroness Lansbury's. The Brents and Natalie, who was wearing crimson organdie by her friend Donald Brooks, were invited to the palazzo of the Countess Cicogna. Marina Cicogna was a part-time fixture of Venice and a full-time filler for the people pages of international magazines. Some years ago, *Time* showed a photograph of the Countess dancing with Richard Burton at a party. The text inferred that their idle fox-trot caused a rift between the Burtons. The item was memorable as perhaps the only Burton-Taylor rift that did not come off.

On this particular night, the Burtons arrived at the Ball in a flashbulb crunch of togetherness. As each of the gondolas drew up to the landing, the cordon of *paparazzi* surrounded the disembarking VIPs. The Grande Dame of Venice, Contessa Volpi. Loel and Gloria Guinness. Rudy and Consuelo Crespi. Douglas and Mary Lee Fairbanks. Andrea and Audrey (Hepburn) Dotti. Luciana Paluzzi. Hubert Givenchy. Truman Capote with Joanne (not Joan or Joanna) Carson. Roy Halston. Fabrizio Mioni. Sonny and Mary Lou Whitney. Brigitte Bardot. Senator John Tunney. Errol and Margaux (Hemingway) Wetson. Carlo and Sophia (Loren) Ponti. Sargent and Eunice Shriver. Zubin and Nancy (Kovacs) Mehta. Princess Luciana Pignatelli. Senator and Mrs. Hubert Humphrey. Secretary of State and Mrs. Kissinger. Jean and Kirk Kerkorian. Garson and Ruth (Gordon) Kanin. Douglas and Lily Auchincloss. Dino and Sylvana (Mangano) De Laurentiis. Senator and Mrs. Ted Kennedy. Yul and Jacqueline Brynner. Candy Bergen. Governor and Mrs. Ronald Reagan. Federico and Giulietta (Masina) Fellini. Roddy McDowall. Rob and Merle (Oberon) Wolders. Ambassador Elliot and Mrs. Richardson. Rossella Falk. The Perennial Partygoers: Jerome Zipkin. Jules and Doris Stein. Michael and Shakira Caine. Lee Radziwill. Baroness Marie-Hélène de Rothschild. Mme. Hélène Rochas. Nan Kempner. Ahmet and Mica Ertegun. Marisa Berenson. Tony and Berry (Berenson) Perkins. Winston and C. Z. Guest. Kitty Miller. The Enemies: George C. Scott and Frank McCarthy. Joan Fontaine and Olivia de Havilland. Irving Lazar and Otto Preminger. William F. Buckley, Jr., and Gore Vidal. Gore whispered wickedly to Elena, "Eat your heart out, Truman." A decade before, Capote had given the Ball to end all Balls at New York's Plaza Hotel—the Ball to end all Balls until von Helsing's.

The international press converged on Venice. Lord and Lady Harlech. Gianni Vozzacchi, who was Princess Grace's favored Italian photographer. Both Dorothys, Manners and Treloar. Jim Bacon, Michael Coady, of *Women's Wear Daily*. Hedley Donovan of *Time,* Inc. Henry Grunwald of *Time*. Andrea Rozzoli of *L'Europeo*. William Fine of Hearst Publications. Osborn Elliott of *Newsweek*. Marshall Field of Chicago's *Sun-Times*. Clay Felker of *New York*. Oriana Fallaci. Radie Harris of the *Hollywood Reporter*. Alberto Mondadori of *Epoca*. Kay Graham of the Washington *Post*. Ivor Davis of the Hollywood Foreign Press. Richard Stolley of *People.* Jean Prouvost of Paris *Match.* James Bellows of the Washington *Star.* Roderick Mann of the *London Sunday Express.* Eleanore Phillips of *Vogue.* Mirella Petteni of Italy's *Vogue.* Stanley Eichelbaum of the San Francisco *Examiner.* Lord Roy Thompson of the London *Times.* Ian Calder of the *National Enquirer.* Liz Smith of the New York *Daily News.* Jacqueline Kennedy Onassis of Viking (if you could call that the press). Irv Kupcinet, Bob Thomas, Eugenia Sheppard, Bill and Tichi Miles, Luigi Barzini, Dick Kleiner, Hank Grant, Earl Wilson. As Suzy was sure to write later, "And on and on."

11

"I don't understand," said Elena. "Grace said she was staying with Merle and Rob in Amsterdam, but they're here."

"Poor Grace is in Santa Monica, having a body lift," said Natalie.

"Pity the doctor," Randy said. "That's one body I wouldn't want to lift."

"Oh, no," said Natalie. "The witch and her warlock are here. Is she AWOL or did she get permission from the coven?" Nancy and Mike were threading their way through the aisles. Elena noticed that nobody spoke to them, and they spoke to nobody. They were like two restless children in quarantine. Unseated parties were awkward, thought Elena, even von-Helsing parties.

"Natalie, be kind. You must feel sorry for Nancy," said Elena.

"I feel sorrier for the dolls she sticks pins in. Take Kip. Deballing him wasn't enough. Putting horns on him with that bilious excuse for a movie star. Deserting her daughter, her very own flesh, if she's made of flesh, to lecture lonely old women on how lucky they are to be widows. Do you know what she calls her lectures? 'The Feminist Rule.' Abandon your children and lovers. Sacrifice pricks to the Devil. Form a circle around the men by moonlight and chop off their peckers."

"That's a woman, all right," said Randy. He was bombed.

"That is not a woman," said Furio. "These lovely ladies are women. *Belle donne*. 'Thank heaven for lee-tle girls,' " he sang, in a deft imitation of Maurice Chevalier. "Your Mr. Lerner wrote that."

"So maybe Mr. Lerner likes little girls," Randy said. "I don't know his hang-ups. Mr. Lerner's a fucking satyr. He knows so much about women he's had six wives and ten million mistresses."

"Good God," said Natalie. "They're heading our way. They'll probably ask to sit with us. Let's say all the seats are taken."

Mike and Nancy were indeed approaching their table, Nancy in a white diaphanous number that, to Elena's trained eye, was the work of Bob Mackie. The sequins were designed to reveal, not conceal. As she moved, Nancy drew the eyes of men and the incredulity of women. The *paparazzi* were shooting from every angle.

As Mike and Nancy joined them, it occurred to Elena that she had neither seen nor spoken to Nancy since the Nathans' break-up. Lately, Elena had often considered the ramifications of divorce. Divorce was war. The battle lines were drawn; one had to take sides. One had to decide in which army to enlist. The Nathans' friends supported Kip, not because he had been betrayed by his wife, but because he was rich and powerful. Loyalty counted for nothing where money and power were involved: in Hollywood, wars were fought by mercenaries. Elena had tried to call Nancy, but the calls were never returned. Mike had forbidden Nancy to see or speak to anyone she'd known during marriage. That included Nancy's only confidante, Pat Lukas. Nancy was thinner than ever, almost skeletal, and she had aged: she looked ten years older. The emotion Elena felt for Nancy was empathy, not pity. Anticipating the contest when she left Randy, Elena wondered which of the two their friends would select. If *Overwrought* was successful, Randall Brent would be sought-after, a star. Elena would be, as Kip put it, another extra woman. She would begin again, in her own self-interest. Elena was shrewd enough to acknowledge the principle by which she lived.

"Who made your dress, dear?" said Natalie, viciously. "The Ninon Curtain Company?"

"I think it's elegant," said Elena. "Nancy, is something wrong? You're ashen." Nancy was supporting her head, her elbows on the table.

"Would you come to the powder room with me?" Her voice was all but inaudible.

Natalie was either contrite or curious, probably both. "Can I help?" she asked.

"Stay here," said Elena, sharply. Natalie was her best friend, but she was a busybody.

They sat on the sofa in the ladies' room. "It will pass," Nancy said, in a frail attempt at reassurance. Whatever she was, she was not a physical coward. At school, she had not been good at games, but she never complained when she was hurt. Her athletic classmates admired her for her good sportsmanship. "I get these dizzy spells—"

"Put your head down," said Elena. "That's right. Have you seen a doctor?"

"No. They always go away."

"Are you nauseous?"

"Yes." She looked at Elena. "I can't see you. Only the spots, bright spots—" It was then she collapsed. Elena caught her and laid her on the couch. Even in this sandbag state of inertia, Nancy was as easy to lift as a teenage girl.

"Forse la signora ha bevuto troppo." The woman spoke with the jaded certainty of washroom attendants, hospital orderlies, soldiers on latrine duty—all those people who have seen too much for too long.

"Oh, no. *È impossible.* The lady doesn't drink. She is ill, very ill," said Elena. *"Lei parla inglese?"*

"Sissignora."

"Then call a doctor. *Un dottore. Presto."*

The woman was clearly perplexed. *"Madonna Santa, dove trovo un dottore a quest' ora!"*

Elena was cradling Nancy's head in her arms. She placed a cushion under the girl. *"Usi il telefono!* The telephone, for God's sake."

"Mamma mia, non so che fare." The woman threw up her hands in frustration. Why, Elena thought, does darkness present an impasse to those who work by night?

"What happened?" said Natalie. "You didn't come back, and I—"

"Never mind," said Elena. "She's very sick. There must be a doctor here somewhere. Tell Furio to find one."

"How can he find one? They aren't carrying little black bags tonight."

"Natalie, this is no time to be flip. Have Furio find Max. Have Max use a megaphone if he has to."

"Good God, she's out cold."

"Natalie, that's what I'm trying to tell you. Now will you go? And hurry!"

* * *

Reade was remarkably organized in crisis. He displayed an executive's logic and common sense. He minimized Nancy's condition to those at their table, persuading Mike and Natalie they could best help Nancy by getting some sleep. Nancy would surely want to see Mike in the afternoon; by then, Elena would be exhausted and Natalie might be needed to take over the vigil. Randy presented no problem—he was unable to tolerate the indispositions of others. Furio made it clear that he was available in any contingency but, with his innate decorum, understood that his presence would complicate matters. Dear Furio, thought Elena. It was he who had arranged for *l'autolancia della "Croce azzurra"* which would take them to the hospital.

Nancy rallied briefly in the emergency boat. Her voice was so faint Elena had to strain to understand her. "Lizbeth," Nancy said. Elena was startled. Nancy's daughter's was the last name she expected to hear. Then Nancy fell away, far away, to the distance and lethargy of silence.

Several hours later, in *l'ospedale dei Santi Giovanni e Paolo,* the doctors told Elena and Reade that Nancy's condition was critical. "We cannot pinpoint the ailment," said the chief diagnostician. "We know it is malnutrition, but there are complications. Mrs. Nathan admits she has hardly eaten for weeks. She has taken amphetamines for too long. She's conscious, but she is unable to swallow foods or liquids. We're feeding her intravenously."

"But people don't die of malnutrition today," said Elena. "Do they? Have you any idea what's wrong?"

"Too many people die of what you might call self-induced starvation, Mrs. Brent. If you are asking for my unofficial opinion, I will tell you. There is a malady called *anorexia nervosa* which often proves fatal. I don't mean to frighten you. It is by no means always fatal. We find it mostly in teenagers who have been taking drugs and dieting."

"Can it be cured, then?"

"That depends on the stage, on the stamina of the patient, on many things. Mrs. Brent, I'd suggest you notify Mrs. Nathan's relatives. Mr. Nathan?"

"The Nathans are separated. They're getting a divorce."

"Mi dispiace, Mrs. Brent. Mrs. Nathan keeps asking for someone—we can't make it out. It sounds like 'Keep.' "

"That's her husband," Elena said. "I'll call him. Can I see her, doctor?"

"Of course. It will do her good. She's depressed. She also calls for an Elena—"

"I'm Elena." The tears came again; during the relentless crawling hours before the dawn, they'd formed streaks on her face.

Reade gave her his handkerchief and walked her to the door of the room. "Elena, if you need me—"

"You're here. Thank you, Reade." She said it simply. "Will you put in a call to Kip? It may take hours—"

"It won't take hours. You forget. I'm an expert at digits. I'm even an expert at getting calls through Italian operators."

Facing the door to Nancy's room, Elena hesitated. She felt suddenly drained as she stared at the sign: VIETATE LE VISITE. She turned to him. "Reade, you will be here when I come out?"

"I'll be here as long as you need me, Elena. Forever. I haven't told you, but I'm going to marry you." He took her by the shoulders, steadying her, and kissed her gently.

She didn't reply. There was no answer. Not now, in this place, in this time of tragedy. Elena tasted the tears once more, but these were for Reade, not Nancy. What mattered was he was here. What mattered was he was supporting her. She brushed the tears away and opened the door.

Nancy looked tortured, propped up at an angle, suffering the discomfort of pumped-up hospital beds. In the twenty-watt shabbiness of the room, she gazed at Elena without recognition. Elena moved closer and spoke her name. "Elena," said Nancy, "thank God. I'm so lonely. What's happened to me? Oh, please don't leave me. Don't you leave me, too." Elena took her hand and pressed it, sitting down on the edge of the bed.

"I won't leave you, Nancy. I won't." She fought back the tears.

"Where am I? In Venice? You know I don't even know what hospital I'm in."

"You're in Venice. This is the Hospital of the Saints John and Paul."

"That's pretty New Testament," Nancy said, "and ominous." She tightened her grasp on Elena's hand. "I'm going to die. I know. Elena, please tell me the truth."

"Nancy, you're pretty sick. Anemia, or something. But nobody's said you're going to die. They're trying to make you well, and they will."

"They won't. That's my negativism. I've lived my life in the negative, in a death wish. Now I'm going to die, and I'm afraid. You know, I never thought about anyone else. But life isn't hating. It's loving. Life isn't taking. It's giving. I wanted to be in the headlines. I wanted to be an intellectual. But life isn't headlines. It's heart. You know what the headlines bring you? They bring you envy and hate. You're a target. There's one of you against all the others who want to be in the headlines. I wanted to be admired. I wanted everyone to like me. Nobody likes me. I haven't got a friend."

"I'm your friend."

"You're here because of Kip—"

"I'm here because of you."

"I didn't even return your phone calls."

"Nancy, the people who care about phone calls aren't your friends. The people who spend their lives on the phone are the ones who haven't got friends." As she spoke them, Elena was struck by the meaning of her words. Was Randy correct about her life-style? Was she on the Natalie Kaufman circuit because she, Elena, had no friends? She let it go. "Nancy, Mike is very anxious about you. Would you like to see him?"

"Mike Richards, the movie star. The man who told me all an actor has to give is his body. Now, that's a line, isn't it?"

"Any man who can say that has nothing to give but his body."

"I fell for it, just to hurt Kip. Elena, Kip loves you. I want to see Kip. Oh, please, will you ask him to see me? I know he won't—"

"Now what were you saying about being negative?" She could no longer contain the tears. She reached for a Kleenex. "You see? You're being silly, upsetting me. Of course Kip will see you."

"Why should he? I've never done anything for him. The one man I loved—"

"He's still in love with you, Nancy. I know. You gave what a woman can give to a man. You married him. You bore him a child—"

"Elizabeth." Nancy began to cry. Elena relived the pain she had felt in the ambulance, the shock she experienced when Nancy called for her daughter. Nancy hadn't been much of a mother, but in the end there was the helplessness of consanguinity. Mother and Child. Mary and Jesus. Elena, who had been raised without religion under Communism, perceived the fundamentals. One could not reject love, except outwardly. Love was intuitive.

Elena wiped Nancy's face with a Kleenex, walked to the basin in the corner and wet a washcloth. She applied it to Nancy's forehead and eyes.

"Take it off," said Nancy. She was panic-stricken, like a small child whose eyes are suddenly covered and cannot see. She tore the cloth from her face, emitting a cry of pain, forgetting, using the arm that was connected to the I.V. "I'm afraid you'll go away."

"I promised I won't."

"The doctors will make you."

"Of course. You have to rest. But I'll be outside. In the hospital. On this floor."

"Elena, you love Kip. I used to hate you for that. I've been so rotten to you. I've been so cruel to him. To everyone. Why are you being so good to me?"

"Darling, there are various kinds of cruelty. There's intentional cruelty, accidental cruelty, and cruelty committed in self-defense. There are murderers, there are innocents. There are victims."

"You will call Kip?"

"I will," Elena said. She didn't say she'd already asked Reade to phone him. What if Reade had gotten him, and Kip refused to come?

"I'm sleepy," Nancy said. "Will you call Kip now?"

"Right away," said Elena.

"Would you—would you kiss me first?"

Elena did. Nancy's cheek was covered with perspiration; the girl was feverish. "Remember, there are all kinds of loving, Nancy. You are loved." By the time Elena reached the door of the cubicle, Nancy was already asleep. Once outside, Elena leaned against the jamb.

"Mrs. Brent," said the nurse. "Are you all right?"

"I'm fine," said Elena. "I just had a chill." She did not say she had a prescience of death.

* * *

Kip was in New York for meetings with the company's president. Reade reached him while Kip was in conference with Cohen. "I'll be on the next plane," said Kip, with an urgency Reade had never heard from a man outside of a boardroom. When Reade hung up, he was puzzled. What he did not comprehend was the loyalty of Jews to their families in times of distress.

Nancy was rapidly sinking when Kip arrived. The doctor told him her illness was terminal. As they were passing the nurses' station, a volunteer worker, a young American girl, shoved a book at Kip. It was one of Nancy's works on Women's Lib. "Would you get Miss O'Brien to sign this for me, Mr. Nathan?" she said.

"Get out," said the doctor. "The woman is dying." The intruder fled in terror. "*Perdonala,*" the doctor told Kip. "The nurses have just discovered that Mrs. Nathan is a celebrity." He shrugged. "It is human nature."

"She—Nancy—didn't tell them?" Kip asked. He didn't know why the doctor's answer meant so much to him.

"But no. She has been—" The doctor corrected himself. "She is undemanding, a wonderful patient. Here we are, Mr. Nathan. You may go right in."

"My darling," said Kip, "quite obviously, I can't let you out of my sight." He tried to conceal his flagging energy as well as his shock. Nancy's skin was pallid. It blended into the gray of the unbleached sheets, which bore telltale signs of the indignities suffered by former patients. He took her into his arms.

She was sobbing. "Oh, Kip," she said. "Kip, take me away. I know I'll die if I stay here. If we can get out, I'll be safe. I know I've been bad, but I won't be anymore. Oh, Kip, I love you so much."

"And I you." He kissed her, appalled by her frailty, her inability, despite her apparent desire, to cling to him.

"Where's Elizabeth?" Nancy said. "Why didn't you bring her?"

Kip was touched and astounded at once. "There was only one opening on the plane," he said. "Elizabeth's fine. You'll see for yourself in no time."

"I won't," Nancy murmured, "but thank you for that. For saying I will. Why wasn't I better to her?"

"Darling," Kip said. He stroked her hair, the red-gold luxuriance which he had loved; it was tangled and damp.

"Forgive me," she said. "I did everything wrong."

"We were both wrong. We made a mistake. There's nothing to forgive." As her eyes brimmed with tears, he realized the error of his words.

"I know our marriage was a mistake. I wish I could die not knowing that."

"I didn't mean our marriage," he said. "I meant our separation. Nancy, I need you. I was a shit. I am a shit to live with. Studio chiefs are the worst. All they care for is business. Creative. Financial. They're caught in the middle. And you got caught looking in. If I have the chance to do it all over—"

"You'll have the chance, Kip. *We* won't.

My God, he thought, can't I say anything right? Please, God, help me. "I mean, I am only going to change one thing—"

"Yes, me," Nancy said. "I know."

"Never you. I'll change me. The hell with the studio, bringing my business home at night, looking at dailies. Nancy—" He choked on the words. "I'll love you. I'll take the time to love you, as you deserve."

"Dear Kip. You talk as though I'm going to live," she said.

He was grateful for the dim light, for the fog, for the haze that spread through the shutters. He looked away from her for a minute, to clear his eyes with the back of his hand. "Now look, Ms. O'Brien," he said.

"Mrs. Nathan," she whispered.

"Have it your way, my love. Mrs. Nathan. We're going to leave here. We're going to get Elizabeth. No Nana. Just you and me and Elizabeth. We're going to take a vacation. Whatever you like—the Caribbean, the Lion Country Safari, the San Diego Zoo."

"Can we buy her a dog?" Nancy said, in a blessed non sequitur. At last, she was talking in terms of the future, not death. Nancy loved animals, and the dog was a sore point in their relationship. When they married, he had insisted she get rid of the champion poodle she'd bred and shown and adored.

"You can pick it," said Kip. "Any dog you want."

"Kip, hold me. I'm cold."

"My wife," he said. "I love you."

Nancy summoned a smile. "No, Kip. You don't love me.

You may be in love with me, as Elena said. A lot of men have been in love with me, Kip, but none of them loved me."

"I loved you. I love you. I was too stupid to realize how much you meant to me, but I've missed you—" He saw her eyelids flutter, wanting to close. She kept forcing them open. He felt her effort, first in the tensing, then in the laxity of her frame.

"Kip," she said, "there's no time. There's never time. Let me say it. I'd rather have had ten minutes with you than twenty years with any other man I've ever known. I was unfaithful to you, Kip, but I never was promiscuous."

"You don't have to say that, Nancy. Not to me."

"I do. I love you, Kip. And love makes you unafraid. I'm not scared in your arms." He bent over her, embracing her tightly. "Kip, will you do me a favor?"

"Anything."

"Kip, it's—it's Lizbeth." She couldn't pronounce the full name. He had to put his ear to her mouth now, to hear her.

"What is it?" he said.

"Kip, please, for Lizbeth. Don't let Elizabeth grow up like me."

He kissed her, but by then she was motionless, dead, in his arms. He set her on the pillow and stared at her, unbelieving. "Nancy," he said. He called her name repeatedly. Then he began to sob. He caressed her lifeless body, stifling his cries in the musty thermal blanket that covered her. Finally he walked to the bathroom, closing the door as if she were present, and vomited into the toilet. When he emerged, he ran cold water into the glass on the basin and rinsed his mouth.

"It's over," he said to Elena and Reade. As they reached the reception desk, he paused. "Room 117," Kip said to the nurse on duty. "My wife is dead."

"Miss O'Brien?" said the nurse.

"Mrs. Nathan. My wife, Mrs Nathan, is dead."

12

San Luis Obispo is a city of eucalyptus and pine, a coastal greenhouse situated two hours north of Santa Barbara. "San Louie," as it is called, is a demographic delight for filmmakers, an overpass for post-collegians and the middle-aged, a crossroad for the aged from nearby retirement compounds as well as for those of all ages traveling to San Simeon. More importantly, San Louie is a haven between Los Angeles and San Francisco, distant enough from each to elude the peripheral eye of the movie press.

For those and other reasons, the sneak preview of *Overwrought* took place at San Luis Obispo's Fremont Theatre. The last two rows in the house were reserved for the Hollywood types—the studio personnel, the creators and stars for whom this one-hundred-minute run of film in a middle-class suburb was crucial. The event held even more significance for its producer, director, and star than most because, as Adam had told Elena, it was a kind of tryout for those who wanted to make the big high-budget movie project, *Rogue's Gallery*. To outsiders, who still believed that Hollywood films are produced on studio assembly lines, the launching of *Gallery* might have seemed like a rather simple operation. In fact, it was not. It had some of the elements of a major business deal, except that the dealers were less predictable than most businessmen. The possible profits were less readily calculated in hard figures, and the psychological quirks of the participants were even more important factors than they would have been in the merger of two companies or the introduction of a new car model.

On one level, a movie package was a technical (and therefore fascinating), occasionally grubby matter of percentages, contracts, and speculation. On another level, it was a battle in which the users tested each other's powers and exploited each other's weaknesses. They were ready to maim and, on occasion, to kill. On still another level, it was an exercise in imagination. Hollywood's men and women bet hundreds of millions of dollars every year that they could captivate the imagination of their audience; but first they were captives of their own imaginations. No matter how cynical or calculated, any Hollywood deal represented someone's conviction that a new picture is a small miracle that can transform lives. And in many ways, it did. The making or unmaking of *Overwrought*, not to mention *Rogue's Gallery*, had changed many lives, and would change many more.

The audience was the incalculable, unknown factor in the new math of moviemaking. The people of San Louie and outlying towns like Morro Bay were of vital significance. They were the night's celebrities, not the New Hollywood folk who were there to observe them and to be guided by their reactions. The night belonged to the paying guests, although they did not know it.

Adam drove up that morning to be sure the corrected print had been delivered and to check the theater equipment. He and Marina took a suite at the Madonna Inn, as much for their own convenience as for that of the company people who followed. The projectionist ran the first two reels, and Adam was satisfied. He had seen the picture dozens of times in every stage, from the rushes to the final cut. He wouldn't admit that he was sick of it. He told himself he was too close to the project to judge it, but in the depths of his being he hated every frame. He thought it tawdry, a potboiler. Adam fought to reshoot certain scenes, but Kip was determined to keep the movie within its budget.

By the time Adam returned to the Inn, the others were there: Natalie, Jack, Elena, Randy, and Kip with his latest girl, a striking model named Madeline Farrell.

"Let's go for a swim," Marina said.

"Are you kidding?" said Adam. "It's fifty degrees." He knew she was serious. Marina had been smoking grass all day. She was stoned.

"I have a better idea," Kip said. "Let's have a drink. I ordered some liquor. Will someone call down for sandwiches?"

"I'll do it," said Jack.

Randy poured himself a triple Beefeaters on the rocks. He needs it, Elena thought. He doesn't know that our marriage, as well as his career, depends on the outcome of the sneak.

Elena accepted a scotch and water from Kip. She wasn't much of a drinker, but tonight she wanted some fortification.

"Tell Ken to make it louder," Adam said to Jack. Ken Watkins, the filmcutter, adjusted the fader on his lap. It controlled the sound. Kip slipped out with Madeline before the picture was over. He didn't like what he saw and heard. The audience was laughing at some of the serious dialogue, and several couples had left the theater during the movie. Anyway, Kip thought, it was the producer's and the director's job to judge the reaction.

When the movie broke, the manager was standing by desks in the lobby, handing out preview cards. "We want to know your opinion," he said. Most of the people were anxious to give it.

"Wasn't that stupid?" a girl in her twenties said to her escort. "I mean, the women were all like sticks. They couldn't read a line."

Randy didn't want to hear any more. "I need a drink," he said. "Are you coming, Elena?" They had agreed to meet in a bar until the cards were counted.

"I think I'll stay," said Elena.

"It will take an hour," said Randy.

"I'll join you soon."

Natalie and Marina left with Randy. Jack and Adam went to the manager's office with Larry Greenberg, Pacific's publicist, to read the cards.

Elena was sitting on the bench in the lobby when Kip returned. "How did it go?" he asked. He spoke even faster than he usually did; he was clearly uptight.

"I didn't hear many bravos." Elena said the words mournfully, as if she were reciting a dirge. Her own.

"Elena, no matter what happens tonight, you've got to leave him. I'm the guy who said wait. I've watched you. You can't go on like this."

"I don't know."

"Come on," Kip said. He took her into the office to read the cards.

"Listen to this one," Larry Greenberg was saying. " 'The actress who was murdered should have been killed before she started the picture. She had one expression. She looked like a bulldog.' "

"Very funny," said Adam. "Hello, Kip. Elena. Welcome aboard the Hindenburg."

"It's that bad?" Kip said.

"Catastrophe time," Jack said.

Greenberg was placing the cards in four piles on the desk, according to the responses to the first question: What did you think of the picture? Was it Excellent, Good, Fair, Poor? The second query was: What actor did you like best? The third allowed for any other comments the viewer cared to make.

"That's it," said Greenberg, after toting them up. "We have ninety-four cards. Forty-seven are poor, thirty-six fair, nine good, and two excellent. That's roughly a seventy-five percent fair-minus result."

"How do we find the two excellents?" Kip said, gloomily. "We'll plant them in every theater throughout the country to lead a standing ovation. This one is for the shelf. I can't release it."

Adam glanced at Elena, then back to Kip. "There's one positive, Kip. A very big positive. Most of the people raved about Randall Brent."

"That's true," said Larry Greenberg. "In general, the women found him sexy and the men said he gave a great performance."

"Wonderful, Larry," said Kip. "So we'll star him in a remake of *Gone With the Wind*. That wouldn't be a bad title for this turkey. I'm sorry, Elena."

"May I borrow the cards?" Elena said.

"What for?" said Kip.

"You'll see. Can I take them to the bar?"

"They're yours."

The place was called The Cigar Factory. When they arrived Marina and Natalie were laughing at the latest Hollywood joke. Randy was telling his troubles to Madeline. That was how gin affected him—as a depressant.

"Well?" said Randy. "Give me the death notice."

"Here are the preview cards," Elena said. "They loved you in it, Randy. And so—goodbye."

He stared at her. "Thanks," he said, "for both the job and the goodbye." She started to leave. "There's one condition." Oh shit, thought Elena. What now? "Never invite me to one of your parties," Randy said.

BOOK THREE
ROGUE'S
GALLERY

1

"I just dropped one of my oldest customers," said Harvey Parkes. "She moved to South Barrington."

"Where did she live before?" asked Elena.

"She had a beautiful house on Sunset. She sold it because her husband died."

"You are a terrible snob," Elena said. "You know you'd still do Jennifer if she moved to South Barrington."

"Mrs. Norton Simon wouldn't be caught dead on Barrington," said Harvey. Barrington, a street in suburban Brentwood, was always jammed with cars. The densely populated, moderately priced apartment houses provided no parking for visitors. "Besides," said Harvey, "I won't drive all the way to Brentwood."

"You drive all the way to Malibu for Dyan and Barbra and Jennifer," said Elena.

"That's different," said Harvey. "So does Jurgensen's. Mrs. Delaney told me that Jurgensen's delivers to Malibu twice a week for anyone else, but they deliver every day to Mrs. Simon."

"Do they really?" Natalie will love that, Elena thought. She'll dine out on the story of Jennifer's daily groceries for weeks. Mrs. Paul Delaney was married to a top executive for Hughes aircraft. Elena didn't know her personally, but she knew that when Harvey dropped a name he had a reason for it. He didn't want the name dropped again, except by himself. So she said, as he expected her to, "How is Mrs. Delaney?"

"She's fine. She gave me this for my birthday," he said. Harvey was pouring some warmed-up Nivea lotion into the palm of his hand. "It's the original digital watch."

Elena was impatient with his chatter this morning. She wanted him to get on with the massage. She had warned him that Edith Head was coming by with some sketches for her wedding dress, but the information didn't faze him. Harvey was behaving like his old sluggish self. No one could hurry Harvey Parkes. She admired the watch, although she really considered it vulgar, with its broad, bulky lines and its rubber-stamp numbers. It reminded her of something a red-neck would wear.

"It cost fifteen hundred dollars," he said.

"How do you know what it costs?"

"I priced it."

You would, thought Elena. You sound like Reade Jamieson. "I'm impressed," she said.

"Now, Mrs. Brent, if you'll turn over." As was his custom, he turned his back and walked away while she obeyed, adjusting the towels to cover her breasts and pubis. Harvey's bluff was pointless. Invaribly, Elena saw him peeking at her while she slipped out of her leotards and climbed on the table. His coyness distressed her more than his curiosity, but Elena went along with his make-believe.

"All right," she said, edgily. "I'm ready."

He strode the length of the screening room in the Holmby Hills house Elena had found for Reade. "I was thinking the other day," Harvey said, "that every one of my clients is either a millionaire or a movie star."

"Except me," said Elena.

"You will be, when you're married."

Do you think I don't know that? Elena thought. Why else would I be marrying that bastard? Reade is a multimillionaire, but Harvey Parkes doesn't know he's a cheap millionaire. Kip was right, thought Elena. Since my divorce I've become just an extra woman at parties. Although attractive single men outnumbered attractive single women in the New Hollywood, most of the interesting men were gay. They had nothing to offer in the way of a future. Elena was a woman who looked to the future. Which is why she moved in with Reade Jamieson and why she decided to marry him.

"I'm taking a full-page ad in SHARE's calendar," Harvey said. "It reads: 'Harvey Parkes, By Appointment.' No phone number, no address. How do you like it?"

"I love it." Harvey Parkes was the only unlisted masseur in the city. Elena had advised him to stay out of the telephone book. She explained that exclusivity meant business. SHARE was an industry charity for exceptional children, whose members sponsored an annual dinner and entertainment. People attended the gala in rented costumes or Levi's; the invitations read "Come in western dress." Such stellar figures as Sinatra, Lucille Ball, John Wayne, Milton Berle, Dean Martin, and Don Rickles volunteered their services for the show. "But Harvey," Elena said, "I'm having second thoughts. SHARE has the kind of angels you'd love for your clients. Janet Leigh, Jo Stafford, Gisela Johnson . . ."

"Who's Gisela Johnson?"

"She's Mrs. Arte Johnson."

"Oh," said Harvey. "Well, I'm busy enough. If they need me, they'll find me. I don't want my phone number floating around. You have no idea how many calls from nobodies my secretary gets every day. I'm not about to take anybody who isn't important."

Elena was hardly listening. "You're right," she said, nervously. "Harvey, if you could speed it up . . ."

"If you want to be paunchy, I'll speed it up. Okay, I've finished your arms. But don't forget the isometrics I taught you. You can do them anywhere. Your upper arms are still okay, but I see the signs of flab." He parted the towels and began on her stomach. He called his method "clipping." Harvey said it distributed the fat from one part of the body to another. He practiced his method long before Nicole Ronsard began writing on cellulite. He didn't believe in cellulite. He attacked any theory that wasn't his own. Harvey believed in clipping and mistresses. He'd passed through the Oriental phase; he now dated mostly blacks. Elena wondered whether the women were a ruse. After all, he was exposed to the most glamorous bodies in the world, and he never so much as made a pass at his female clients. Having finished her stomach, he tucked one towel between her legs with decorous care and started to clip her thighs.

"I've always wanted to ask you something," she said. "Why do you make people lie on their stomachs first and begin with the back? Isn't it more relaxing to do it the other way around?"

"It's funny, nobody ever asked me that," he said. "I'll tell you. When I got out of the Army in the forties, I had the fags. Men were wearing gabardine pants—and I lost more pants that way. They'd get so excited so quickly when I did them front first, they'd spurt all over me, or grab me, or both. So I worked into it gradually. Then, through the fags I was introduced to older women, and they became my customers."

"I'll bet you had problems there," said Elena.

Harvey smiled. "I certainly did. Older women have special demands. They're lonely, and most of them are neglected by their husbands."

"So what did you do?"

"I did what they wanted, but I was young then, and foolish. Their husbands would sometimes come in. I lost more customers that way than I lost pants with the faggots. Through the old ladies, I finally got the young girls."

"Weren't you tempted?"

"Sure. But I learned my lesson. Never mix business with sex. Then, through you, I got onto celebrities. Now it's too dangerous. I'm not taking any chances on losing my clients. Everyone asks me what it's like to handle the most beautiful bodies in the world."

"And what do you say?"

"I say I wish I was younger."

Elena laughed to disguise her restlessness. "I have to shower, Harvey. Edith is coming. She'll be here any minute."

"All right," he said, in a tone of complaint, "but this was too short a session." Still, he sounded relieved. "I'll get you next time. We'll work for two hours." He consulted his appointment book. "How's Thursday at two o'clock?" He watched her surreptitiously as she belted her terry cloth robe.

"Two o'clock is fine."

"And no cancelations. You're always saying you're tired, or sick, or have to rush out. You're worse than Mike Richards. Every time I came up to do him on the set he was hiding. I had to ask the other actors where he was and then chase him around the scenery."

For what? Elena wanted to say. What she said instead was, "I'll see you on Thursday."

"Do you realize what we've done for your figure? You'd begun to put on weight. Since we've been working two times a week, everyone has told me how great you look. I can't afford a fat student, Mrs. Brent. Being engaged to a millionaire seems to suit you, but you have to watch the food. Those chinks, Ching and Chong, can ruin you." In

Harvey Parkes' terminology, "Ching and Chong" translated as Tai and Eddie, the couple Elena had hired to run the house. Elena accepted Harvey's bigotry. He referred to Orientals as "chinks" and to blacks as "niggers"—and that, despite his penchant for Oriental and black girls.

"Tai is an excellent cook," she said, defensively.

"You should fire him. Meanwhile, stay off the noodles and rice."

"Look, Harvey, I have to go . . ."

"I'm a little early for my next appointment," he said. "Do you mind if I use the telephone?"

"Of course not. Watch the television. Anything. Would you like some coffee? I'll send some in."

"Okay, but no cream or sugar. Those chinks will kill you. By the way," he said, "do you have any more of those pills? The ones that give you energy. I get awfully tired at two o'clock in the afternoon. Just sometimes. I don't get tired very often."

"You shouldn't, although they're safe enough. They were invented for pregnant women. I'll send some along with the coffee."

"Thanks," said Harvey Parkes, who was disturbed by her ripening body. He knew she wasn't pregnant; she'd told him once she could never have children. She took the pink pills—Preludin, she called them—to curb her appetite. "Remember, don't eat."

"I'll remember." Elena felt sorry for Harvey Parkes. At fifty-two he was doing a young man's job. She rushed out of the room; she couldn't wait to get to the phone. She wanted to speak to Natalie about Jurgensen's special-delivery service for Jennifer Simon.

Edith Head had the greatest collection of cacti and one of the few authentic adobe houses in Beverly Hills. She also had eight Oscars, two more than Billy Wilder. Edith was revered and respected by her peers. However they might revile one another, designers in the New Hollywood paid obeisance to the tiny, ebony-haired duenna with bangs. Edith Head, who was otherwise known as Mrs. Wiard Ihnen, wore tortoiseshell spectacles long before they were fashionable. Like the now historical MCA agent, Edith believed in basic black for herself ("with pearls"), but she pioneered glamour for her clients, the stars. Edith was a holdover from the Golden Era of Hollywood, when dress was dictated not by the Paris salons or Seventh Avenue but by the silents and talkies that were the fables of the world. She had dressed everyone—Bette Davis in *All About Eve,* Grace Kelly in *To Catch a Thief*, Jill Clayburgh in *Gable and Lombard.* Like the goddesses of ancient Greece, she gave her beautiful charges wings, while folding her own unmanicured nails behind her. Edith Head was to fashion what Edith Hamilton was to mythology. And so Elena had chosen her to design her wedding gown.

Edith's sketches covered the coffee table in the living room. "As a second bride," she said, "you can't wear white. A long veil isn't proper either. I'd like to do ivory or pale beige chiffon. Beige would be flattering to your blondness. Although I did that for Elizabeth Taylor at her second or third wedding, I can't remember which. She was dazzling."

"I'm sure she was," said Elena, without enthusiasm.

"Don't you like Elizabeth Taylor?" said Edith.

"I love her. But I wanted something original."

"My dear, this *is* original. I was only referring to the color. I'm partial to beige and this sketch. I've never done anything like it before. Since you're being married at noon, I like the ankle length."

Elena lit a cigarette and studied the drawing. "I love the soft, full sleeves," she said.

"And notice the cowl neck," Edith said. "The cowl has a drape that falls forward over the head, like a scarf. It's very plain and very simple and very understated and very expensive-looking. Creamy beige with real creamy pearls."

I have no real pearls, Elena thought. I can borrow some from Marvin Hime. Hime was known as "The Jeweler of the Stars." He loaned his high-priced baubles to the already gem-laden ladies of the New Hollywood. Did the outside world really believe that all those Gabors acquired all those diamonds as gifts from ex-husbands and suitors? "Furio, what do you think?" Elena asked her collaborator.

"I think it's perfect, stunning," he said. "Edith, what about the matron of honor?"

"I don't know why I feel anti-color. The pinks and blues have been overdone. But we must have a contrast. For Natalie, who's a brunette, I'd do pale green or lavender."

"Good," said Furio. "The palest lavender, but make it midcalf, so she doesn't compete with the bride."

Tai announced lunch, and Elena, thinking of Harvey Parkes, felt guilty. She'd ordered fried chicken and a Waldorf salad with lemon soufflé for desert. "At this rate, I may not fit into the dress," she told Edith.

"We'll manage. You'll look divine," she said. "Now, about the bouquet. I see orchids and baby's breath—*Phalaenopsis*. You know what they are? White butterfly orchids—the very expensive ones."

"How about Reade?" Elena asked. "What should he wear?"

"A dark business suit. Would you like me to dress him?"

"You dress a man? That's a first," said Elena.

"Not at all," said Furio. "*Cara,* Edith dressed Redford and Newman for *The Sting*. She won an Oscar for the picture."

"Imagine," Edith said, "dressing Newman and Redford. Such beautiful men. It's much more fun dressing men than women. Which is partly because you can put a man into anything nowadays and you don't go wrong, where you can with a woman. The accepted looks for men can be brocade jackets, velvet jackets, anything."

"But not for a wedding at noon," said Furio.

"And not for Reade, the reactionary," Elena added. "Let's stick to the business suit."

"Of course," Edith said.

"Could it be a pinstripe?" Elena asked. "Bill Blass was wearing a pinstripe recently at Doubles in New York, and he looked so smart I told him he'd bring the pinstripe back in. He grinned and said, 'As far as I'm concerned, it never went out.' "

"Bill's a handsome man," Edith said, "But Bill would never wear a pinstripe suit to his wedding."

"Is Bill getting married?" Elena asked.

"If he is," said Edith Head, "he certainly has the talent to design his own suit for the ceremony."

Elena put down the needlepoint canvas she was making for Furio. She could not concentrate now that her wedding was imminent. She had few illusions when she agreed to marry Reade. As with Randall Brent, she was striking a bargain. Marriage, she believed, was a synonym for compromise. Randy had wanted her as a front for his bisexuality; Elena needed him as a guise for her sordid past. Each of her alliances was a subterfuge. Through Elena, Reade became an initiate to the salons of the celebrated. In Reade, Elena was seeking a sponsor for her own salon.

She did not love him, nor was she happy living with him. Happiness was transient, a moving target; it was not her aim in life. In the absence of Adam, Reade resurrected her sexual hang-ups, her conflicts, her lifelong concern that she was unable to love. Adam had awakened her in a way she had never known, in an arousal of sex accompanied by the feeling of love, in an evocation of passion and emotion at once. The experience had frightened and disturbed her. She had devised a philosophy that felt far safer, the tenet that love was a myth, a romantic conceit, a kind of neurosis.

She had been scrupulous with Adam, never letting him guess the degree of her caring, her terror of flying too high. She had gone even further, damaging Adam's ego. Adam had proposed to her during their second weekend together at the Kaufmans' beach house; Elena laughed, perversely. She continued, all through their affair, to dispel his persuasions. Had she driven him back to Marina, or had he gone of his own accord, through opportunism? Elena would never know. She persistently concealed her longings from Adam, fearing that if she expressed them she would be vulnerable to rejection, in danger of being destroyed.

Elena looked out at the masses of flowers that glistened in the arcs of the sprinklers on the lawn. She shrugged and turned on the TV set.

She was watching the Mike Douglas show when she heard Reade enter, his unmistakably arrogant voice giving orders to Tai about dinner that night. She sat up abruptly and doused her cigarette. Reade despised cigarette smoke. She slipped on her shoes, since he also despised her habit of kicking them off. She fanned the smoke and opened a window to clear the air.

"I might have known you'd be wasting your time," he said, "on television. Well, at least it keeps you out of the department stores."

She decided to disregard his bad humor. "Darling," she said as she kissed him, "how did it go?"

"How could it go? Those goddamn directors' meetings. They want a token woman. They'll probably put Pearl Bailey on the board. Let's not discuss it. I need a drink." He took the vodka out of the freezer and mixed a couple of martinis. The drink relaxed him. "How did my bride spend her day?"

Elena was expecting the question: he always wanted to know where she was every minute. She had to answer him and she did, with misgivings. "Darling. I think I've found my wedding dress. So does Furio. I want to show you the sketch." She crossed the room to the baby grand. Edith, with her usual wit, had left it beside the photograph of Elena and Cary Grant. How fitting, Elena thought; she likes beautiful people, and so do I.

"This is signed by Edith Head," he said. "I'm not sure about this, Elena."

"She's the best in the business, Reade."

"And the most expensive, I bet."

"Reade, Edith is a close friend of mine. Don't worry."

"I'm worried. Did you discuss the price?"

"Not exactly. I told you, Edith's a friend."

"You'd better invite her to the wedding."

"Of course. I promise you, Reade, there won't be a problem."

"There'd better not be. Settle the price in advance."

"I will," she said. "I'm sure Edith will do it at cost."

The Jamiesons' wedding day dawned like a postcard of Southern California, a *trompe l'oeil* of sunlight slicing the landscape, streaking the hedges, and stippling the palm trees. But the focus of attention for the invited and uninvited—the celebrities and the plainly curious—was All Saints' Church, the only Episcopal church in Beverly Hills.

Reade was waiting with Kip, his best man, when Elena came into the vestibule with Natalie. "What a breathtaking bride," Kip said, as he kissed her. Reade was customarily astonished. He didn't understand Kip's remark. To me, she is hardly breathtaking, thought the groom, as the organist struck the first chords of the wedding march. Natalie and Kip took their places in front of Elena and Reade, and they started the torturous measured gait toward the altar. Elena took Reade's arm, and they followed. To me, this woman's a peasant, Reade reflected. She has no beauty. She is coarse, not refined. He nodded stiffly to their friends in the pews on either side. But all these people think she has beauty and style, so I must be wrong, Reade decided.

He didn't even say I look lovely, Elena thought. A gown

by Edith Head, my makeup and hairdo by Sydney Guilaroff, and Reade is not even impressed. I know he has no breeding, but why won't he learn? He never will. She found herself smiling at a row of strange men with flat ears and bent noses. How did they get in? she wondered. I've never seen them before. They look like thugs. She shivered. The men must be friends of Reade's. They were standing on the epistle side, the groom's side of the church. Why am I here? thought Elena. What am I doing here? She was overwhelmed by the urge to flee.

With my money, thought Reade, I could have gotten a much younger, prettier woman. But this one has the status I need. She moves in the glamorous circles I've never been able to dent. She has the ineffable charm of an enchantress. That's it, he thought, Elena is a witch. She's an ugly witch, but she's useful. She'll get me the good publicity I need. I can use her for a couple of years, if I don't wind up in the trunk of a car.

He's mean, thought Elena, as she nodded to Loretta Young and her popular escort, Max Factor. But I can use him. God knowns Randy was mean, and I didn't use him. He used me. She acknowledged Pat and Bill Buckley, who were on the gospel side—her side—of the church. I don't want to introduce them to Reade, she thought. They'll see right through him. The only thing Reade has is money, but money is power. Money spells security. I've never had security in my life, at least not since my father died. I'm tired of standing on my own.

She'll give me position, Reade thought. I'm rich, but in the jet set I'm just a professor from Cambridge, a money man who made good. Thank God they don't know how I made good. They don't care. With Elena, I can keep them from finding out.

Reade came to the church by taxi, Elena thought. I'm surprised he shelled out the money for a cab. I made sure he didn't see the limousine that I hired to bring us—Edith, Sydney, and me—but what will he say when he sees it after the ceremony? The hell with what he says. He won't say anything. There will be people around. I'll face his reprisals later, alone. I've done it before; I can do it again.

They had reached the altar, and, as Elena looked up to the pulpit, she experienced a sudden headiness. The smell of the incense, the sweetness of it, assaulted her. She listened to the voice of the Reverend Clarke Oler, but the words of the traditional service came through to her like an incantation. Elena was mesmerized by the prismatic colors of the candles, by the starkness of the lilies, and by the majesty of the cross. Kip handed the narrow gold wedding band to Reade, who slipped it on her finger. Elena heard someone say, distinctly, from the row of the pews behind her, "Aren't they handsome together? Look how in love they are."

2

Elena stepped out of the shower at Washington's Madison Hotel. The Jamiesons were in the nation's capital at the invitation of Victor Kroll, the National Economic Adviser. Kroll was the most considerate of hosts. He had arranged a luncheon that afternoon with the true (and few) bright members of the Administration—Vice President Rockefeller, Defense Secretary Donald Rumsfeld, Treasury Secretary William Simon, and Attorney General Edward Levi. Kroll was cheery throughout the day, since the President's stock had jumped in a popularity poll released that morning.

They left Sans Souci, the National Economic Adviser's favorite restaurant, flanked by Secret Service men. San Souci was a brisk five-minute walk from the White House, and the limousine was waiting outside, but Victor preferred to walk. "Is there anything special you'd like to do?" he asked Elena.

"You've taken too much trouble already," Reade said. Elena agreed to that. Her husband had urged her to call her friend Victor Kroll from New York, a gesture which was tantamount to an invitation. Reade was not only a cube, he was a climber.

"I'd like to visit the Kennedy graves," Elena said.

They had reached the east gate of the White House. The government car, which had been trailing them slowly, stood at the curb. "Take my car," Victor said. "You'll get right through. If you go any other way, you'll have a long walk."

"Are you sure?" said Elena.

"On second thought, I'll go with you," Victor said.

My God, I could love this man, Elena reflected. I do love him. Victor Kroll, the Republican, was a patriot. His respect for the Kennedys and his adopted country transcended political parties. His achievements belonged to history, but his morals belonged to the world. Elena recalled the weekend when Kroll stayed with her and Randy at Malibu Beach. They were giving a party in his honor on Saturday night. The day was so glorious, and Victor was so enjoying it, she suggested he send his car and driver to town to pick up his date. "Why waste ninety minutes of sunshine?" she said.

"I would never use a government car to pick up a girl," Victor said, without a trace of smugness. He was simply making a statement. Had she been in his place, Elena would not have detected the moral scruple. She learned a lot that day about Kroll's integrity.

They took the usual safety precautions on the drive to Arlington. One of the Secret Service men drove; another sat beside him. Reade and Elena sat on the left behind the driver. Kroll always sat on the right behind the man who was free to act (or fire, Elena knew) in case of trouble. That was only one facet of the government's anti-assassination procedures. The cemetery was graded: they climbed several levels to the tombs, accompanied by dozens of tourists who wanted, like them, to pay homage to the brothers whose radiance had been blotted out by the untimely flash of a murderer's gun.

"We adore them, but what do we do for them?" said Elena. She was crying as she gazed at the stark memorials. "Death is nothing. It's the hurts along the way that count. Life is aloneness." She was thinking of John and Robert Kennedy, of Nancy, and of herself.

" 'No man is an island,' " said Victor. "John Donne wrote that in the 1600s. Has any writer ever written on any other theme?"

Reade remained silent. He only read books on computers.

Elena was moved by Kroll's comment. She grew anxious. The Secret Service men had disappeared. She finally spotted them on the level below. They were vigilant, scanning the crowd, but Victor, Reade, and Elena stood alone, alone on the palpable ground of death and the finite. Elena, with her atheistic training, could not conceive of infinity except as a mathematical postulate. The countless, unpredictable strangers made her apprehensive. She shifted purposely to the outside of the step, facing Victor, using her body as a shield between him and the tourists below. She felt compelled to do so when she was with Victor Kroll. Elena was not courageous, but his virtue and vulnerability incited temerity in her.

Later, in the car, she raised the issue she had suppressed when they were together in public. "Victor, anyone there could have killed you if they'd wanted to. If someone fired at you, the Secret Service would have been too late."

Kroll smiled. "Undoubtedly, Elena. The Secret Service is more a deterrent to kidnaping than to assassination."

"Aren't you through in the bathroom?" said Reade. "We'll be late." Victor was taking them to the Jockey Club for dinner.

Elena shuddered. Reade's impatience with her was interminable. Reade was forever chiding her on the go; Randy, at least, mostly sulked in his room. When he ventured out, she escaped his aggressions. Elena wiped off the excess body lotion with her towel. "I'm almost ready, darling," she called. "We won't be late."

When she joined him in the living room of their suite a few minutes later, she was fully dressed. "You see?" she said, in a placating voice. "We're early. Victor's calling for us at eight." She opened the cabinet that the management stocked with bottles of liquor. "Why don't we have a drink?" she said.

"You think just because it's in the room it's complimentary?" he said. "They count the bottles and replace them. It goes on the bill. Can't you wait until we get to the restaurant?"

"Of course. I just thought . . ."

"You don't think, my dear. Not about money. Tell me, what did you do when you were married to that impoverished ham?"

"I spent money," she said. She said it defiantly, although Elena was normally too frightened of Reade to defy him. She had been drinking more since her marriage to Reade. He drank heavily, but on the liquor of others. Why do I want a drink? she thought. Because I need an outlet. Because he is dull. Because I am bored.

"Maybe you'd like to go back to your has-been."

Not that, she thought. "Randy's not a has-been. You know he's a star on TV. Let's forget him. Darling, I forgot to tell you. Bill Fine called today. He wants to do a layout on our new villa in *Town & Country*." The house in Cap Ferrat was a sore point. They had traveled from Paris to the south of France on their honeymoon, and Elena had urged Reade to buy it. He called it "a useless extravagance." She didn't want to spend all her time at his house in Cambridge or their new mansion in Los Angeles. Now that she was married to a millionaire, she wanted to travel. When they stayed at hotels, Reade invariably asked for the cheapest suite at the cheapest A hotel. Elena had convinced him they needed houses in which to entertain; Reade loved society. She was taking a chance by mentioning the retreat on the Riviera, hoping the spread in *Town & Country* would assuage his annoyance over the cost of the real estate. Aside from his bank account and hobnobbing with the famous and frivolous, Reade valued nothing more than a line in a column.

"That's some excuse for spending a million dollars on a white elephant, especially one that's painted pink," he said. Elena, who understood semaphore, knew he was pleased. "Tell him yes, if you think so." That signaled "tell him yes." "I suppose they want pictures of you in the house?"

"They want us both," said Elena. "I told Bill we'd be there next month."

Reade's surprise turned to conciliation, as it usually did in what Elena called their verbal swordplay. His ego told him Elena's frequent portraits in *Vogue* and *Harper's Bazaar,* which were virtually house organs, emanated from her stature as Mrs. Reade Jamieson. "That wasn't a bad idea of yours," he said. "Let's have a drink." He smoothed his mustache in the mirror over the cabinet that concealed a small refrigerator, and then he broke out the ice.

"My aides investigated your jet," Victor said during dinner.

"Did it pass?" said Reade.

"I could make a bad pun and say 'with flying colors,'" said Victor. "In fact, I will. What I won't do is show their report to the President. According to their research, it's safer than Air Force One."

"My husband could be a mechanic, if he weren't a genius," Elena said. "You don't think he'd own a plane that wasn't the best?"

"Since my Grumman Gulfstream passed muster, we leave at noon tomorrow," Reade said. Kroll and a date were accompanying them to New York. They had tickets for *Equus* the following night.

The maître d' hovered over them. Kroll ordered liqueurs all around, and Elena reflected the service was excellent—if you were Victor Kroll, Jack Valenti, Joe Alsop, or anyone close to the center of power. Washington's Jockey Club reminded Elena of a mock-up of Manhattan's "21." The Jockey Club could have been, in fact, a long-distance TV monitor for the famous restaurant in New York. The decor, the food, the dignity of the patrons were almost identical. Except that the Washington clientele consisted largely of politicians and the well-heeled or expense-account press. Like its northern counterpart, the Jockey Club's theme was equestrian: its walls were multidimensional, with saddles and photos of horses. The effect was soothing—leather and suede, brown and white, with touches of red.

The Jockey Club had an advantage over dinners at home in Washington. The host couldn't separate the men from the women for coffee, cigars, and political talk at the end of the meal. The custom was unique in the nation's capital and, Elena thought, outmoded. Elena enjoyed the stimulation of men. How often, in the elaborate townhouses of Georgetown, she had been caught in the arid conversation of wives. Political wives, she was amazed to discover, were like hausfraus everywhere else, only more so. They were caught up in the humdrum—discussions of diaper rash, house painters, marketing. Elena was more taken with statistics on the high cost of living or the latest Russian defections than she was with the efficacy of soaking your grimy utensils in Spic and Span.

3

They registered at the Gotham Hotel in New York, which satisfied Reade because it had a good address. "It's just across the street from the St. Regis," he told Elena, "and the suites are one-half the price." (They're half the size as well, she thought, as she unpacked and jammed their belongings into the dingy closet.) Kroll and Eileen Witt, who was a Washington socialite, were staying at the Park Avenue apartment of NBC's Herb and Judy Schlosser.

After theater, the six of them went to El Morocco, the private supper club on East Fifty-fourth Street. Elena was dancing with Herb when she felt a tap on the shoulder. "Hello," said the man with the thinning platinum hair. "Long time no see." She recognized him at once; he was unmistakable. He was Wally Swoboda. "Can I cut in?" he asked.

"If you don't mind," said Elena, "we just started dancing—"

"I hate to lose her," Herb said, simultaneously. "But okay. I'll get you later, Elena."

"Thanks," said the blinking man. "I'm Walter Sands." The name hit her like a piece of shrapnel. Randy had told her about the new producer at Pacific while he was filming *Overwrought*. "He's the 'King of the Cunt and Cock Films,' " Randy explained. Elena let it pass. How could she have made the connection? The name was different. Besides, she hadn't seen or heard from Swoboda in fourteen years. She was still a novitiate, having made three dirty movies for him, when she left West Berlin with Fred Hunt, the American correspondent of *Life* magazine. "I've been meaning to call you," said Sands (Swoboda, Elena thought grimly). "I'm in Hollywood now, you know."

"I didn't know," she lied. "I hope you're doing well."

"I can't complain." He looked towards their table,

towards Reade and Victor Kroll. "You've done extremely well," he said. "Is that Victor Kroll?" He squinted in the dim light.

"Yes," she said. "He's a friend." She struggled to maintain her composure and to keep up with him. He scrambled when he danced, like an acrobat.

"I'm out of the fuck films, you know." She flinched at the phrase from his mouth, from her past. "I'm with Pacific."

"Mr. Sands?"

"It's Walter to you, Elena."

"Do you mind? I'd like to rejoin my table, Walter."

"In a while. I've been wanting to talk to you. How about a drink at the bar?"

"I'd rather not, just now. Another time. My husband . . ."

"Your husband might be very interested in what I have to say." She stopped dead on the floor. Her stomach capsized like a boat. "You see, I have these movies I made in Berlin."

"I don't know what you mean. . . ."

"I'll explain, at the bar." She glanced at their table, relieved that no one was looking their way. Sands slipped his arm through hers. She let him guide her to the bar in the Casbah room.

"Really, I have to get back," she said.

"Then I'll lay it all out for you. I have these pictures you made. . . ."

"I did that to help you."

"Come now, Elena. You needed the money. You're talking to Wally Swoboda, not Reade Jamieson." So he knew her husband's name. What else did he know about her? She shivered. "You cold? We'll fix that. What are you drinking?"

"I'm not drinking," she said.

He ordered a gin martini. "Okay, Elena. Here's the pitch. You have something I want, and I have something you need very much."

"You want money? I haven't got any, Mr. . . ."

"Walter." He laughed. "No, I don't want money. Elena, I could buy and sell your stuffy, professorial husband a thousand times. You think he's self-made? *Fortune* magazine listed me as one of the fifty richest men in the world."

"Then what do you want of me?"

"Sit down," he said. She took the barstool she had refused before. "It's simple. You are the number one hostess in Hollywood, maybe in all the world. Oh, you're not exactly royalty, but I can wait for that. What I want, Elena, is prestige. You're the one who can give it to me."

"I don't understand," she said, weakly. She thought she did.

"I want to go to your parties. I want to be photographed with you. You might say . . ." He leered at her. "You might say I want to be your closest friend." His droning voice conveyed to Elena that skirt of madness she'd detected when he told her about his fantasies of making the Busby Berkeley fuck film so long ago in Berlin.

"I have to go," she said.

"Where are you staying? I'll call you."

"No, no. We leave tomorrow." She couldn't let Reade, or anyone, discover her past.

"Then I'll call you in L.A.," he said. "Unless, of course, you have no interest in the negatives."

"How about prints?" she said. "What good are the negatives without the prints?"

"You'll get them all," he said. "Both. Elena, I'm a man of my word. If we make a bargain, I'll keep it." (I bet you will, she wanted to say.)

"Why don't I call you? Tomorrow morning, before we go back?"

"That's better," said Walter Sands, the entrepreneur. "I'm at the Waldorf Towers. I'll expect your call. My first appointment's with Cohen, at two."

Her compulsion was not to return to the table. She could leave, sending Reade a message that she had a splitting headache and didn't want to spoil the party. She had no money. She had left her purse at the table, but she could easily walk the half-dozen blocks to the hotel on Fifth Avenue. No, she decided. She had to be by herself. If she left without saying goodbye, Reade would follow her. Whatever her story, it must have the substance of truth. Reade knew she had gotten her period that morning. He also knew she suffered badly from menstrual cramps. Reade was nothing if not a logical positivist. He believed her story. She took a taxi to the Gotham.

Since Reade was sure to examine the calls on the hotel bill, she phoned Kip Nathan collect in Beverly Hills. "Mr.

Nathan is finishing dinner," Peter told the long-distance operator. "Can he call Mrs. Jamieson back?"

"No. Tell him it's urgent," she said.

"Kip, what can I do?" she asked, when she finished recounting her conversation with Sands.

"Call Ted," said Kip. "He's the smartest man I know."

"So much for Warren's theory," Elena said. "Agents may run the studios, but attorneys run the world." One of Ted's dummies answered the phone, but he came on immediately. "Ted, will you help me?" she said. "Not only my marriage but Reade's reputation is at stake."

"His reputation? Elena, I thought you were brighter than that. Don't worry. I'll take care of it. It's done. You'll have your negatives and your prints."

"Ted, what do you mean, 'his reputation'? What did you mean about Reade?"

"I men there are only two men in the world who can settle this by a single phone call. Reade is one, and the other is me. Elena, your husband is deeply rooted into the Mafia. How do you think he made his money? How do you think he met Kip? I introduced him to Kip. Your husband, Reade Jamieson, put me in business."

4

"Have you read Clare Ballen today?" Ted asked.

"I haven't had time to read a phone message," Kip said. He was lying on the hospital bed in his screening room at Pacific.

"I thought her lead might interest you, so I brought it along." Ted put on his glasses and unfolded the column. "Mr. X. is the King of Smut, or he was until not long ago, when he joined our second most productive studio. Mr. X., unfortunately, has so far been unproductive there. Now poor Mr. X. is even losing his past productions. On Monday, Mr. X. flew in from New York and conferences with his studio's president, Mr. Y. Mr. X. went directly to his office—only to find it pilfered. A rapid inventory proved that nothing had been taken.

"Minutes later, Mr. X. got a call from Mrs. X., his slightly older and somewhat blowsy wife. Mrs. X. had just returned from San Francisco, where she had been visiting relatives, to discover that someone had broken into their house while the servants were away. (Their servants cover five letters of the alphabet, A through E.) The safe in the X.s' library had been blown. Mrs. X.'s jewels, which are valued at something over two million dollars, were intact. What was missing? Ah, there's the rub, or the shakedown, or whatever. Gone were the negatives—and the positives—of three pornographic movies Mr. X. produced and directed years ago in West Berlin. What did the films have in common? They starred Mrs. Z.

"Mrs. Z. is one of our city's super-A hostesses now, as she was before she married Mr. Z. Her first husband was Mr. S., who is one of the biggest stars on television. Her present husband, Mr. Z., is an Easterner with an engineering background who's so rich he can afford to buy IBM. His favorite pastimes, indeed, are working with computers and playing with abacuses. The moral: If you've been fooling around displaying your assets in front of a camera, you're apt to marry a man who has plenty of assets."

"You dog. You pulled it off for Elena. Terrific. But couldn't you keep it out of the papers? What will Jamieson think of that one?"

"He's thought already. Clare told me at lunch he's threatened to stop publication of the novel she's writing."

"That's pretty rotten. Her mother's very sick, and she needs the money. Can he?"

"Who knows? Not if I can help it."

"She's a damn good reporter. What's happened to honest journalism?"

"Except for the Washington *Post,* it went out with Watergate."

"But Clare had everything right?"

"She was accurate down to the last detail. That bastard even plays with abacuses. All she left out were the tape recorders. He uses them to his own advantage, too."

"I agree he's a bastard, but he's got the money Elena needs. And he started you off with his pals."

"I've paid him back, with interest. Including this latest caper. Getting back those pornos wasn't exactly easy. And staying clean in the press."

"Then you planted the story with Ballen? I see. To keep the story out of cityside, where it could have caused trouble—at least an investigation."

"You're getting too shrewd, Kip."

"Where are the prints? We can screen them sometime. I bet Elena's not bad."

"I wouldn't know. She turned me down."

"You never told me. During Randy?"

"Before. In Rome, when she lived with Fred Hunt. My timing was bad, I guess. You've never had her?"

"Never. We joke about it. Why spoil a good friendship?"

"I can't think of a better reason to spoil one. Listen, Kip, I came early on purpose. You're not going to like this, but the boys told Cohen they want Mike Richards for Bellamy."

"He's too young."

"They'll use makeup."

"That shit Richards has Mob connections? He'll never work in this town again."

"You son of a bitch. Is that why he's been auditioning? Not even testing. Reading. His picture with you is making a fortune."

"He'll spend his life auditioning. He'll be lucky to carry a spear at the Met."

"I believe you. Okay. So Richards is out. So you've got no cast."

"We've got Marina, or so Adam tells me."

"He's got her, you mean. By the pussy. Marina Vaughan, The Constant Nymph."

"Help yourself to a drink. And get me one. Scotch, neat."

Ted walked to the table along the far wall. It was stacked with booze and sandwiches. "Have you looked at these tests?"

"Just once, with Baker and Kaufman. Charlie Finestein, Kaufman's replacement, is coming tonight."

"Finestein was good in the forties, but don't you think he's old-fashioned for this one?"

"He's so old-fashioned Hollywood loves him." Kip smiled at Ted. "He's so old-fashioned he's getting the AFI award next year. He's been broke. He's been sick. He's been an alcoholic. If he directs *Gallery*, it will cop every Oscar in sight. The Oscars are a popularity contest, baby."

"What isn't?" said Ted. "That's why I'll stick with the power."

"I like the two guys in the last one," said Harry Waller, as the lights went up in the screening room.

"That guy in the first—what's his name?" said Finestein. "I've seen him on television."

"He's too pretty," said Waller.

"He's not too pretty for me," said Marina, taking one last drag on the roach and stifling it in the ashtray beside her. Marina was wired. Adam looked at her darkly, and not in the biblical sense.

"The president says he won't go with unknowns. I told you that, Harry," said Kip.

"I don't give a fuck what the president says," said Waller. He was pouring himself another drink. "Who the hell do you think I was writing about? Paul Newman? This picture needs new faces. Wop faces. Jew faces. Newman doesn't even look like half a Jew, for Christ's sake."

"Take it easy," said Ted. "There must be a compromise, Waller. This is a nine-million-dollar picture. That means the break-even point is twice the negative cost, eighteen million dollars. We can't go with the Smothers Brothers."

"StuGazzu," said Waller.

"In classic Italian," said Adam, "it means fuck you." Waller gave Buckley the finger.

"The president had an idea," said Ted. "What do you think of George C. Scott?"

"StuGazzu," Waller repeated.

"George is one of the finest living actors," said Kip.

"Touché. He's also one of the finest living pains in the ass," said Finestein.

"That's because you're not a woman," Marina said. "He's sex-y."

"So are you, baby. That doesn't make you right for the part of my buddy Carmine. The moll you can play. From what I hear, you can play the whore to perfection."

"I don't like your friend," said Marina to Adam.

"Well, that's a first," Adam said. "Marina, why don't you stay out of this? We'll discuss it later."

Marina slumped over, her head on his shoulder, and played with the hairs on his chest. "Honey, later who wants to discuss?"

"Shut up," said Adam. Among other things, Adam was tired. He had been smoking, too, but he never allowed himself to get out of control. If he scorned the Establishment, he was becoming even more disillusioned with the youth scene. Adam was a man with a passport and nowhere to go.

"It's funny you mentioned Paul Newman," said Kip. "I'm considering him. I think he'd be great as Bellamy."

"He'd be lousy," said Waller.

"You'd have to pay Newman a million," said Ted.

"At least," said Kip. "And why? Because he's worth it."

"Mmm-hmm," said Marina. "I'll play with Paul Newman anytime."

"I think we need some food," Kip said. "Why don't we adjourn to Trader's?"

"Sounds good to me," said Waller, "as long as there are broads and a bar."

"Listen, I'll buy you a supper," Kip said. "But I won't spend a dime on this project if it's cast with unknowns."

"In that case, you'd better get yourself another project, Nathan. I only said yes to this dandelion because my buddy is fucking her. He's a starfucker, aren't you, Adam?"

Marina lunged at Waller. "I'll kill you," she said. She beat his chest with her fists. "I wouldn't be in your lousy movie now for ten million dollars."

Adam pulled her away and patted her head, as if she were a little girl. "I think I'll take you home," he said. Then, to Kip, "I'll join you, if I can." Kip nodded. Actors, he thought, and actresses. And writers.

Waller, true to his image, spent most of his time at the bar in Trader Vic's. Adam never arrived. To Kip's relief, he was able to talk with Charlie and Ted.

"I know this script will go over with newcomers," he said. "Are you sure Pacific won't back me?"

"I hate to say it, baby, but after *Community Future* and *Overwrought,* two flops in a row, your credit's run out."

"The Richards film has grossed three million so far, and it hasn't hit the neighborhoods or the foreign market. That's a failure?"

"Boards of directors don't figure on single hits. They amortize. You shelved two movies that cost the company four million bucks. You've made a million back on the third. It doesn't balance, Kip."

"But this will be our big one. *Gallery* is Pacific's *Sound of Music.* I know. I have to make it, Ted. What do you think, Charlie? Am I a lunatic?"

"It's the best screenplay I've read in ten years. It's a natural."

"Okay," Ted said. "I read you. You think it's a natural. Then try rolling it in Las Vegas."

"What about outside financing?" Kip said.

"The IRS has made that tough, with its latest rulings and positions. Businessmen are reluctant to get involved in movie tax shelters now because of potential congressional action."

"I didn't ask if it's tough. I asked if it's possible."

"Anything's possible," said Ted.

"That's what I figured," said Kip. "Can you get it?"

"You want it that badly?"

"Yes."

"I can get it."

"How?"

"Does Ballen give sources?" Ted lifted his glass in a toast. "To some negatives I happen to have in my possession."

"You wouldn't do that to Elena?" Kip said.

"I won't have to. Relax. That Bourbon-headed New England social climber won't take the risk. He'll pay. He'll invest."

"Here's to justice," Kip said. He raised his Navy Grog.

"Which justice, legal or moral?" asked Ted. "They're quite different, you know."

Charlie Finestein clicked glasses with them, and took a sip of his Mai Tai, and stared. He hadn't the slightest idea what they were talking about, but he had the conviction that *Gallery*, at last, would get off the ground.

5

"Have you heard what Barry did to Helen?" said Natalie.
"Who are Barry and Helen?" Marina asked.
"The Springfields. You don't really know them, of course. You met them at Elena's party. The tiny man and the big-assed woman from San Marino. He's loaded."
"He's drunk?"
"Darling, there are other things in the world than drugs and booze. I meant money. He's stinking rich."
"Is it interesting?" Marina said. It was five in the afternoon, she had just gotten up, as she always did, at four, and she had a miserable headache. It must be the pills, she thought, yawning. She had taken three when they went to bed; Adam had told her that was the limit. After he left the house in the morning, Marina swallowed three more.
"It's fascinating," Natalie said. "Just listen. Do you want to get a cigarette?"
"As a matter of fact, I do." Marina went to her bone china bust of George Washington and got a joint. She found it amusing to conceal her reefers in a replica of the "father of our country."
"You're back," said Nat. Marina smiled. Natalie had no idea she was smoking a marijuana cigarette. "Well, I went to this lunch at Le Boîte for Helen today. I knew what a bore it would be, but I've turned down like eighteen lunches for Helen, so I thought I should go." Marina didn't ask why. Marina never went to anything she didn't want to go to, but she understood Natalie. Natalie was compulsive about the Establishment.
"Who was there?" the girl asked.
"The usual deadly bitches of Grace's. Why *they* pay her I'll never know." They both knew why—to get their names in the columns. "Anyway, who was there doesn't matter.

Except maybe Iris Gordon. Imagine the nerve of him, sending that tramp of his to a lunch for his wife. . . ."

"Who's Iris Gordon?"

"You met her at Elena's too. Oh, I forgot. You were busy with Adam that night. Iris is a starlet—darling, read prostitute—she's Barry's mistress. She used to be one of Ragged Dick's dummies." "Ragged Dick" was the term used in Hollywood's locker rooms—ladies' locker rooms—to describe Ted Buckley. One of his women had coined the nickname because he was such a bad lay, and it stuck.

"Natalie, can you get to the point? I have to dress. Or do I? Does one dress for an orgy?"

"You dress to enter." Natalie laughed. "Now, be ready. I'm picking you up at nine. My God, Grace will be there. I'll have to call and tell her what happened."

"Tell me," Marina said, wearily.

"Barry Springfield called poor Grace last week and asked her to give a lunch for Helen. He said she needed a lift and to spare no expense. He paid for it, naturally. Drinks before, a different wine with each course—"

"So what?" said Marina.

"I just got it. Iris was there as a spy. God forbid Barry's wife should leave early. Darling, have you any idea what that prick was doing for those four hours Helen was gone?"

"He was fucking?" Marina said.

"She should only have been so lucky. It's worse. He had moving vans take all the furniture out of the house, every antique and every painting. She came home to find the place ransacked. That poor woman—"

"I thought you didn't like her."

"I don't. But I like him less."

"There's community property in California."

"Darling, possession's nine-tenths of the law, or something like that. Their art collection alone is worth millions. That bastard. I'm surprised he didn't take her Norells."

"Natalie, how come you always know everything first?"

"I have my sources," she said. "Which reminds me, I must call Ballen."

"Why? Why give her a tacky story like that?"

"My dear, someone's bound to print it. This way, I'll have a credit with Ballen for future use."

"Natalie, you are a bitch. I don't know why I like you."

"I have to go. Remember, nine tonight."

"Are you sure it's okay? I mean, I'm nervous. If Adam hears . . . "

"He won't hear. He has another meeting on that damned movie of his, doesn't he? So you and I are going to a new play. . . . "

"What's it called again?"

"For God's sake, write it down. *Same Time, Next Year*. At the Music Center. Just remember not to answer the phone after eight."

"What shall I wear?"

"Jeans. Boots. A mini-skirt. Anything. They don't take the pictures until the action starts. Okay?"

"That's another thing. You're sure the pictures won't get out?"

"I've told you. Nobody sees the tapes except the participants. You think these people want to advertise?"

Marina felt like another joint. "See you later," she said. She headed for the den and the ceramic head of George Washington.

Grace St. George was humming as she tweezed her eyebrows in front of the magnifying mirror. All in all it had been a good day. She had done Barry Springfield a favor, and now she was sure she would keep Helen Springfield's account. Barry seldom asked favors. Besides, he always paid her a bonus when something appeared in the press. Ballen, of the *Chronicle*, had declined Grace's invitation, saying, "Just send me the guest list." Ballen never attended Grace's lunches, nor did she use anything from the *tabula rasa* Grace passed off as news. The names of the innocent were misspelled, the descriptions clichés. In the beginning, Clare had been burned when she ran any item from Grace.

When St. George didn't know what someone did or why they were important—and none of her clients were important—she'd simply invent. Her inventions were uninventive. Every male was "a millionaire playboy" or "the most desirable bachelor in town." Every female was "the wife of that famous actor"; the actor was, invariably, second-rate. He was yesterday's non-news. On the few occasions when Ballen had publicized Grace's clients as "millionaires," either the men themselves objected (they feared the IRS) or others told Clare she was a laughingstock because the men were frauds. Poor Grace was too stupid to know why her items never made Ballen's column. Since she didn't read, she was even too stupid to know that they never did. Hope springs eternal in the breast of the bumbling. Grace intended to take her guest list to Clare in the morning.

Tonight, she had another job. She was introducing a man named Walter Sands to the videotape-cassette crowd. She couldn't remember exactly who he was or what he did, although Warren Ambrose had given her a docket so complete it would have satisfied the FBI. Anything more than a garbled phrase was perplexing to Grace. All she remembered of Warren's conversation was that Sands was crazed for publicity. She would try to discover more from the man when he called for her. If she couldn't, no matter. Poor Grace had her tag all ready: Walter Sands was "a millionaire playboy."

Natalie gave her story to Clare and dialed Grace. As soon as she heard the ring at the other end of the line, she hung up. How stupid of me, she thought. Grace will call Clare, or plant the Springfield item with someone else, and I'll lose points with Ballen. Grace St. George could learn it the hard way. Let her read it when it appeared in the *Chronicle*.

Natalie slipped into a pair of dungarees, not the French ones she had to lie down on the bed to zip up, the form-fitting ones that compressed your stomach and hips. They left marks on your body; Nat never wore them on Monday nights. She selected a boat-neck T-shirt of red velours. Natalie was applying her mascara when she heard Jack's key in the lock. She shoved her makeup into the drawer of the dressing table. She couldn't let him see her putting on her makeup. That was the last of her dressing rituals, and she was in jeans. One didn't wear jeans to the Ahmanson Theater.

"Darling, you're early," Natalie said. "I thought you had meetings tonight."

"So did I," said Jack. "I was informed that I'm out of the project. Kaput."

"They can't do that to you. They've lost their minds," said Natalie.

"They did it," Jack poured himself a drink.

"But why?"

"How should I know?" He fell, almost literally, onto the

couch in the living room. "They needed a patsy, I suppose. Somebody had to take the blame for *Overwrought*. We drew straws, and I got the short one. I'm the straw man."

"Why not Kip? Why not Adam? They saw what was happening."

Jack took a cigar and lit it. "I'm afraid the director was outnumbered. It's three against one. Kip, Adam, and Waller. They have to answer to Cohen and the stockholders. *Rogue's Gallery* must go on."

"Have you eaten?" said Natalie. She glanced at the clock, a reproduction that came with the furnished apartment. "I'll make you something."

"Thanks, but no. I'm not hungry. Besides, it's eight-fifteen. You're very late. Or aren't you going downtown with Marina?"

"Of course we are. So we'll miss the curtain."

"Natalie, please. No games. I'm too tired for games. I know where you're going. My office—my former office—at the studio is next to a new guy's. He's the king of the skin and snatch flicks, or something like that. He gave me the time, the place, and the cast. Plus the script."

"I don't know what you mean."

"I mean you know I know about your Lesbian pranks. So now I know about Monday nights. What's the difference? I've never objected to your girlie sessions, have I? Go to it. I think I'll go to bed. I'm tired."

"Darling, why don't you come along? Why don't you try it? You might like it."

"I have tried it, and I like it," Jack said.

Natalie couldn't conceal her astonishment. *"You?"* she said. "You, of all people? You wouldn't watch a 'circus' in Mexico."

"I'm not a voyeur. I like to participate."

She felt a new respect for him, an identification. Could Jack be a swinger? Natalie took his glass and fixed him another drink. "Marina's expecting me—us—at nine."

"My dear," he said, "there are times when I think this marriage might work."

Jack was so smashed that Natalie had to drive to Marina's. "What have you heard from Elena?" he said.

"Darling, nobody's heard from Elena since she married that computerized Silas Marner."

"Aren't you being a little bit rough?"

"How would you like to be fucked by a one-armed bandit that pays in slugs instead of sperm? Jamieson is so cheap he's been barred by every restaurant from Matteo's to Annabelle's. Do you know what he gave her as a wedding present? A silver identification bracelet from Gucci. Silver, not gold."

"No wonder, my dear," Jack said. "You cornered the market on jewelry before gold bars became the thing."

"You know he wouldn't even let her go with him for the wedding ring? He thought she might choose one that cost him more than $5.95. He bought her the cheapest gold band at Tiffany's. I checked. Imagine. It sells for twenty-seven dollars."

"You are a bitch. But I've seen her wedding band," Jack said. "It's made of baguettes."

"That's the one Randy gave her."

"But Randy couldn't afford it, not then. Not before his new series."

"That's precisely my point. Randy couldn't afford it, but Randy at least is generous."

"Let's hope he's generous enough to hire an out-of-work TV director."

"His series is that successful?"

"His series is number one. It's tops in the Nielsen ratings every week. Norman Lear should have him." Natalie had learned from Jack that television stars were more famous and more admired than movie stars. They were the real household names. Robert Blake, of "Baretta," reached fifty million Americans in a single night, more than Marina Vaughan in all of her pictures. The New Hollywood caste system was inverted: Robert Blake would be fortunate if he encountered James Caan at the Premier Market. With few exceptions, only movie stars went to Establishment parties. The line was rapidly being honed. Although filmmakers persisted in saying TV stars were overexposed, they knew that in terms of public recognition one could pit Elizabeth Montgomery against Faye Dunaway, or Carrol O'Connor against Gene Hackman. Angie Dickinson was more apparent than Glenda Jackson, Danny Thomas than Dustin Hoffman. Lucille Ball was in more living rooms than Mae West had been in beds. Why else had Miss West, the legend, at last consented to make her TV debut on a Dick

Cavett special? The money was in television, big money from reruns and from commercials. The movie and stage stars were beginning to realize that. Why else were Lord Olivier, Bob Hope, Tony Martin, Henry Fonda, and Rex Harrison endorsing products from Polaroid to Chrysler?

Natalie pulled into the driveway. The house was dark, except for a light upstairs in the master bedroom. They rang the bell three times before Teresa opened the door. "*La Señora Vaughan no está buena,*" she said. "*Yo no se qué hacer.*"

"My God," said Natalie. "Jack, come along." Marina was lying face down on the bed, a half-empty bottle of scotch on the table beside her. She was naked. "Help me," said Natalie.

"My dear, are you sure this is decorous?"

"Jack, don't be a fool."

"Well, it's decorative, anyway." He leered at Marina's breasts as Natalie struggled to turn her on her back. Marina had the mammaries of an eighteen-year-old. Her body was yielding in her unconsciousness as Jack flipped her over. "Very nice," he said.

"She's ripped," said Natalie. "Where's Teresa?"

"How the hell should I know?"

"Well, find her. Tell her to make some black coffee." Natalie rummaged through the medicine chest in Marina's bathroom. It was packed with downers—Seconal, Nembutal, Amytal, Tuinal. Finally, she found an upper: a bottle of Dexamyl.

She was about to extract one when Jack came up behind her, swathing her breasts with his hands. He hadn't done that for months. "The coffee is on the way. I'm horny," he said. "How about it?"

"Not here. Not yet," said Nat. Slipping out of his embrace took more of an effort than she would have conceded. Marina's buoyant breasts and the baby down of her patch had turned both of them on. Group sex, thought Natalie, has its advantages, even—maybe especially—for couples. Marriage breeds contempt. Jack caught her once more, this time lifting her blouse and licking her like a suckling child; she held his head, unwilling to let him go. Jack wasn't so drunk after all, she decided; or, if he was, he should take to the bottle more often. And to the tit.

Marina leaned on the door. "What's going on?" she said.

In her state, Natalie thought, she wouldn't know. Jack straightened. "You can certainly tell he dresses to the left," observed Nat. Marina was observing very little.

"Oh, it's you," Marina said, drowsily. "I have to tinkle." She staggered to the toilet.

"Jesus," said Jack. He stared at her, his urgency unabated.

"Whatsa matta?" Marina said. "Haven't you ever seen a girl pee before?"

"No. darling, he hasn't," said Natalie. "He'll see a lot more before the night's over. Now be a good boy," she told Jack, "and contain yourself. Why don't you wait outside while I pull her together? But don't pull your pud, or later on you'll regret it."

6

The apartment was two floors up in a three-story building just south of Sunset Boulevard. Below it, running to Santa Monica, was the area that had been dubbed "Fag Hollow" by Hollywood's fags. As the epithet implies, it was populated mainly by gays and its atmosphere was that of an artists' colony. The late Dorothy Parker had lived there. Designer Tony Duquette and Beegle, his wife, inhabited Tony's elaborate, tapestried studio-edifice. Margo Leavin, who was one of Hollywood's foremost art dealers, had her gallery just below the Duquettes. The split-level streets were lined with cottage-houses which had been bought and remodeled by their occupants, many of whom were accredited interior designers.

The overall expanse that was known as West Hollywood was bounded by Beverly Hills on the west and Hollywood on the east. The sheriff's department patrolled the district, which was notorious for its topless bars and restaurants, its striptease joints, and its head shops. One could find almost anything in its confines, from hard drugs to aphrodisiacs to Accu-Jacs or the most updated traditional sexual gimmicks. West Hollywood had the scent of vice and crime. Sheriff Pitchess' men played Big Brother to the pushers and prostitutes who roamed the Strip and to the dopers who robbed to get money to pay them. Women and men were mugged or molested by daylight. Cars were stolen; auto-insurance rates were high. Utility companies asked for deposits. Liquor and grocery stores refused to extend their customers credit. Landlords demanded three months' rent in advance. Their tenants were vagrants who rented furnished apartments, ran into arrears, and vanished by night, toting their worldly possessions in a suitcase or two. West Hollywood was nobody's Bali Ha'i.

Alan Rosenfield let himself into the four-room apartment. He took pride in the fact that he had a key. He was trusted by all his employers. He deposited the platters of food he'd picked up at Scandia. Alan was the first to arrive, as usual. He always made it a point to be early, like any respected member of the projectionist's union, to check the Videocameras and the tapes. Alan was not a projectionist. He was a TV repairman who moonlighted. Alan supplemented his income by filming mass encounters on weekends and at night. To Alan, this was merely another job. It never occurred to him that he could make a small fortune recounting what and whom he saw in the covert passageways of sexual intercourse. Alan was satisfied with his wages. Like a bartender or a projectionist, he set a flat rate for a minimum number of hours' work. Alan's minimum, like the projectionist's, was six hours a night. When he provided the camera, his charge was eight hundred dollars. For groups like this, who supplied their own equipment, his price was four hundred.

Warren pressed the button for the automatic elevator.

"Sweetie, how are you?" said Iris Gordon. She fairly gushed, encircling him with her arms, and planting a kiss on each of his cheeks, then his mouth. He pushed her away from him gently, not because he didn't enjoy the contact of her pendulous breasts, but because he preferred to look at them. Iris was stacked in a melon vendor's sort of way. Her T-shirt was either two sizes too small, or Iris (More likely, thought Warren) was two sizes too big. Her nipples puckered; Warren imagined he could see the wrinkles around them. Her midriff was bare where her shirt and her slacks failed to meet. Her pants were so tight her gash resembled a seam that was going to split.

Barry joined them, entering through the door to the garage. He carried a white paper bag. "Hello, Warren," he said. "Are you set for another evening of fun?"

"I wouldn't say set. I'm unsettled," said Warren. "How about you?"

They stepped into the elevator. "I'm—how shall I say?—quite prepared." Warren wondered what the bag contained. He was always aroused by new tricks, and Springfield was one of their most imaginative tricksters.

Warren accepted a drink from Barry, glanced at Iris' tits, and consulted his watch. "The others are late," he said, nervously. "We could go ahead. How about it, Rosenfield?"

"Everything is in order, Mr. Ambrose," said Alan.

"Let's give them another few minutes," Barry said.

"We could get undressed," said Iris, wriggling suggestively. "It's so warm in here."

"I'll buy that," said Barry.

Iris preceded the men to the bedroom and kicked off her wedgies. She raised her shirt, exposing her globes, but couldn't get the tight garment over her head. "Someone help me," she said.

Barry noted the swelling in Warren's Jockey shorts. He was staring at Iris lasciviously. "Be my guest," said Barry. "I have an idea. We'll make a trade. You can take her clothes off, providing you take off mine." For a square, Warren thought, this guy is perceptive. Barry had only been to their parties several times, but he understood that Warren turned on to men, just the sight of them, as much as he did to women. Warren was even more anxious to undress Barry than his mistress. Barry was short, but he had a huge dong. With commendable restraint, Warren tended to Iris first.

"Oh, whee," she said, stretching, raising her arms above her head, the better to display her Amazonian charms. "That's coo-oo-l." She giggled, tapping Warren's bulging prick through the shorts. "And look at you. Look at him, Barry. He's hard as a Tinker Toy."

"I'm going to tinker with you," Warren said. He tweaked the slot beneath the dense hairs that formed a V between her legs. "But later." Warren turned his attention to Barry. He managed to brush the tip of Springfield's cock with his palm as it sprang forward, erect, when Warren lowered his shorts. Ambrose wanted nothing so much as to take it into his mouth, to trace the rim with his tongue. That's for later, he thought, that's for the camera.

Alan was perched on a stool in the open kitchen, which was separated from the living room by a counter. He seldom watched the revelries, not because anyone would have minded if he had, but because, by and large, he found them tedious. He had seen all the variations on sex. Alan preferred to read; he got his kicks from dirty pictures and books. Joe Wambaugh's *The Choirboys* lay open before him. Alan had stopped to buy it earlier on his way home from a TV repair at Metro-Goldwyn-Mayer. The studio's veteran east gateman, Ken Hollywood, was reading it. Hollywood (Can that be his real name? Alan wondered) told him the novel was "sizzling." Alan was playing it safe tonight. He stashed his alternate reading, *Penthouse* and *Playboy*, in one of the empty kitchen cabinets. Wambaugh might not be racy enough.

Walter Sands arrived with Grace while the others were nibbling on the appetizers from Scandia, drinking and talking as though they were fully clothed at a formal dinner party. His eyes were no longer seeds, but saucers. He ceased blinking as he took in the scene. The men had managed to lose their erections, but Iris was leaning back on the couch, her legs parted, laughing at something one of them said.

"This is West Berlin all over," said the present "King of Smut" and the former Wally Swoboda.

"What about West Berlin?" asked Grace.

Sands ignored her as Warren introduced him to the regulars. "My dear," Walter said to Iris, "I've never seen a more beautiful cooze."

"It's spread-beaver time," said Warren. "You don't even have to pose this one. The pussy, I mean."

"Oh, isn't he sweet?" Iris said to Barry. "You never say things like that." Barry threw Sands an icy glance.

While the next arrivals were taking off their clothes, Grace and Walter emerged from the bedroom. Sands asked to be shown how the Videocameras worked.

"This one," said Alan, indicating the Sony, which was attached to the wall on hinges, "is the top of the line. It costs fifteen thousands dollars, including all sound equipment, and it records in color." The back-up model was an Akai. It stood on a tripod. "These sell for as little as two hundred and fifty dollars," Alan said. "They take pictures in black and white, without sound. The pictures develop instantly on the cassettes. The Videocameras work much like a Polaroid but, once I start them, they go automatically."

"Both of them?" Walter asked.

"Yes, but not simultaneously. They operate on normal tapes, which means each plays for an hour. I start with the Sony. I've set the Akai on the timer. It will begin to record when the Sony goes off."

"That way," Sands said, "you miss none of the action, eh? Very clever. I'll have to get one."

"If you want one, I have the connections," said Alan. He was nothing if not a hustler. "I can even get you the Sony 1600 Videotape cassette. That model is out of production, but it's the simplest to operate and the most compact. It will cost you, though. They're up to five thousand dollars on the black market."

"I have the cassette," said Walter. "I'm interested in the camera. Is it legal? Not that I care," he added.

"Completely legal. The Videocamera was designed for government surveillance."

"Now that I believe," said Marina. Natalie's ministrations had been effective. Marina was sober; she had clearly come down.

Walter, surveying the naked girl who stood beside him, began to turn on. "My dear," he said. "You are ravishing. Who are you?"

"My name is Marina."

"I'm Walter Sands," he said. His eyes traveled over her faultless body. He did not blink.

Marina, enjoying the visual tour of the odd little man, said, "That's what I was talking about. We have no privacy, have we?"

Walter connected. "Do we want privacy?" he said. "Do you? Don't you like me to look at you? Don't you want connoisseurs who appreciate your nakedness? Isn't that why you're here?"

"I'm an exhibitionist," she said. "We're all exhibitionists."

"You get to my groin," Walter said. "I want to fuck you."

"So do a lot of us," Natalie said. "When do we start?"

"Right now," said Warren. "Alan."

"Yes, Mr. Ambrose." Alan switched on the camera.

Walter looked at Natalie. "Why don't you take her first?" he said, referring to Marina.

"Why all the generosity?" Natalie said.

"I like to watch. It excites me."

Well, thought the uninhibited Natalie, he is uninhibited, that's for sure. An admitted voyeur. "Marina, we have another Warren Ambrose. Another bird-watcher," Natalie said. "What do you say? Shall we let him watch our birds?"

"Which bird do I get?" said Jack.

"Marina's, of course," said Natalie. "Mine you can have at home. But don't expect me to watch. I'm an activist."

"Do what you want," said Jack. "I'm broad-minded."

"That's a lousy pun," said Natalie. She scanned the room and headed for Madeline Farrell, Kip Nathan's latest conquest. His latest concubine, Natalie thought. She'd been astonished to see Madeline earlier, arriving at all, much less unescorted. My God, Nat reflected, if men had any idea what their women do.

"How do you want it?" Jack asked Marina. "It's up to you."

"I like your gong," she said, taking it in her hands.

"You keep doing that, this will be a bunny fuck. Wham, bam, thank you, ma'am," Jack said. He pulled her to him. She ground her flat stomach and glorious tits against him.

Walter Sands retreated, gazing about the room, and massaging himself. He was hot, but not hot enough yet. He saw Warren Ambrose, who, to Sands' dismay, was already into the action. Sands had lost a fellow voyeur.

Warren was literally enveloped by Iris Gordon and Barry Springfield. Walter moved closer to them, still stroking his flaccid prick, assuring himself he had made no mistake. Ambrose was giving Springfield a blow job, while Iris caressed Warren's balls. "You want to join us?" she said to Walter, looking up from the sofa. "Baby, I know what you need." She grabbed his buttocks and pulled him down beside her, clasping his dick between her hard, unyielding silicone breasts. Sands found them a turnoff. When he didn't react, Iris whispered, "You're my dish. Follow me."

Both Walter and Barry were small of stature, but Barry was not so well endowed. Even when it was partially erect, Walter's cock was enormous. Iris led him to the second bedroom. They stepped over mounds of discarded clothes; the floor and the beds were strewn with them. Panties, Jockey shorts, bras (not many of those: brassieres were passé), outer garments of every size, shape, and quality.

"Now, what would you like me to do for you, honey?" said Iris.

"If you please." Walter's eyes were blinking rapidly as he handed her a sweater, a man's black sweater, from one of the piles on the bed. "Put this on. Now button it. Now unbutton it." The cardigan barely covered Iris' parts when it was closed. Iris put her hands on her hips and moved sideways, displaying her profile, then her behind, then a straight-on view with the sweater parted. She turned slowly, completing a circle, like a professional model.

"Does this excite you?" she said.

Sand was breathing heavily. "Button it up," he said. "No, all the way up."

"Oh, look at your pecker," Iris said. "It's so long." She giggled.

Sands didn't have to look. He could feel the tumescence. He lurched forward and dropped to the floor. She started to lie beside him. "No, stand. I want to look at your pussy from below. Spread your legs." He reached up and thrust three fingers into her cunt.

"Ooooh, that's nice," she said. "That's more like it."

Walter stood up and pushed her onto a heap of clothes on the bed. He unbuttoned the sweater and took her with sawlike movements.

"Ooooh, you're so deep," she moaned. "Can you feel it? You're touching my uterus. The doctor says I have a low uterus." To another men, her use of the clinical term might have been a turnoff. To Walter, it was the opening of a faucet. His come rushed into her with a force that was uncontrollable.

They rejoined the others. Warren and Madeline were going at it now. Natalie and Marina. Some of them were passing around a bottle, rubbing one another all over with the contents. "What's that?" said Walter.

"Vanilla extract, diluted," said Barry. Warren reacted before reverting to Madeline's daisy-petal breasts: "So that's what Springfield was carrying," he observed.

"Has anyone ever tried this with a hand-held camera?" Jack said, eliciting general laughter.

Barry retrieved his bottle and spread the vanilla liquid over Iris' body. "I hope," she whispered to Barry, "we're using both cameras. It takes at least two hours to get this guy to come. He has a sweater fetish."

"Haven't we all?" said Barry. "Just wait," he told Walter aloud, "until you see the playbacks of the cassettes." The suggestion roused Sands, who would never make the ultimate porno movie, but was the ultimate voyeur.

Walter licked his lips as he surveyed the pulsating, undulating bodies before him. The camera was panning the room as Barry began to lick the vanilla from Iris' body. Barry began at her feet.

Alan Rosenfield was reading *The Choirboys.*

7

Reade was opening mail in his study in Holmby Hills. "Those bastards," he said to Elena. "Who the hell do they think I am, the Bank of Ámerica? Have you seen this bill?"

You show me every bill, thought Elena. "What is it, darling?" she said.

"It's for that dinner-dance you insisted we give for those grocers, the Borys." Margot and Edmond de Bory owned Paris' famed Fauchon.

"But they had a reception during our honeymoon, Reade," she said. "You agreed we have to reciprocate."

"We didn't have to reciprocate to the tune of four thousand dollars. Those crooked bums at La Boîte. I don't like to be taken. Nobody cheats Reade Jamieson."

"Of course not," Elena said in a placating voice. "But I can't believe La Boîte would cheat us. We've given parties there before, and it always runs around that. It's twenty dollars a head for their cheapest entrée, minus thirty percent. We had thirty-six people. With the discount, that seems all right."

"Since when has a nudie movie star become the mathematician in the family?" he said, his face reddening. "What would a goddamn hooker know about cost? How much did you get for soliciting on the streets of Berlin and Rome? A hundred dollars a night? A ten-carat emerald? What price did you put on your charms?" She trembled. "Oh, I know about that. I knew it before I married you. What do you think I am—a goon? I knew what I was getting. Do you think I'm deaf? Your background, my dear wife, is the talk of both coasts."

She took a cigarette from the silver box on the table, then put it back. Before they were married, Reade simply objected to her smoking. Now he forbade her to smoke in the house. She clasped her hands on her lap so he wouldn't see they were shaking. "Why did you marry me, Reade, if you hate me so much—"

"I don't hate you, my dear. I hate your extravagance. As a matter of fact, I find you very useful, when you deliver. But sometimes you don't deliver. This marvelous party of yours was to be my introduction to Alexis de Rede, wasn't it now? He's the only guy I wanted to meet. He's the only guy who has class, and he didn't show up. I know all your other cronies. I didn't have to spend four thousand dollars on them. And I won't, for Christ's sake. I went to all the trouble to choose a two-dollar wine. Do you think it's easy to find a two-dollar import at a French restaurant? How could the bill come to this?"

She needed a cigarette badly. She also wanted to get away from him. "Why tell me?" said Elena. "Talk to George. He's the owner."

"Don't think I won't. And right now. Where's the goddamn phone book?" He dialed the number. "Who is this? Caspar? Yes, this is Mr. Jamieson. I want George." He waited, tapping his fingers on the tape recorder he used for dictating letters to his secretary in Cambridge and for mental notes to himself. "George? Forget the amenities," Reade said. "What's this bill for the party? A hundred people couldn't have cost that much. You must be trying to make your payroll. Well, I can't afford it. What's more, I won't be chiseled." He motioned to Elena; she picked up the extension. Reade loved to be tough, and he wanted witnesses to his misanthropy.

"Mr. Jamieson, if there's some mistake, I'm sure we can correct it. Let me get the bill. Would you like me to call you back?"

"No. I'll wait."

"I have it here," said George. "Now, just what is it you object to?"

"I object to the bill. Your whole lousy bill. It's padded, and I'm not going to pay it. Does that answer your question?"

Here it comes, thought Elena. You don't accuse George of cheating.

"Mr. Jamieson," said La Boîte's maître d' and owner, "there's nothing wrong with this bill. We haven't even added on a gratuity for the waiters. We've charged you only for the food and liquor and labor. We've been doing that for Mrs. Brent—I mean Mrs. Jamieson—for years."

"Bullshit." Reade was shouting now. "You're a bloody swindler."

Elena blushed. She was mortified.

"Mr. Jamieson, I don't like being called a crook and a swindler. So I'll tell you what I'm going to do. I'm going to give you this party as a present. It's on the house. But I will be very happy if you never enter La Boîte again." George hung up without saying goodbye.

Reade grinned at Elena maliciously. "You see how to handle people, my dear? That's a lesson in economics." He was again in good spirits because he'd gotten his way. For Reade, the only way was his. He looked her up and down, as he would have one of his sculptures. "Where are you going?" he said.

"I'm taking Alice to lunch." She wanted to say, "I'm going to lunch with Alice," but she knew she had better clear the expense with him.

He didn't argue for once, because he was complacent in his victory over George. Sometimes Elena considered him a manic-depressive. Reade was pathological in his sudden turns of mood. He could be the most charming and the most miserable wretch she had ever known. His temper depended on what he had to gain in terms of society or business, and what he had to lose in terms of money. His behavior was determined by a checkbook and public acclaim. "Good," he said. "Aren't the Ambroses giving a party for Alexis de Rede?"

"On Saturday," Elena said. "I accepted." She wondered how she was going to tell him that no one referred to the Ambroses' guest of honor as "Alexis." Members of the Jet Set called him "Alexei."

"Where are you lunching?"

"We haven't decided." Elena was lying. She'd made a reservation at La Boîte, but now she had to cancel it. She walked to their bedroom, called Alice, and suggested they meet at L'Hermitage instead. At least Elena could still sign a check at L'Hermitage.

Alice wanted to do some shopping after lunch. As they entered Giorgio in Beverly Hills, Mary Jones was leaving. She was trailed by a male employee carrying two new evening gowns to her car. Elena and Mary exchanged hellos.

"Who's that?" said Alice.

"Her husband went to Harvard with Elliot Richardson," Elena said. "She's Mrs. H. Bradlee Jones, of Pasadena and Giorgio." Alice laughed. "You must have missed Ballen's column, the one in which she gave presents to famous people last Christmas."

"What did Mary get? Ambassador Richardson?"

"No. Ballen gave her a private freeway to Giorgio's and a room above the store."

"Did she like it?"

"She loved it."

Gale Hayman, the owner's wife, came up to them. Gale was a perfect model for her own clothes. She was slight, a size six, and pretty, with black hair, a pert nose, and commendable taste. She waited personally on Giorgio's most distinguished patrons. Strangers drew one of the many aggressive, hard-selling saleswomen. "Elena, Alice," Gale said. "It's so good to see you. What can I do for you?"

"I need a long, informal dress for the party we're giving on Saturday," said Alice.

"And you?" Gale asked Elena.

"Reade and I are going East next week. If you have something for daytime and also for dinner—the boring things they wear in New York. Short dresses."

"They have to wear short in New York, because the streets are so dirty," said Alice. "Why don't we look around?"

"Go ahead," said Gale. "In the meantime, I'll gather some things I think you might like."

As they separated the clothes, which were tangled together on their hangers, Elena said to Alice, "Do you know Jerry Blum?"

"You mean Lord & Taylor's vice president?"

"Yes. Well, Jerry was out here two weeks ago and I told him he had to see Giorgio's. He'd never seen anything like it. He said, 'My God, there are two-thousand-dollar dresses crushed together on the racks. They're being destroyed by handling. It's unbelievable.' "

The store itself was unbelievable. Giorgio was Los Angeles' complete boutique. You could live overground in Giorgio's and never have to set foot outside. For one thing, it had a men's department adjacent to the spacious women's section. For another, it carried lingerie, furs, and accessories such as jewelry, belts, and handbags—a woman could be entirely outfitted there. It she wanted a bra, a body suit, a pair of shoes, or a meal, the Haymans would send for them. Gale and Fred had already taken care of the luxury, the diversions, and the drinks. They had a limousine service for their best customers, a pool table, and a bar complete with bartender. Frank served everything from orange juice through cappuccino to wine and hard liquor. All was free, an accommodation to customers. The customers, too, were remarkable. Nowhere else in one hour in Beverly Hills could you meet so many stars and socialites, or see so many signed photographs of the fabulous and the famous.

Roger Smith was sitting at the bar. He was drinking white wine on the rocks and assessing a gown his wife, Ann-Margret, had chosen. Jill St. John told Elena she'd sold her house in Benedict Canyon and was living permanently in Colorado. "Skiing," said Jill, "has given me a new life." The shapely redhead no longer needed Harvey Parkes: she got her exercise in the fine powder of Aspen.

Gale reserved the largest dressing room for Alice and Elena. Like the others, its walls were crammed with autographed pictures. "We would get the room with Joyce Haber," Alice said, referring to the columnist for the Los Angeles *Times*. "Just the sight of her makes me sick. There hasn't been a decent show business column since Hedda died."

"You know what Burt Prelutsky called her when he wrote a parody of her? Joy Saber," Elena said. "And someone else referred to her as Hedda Haber. But Alice, what has she done to you? You like almost everyone."

"She's vicious. She wrote that Warren tells his clients there are two things they have to learn—they must never pass anyone else's office on the way to their own, because then the executives will forget they're working there. And Haber said Warren instructs his people to learn to read upside down, so they know what's on the memos, in case they're called into somebody's office."

Elena laughed. "That sounds like something Warren would say. But actually Frank Orsatti told his clients that. He perfected it in his own life. He couldn't read straight up. He could only read upside down."

"Do you like this?" Alice asked. She was wearing an Albert Capraro dress with slits that went up to the thigh. "Or is it too daring?"

"I love it," Elena said. "It's perfect for Saturday. You have the figure for it, darling. Why not?"

"But will Warren like it?"

"Warren will like it. Besides, you don't dress for your husband, Alice. You dress for other men."

"That's strange, Elena, coming from you. You've dressed so differently since you married Reade. I mean, so sportily."

You mean so tackily, thought Elena. "He likes simple clothes," she said. She didn't add, "He likes bargain-basement clothes."

"Then you do dress for Reade?"

Alice was trying to draw her out. Sweet Alice liked gossip as much as anybody, so long as it didn't relate to her. "Darling." Elena said, "at thirty-two, I'm still a bride. I'm still being tested. Later, it will be different. You have to mold a man slowly."

"I see what you mean," said Alice, noticing, as she had before, that Elena had aged since her recent marriage to Reade. Her face was drawn and her movements were hesitant, tense. She was not the old—or the younger—Elena who had been married to Randall Brent. Randy may not have given Elena security, Alice decided. but Reade had given her insecurity: there was a distinction. Everyone knew that when Reade received the first week's bill from the Ritz Hotel in Paris during their honeymoon, he demanded a discount and was refused. The Jamiesons had to move to the Hilton. Even today, Elena selected the least attractive and least expensive dresses Gale offered her. Reade was a multimillionaire and a bastard. Randy was a bastard who was about to become a millionaire. Elena, with all her insight, was myopic about her men. She had traded a diffident husband for a shabby one.

Marguerite, the salesgirl, was covering their purchases in plastic bags. Alice was taking the daring Capraro, a delicate Stephen Burrows pantsuit, and a stunning black-and-white outfit by Mollie Parnis. Elena had chosen two daytime dresses by no-name designers. Gale, who seemed nervous, handed Alice Ambrose the sales slip to sign. "Do you have a Master Charge card?" Gale said to Elena.

"Darling, just put it on my account," Elena said.

"I don't know how to tell you this," said Gale Hayman, "but your husband closed your account with us last week."

Alice looked at Elena, hard, as did Lynda Day George, who was standing nearby.

Elena was stunned. "Are you sure? There must be a mistake."

"I'm afraid there isn't," Gale said. "We got a letter. We checked it directly with Mr. Jamieson. Elena, we've always been friends, and I was worried. I thought we'd somehow offended you. So I also checked Saks and Bonwit Teller. Your husband has closed your charge accounts at every store in town."

Fred Hayman put his arm around Elena to steady her. "You'd better square it away with your husband," he said.

8

Furio was disturbed about Elena's comportment since her marriage to Reade. She had put on weight, and she paid less attention to her appearance. More often than not, she wore no makeup, allowing the puffy flesh she had acquired (From drink, or starch, he thought) to eclipse her doe-like eyes. She neglected her hair, refusing to use the rinse that put highlights into its natural blond, revealing the darker roots beneath weeks-old Clairol. She had cut it short, using falls and other hairpieces to substitute for its old luxuriance. She was photographed more often than ever, whether window-shopping on Paris' Faubourg St. Honoré, entering Manhattan's Côte Basque, or attending major events like the Los Angeles gala for the American Ballet Theater. Black and white replaced color in her wardrobe, mostly white silk blouses and long black shirts, which Furio hinted to her were stark and unbecoming. "Darling," Elena said at such times, "they're so practical. Easy for traveling. And then you don't need so many dresses. People remember colors. They don't distinguish black or white. Reade taught me that." Cheap bastard, I'll bet he did, thought Furio.

Tonight Elena looked pale in a black wool shirtdress with not a touch of color. She wore no jewelry apart from the narrow gold wedding band Reade had given her. "Where is your diamond ring—Randy's?" Furio asked.

"Reade doesn't like me to wear it," she said. "It's in the vault." *His* vault, no doubt, thought Furio.

Reade was away on business. They were dining in the enormous, stadium-sized house in Holmby Hills. Holmby Hills was an area between Beverly Hills and Bel-Air whose residents had perhaps the highest per capita incomes in the United States. Elena was restive; Furio was trying to entertain her.

"Cara, you haven't heard about Kenneth Larsen and

Kip?" Larsen was one of Hollywood's top composers. He ranked with Mancini, Bacharach, Hamlisch, and Legrand, although Larsen was younger. He had won four Oscars, two for Best Song and two for Best Original Score. "Kip decided on Larsen to score *Rogue's Gallery*. When Larsen came to his office, Kip told him, 'This is the kind of score I want,' and played the theme from *A Man and a Woman*. 'You want Francis Lai,' said Larsen. 'I suggest you go to Paris and get him.' With which Larsen left Kip's office in a rage, slamming the door behind him."

Elena laughed. "What happened?"

"What else? Kip flew to Paris and signed Francis Lai to score *Gallery*."

"I love it," Elena said. She drained her espresso. "Furio, will you excuse me? I have to call Reade."

"Why now? He left for Las Vegas only this afternoon."

"He told me to call him at ten. He gets nervous about me if I don't call." *Cristo,* thought Furio, what a marriage. It's like a jail term. It's like Elena's on parole.

She joined him in the library. "Furio, do you know a Mr. Esposito?"

"In Las Vegas? That would be Rosario Esposito. Why do you ask?"

"Who is he?"

"He runs the town, but always through front men. He's not allowed in Las Vegas. He's there? If the Gaming Control Board knew . . ."

"He answered the phone. He's with Reade. Oh, Furio, what will I do? I didn't know about Reade's connections until a few months ago. I was afraid to tell you. Do you understand?"

"Ma non é possibile! Ho capito. I didn't know, either. When I said Reade was good for you, I meant he was rich, and I thought he was—how do you say?—a father figure."

"A Godfather, maybe. I'm terrified of him, Furio. He's a bully. If I had to marry into the Mafia, why didn't I marry a Jew or a Sicilian? I had to marry the only WASP in the Mafia."

"Ted Buckley's a WASP."

"Ted's a Jew. He changed his name from Bernstein."

"How do you know Reade Jamieson didn't change his name?"

"I don't. Come to think of it, nothing about him would surprise me—except to discover he's decent."

"It is that bad?" said Furio.

"Worse. The last time Reade went to Vegas he had to buy back those dirty movies I made in Berlin. Remember? You're the only person who knew about them. Somehow Randy found out—I don't understand—but now everybody knows."

"Elena, when I called you, you said it was settled."

"Apparently not. It's true that Swoboda—Sands—no longer had the films. But somebody else did. Reade had to put money into *Rogue's Gallery* to get them back. You know what my charming husband made me do? He made me watch them. He forced me to sit there with him, seeing myself doing all those things on the screen, for public consumption. It was disgusting, Furio. And he kept making filthy remarks, and he kept asking, 'Why haven't you done that to me? I'd like some nookie now.' He felt me. He tried to undress me right there in our screening room. I had to fight him off."

"*Cara,* no wonder you seem so upset. Why didn't you tell me?"

"I was frightened. Terrified. The photos that Randy used to show me were nothing. When Reade heard about the movies, he hit me, Furio. No man has ever hit me before. Not Randy, not in his drunkest revels. I was just sitting there, and the next thing I knew I found myself on the other side of the room. I had a carpet burn on my back for weeks. Reade called me every four-letter word in the book. He taught me a few I've never heard before." She laughed bitterly. Her voice was hoarse. "He said, 'It doesn't bother me that you made the movies. What bothers me is you're so fucking stupid, you cunt, you didn't have any control of them.' "

"What did you say?"

"I said, 'I didn't have control, but *your* people did.' That's when he beat me up. The irony is he doesn't give a damn that I acted in pornographic movies. All he cares about is the money it's cost him to get them back."

"I don't understand about *Rogue's Gallery,*" Furio said. "Why did they need Reade's money?"

"Ted explained it to me. The author insisted on using

nobodies for the leads, and Cohen refused to finance it unless they got bankable stars."

"Elena, you told me Ted had the movies. Now you're saying he wanted to let them out, that he used them for outside financing from your husband."

"Furio, I am guilty. I'm in the conspiracy. Ted assured me that even if Reade did not come across with the money, the movies would disappear. He did me a favor in getting them from Sands. Swoboda. I owed Ted a favor. I owe Kip a number of favors. So I agreed to go along. I think it's a good investment. And even if it weren't, that bastard I married can well afford it. He's made it up on my wardrobe. I can't buy a dress that costs more than a hundred dollars, and I even need his permission for that. He closed every one of my charge accounts." Furio looked at her curiously. "You must have realized. You've hinted at how tacky my clothes are. Do you think I like it, Furio? Have you any idea how ashamed I am?"

"Elena." He put his arm around her. "I understand you so well. I'm sorry I ever mentioned your clothes. The important thing is that you are you. You have panache. Élan. You have *classe* as we say in Italy. You are unique. The unique are indestructible."

"We are expendable," she said. "I feel every minute like a *soldato* on a demolition squad. I'm tired of wondering what will happen next. What good is this life I've struggled for? Money? He has it, and I can't spend it. Everyone thinks I am lazy and coddled by luxury. Ha! I work harder than any suburban housewife who pops a television dinner in the oven and I work a lot harder than most career girls. I read six newspapers a day in three languages. I read all the magazines. I know enough about the stock market to write an investment letter. I know as much about who makes how much money, about who is going broke and who is getting rich, as the Internal Revenue Service. I know all the beautiful people and I must admit I have fun with them. But do you think I enjoy having lunch at Perino's with the chic Mrs. Olive Behrendt when I'm wearing rags? It's humiliating. I also have to listen to more bores than the Queen of England at a garden party. I've taught myself all about computers, so I can talk about software and remote terminals to Reade's friends. I've never used more than an Instamatic camera, but I've learned to use tape recorders because Reade prefers them to notes. Sometimes I wish I were back with Pasquale, our mobster friend in Rome. He didn't expect me to talk at all. He was generous. I've gone full circle, haven't I? From Pasquale Caruso, our mutual friend, to Reade Jamieson and the Mob."

"When will you learn, Elena? Honesty has nothing and everything to do with money. There are the crooked rich and the crooked poor, but only the crooked rich man has the resources for expertise at swindling. It's opportunism—Robin Hood in reverse. The rich man steals from the rich, and he gives to the rich—himself. The prisons are filled with poor men. Poor men don't steal for themselves. They steal in order to feed their wives and children. A poor man will steal from strangers, but not from his friends."

"What you're talking about," said Elena, "is the Establishment."

"What I'm talking about," said Furio, "is humanity. The brotherhoods. Not the Brotherhood of the Teamsters, but the brotherhoods of elected officials, the brotherhood of Big Business, the brotherhood of the media, the networks and the press. I'm talking about the self-seekers. The people who do not do what is honest, but what's self-serving. The people who publish not what is true, but what is beneficial to them. Think of that when you watch the late-night news or read your morning paper."

"Furio, I was raised under Communism. In the United States, we have communications."

"Elena, we have edited communications. I am no Communist, but we don't have freedom. 'Liberty' is a word that was coined by the propagandists and spread around by the founders of our country. It's a term on a bell in Philadelphia. Maybe then it had meaning, but has it validity today? Our government has invaded our privacy. We've been tapped and bugged from the highest places. Forget the Bill of Rights. This is *Brave New World,* a fiction in which the scientists solve all human dilemmas. But who is the scientist? He is your husband. Reade Jamieson, wife-beater, is the scientist."

"I think you exaggerate, Furio. My phone isn't tapped."

"Elena, you are naïve. You know Victor Kroll. You knew him in the Nixon Administration. You call him. Your phone is tapped. Ask Clare Ballen. She'll tell you. She finally got an honest telephone repairman who said, in confidence because he would lose his job if the government knew, that all four of her lines are tapped."

"Did he fix them?"

"No one can fix an outside tap, except the people who installed them—or government men. Most often, they are put in by government men."

"My God," said Elena. "It's 1984."

"It's 1976. Can you imagine what it will be like in 1984?"

"The White House must have a dossier on me," said Elena.

"If this keeps up, there won't be any White House. The people are too sophisticated. They're just beginning to learn that what they read in the papers isn't necessarily true, and what they don't read in the papers is probably true. Oh, there are the exceptions. Some people don't read. The spaced-out, the performers who only follow their notices, like your friend Marina Vaughan."

"Marina's intelligent."

"Marina is so intelligent she thought Watergate was a new drink," said Furio. Both of them laughed. The telephone rang. "Aren't you going to answer it?"

"Let Tai get it," said Elena. The Jamiesons' Chinese houseman buzzed her. "Missy, is Mr. Baker. He says it's important." Oh, God, what now? thought Elena. "I'll take it," she said. She smiled at Furio. "It's Adam Baker, your favorite. Here goes. If what you say about wiretapping is true, this might just provide a sequel to Francis Coppola's *The Conversation*."

Marina had overdosed. Adam found her when he came back from his meeting with Waller and Kip. She was lying on the floor in the bedroom. He thought she was merely asleep until he saw the fifth of J&B, three-quarters consumed, on the night table. Adam tried to wake her, but he could not. He was sure she had O.D.ed when he discovered the empty bottle of Nembutal in the bathroom.

Adam panicked for the first time in his carefree life. Susan McConnell could get away with O.D.ing in Europe where suicide attempts, even those of American Superstars, were looked at askance by the doctors and the police. Psychoses were dismissed as idiosyncrasies. But this was America, where everyone wanted to believe the worst:

America, which—like Europe, he had to concede—thrived on gossip and scandal. In the Old Hollywood, the studio system protected its contract players. The system was money changing hands, cash advanced by the company publicists or attorneys. In Hollywood's "Golden Era," the police and the press were silenced. The New Hollywood had its silencers, but they were more lethal and harder to buy. Movie stars had become independents: they stood up or freaked out on their own.

Adam had had enough experience with the "future scene," as he chose to describe Marina's kinky milieu, to anticipate such a crisis. Nonetheless, the notion was not the event. Adam was into alcohol long before he heard the name Harry Waller. Adam smoked marijuana as a kid of fifteen in Omaha. He was clued-in to the fact that one did not O.D. on marijuana. One did O.D. on a combination of depressants. One did O.D. on barbiturates and alcohol. Take Monroe and Kilgallen.

Adam's first impulse had been to call Kip. *Rogue's Gallery* was completed; Marina was the star, and Kip had a vested interest in protecting his players. On the other hand, Adam considered calling Ted; no one was more proficient at the fix than Pacific's lawyer. But Adam hesitated in using his most powerful connections; he might need their favors on other occasions. That is why he turned to Elena.

Elena's physician, Tom Abraham, was already there when Adam arrived. Together, they carried Marina to the downstairs bedroom. "I stopped at the office to get an I.V. bottle and a stomach pump." The doctor was trim and graying with slightly hunched shoulders, like those of a man who'd been applying stomach pumps for most of his life. "I'd better get started," he said. It was a dismissal.

Adam found Elena and Furio in the library. "Tom's the best," she said, fending off Adam's question. "If anyone can bring Marina around, it's Tom. He treated her mother, Bobbie Shaw. I can't tell you how often he saved her. She tried to kill herself a dozen times when she was married to that worthless chorus boy."

"Elena, I'm sorry for the imposition. If I'd called another doctor, I know he'd have recommended an emergency hospital. There'd have been a record."

"Adam, this is Hollywood. Marina's a star. A big star.

Even doctors protect their own. They're supposed to report this sort of thing to the police, but none of them do."

"If they did, the cops would be so deluged with paperwork," Furio said, "they wouldn't have time for anything else."

Tom Abraham stayed on to treat Marina long after she regained consciousness. He and Elena were finishing lunch when Adam arrived. "You can see her," the doctor said. "But not for long."

"Will she be all right for the promo tour?" Adam said. Trust Adam Baker, Elena observed, to think of that.

Elena canceled a three o'clock sitting with *Vogue's* Richard Avedon and a dinner at Rod McKuen's. Reade phoned to say he'd be home the next day: "I have some more business in Vegas." I'll bet you have, she thought. She did not tell him about Marina. Dr. Abraham recommended that the girl remain in the house for a couple of days, and Elena was wary: she didn't want to provoke Reade's treacherous temper. She had learned to procrastinate; he was capricious. His humors were unpredictable. She would face his rage, his irritation, whatever, when he discovered Marina was there. On the other hand, he might be pleased. Marina Vaughan was a superstar, and Reade was a sycophant. Whatever his disposition, she would face it tomorrow.

The telephone rang. "Mrs. Kaufman is calling," Tai said. My God, thought Elena, if Natalie hears about Marina O.D.ing, the world will learn on CBS and NBC at five o'clock. "Please tell Mrs. Kaufman I'm out," she said.

The weather was August in November. Elena decided to take a swim. She was on her fifth lap when Adam appeared. "What's this Esther Williams act?" he said. He handed her the towel as she stepped out of the pool.

"How is Marina?" she said.

"She's fine. Elena, how are you?"

"Can't you tell?" she said. "I'm rich, and fat, and healthy. I've never been better. By the way, I hear good things about *Gallery*. They say it's a smash."

"Who knows? Kip insisted on rushing it through to qualify for the Oscars. 'They,' the technical people who've seen it, don't represent the general audience." He sat down beside her, dejected.

" 'They' usually know. They're quick to knock somebody else's picture, but reluctant to praise it. Jack Kaufman says you'll win the Academy Award. He thinks Marina will, too."

"If she doesn't stay off the stuff, it will be a posthumous Oscar. We went through hell with her, but it was worth it. She's going to startle a lot of people. Yes, she has a good shot at the Oscar."

"You see? I'm right. So cheer up. There's one thing about me, Adam. I only lie about things that are unimportant."

"You're pretty skilled at that," he said. "I'm kidding, Elena, or maybe not. You lie to yourself. You may be rich and healthy, but you're not fat. Only the self-indulgent are fat. Marina is fat."

"She's skinny."

"That's not what I mean. Ask the doctor. Ask Kip."

"Why Kip?"

"Since she's going to be all right, I'll tell you. She caused us more than a couple of problems on *Gallery*. Like locking herself in her dressing room because she hadn't been laid. We ended up, Kip did, in finding a stud who was at her beck and call between takes."

"That has to be the lowest," Elena said. "You were living with her. Are you trying to tell me you were inadequate?"

"Anyone is inadequate for Marina. Sex is ninety-nine percent mental. Marina is skinny, as you said. Marina's beautiful. Marina's also hung up on sex, and sex without love is nothing. It's fine for ten minutes, but what do you say to the woman after that?"

"I've never known love," Elena said.

"You've never acknowledged love. There's a difference."

"It's chilly," she said. "Why don't we go inside?"

When Elena phoned Reade, the man named Esposito said he was out. "Please tell him I called," she said.

Adam stayed for dinner. Elena knew she was wrong to

encourage him, but she was depressed. There was still something about him that made her lose control. When they were lovers, she had confessed her sexual need for him but no more. She sent him away because she knew if she succumbed to his pleas that she marry or live with him, he would have the upper hand. Elena would have been willing to relinquish all she had gained—her social position, her power, her self-respect—to please Adam. If he asked her to go with him to the wilds of Canada, to share a mountain cabin in isolation, she would have done so. Adam was the most dangerous game Elena had ever played in her life. Because if he changed his mind, if he abandoned her, she would be adrift. She could not put that much faith in love. His attraction for her impelled her to conceal her emotions. Tonight her feint was idle chatter, relating gossip and anecdotes.

"Warren Ambrose is something," she told him. "We all know he doesn't read his manuscripts, not even his authors' outlines. Alice does. She gives him notes. Well, Ross Hunter called Warren the other day to ask about a property, and Warren said, 'I'll send it to you. Read it. The author tells the story best.' "

"Elena," Adam said over brandy, "I haven't thanked you for convincing Reade to invest in *Rogue's Gallery*. Without him we wouldn't have a film."

"I didn't convince him," Elena said, "so save your thanks."

"What does that mean?"

"I told you, I never lie about major things. Someone else convinced him. Let's forget it."

"If you mean those silly movies," he said, "who cares?" She was shocked. How had he learned? Had he understood Clare Ballen's column, or heard about her early transgression in the gossip mills of Hollywood?

"I made them," she said. "I trusted a man named Wally Swoboda. You know him as Walter Sands."

"The best I can say about Walter Sands is he wears short socks," Adam said. "You can never trust a man who wears short socks."

"Lee Anderson called me today to ask me about the pornos."

"Who is Lee Anderson?" Adam said.

"The press agent," said Elena. "I lied. Lee knew I was lying, but she's a friend. She won't use it. Oh, Adam, does everyone know?"

"My darling," he said, "believe me, only a handful of people know. And we are your friends. Besides, considering Reade's connections, no one would dare to let it out."

"I suppose," Elena said, recalling her discussion with Furio, "there's something to be said about high people with high connections."

"Elena, is that what you really want out of life? High people with high connections?"

"I don't know what I want," she said.

"What would you think of a failed producer whisking you off to an island in the Caribbean?" he said.

There it is, she thought. The Caribbean, not the wilds of Canada. "It's too late," she said.

"Elena, it's never too late. Not as long as you're breathing. The people who vacillate tend to crash the rail like racing car drivers. Elena, marry me. Say you'll marry me now, before *Gallery* premieres. Without the confetti, without the tinsel, without the fame or the money or the Oscar you think I'll win, without the discredit or the failure that I consider distinct possibilities. I love you, and I think you love me. But the only way I'll be sure is if you accept me now, before the returns are in."

"I don't know," said Elena. "Adam, I just don't know."

"Let's go upstairs. I'll convince you."

"I couldn't. Not in this house. Not in his room."

"My darling, it's your room, too. There are times when I think you need a psychiatrist."

"There are times I agree."

"All I want is to love you."

Elena already loved him. "All I want is to survive," she said.

10

Adam left her at 5:00 A.M. Elena couldn't get back to sleep, so she brewed some coffee and took a thermos up to her room. She propped herself against the backrest to read, but she had no concentration and put the book aside. Her senses, her being, converged on Adam as she lay in the bed that, less than an hour ago, they had shared. Again he had hightened her acuity; again he had proved himself a prodigious lover, the best-adjusted lover Elena had ever known. He dispelled her conviction, from her earliest days with Karl and Helmut, that women were objects—or subjects at best—to please a man sensually. Adam seemed to have no hang-ups, no qualms about sex. He enjoyed making love to a woman for the woman's sake, as well as his own.

They had conversed for hours intimately, exchanging the deeply secreted beliefs and ambitions that those who love (as opposed to lovers) reveal to one another. Adam told Elena he had used the Establishment ("*Your* Establishment," as he put it) to attain success. He considered the A Group phony, superficial, and passé, like the outworn rung of a ladder which is the only ladder around. He talked freely about his liaisons with Marina, explaining that she represented the "with-it scene," his rebellion against the evanescent aboriginals of the New Hollywood. Adam admitted that when he resumed his affair with Marina he got caught up in the drug crowd and a whole other kind of sybaritic sexual life. He took part in sexual experiments but refused to be drawn into homosexuality, except vicariously through observing her. Adam had gone along with everything else because he was unafraid, because it was In, and because he dug sex.

Most importantly, Adam told Elena she turned him on more than any woman he'd ever known: "You have the ability to respond so naturally and so fully, my darling," he said. "That is so rare it's wondrous to me." Elena was honest in that area because she had the instinct to feel, the very instinct which she had trained herself to hide and curb. Adam alone brought her out of her self-imposed repressions in bed. Adam alone evoked in Elena the state of sexual awareness and desire, which were all the more intense for her lifelong sublimation. Elena and Adam, who were both in their early thirties, had the distinction of sharing their love as first lovers do.

Elena reached for a cigarette, but the pack was empty. She had consumed its contents in an hour. "What's happening to me?" she said, aloud. Her longing for Adam was sentient, another presence in the barren room. She wanted desperately to tell him at last that she loved him, that without him her life was untenanted.

Then she thought of Reade, and her acclimatization to self-restraint took over. Reade had not returned her call, which was unlike him. Elena dialed the number that went directly to his suite in Las Vegas. This time it wasn't Mr. Esposito who answered, but a stranger who spoke with a menacing accent Elena related to Brooklyn, Long Island, Manhattan, Queens, and the Bronx—in short, what is known as Greater New York. "Who's dis?" the man asked.

"It's Mr. Jamieson's wife," she said. "I'd like to speak with him. It's important."

"Sorry, lady. Jamie's not here."

"How do you mean, he's not there? It's seven o'clock in the morning. Reade never goes out before seven."

"Let's say little Jamie's changed his habits. Or let's just say he's busy. He's at a meeting. He ain't gonna come to the phone."

"Reade is supposed to come home today," she said.

"I wouldn't count on dat if I was you, lady. Jamie ain't goin' nowhere. Not today. Not maybe for a long time."

"But he's there? He's all right?" she said.

"Listen, lady, I don't like talking on telephones, see? I don't know who you are, and that ain't my business. Jamie ain't your business, get what I mean? That's advice." The pellet-voiced man hung up.

Elena was terrified. She had never failed to get through to Reade wherever he was. He was clearly in jeopardy. She dialed Ted's number. The answering service picked up. "I have no location for Mr. Buckley."

"Do you expect to hear from him?"

"I wouldn't know, madam. Just a moment." The woman put her on hold to take another call. Elena found nothing so irritating as snappish females who put you on hold. The only social improvement she'd noted, in the last decade, was the accession of the male telephone operator. Men were far more polite. She waited for what seemed to her five minutes, then decided she'd been disconnected. She dialed again.

"This is Mrs. Jamieson. I'd like to leave a message for Mr. Buckley."

"I'll ring him," said the woman.

"He's not at home. You just tried. Please tell him to call Mrs. Jamieson. Say it's very important."

"I don't know when I'll hear from him, madam."

"Just give him the message," Elena said.

She phoned Kip; in fact, she woke him. He told her as far as he knew Ted was still in town. That means, Elena thought cynically, he's in Chicago.

Ted called her at nine-fifteen from Hillcrest. "How soon can you get here, Elena? I had a breakfast meeting. I want to talk to you, but I haven't much time. I'm leaving for Vegas."

"Ted, what is it? I tried to call Reade. . . ."

"I'd rather not talk on the telephone," he said.

"I'll be there in fifteen minutes," she said, "if not sooner."

Ted was waiting for her in the private room of the country club. He was on his fourth Bloody Mary. "Do you want a drink?" he said. "You may need one."

"No."

"Some coffee?"

"No, thanks. Ted, what's going on? I can't get Reade."

Ted waved the waiter away. "Elena, I'm going to give it to you—but neat. Can you take it?" She nodded. "I told you Reade's into the Mob. Something happened yesterday. One of his dealers . . ."

"You mean drugs?" she said.

"The heaviest. Reade controls every hard drug that comes through Mexico and South America. Heroin, coke, you name it." Elena grew pale. "Here, take a sip," he said, offering her his drink.

"No, no. I'm all right. Go on."

"Reade's man was found by the cops at Zuma Beach. He had a couple of bullets in his head. The stuff was still in the car. Whoever got him wasn't a junkie. This is more serious. Whoever went after him was either a nut or a pro."

"Meaning what?"

"Meaning anything. Somebody wanted to put the finger on Reade. Somebody wants his business, or a share of the take. Somebody close to somebody else who O.D.ed on heroin. Somebody who had it in for the dealer. For all we know, it could be the simple crime of passion, revenge by some guy because the bagman slept with his wife. It could also be an accident, one of those snipers who shoots at anybody."

"Have you spoken to Reade? Is he all right?" said Elena.

"You can't get to him; I can't get to him either. I spoke to New York. They've told him not to move, to stay put. They're sending guys out from there, and New Orleans, and Texas. They're sending me from L.A. The heat's on. Reade has to clear himself with the organization, his organization. He's being guarded like he's in a fucking penitentiary. The only crime you can commit in the Mob is to make a mistake. Your husband's committed a blooper. A gigantic blooper."

"And now?"

"He's in danger. If I had to guess, I'd say he'll smooth it over. I don't know the facts. I can't assure you, Elena, as much as I'd like to. This goddamn situation may never be squared away."

"Can you help him, Ted?"

"You know I'll try. I told you, he started me in business. Reade is a shit, Elena. Still, that has nothing to do with it. Some of us pay our dues. Reade has double-crossed me. He's double-crossed everybody. He works for himself. I'm not exactly into that New Testament crap about turning the other cheek, and, even as a Jew, I don't subscribe to the eye for an eye and the tooth for a tooth. That's not what life is about. My God, that sounds pompous. What I'm trying to say is—if you can understand a pragmatic theory, one that I've lived long enough to evolve—we're taught wrong. We're told that you get what you give. Believe me, giving is charity. Getting back is a miracle. The Mafia doesn't exist because there's justice. The Mafia exists because there's injustice. The Mob exists—and a lot of guys who are into it are the best, not all, but a lot—because of the corruption in our sainted, so-called institutions. For me, the worst sin is hypocrisy. The sinner is not the assassin. The sinner's the bastard who hires the assassin."

Elena recalled her conversation with Furio about thieves and deception, about the rich and the poor. She put it together now, and somehow it all made sense. As Reade would say, it added up. As he said more often, "Q.E.D." She patted Ted's hand. "You're right. You are the best. The people who are sitting up there in our capital tapping phones are the worst. I've never known you to hurt a human being. Ted, I've never known you to take. You give."

"I'm no saint, Elena," he said. "But those who give are the winners. Ironically, the winners are the ones who lose. You know why? Because the losers have nothing to do but sit back and sue. The losers are the drones. The winners are busy. They're the workers. The workers are the ones who are sued. You know what I've learned in thirty-five years at the bar? The plaintiff is mostly wrong, and the plaintiff too often wins. The defendant is the pigeon, the sitting duck. If you'll pardon my switching my metaphor from the bees to the birds. Who's there in the courts protecting the little guy? Who's there defending him, rich or poor, from the professional litigant? The drone is the fellow who'd rather slip on the pavement in front of your house and sue than use his God-given faculties to repair the crack in your pavement."

"That's a Los Angeles thing," she said.

"No, Elena. That's a national thing. It's Portland; it's Indianapolis, and it's Kansas City. God help us, it's Miami. I've seen a lot, a lot of what good men go through because they're good, and I'd say it's time the defendants of this world rose up against the plaintiffs. The lazy. The rich. The powerful. The publicity seekers. The nuts."

"We should have more Cuckoo's Nests," Elena said.

"The reason we have the Mafia is we don't have more Cuckoo's Nests." Ted drained his glass. "The defense rests."

"I never think politically," said Elena, "but it's difficult not to be a liberal, isn't it?"

"It's getting more difficult not to be a radical," said the

lawyer. "Right now I have to catch a plane to defend an ultraconservative. Your husband."

"The woman who came to dinner is leaving tomorrow," Marina said.

"Are you sure it's not too soon?" Elena said. She wanted to say "Please stay. I need companionship. I don't want to be alone." But she didn't.

"Tom came while you were out, and he says I'm fine. Besides, I got my marching orders from Adam. He called and practically ordered me out of the country. He suggested a rest in Hawaii or Mexico. Isn't that sweet? It seems the powers that be are nervous about their picture. Imagine what would happen if it leaked out that Marina Vaughan, the only bankable star in *Rogue's Gallery,* tried suicide."

"Did you?" Elena said. "I thought it was an accident."

"There's a very fine line in playwrighting," said Marina, "between an accident and a denouement. I watched my own mother's dissolution in alcohol and drugs. I saw her lacerated, literally, by my father. He used to beat her. Daddy—they all—convinced me Bobbie's death was a fluke. Do you know how I discovered she killed herself? I read it months later in one of those lousy fan magazines. The headline, as I remember, was: 'Bobbie Shaw: Her Suicide—The Star Who Was Scarred and Scared to Death by Her Family.' Her family. Me. My father, the hanger-on."

"I didn't know," said Elena. "But won't you stay longer? You're welcome here. You're fun, Marina. You're company."

"I can't thank you enough for that," said the girl, "but as I told you, I got the word. It's get out of town, and it wasn't even from Mel Torme."

"If Natalie were here, she'd say Torme has the best pipes in town," said Elena.

"Anyone else might say that. What Nat would say is he has the biggest pipe in town."

They laughed. "Dear Natalie," said Elena. She strained to conceal her disquietude as she asked the pertinent question. "Are you going with Adam?" she said.

"Are you joking? Adam is through with me. Isn't that nice? Oh, I know about you and him, Elena, just as you know about him and me, but the older I get the more I'm attracted to women. Don't cringe. I'm not making a pass. I'm saying that men are creeps. They use you. Adam used you to get me. He used us both to get everyone else. It's a formula. Tell a man you're sick, and he'll run. Tell him you have a headache, or you have the curse, or you need an abortion, and what does he say? 'Don't tell me, tell the doctor.' Adam is calling Radie Harris to plant the story I'm on vacation and grooving in Mexico."

"You're not going alone?" Elena said it with authentic concern.

"You'll never believe this, but yes. I'm going to Acapulco by myself. No man and no woman. I'm staying with Sloane." Sloane Simpson was the ex-wife of New York Mayor William O'Dwyer and the First Lady of Acapulco.

"In that case, you'll have a ball," Elena said.

"I'll go to all the right parties, if that's what you mean," Marina said. "But all I want is rest."

"Does anyone ever get what he wants before he dies?" said Elena. She was paraphrasing her favorite line from Euripides' *The Trojan Women.* In the version Elena had seen performed as a girl in East Berlin, the line was: "No one is ever happy, however fortunate, before he dies."

11

Elena switched on the pocket-sized tape machine Reade had given her for her birthday. (What else? she thought at the time. He makes them. They're free.) "Dear Reade," she said, somewhat self-consciously, "Ted called me this morning to say that whatever the trouble was, it's all over. Darling, I've been so worried about you, and I'm so glad. You know I tried to reach you, but I couldn't. Maybe—maybe that's just the story of our marriage. We never seem to reach each other. Ted told me you're both flying home this afternoon and that you've been cleared. I don't know how to say this exactly, but Ted was giving me my clearance, too. I wouldn't have left you until—unless—it was all resolved. I've missed you very much. You may not believe that after you've listened to all of this, but it's true. I've missed you, and I have thought about you. I've agonized, Reade. I really have. Not knowing if you were safe, if you were alive, if I'd ever see you again. But I've agonized about something else. Or somebody else. I think you know. It's Adam. I'm not sure this is right—I never seem to do anything right—but I have to go to him." She felt the tears welling up in her eyes, and heard her voice. It was quivering. "Darling, I would never have married you if I hadn't believed it would work. But one can believe—and make a mistake. We all make mistakes. I made a bad mistake. Forgive me, Reade. I can't live without Adam. I'm sorry."

Elena switched off the recorder and tried to compose herself. She placed the recorder on his pillow, where he was sure to find it when he returned. "I'm going shopping," she said to Kam, who cleaned the house when the Tais were off. "I probably won't be back before you leave, so just let yourself out."

"Yes, Missy," Kam said.

Elena took the new Rolls, which, like everything else in

the house, was Reade's. She found it grimly amusing that Reade, the computer genius, had never learned to drive. He claimed that one didn't have to drive in Boston. In Boston, that might be true, but in Los Angeles it was a definite handicap. Since Reade was too cheap to hire a chauffeur, or even to take a taxi, his friends had to pick him up and take him home when they were on the West Coast. When they stayed in hotels, Reade never leased cars. He discouraged Elena from taking cabs, so she too relied on acquaintances for transportation. Elena intended to return his car, of course. She didn't want anything that belonged to him and she felt guilty about leaving him. *Weltschmerz* was the companion to her exhilaration at having made the decision to go to Adam.

She anticipated Adam's surprise, his elation, on seeing her. Thank God, she thought, Kip's secretary is so efficient. Carol kept tabs on everyone's whereabouts. Adam was in Palm Springs, at La Siesta Villas. Carol even knew his bungalow. It was number three. Elena smiled, recalling a story she'd heard about Rex Harrison's latest stay at the Beverly Hills Hotel. Harrison's male companion (a secretary, no doubt) told the reservations man: "Mr. Harrison wants no bungalow higher than number eight." Elena was sure that Adam Baker outranked Harrison in one-upsmanship. Despite Adam's protestations about the Establishment, the A's, the In's, and status, he undoubtedly rejected any bungalow numbered higher than three.

She stopped at the jeweler, Marvin Hime's, on Beverly Drive. Elena had called him impulsively that morning because she wanted to take her lover a token of her adoration. Hime agreed to inscribe a miniature gold Oscar "For The Rogue—Love, Elena." Marvin sold the charms, which could be worn on a bracelet, a chain, or a key ring, to favored customers. Officially, it was taboo to duplicate the Oscar, but the Motion Picture Academy had its progressive side; the directors looked away. Some of them, and many of their wives, owned replicas of the sexless statue which was the industry's highest accolade to its members.

Elena found freeway driving an emotional release. She was a speed freak, ignoring the limits, and she was lucky. She had never been caught. She reached Palm Springs in two hours. She had never been to Frank Merlo's La Siesta Villas, but she knew a great deal about the resort. Mario

Puzo wrote *The Godfather* there. Steve Shagan made it his hideaway for revisions of *Save the Tiger*. The place was famous as a retreat for such as Peter Lawford, Doris Day, and George Peppard. She headed directly for Stevens Road, remembering the hotel was across from Liberace's extravaganza, which Randy called "Lee's excuse for a house in the desert."

As she drove up to the cottage, she glanced at the clock on the dashboard. It was twelve-fifteen. She had a sudden premonition. My God, Elena thought, Adam may not be here. He may be at lunch. He may be playing tennis. Why didn't that occur to me? She would not share this ultimate moment, this sweet submission, with strangers. If Adam was out, she would wait for him. It's as simple as that, she decided.

She tried the door. It was unlocked. Elena's apprehension was confirmed. Adam was out. She placed the tiny gift-wrapped box containing the Oscar on the coffee table, noting the clutter of scripts and dirty glasses. She thought of calling room service, but changed her mind. She would freshen up. She opened the bedroom door.

Adam was there, after all, although she saw Randy first. They were naked, performing the classic act that is known as sixty-nine. Elena put her hand to her mouth. She thought she was going to vomit. Instead, she gasped, involuntarily. The men looked at her, and, in her humiliation, she tore through the living room, jumped into the car, and broke a nail in her violent attack on the ignition key. She drove blindly, uncontrollably, afflicted not only by her tears but also by one of the sudden sandstorms that are characteristic of the desert. The vision, the nightmare vision, of Adam in bed with Randall Brent, her ex-husband—Randall Brent, the aging and leading star of television—kept rising before her. The horror of that scene in the villa would never disappear—the realization that when Elena finally went to Adam, daring at last to put her faith in love, he had betrayed her. She could not see through the windshield now. She stopped the car, rested her head on the steering wheel, and cried. She cried frantically—as Elena Schneider Brent Jamieson had never cried before.

By the time she collected herself, it was one o'clock. What of Reade? The tape? He could not discover the tape. She had to destroy it. Kam usually left at one, but there was the chance, the slightest chance, that Kam was still there. She drove into a gas station on Palm Canyon Drive and called home. Kam was gone. She got the Phone-Mate machine: "This is Mrs. Jamieson's residence. Mr. and Mrs. Jamieson are not at home. If you will leave your name and number and the time you called when you hear the signal . . ." The goddamn contrivance would go on endlessly. Elena hung up and phoned on the answering service line. "This is Mrs. Jamieson," she said. "Are there any messages?"

"Let me check," said the woman. She disengaged herself for what seemed an eternity. "There is one, Mrs. Jamieson. Mr. Jamieson called to say he'll be home at three o'clock." My God, thought Elena, even I—at seventy miles an hour—can't make it by then. On reassessment, Elena, the indomitable, came to the fore. I have to make it; I will.

The sandstorm had gained in velocity. She knew that if she drove fast, the sand would pit the windshield: she would have to admit to Reade she had been in the desert. I'll think of a cover for that, she thought. First things first. I have to retrieve the tape. I've lost Adam. I cannot lose Reade.

She skidded into the driveway in Holmby Hills, alarming one of the three new guards who had been added to their entourage in the last, tumultuous week. He greeted her, his pistol half-drawn. "Mrs. Jamieson . . ."

"Is Mr. Jamieson here?" she said.

"He arrived twenty minutes ago," said the man.

She put her key in the latch, and Reade opened the door. He was waiting for her. Now she was more than apprehensive. She was terrified. He must have listened to the tape. It was their usual method of communicating with one another. Why didn't I leave? she thought. Why didn't I go to Kip's, or to Furio's?

He did not kiss her, as he ordinarily would have. Still, there was something about his bearing that belied his usual arrogance. He looked worn, like one of Randy's old terry cloth robes.

"Are you all right?" she said.

"How else would I be? You know we're both survivors."

"I know," she said, cautiously.

"I thought you'd be here to meet me, but I found your

tape. I ran it." Oh, my God, thought Elena. She just looked at him. "I played it," he said. Elena continued to stare at him, aghast. Reade laughed. "There was nothing on it," he said. "Imagine me, the computer expert. I pushed the erase button by mistake." She understood. He had heard it.

He took her into his arms with a compassion he had never displayed before. "We all make mistakes, Elena," he said.

12

"This is the greatest party I've ever been to," said Furio. "Elena, you could write a guide to the water closets of the world."

"The water closet is Marina's territory," Elena said.

"You couldn't be more right," said Furio. "*Scusami.*"

It was Oscar night. To the uninitiated, the excitement belonged to the telecast at the Music Center and the ensuing Governors' Ball. In reality, any member of the Academy, or his intimidating brother, was able to attend the presentations and the supper at the Beverly Hilton. The awards at the Dorothy Chandler Pavilion dragged on for hours and could better be seen on television unless, as a nominee, one had the front seats in the orchestra on the aisle. The Ball was a soporific, a stultification of humanity consisting mostly of the despondent losers, the marginal celebrities who wanted their pictures taken, and those reluctant good citizens who were drafted into attendance. The anticlimax of Hollywood's biggest night was a dinner of cold prime ribs, one stuffed artichoke heart, an over-stewed tomato, and wilted greens.

The cognoscenti of the New Hollywood collaborated, giving private parties to view the Academy Awards. Each year there were dozens of parties-at-home; each year there was one most coveted invitation. This year the place to be was the Jamiesons'. The rites were similar: one had a pool in which his guests invested money for winner and second winner and loser take all, or the host and hostess provided the prizes. People came by for cocktails, the telecast, and dinner, which was served continuously, even into the morning hours—participants kept dropping in after attending the tedious ceremonies.

Elena's party was catered by Chasen's. Reade had been so contrite since his return from Las Vegas they had no quarrels on money matters. Indeed, he was indulgent (For him, thought Elena), allowing her to hire Chasen's as a supplement to the Tais. Reade even suggested she ask their friend, Jean Louis, to design her costume for the evening. Elena chose a brilliant contradiction in terms—a man-tailored, feminine, chiffon concoction of party pants. The color was emerald green for two reasons, because it matched her jewelry and because she was superstitious. She detested Adam, but still she wanted *Rogue's Gallery* to win the Oscar. Kip was in trouble; he needed the win. She knew as well as anyone in town that Kip believed in using green ink for notes that related to money. The elusive Hollywood information network, with its barometric sensitivity to impending sensations or failures, was on the mark. *Gallery* was a tremendous hit. In the backbiting atmosphere of the New Hollywood, box-office grosses could be a deterrent to receiving the industry's most desired award—or its most impressive doorstop.

George Schlatter, the producer, gave Elena a bear hug. George was the funniest, most ribald character Elena knew, except for his wife, Jolene. Being in a room with them was like being in the ring with both Joe Louis and Max Schmeling. "You know what you are?" George said. "You're twenty-nine, you're beautiful, and you're witty."

"Don't believe him, Elena," said Jolene. "In Hollywood, that all too easily translates into being forty-two, having had a good nose job, and having carefully collected Billy Wilder's wisecracks."

"Who's taking my name in vain?" said Bob Hope, the perennial host of the Oscars, who had relinquished his title this year.

"We were speaking of Billy," said Jolene.

"We are one," said Bob. "Have you ever seen us in the same room together? Wilder has been living on my jokes for years."

"Let's not kid a pro," said Schlatter, who, as the master of "Laugh-In," knew comedy better than anyone. Except maybe Jolene. "You've been living off Wilder's lines for years."

"You've been living off your wife's," said Hope. "I'll trade you Billy for Jolene."

"As long as you send Dolores to The Big Apple," George said.

"I warn you, Elena, I'm trying to win the booby prize tonight," Bob Evans said. "I'm the worst at ballots." He handed his to her, folded.

"My God, Bob," she said, "I hope you win anything but the booby prize."

"Why?" Evans asked. "Is it Roman Polanski?"

"You'll see," said Elena.

"Last year, when I came out of the Oscars and *Chinatown* lost, I felt as though I'd been sparring with Ali."

"Which Ali?" said Lisa Taylor, the top *Vogue* model Bob was currently dating.

"Both Alis," said the producer who had been married to Ali McGraw.

"Bobby," Ted Buckley said, "what the hell is Audrey Meadows doing with one more bodyguard than I have?"

"She's prettier than you," said Evans, "and more likely to be raped."

"I'm serious. She arrived with two men who are armed."

"I would hope so," said Natalie, joining the group. "Were they short arms or long?"

"That's my wife," said Jack, smiling resignedly.

"Darling," Elena said, "so Audrey's husband, Bob Six, is away. So he's tending to Continental Airlines. So who isn't worried about their safety, nowadays? Of course, it does seem extraneous, since we have four guards of our own."

"That's only because I love you, Elena," said Ted. "My friends put them on."

"I thank you," she said. He kissed her.

"Do you know how Audrey took her last test for a driver's license?" Natalie said.

"Who cares?" said George Schlatter.

"I care," said Jolene, whose bills with the telephone company were exceeded only by Natalie Kaufman's. There were those who said that George bought a houseboat to keep Jolene away from the phone.

"All I can tell you," said Natalie, who was virtually panting to tell them, "is that Audrey went to Culver City with two armed guards. And this is the clincher—they stayed while she took her test in a private room."

"With that kind of company," said Bob Hope, "she must have gotten one hundred percent."

"With that kind of privacy," said Nat, "she should have gotten two hundred percent."

"Two hundred percent of what?" said Reade. (Nothing intrigues him, Elena thought, except figures. She couldn't resist a smile. Mathematical figures. Not Natalie's.)

She left the group to greet Jimmy and Gloria Stewart and Paul and Joanne Newman, who had just arrived. Elena moved on to Rex Kennamer, who was Elizabeth Taylor's doctor. "I've never seen such a horde of photographers," Kennamer said. "They asked me if it's true Victor Kroll and Susan McConnell are coming."

"They are, after the Oscars. As you know, the party's in honor of Victor, not the Awards," Elena said. Kroll was on this particular foray to the West Coast to speak to the World Affairs Council. Elena seized the occasion both to dignify her party and to augment the political tensions. Apart from Victor, the Republican faction was well-represented. Senator and Mrs. Jacob Javits were in town and accepted. California Attorney General Evelle Younger was an ally of the Administration; he was Ford's campaign chairman for the presidential primary in June. The Democrats in attendance were Governor Brown, who had recently declared his own candidacy for President, Senator and Mrs. Alan Cranston, and Mayor and Mrs Tom Bradley. Since her marriage to Reade, Elena had amassed a whole new collection of VIPs. She might be reined-in, but she was the reigning hostess of California.

"I can guess who put Victor Kroll and Susan McConnell together," Rex Kennamer said.

"You'd be wrong. Victor's date is Marina. Susan's with Adam tonight. The unflagging Adam Baker, who programs his public appearances as carefully as a presidential hopeful." She couldn't resist the comment.

"How do you mean?" asked Rex.

"Marina and Susan are rivals. He used Marina to get her for his picture. He threw her over when he no longer needed her. He got her the nomination for Best Actress through expediency, not love, my darling. In fact, he got ten nominations for *Gallery*. But Susan's a bigger star than Marina Who else would he take to the Academy Awards?"

"Well, I don't know what photographers are covering the Music Center," Rex said. "It appears to me they're all on Delfern Drive. Listen, I have an idea. Who do we hate? Let's tell the press Kroll and McConnell are going to their house. Let's send them there."

Elena loved Kennamer's banter. He was one of the most clever men she knew. "You're delicious," she said. "I adore you." Clare Ballen appeared.

"So do I," she said.

Elena told Clare that once, when Reade was in the East on a business trip, Rex took her to dinner at La Scala. The ever-vigilant fan force saw them drive up in Rex's cream-colored Jensen and assumed that she, Elena, was Elizabeth Taylor in a blond wig. Elena was assaulted by the autograph hounds. On a whim, she signed half a dozen books "Best Wishes Always, Elizabeth Taylor."

"You can go for broke," Rex had said, when they were safely inside the restaurant. "You can work for me and forge my name to prescriptions."

"If we're telling Rex Kennamer stories, I can top that one," Clare said. "Remember when Edie Wasserman gave the benefit for Cedars-Sinai at Universal? The one with Frank Sinatra and Kelly doing 'Singin' in the Rain'? Rex and I were in Edie's party, which meant the front row. I mentioned to Rex that Frank likes me, as far as I know, and I'm just about the only woman reporter he hasn't hit in his acts. I'd written something in one of my columns like 'If Sinatra says one more thing about female reporters being two-dollar whores, he'll hear from my lawyer.' Rex offered me a twenty-dollar bill. 'If Frank says a word about women journalists tonight,' he said, 'I want you to go up on the stage, throw this at his feet and say, "You're behind the times, Frank." ' Sinatra's lawyer, Mickey Rudin, heard us. He said, 'I'll contribute twenty dollars myself. Clare, why don't you take up a collection from the audience for the hospital? Two dollars from everybody. Then I'll tell Frank to stage it.' "

"Did he?" Elena said.

"Unfortunately for the hospital, no. Frank was the perfect gentleman. He said something like 'At this point, I usually attack the press. Tonight, I'm not going to. Which doesn't mean I won't do it again. But I want you to know I only go after the bad cats.' "

"Some have been pretty rotten to him, like in Australia," Elena said.

"Yes, but in my opinion he should ignore. He's made the rotten ones famous. It should happen to me. Maybe I'll ask Mickey Rudin to stage something after all." They laughed.

"Wasn't that the night Johnny Carson led the standing ovation for Kelly?" Elena said.

"One of the standing ovations. Which is my only reason for liking Johnny Carson," said Clare. "Somewhere beneath that hackled midwestern exterior there must be taste and a heart."

"Johnny's coming tonight," said Elena, anxiously. "I didn't know you were enemies." Secretly, nothing so invigorated Elena as pitting opponents against one another. Gore Vidal, who was suing Capote, was asked; so was Truman. Agents Kitty Hawks and Sue Mengers ("Sue may be conniving," Elena decided, recalling Ballen's words while drawing up her invitations list, "but she's powerful. And she's funny.").

"Johnny and I are no longer foes," said Clare. "At least not on my part. I like his wife."

"Joanne?" Rex Kennamer said.

"Not Joan or Joanne, but Joanna. The reason Johnny said he disliked me was 'You're a friend of my ex-wife's.' He meant Joanne. Now, isn't that silly? Why shouldn't I like Joanne?"

"Because Johnny's paying her alimony," Elena said.

"I should have his problems," Clare said. "He earns four million a year."

"I'm confused by the names," said Rex. "Who are all these Joans, Joannes, and Joannas?"

"I've got it," Clare said. "No wonder Johnny led a standing ovation for Kelly. His first name is Gene. Mr. Carson has a hang-up. He doesn't like me because my first name's not Jean, Joanne, or Joanna."

Ted Buckley had joined them. "Elena," he said, "which Joanne shall I put my bodyguard on tonight? Joanne Woodward?"

"No. Put him on Johnny Carson."

The Jamiesons' screening room was set up for the telecast and the dinner buffet. Elena's projectionist, Clarence Woerth, constructed the pedestals that raised the TV sets for easy viewing. There was one on each side of the cavernous room, which had a sixty-foot throw. In the New Hollywood, Maude Chasen, the eminent lady who owned the restaurant (and was a guest of Elena's), rated the parties. Maude assigned both Ron Clint, her manager, and her captain, Tommy Gallagher, to the Jamiesons' mansion that night. The hosts and hostesses of the peripheral Oscar party gatherings catered by Chasen's were on their own.

The cliques assembled, of course. Marlo Thomas was sitting with her charming beau, David Geffen, the Kaufmans, producer Douglas Cramer, who escorted ABC's Sue Cameron, and the Leonard Goldbergs.

"What are we eating?" said Marlo, whose dark-haired beauty was complemented by simple white jersey.

"I think it's Chicken Jerusalem," said Natalie.

"How can you say that to me," said Marlo, dropping her fork on her plate in a typical comedy gesture, "after what they've done to Beirut?" Marlo's father, Danny, was a Lebanese-American.

"How dare you?" said Nat. "We're Jewish."

"So am I," said David. "No. Correction. I'm a nihilist."

"You're Jewish," Marlo said. "You'd better be Jewish. All the men I love are Jewish. Show me a guy with curly hair and I run to him like he's a magnate."

"So eat," said Wendy Goldberg. "It's Chicken Beirut."

"I'll be damned if I want to see the boring technical awards," said Priscilla Helburn. "I'd rather be balled."

"Since you put it like that," said Ted, "I'm not averse." Priscilla was despised by producers, directors, and fellow actors, but the networks loved her. She had what executives called a high TV Q, although no one believed them. Her previous series lasted thirteen weeks, or less. Her current series was, for reasons known only to Nielsen and the American viewer, a smash. Priscilla was a bitch who came late to the set, rewrote her lines, and spouted foul language to anyone within earshot. If it weren't for the network bosses, Priscilla would have been collecting unemployment in Santa Monica. As it happened, she was earning twenty-five thousand dollars a week. Why did producers hire her? Because if they employed someone else, someone better, for their pilots, they understood that the series would never get on the air. The public airways were a private trust. They were regulated not by the FCC, but by a few top-income media-men who deferred their enormous salaries.

Priscilla, who was older and less attractive than most of Ted's mistresses, pursued him because he was powerful and intrigued him because of her perversity. Priscilla was a masochist. She liked to be abused by men. "Do you want to ball me? Say so," she said.

"I want to ball you," he said. He led her out the door and past the profusion of bodyguards to the pool house. The guards simply nodded and smiled. Ted Buckley's reputation, along with Priscilla Helburn's, preceded them.

She stripped, and Ted was astonished once more by what a good body she had for her age. Priscilla admitted to forty-five, which, in Hollywood jargon, meant fifty. She gave him the Mason-Pearson hairbrush she carried in her purse and gripped the upholstered couch with her hands, exposing wide hips and taut buttocks. "Hurry up," said Priscilla. "Hit me. Hit me hard."

Ted undressed and shoved his cock, which was normally like a spindle, into her anus. "You have a beautiful derrière," he said. "It makes me want to fill it."

"You fill it," Priscilla answered. "My God, you're as big as a codpiece." He was, and he was aware of it. After he came, he succumbed to her pleas. He beat her, but not with the tiny hairbrush. He went to the sink and wet a towel, and slapped her until she cried out in exaltation.

"Here we go," said Liza Minnelli Haley to her husband, Jack, as they sat in the screening room. "This begins the sweep." *Rogue's Gallery* had received the early, often-telling award for Best Achievement in Editing.

Liza's effervescence was contagious as the Benjamins, Dick and Paula Prentiss, took the stage. *Rogue's Gallery* won for Art Direction.

"You must have ESP," said Rock Hudson.

"She's better than that. She has talent," said Liza's father, Vincente Minnelli, whose latest movie Liza was starring in. The film had gone through so many changes that no one, absolutely no one (except maybe Vincente and Liza), was sure of the current title.

Gallery missed the next Oscar, for Costume Design. "Oh, oh," said Mary Benny to Rosalind Russell Brisson. Clearly, the vote was not split: the coterie at Elena's was rooting for *Gallery*.

"That means nothing," said Alice Ambrose. "How can a picture about prison breakouts, sodomy, and incest possibly win for its costumes? Besides, Edith Head and Irene Sharaff weren't designing."

"Alice, shut up," said Warren. "You don't understand the movie. It has social significance. It doesn't take place in a jail, for Christ's sake. The setting's America. They're not breaking out of prison. They're breaking out of bondage. They're rebelling against the Establishment."

Alice was mortified, once again, by her Ivy League husband. She stared him down. "If you're the Establishment," she said softly, but firmly, "I don't blame them."

George Burns and Ann-Margret were announcing the Cinematography award. "And the winner is . . . *Rogue's Gallery*."

"Wow," said Cary Grant. "This *is* a sweep."

"Isn't he beautiful?" said Sue Mengers Tramont. "You know Cary's in love with me, but my husband is jealous. Jean-Claude won't let me talk to him."

Ted Buckley slipped into the room and plopped down on the sofa beside the Hugh Lamberts. His vested interest in Pacific Pictures superseded his unvested interest in Priscilla. Ms. Helburn's series was airing (absurdly) against the Oscars. "Let's see my show," Priscilla had suggested. "I never miss it. I'm especially good in the segment tonight."

"You'd better be," Ted said. "With this competition, I wish you a whopping four share in the ratings." Priscilla was in the gameroom enraptured by her image (As in a fun-house mirror, distorted, Ted thought). "What's the score?" he asked Nancy Lambert, who had recently given birth to Frank Sinatra's second grand-daughter.

"We've won three so far," said Nancy. Cicely Tyson and Roger Moore were presenters for Best Foreign Film.

"Now this is a dud of a classification," said Ted. "*Rogue's Gallery* doesn't qualify."

Eventually, *Gallery* qualified well enough to win seven out of its ten nominations. When Francis Lai accepted the Oscar for Best Original Score, Elena said, "Kip has an ear. He flew to Paris for this one." Kip also had an eye. His movie took Best Screenplay, based on material from another medium, as well as Best Director, Charlie Finestein. And best of all for the box office and for Kip Nathan, *Rogue's Gallery* won Best Picture.

Marje Everett and Sylvia Kaye, who had been tabulating the ballots, brought the results to Elena. "You announce them," Elena told Sylvia.

Nobody could have predicted the winner in a room

where so many industry people were so astute. Except Joyce Easton, who would have chosen her love, Ted Ashley. Warners' canny two-time Chairman and Chief Executive guessed correctly on eleven of twelve major categories. He and Joyce won a case of 1969 Château Mouton Rothschild, each bottle of which was numbered and signed "Philippe Rothschild."

Berry Gordy was the runner-up by only one point. His reward was a dozen RCA Red Seal classical albums. "I think someone is trying to tell me something," the multimillionaire owner of Motown said to John Denver, who added, "Maybe they're trying to tell me something, too."

Bob Evans did not win the booby prize. George Cukor had been more successful in his manipulations. Elena handed George a plaid carrier. "What's in there?" said George. "The remains of Clark Gable?" There was general laughter. Gable, of course, had caused Cukor to be replaced by Victor Fleming on *Gone With the Wind*.

"I'm so glad you won," said Elena, looking from Cukor to Evans, "and that Bobby did not." She unlatched the cage and extracted a coal-black kitten. "Her name," Elena said as George stroked the animal, "is Ali."

"Which Ali?" said Barry Diller.

"Who knows?" said O. J. Simpson. "They're both brunettes." Elena was supremely proud to have lured the football player after he had presented an award at the telecast.

They moved to the living room, where Warren convinced Saul Chaplin to play the new songs he co-wrote for *That's Entertainment, Part II*. "Come on, everyone," Warren said. "This is Oscar night. Perform." Steve Lawrence and Eydie Gorme sang a medley from Irving Berlin.

"Eydie's never looked better," Françoise de la Renta said.

"Thank God they didn't bring their photographers with them," said Natalie, bitchily. "How can they be the only couple who are always followed by half a dozen photographers?"

"Because they're divine, my dear," said publicist Richard Gully.

"They must have twenty-five scrapbooks," Irv Kupcinet said.

"Jane Withers has fifteen of Gene Kelly alone," said John Schubeck of NBC.

"How many do you suppose Withers has of Jane Withers?" said David Sheehan, who was CBS's below-the-black-belt man for the movie colony.

"Who's next?" said Ambrose.

Peggy Lee sang "Do You Know Where You're Going To?," the theme from *Mahogany,* with a dedication to Berry Gordy.

"If you're trying out for ABC, you've got it," said Fred Silverman, who was that network's president for entertainment.

"Carol," said Marge Champion to Carol Lowe, "you must do your imitation of Denise Minnelli Hale."

"I'm leaving," Vincente Minnelli, Denise's ex-husband, told Lee Anderson.

"Vincente," said Audrey Hepburn, who was perhaps the most stunning woman in the room, "would you mind sitting down?"

Carol Channing took the stage in all her white-platinum radiance. "This is just a little thing I do at private parties," she said, "and on Broadway." She went into her impression of Denise's Yugoslavian accent, the one that stopped the show *Four on a Garden* at every performance.

Mikhail Baryshnikov, the principal dancer of the American Ballet Theater, seemed edgy. "Misha, relax," said Danny Kaye. "We won't call on you." Then Danny did a hilarious monologue on the Oscars, on its presenters, its winners and its losers.

Altovise Davis and Lola Falana were dancing together to Sammy Cahn's rendition of his Oscar-winning "Three Coins in the Fountain." "This could be the start of something big," Steve Allen said to Sammy Davis. "If you play your cards right, I can get the three of you an act on Merv Griffin. And for more than three coins."

"Forget it," said Sammy. "I just bought the theater Merv broadcasts from." Both Lola and Altovise were protégée-dancers of Sammy's. Alto and Lola, then Lola and Sammy, were roommates before Sammy married Alto. "Besides," Sammy added, "we only do our act privately. How do you think I got custody of their jewelry?"

"Elena, we have to go," said Sidney Korshak.

"Oh, Sidney, the fun's just beginning."

"We should have left three hours ago," Sidney said. The

famous attorney chose to arrive at parties at six o'clock, and depart at six-fifteen.

"I have an early tennis date with Dinah tomorrow," said Bea, Sidney's wife. Bea was the most delightful and affable of Hollywood wives. She not only knew how to take her cues from Sidney; she collaborated with him on the cue cards.

"I love you," Elena said, kissing Bea. "I love you both."

"Jesus Christ," said Harry Waller to Madeline Farrell. "Look at this. These fucking snobs have a guest book."

"That's propriety, Waller," said Madeline.

"That's a dodge for the IRS. You sign it; they write the party off."

"Just sign it, Harry," she said.

"I'll sign it all right. We'll both sign it. In fact, let's have everyone sign it. *That* will give them a big deduction."

"What do you mean?" asked Madeline, querulously. She was annoyed. He'd been tanked the entire night.

"I'll show you," said Waller, collapsing on the love seat. He turned the page. "Here's Sammy Davis," he said. "All he did is sign his goddamn name. I can improve on that." She sat down beside him. "I've got my eye on you," Waller wrote above Sammy's signature.

"I get it," said Madeline. "It's a game."

"Has anyone ever told you you have the IQ of Jimmy Breslin and Norman Mailer minus 306?" said Waller.

"Who are Breslin and Mailer?" Madeline said.

"They're nobody, baby. Only two studs who tried to take over New York before it collapsed."

"New York has collapsed?" she said.

"I swear to God, I can't imagine what Nathan saw in you."

"He saw my tits," she said.

"Okay. Stay in the hay. That's your specialty, honey. That's what you excel at." He continued to write in the ledger.

"Veronica Lake is polluted—Ralph Nader."

"I think I'll have one last cigarette, and go—Edward R. Murrow."

"Listen, schmuck, I wouldn't lift a finger for you—Hedy Lamarr."

"The doctors are wrong. He has phlebitis of the brain—Pat Nixon."

"Dear Elena and Reade—I never see or hear from you guys anymore—Helen Keller."

"Talk about being hung—Fay Wray."

"Why does Charlie say I'm over-bearing?—Oona Chaplin."

"If at first you don't succeed, pull yourself up by your ankle straps—Joan Crawford."

"Save the empties for me—Fatty Arbuckle."

"My career is going downhill—Jean-Claude Killy."

"You're lucky, Elena. You've always been lucky. You'll be lucky again—Bette Davis."

"I don't get that," said Madeline.

"Naturally," Waller said. "You can't read. Nonetheless, I'll buy you a copy of Lillian Hellman tomorrow."

Betsy Bloomingdale said to Barry Diller's date, designer Diane von Fürstenberg, "I can't bear short dresses, those luncheon dresses. But darling, I bought a couple of yours, in case I go to a funeral."

"That's all right," said Diane. "I never watched your TV show either. Only once, before it went off the air. You were wearing a strapless chiffon dress with diamond earrings at two in the afternoon. As I recall, it was dubbed 'For People Who Are Going Places and Doing Things.' You asked that gourmet, George Christy, if he thought you should serve French wines. He said, 'I think so. It's cosmopolitan.' David Jones, the florist, was arranging rare orchids. In a crisis economy. My dear, I told Barry, 'If you think Tiffany has good place settings, watch Betsy's show.' "

"You are a love. You are deep," Betsy said, "as Barry said in your *Newsweek* cover story."

"I want to show you something," Marina said to Victor Kroll. "You told me you like Giacometti. The Jamiesons have the best Giacometti I've ever seen."

"Where is it?" said Victor.

"It's in Reade's office."

"I can't leave right now," Victor said. "I'm the guest of honor. I haven't said my hellos yet."

"Say your hellos," said Marina. "These people bore me. I can't stand parties. I'll meet you upstairs."

Victor Kroll, the Administration's darling, felt he had

not been on shakier ground since Harold Wilson resigned. Marina had been spaced out all evening. There was a kind of schizophrenia lurking in his psyche. On the one hand, Victor appreciated beautiful women. Kroll was drawn to the kook. He accepted the fact that starlets and stars were characters out of P. G. Wodehouse. They were dotty. On the other hand, Victor was a statesman more subject to calumny than other public figures. He had not the slightest intention of joining her, but when Marina failed to reappear, Kroll was genuinely concerned.

What he found in the office was more Henry Miller than P. G. Wodehouse. Marina was sitting spreadeagled on the sofa, nude. "Welcome," she said, "Mr. Economic Adviser. My goodness, how did you find the time to come? I mean, you're so busy. You're so busy greeting our great electorate, devaluing the dollar or pound, or whatever it is you do. I'm flattered."

Victor was horrified. "Marina," he said, "you'd better put on your clothes. I'll take you home."

"I told you, Mr. Adviser, I have something to show you first. You know what it is? It's not Giacometti. It happens to be the Motion Picture Academy." Then he saw the Oscar. "You know I've been screwed by everything. Everything, as of tonight. Men, women and children and animals. You looked shocked. We had a beautiful poodle when I was fourteen. I've been screwed by more than anything you can think of. You know what I haven't been screwed by? I haven't been screwed by the Oscar. Until tonight. *Rogue's Gallery* won seven—Best Picture, Best Director, Best Editing, for God's sake. But not Best Actress. You know those people down there in this house, who voted? They hate me. They hate me because I have a bad reputation. They're reputable people, all of them. The Establishment."

"Marina, please," said Kroll.

"Here it is," she said, holding up the sexless statue. "I want you to see it. I want you to see the Black Mass, the ultimate desecration of Hollywood. I am about to be fucked by the Oscar. Mr. Kroll, have you anything as valuable as the Oscar?"

Victor Kroll escaped down the stairs, seeking out his hostess. "Elena, thank you," he said. He was frantic. "I have to leave."

"Why so early?" she said. "I don't understand."

"You walk through the door to Reade's office. You'll understand."

Elena was still in the hallway when a drunken Adam appeared. "Who the hell has my Oscar?" he said. "Where is it?"

"It's here. Your goddamn Oscar's right here," said Marina. She was standing at the top of the stairs. "You know what your shitty Oscar has done to me? It fucked me. I made it fuck me," she said. "My dear producer, the only trouble is it couldn't come."

"Now that's a comment on Walter Mirisch," said Billy Wilder, who had wandered into the hall. Mirisch was the perennial President of the Motion Picture Academy. He was ineffective, but he didn't want to give up the job. He kept on running, and kept being re-elected.

"I've never seen an A party like this," said Doris Stein. "Jules, call the driver. I want to go home."

Elena was relieved that Anthony Newley and Leslie Bricusse were entertaining her other guests in the living room. Any diversion was welcome. "Doris, she's just had too much to drink," Elena said. "I'll take care of it. I'll be right back."

"Well—if you say so," said Doris Stein. "Jules, cancel the driver."

"Are you sure? I'm tired," said the founder of MCA.

"I'm sure. It's the shank of the evening," said Doris. "Where is Susan?" Susan Shiva, their daughter, was in the living room listening, like everyone else, to Tony Newley's rendition of "What Kind of Fool Am I?"

Marina didn't come out of her hysteria until Elena reluctantly slapped her face a couple of times. "I'm a mess," the girl said. "I'm sorry, Elena. I'm sick."

"Marina, you're beautiful. Why do you have to behave like this? Why don't you take care of yourself?"

"Susan, that bitch, takes care of herself. Is that what you're trying to say? That bastard Adam is down there with her, not me. He won the Oscar. I didn't. So give me a reason. Why should I take care of myself? There isn't a soul who cares for me."

"Caring is a myth," Elena said, "and love is a delusion. That bastard, as you call him, reinforced my belief in that."

"You can talk," Marina said. "You've got everything. Money. Power. Intelligence. A husband who pays the bills. Elena, you know where all the closets are and what's in the closets, and you've got it made."

"You think so?" Elena's laugh was strident. "I fell in love with a *pédé qui s'ignore,* since you're speaking of closets, and I didn't even know it."

"What is a *pédé qui s'ignore*?"

"My darling, it's French for a closet queen. A pederast who refuses to admit it."

"You must mean Randy," Marina said.

"I mean Adam," said Elena.

Marina's joy was unbridled. Her laugh was as potent and venomous as the songs she belted out in an amphitheater. "The French must surely have a better phrase than that one," she said. "You're telling me Adam Baker is gay? The great lover is gay?"

"Marina, you're disconcerted. You know this town. You lost the Oscar tonight. He won. It's a popularity contest. Tomorrow the scripts will start coming to you all over again. You're a star. Mr. Baker's a user. *Rogue's Gallery* was a user's triumph. I was the Queen of the Users, and I was totally used by Adam. Adam is the new Queen of the Users."

"Elena, you have it made. What is your secret, Elena?"

"Darling, nobody has it made, and it's not a secret. Have faith, but never in love. Have faith in life. Marina, there's always something better coming up."

"How is Marina?" Adam said.

"Don't you really mean how is your Oscar?" said Elena.

"I wouldn't mind if you had it washed."

"I'll have it washed the day you give me my Oscar back. The one you and Randy undoubtedly laughed about in Palm Springs."

"Nobody laughs at you, Elena."

"I'm serious, Adam. I want it back. Marina and I have more than one thing in common. We've both been fucked by an Oscar."

"I'll return it tomorrow."

"You'd better. When you return mine, I'll give you yours. You won the Oscar tonight, and that excuses a mul-